Praise

Sky of Red Poppies walks th ....g and thought-provoking narrative to provide answers to Iran's brilliant past and brutal present. Well worth considering!
—Dr. Ahmad Karimi Hakkak, *University of Maryland*

Sky of Red Poppies takes its readers on a fascinating journey through the landscapes of Iran and provides a glimpse into a far too often overlooked side of Iranian culture and history. A must read!
—Melody Moezzi, author of *War on Error*

Ghahremani is that wonderful kind of writer who tells compelling stories in rich and lyrical language. *Sky of Red Poppies* is an illustration of her mastery of both.
—Judy Reeves, author of *A Writer's Book of Days*

Ghahremani understands the many conditions of the human heart... *Sky of Red Poppies* is a compassionate story of universal truths.
—Yvonne Nelson Perry, author of *The Other Side of the Island*

Sky of Red Poppies is the moving story of relationships tested under the most stressful of human conditions, that of a repressive government. Zohreh Ghahremani writes with warmth, humanity and a poet's vision.
—Claire Accomando, author of *Love and Rutabaga*

Set against the backdrop of a pre-revolution Iran, *Sky of Red Poppies* is a poetic epic and a powerful read.
—Jonathan Yang, author of *Exclusively Chloe*

For many years I have had the privilege of publishing Ghahremani's charming, nostalgia-laced words of wisdom on the pages of iranian. com. Now it's time for a broader audience to enjoy a heartfelt journey into a fascinating life.
—Jahanshah Javid, *iranian.com*

Praise for The Moon Daughter

The Moon Daughter captures the bittersweet yet triumphant story of an Iranian mother and daughter who immigrate to the United States in the 1970s. In this delicately wrought novel, each woman struggles against the hand that fate has dealt her with intelligence and strength, illuminating the paths of two very different generations of Iranian Americans. But rather than settle for easy answers, this skillfully-woven tale lays bare the emotional truths at the core of the immigrant experience: the complications afforded by loss, the changes of heart that make us all human, and the power of love to bind us together across continents and generations. The Moon Daughter is captivating, heartfelt, and deeply meaningful.

—Anita Amirrezvani, author of The Blood of Flowers
and Equal of the Sun

In her new novel, Zohreh Ghahremani leads her readers into the town of Shiraz which, like its wine, intoxicates us.

—Shahrnush Parsipur, author of Women Without Men

Just as in Sky of Red Poppies, Zohreh Ghahremani's The Moon Daughter offers readers a riveting and poetically rendered window into Iranian culture, this time through the story of a woman and a baby whose flaw speaks to much deeper defects in families and cultures. Prepare to lose sleep--you will not want to put this book down.

—Laurel Corona, author of Finding Emily and The Four Seasons

"Brilliantly portrayed with vivid imagery, intriguing characters, and lyrical prose, The Moon Daughter reveals rare insights from both mother and daughter in their search for love, compassion and justice. At once tragic and triumphant, this spellbinding drama is riveting through the final page."

—Marjorie Hart, author of Summer at Tiffany,
a New York Times bestseller

This eagerly awaited second novel from the remarkably talented Zohreh Ghahremani... offers readers a glimpse into the troubled lives of women in Iranian culture, past and present, in a voice at once personal and immediate. The author's love of art and poetry animates her prodigious storytelling gifts in a powerful exploration of pressing women's issues in Iran, creating a memorable tale of love, revenge and ultimate belonging.

—Kathi Diamant, author of *Kafka's Last Love*

Zohreh Ghahremani's *The Moon Daughter* captures an important period of Iran's tumultuous history and draws a detailed and intimate portait of the lives of one Iranian family and the changes they endure. Her ability to tell the stories that have not yet been told about Iran enriches the fictional landscape of American fiction and evokes the powerful voices of an emerging Iranian-American voice.

—Persis Karim, Director of Iranian Studies, *San Jose State University*

A testament to the transcendent power of fiction, *The Moon Daughter* takes its readers on a journey through, across and between two strikingly distinct, yet decidedly connected worlds. Zohreh Ghahremani manages to enlighten, engage and entertain her readers in a way all authors aspire to and few ever achieve.

—Melody Moezzi, author of *Haldol and Hyacinths*

In *The Moon Daughter*, Zohreh Ghahremani takes us again to her native Iran where we discover that no matter the country or the culture, heartbreak and joy, loyalty and betrayal, love and simple kindness are common denominators in human relationships. Both new and returning readers of Ghahremani's work are promised another novel that combines lyrical prose, exotic setting, and compelling story.

—Judy Reeves, author of *A Writer's Book Of Days*

Other books by Zohreh Ghahremani

SHAREEK-E GHAM (PERSIAN, 2000)
SKY OF RED POPPIES, 2010

Zohreh Ghahremani

The Moon Daughter

a novel

TURQUOISE BOOKS

First trade paperback published in the United States of America by Turquoise Books.

Turquoise Books and the "t" logo are trademarks of Turquoise Books.

For inquiries, please contact:
Turquoise Books
turquoise@turquoisebooks.com
Visit our website:
www.turquoisebooks.org

Book layout and typesetting by Anton Khodakovsky
Cover painting entitled The Moon Daughter © Zohreh Ghahremani. 2013, oil on canvas, courtesy of the artist.
Cover design by Susie Ghahremani
Author photograph © Elvee Froehlich

Library of Congress Control Number: 2013932493

978-0-9845716-3-9/SAN

10 9 8 7 6 5 4 3 2 1

Printed in the United States of America

Acknowledgement

If "IT TAKES A VILLAGE TO RAISE A CHILD," it took an entire city to help me raise my first. A book is indeed a writer's child and I am beyond grateful for the support I have received across the city of San Diego and through the One Book, One San Diego program. The number of people who helped me along the way makes it harder to narrow down the list of those who should be acknowledged and I will be a dreamer to think I can name them all. Please accept my heartfelt apology for any names I fail to list here.

Once again, I am indebted to my loving family: Gary, Lilly, Susie, and Cyrus. They continue their relentless support and enthusiasm, showing up for my events time and again. It was their encouragement and patience that gave The Moon Daughter a chance to come alive. A simple "thank you" will never make up for the sacrifices they have made.

My dream editor Kyra Ryan believes in me enough to never give up. If my English is any better, she is the reason. A master of her craft, she is also a powerful writer who inspires me to give my stories the life they deserve.

Deep gratitude goes to my good friends Barbara Sack and Katherine Porter and to my darlings Lilly & Susie for taking the time to read the entire manuscript and offer their fine editorial comments. And if you like the cover design, it is owed to my Susie's artistic touch and the way she brought out the best in my simple painting.

I am grateful to the best circle of writers: Michele, Anne, Pennie, Kathi, Laurel, Susan, Caitlin, Marjorie, and all the good members of San Diego Writing Women as well as the Association of Iranian American writers for offering camaraderie.

I feel fortunate to know Judy Reeves not only as a teacher, but also a true friend. Her selfless dedication to San Diego Writers, Ink was the reason I became a charter member and in fact, it was Judy who encouraged me to submit the first chapter of this novel to A Year in Ink. I am most indebted to her as well as its two editors Sandra Alcosser & Arthur Salm, who approved its inclusion in Volume 2.

The support of my Iranian-American community has been my column of strength. As long as I have that, nothing can stop me.

Above all, I will forever be indebted to you, my loyal readers, who not only read, share, and support my work, but invite me to your lives and ask me to keep writing. I hope my heartfelt words will once again settle in your hearts.

Dedication

To the loving memory of my mother Sarvar
Khazai, who remained a lady to the very end.
Thank you, *Maman*, for your gift of life.

Part One

Rana

.

Chapter

· *One* ·

THE FIRST TIME RANA HELD HER NEWBORN, she did exactly what she had done with her other two children—she reached for the tiny fist and gently peeled back the fingers and counted them. Finding all ten, she took a deep breath and exhaled. Despite the faint smell of kerosene from the corner heater, the bedroom felt cold. Rana decided she'd count the toes later when the baby's feet were exposed.

Like most Iranian women in the 1970's, Rana had planned to deliver her baby in a hospital and with her doctor present. But the first contractions had come late at night while her husband was out. No taxis ran at such a late hour, but after the unforeseen snow had covered the streets of Shiraz, getting around town would have been difficult in any vehicle. Dayeh, the old nanny, had known a midwife who lived nearby and Rana was grateful they had found anyone at all.

The middle-aged midwife acted frantic, as though she blamed her patient for the way things had turned out. Her plastic gloves felt cold on Rana's skin. "Such a head on a baby," the woman said, "let alone coming out of a woman with *your* small frame." She wiped her forehead with the sleeve of her uniform. Her plastic gloves glistened with some form of fluid, though it was hard to tell what it was. "Mrs. Moradi, I'm afraid your tear is too irregular to stitch." And she hurried about, muttering more indistinct words in her frustrated tone.

Rana closed her eyes and tried to mask her anxiety. After a moment of absolute silence, she felt a rolled towel being pushed between her thighs.

"Hold that tight," the midwife commanded. She took Rana's hand and placed it on her abdomen over the area of the worst cramps. "Press hard here. That should help to stop the bleeding." She pulled the bedcovers up to Rana's chin and tucked them tight around her.

Rana heard water splashing, followed by the infant's cry, now softer than the previous loud wails. Before she had a chance to take a look, the cries turned to a soft murmur and then faded into the next room. She smelled burning wild rue and knew it to be her old nanny's way of wishing good health for mother and child. The smoke mixed with the odor of fresh blood and iodine vapors, turning the air too heavy to breathe. Following hours of labor, Rana felt woozy, and the pain that shot through her made it hard to focus on the midwife's instructions. She heard muffled voices in the hallway and felt the draft as someone opened the door, then came Dayeh's cheerful voice.

"Congratulations, Major Moradi. You have another little lady."

Rana perked her ears, unable to predict her husband's reaction to the news of a third daughter. There was a long pause.

"How surprising!" His sarcastic response sounded like a grunt.

Dayeh chuckled as if it had been a joke. "God's gift, and what a beauty at that."

Another silence.

"*Farhad,*" Rana tried his name, but her dry lips were stuck together and her voice wouldn't come out. What was there to say to him anyway? She held the bedcovers in clenched fists, listened and hoped, but soon heard the hammer of his heavy boots fading down the marble hallway. Somewhere in the distance a door slammed. Nearby, women whispered.

Rana wondered if the energy that drained from her and the emptiness it left behind could be what it felt like when the soul left a body. As her mind filled with images of her other two children, her grip loosened, allowing her hand to slip away. Weightless, she felt herself being pulled into shadows and sank deeper and deeper into a dark well.

The warmth that caressed her face carried the promise of a bright sun. Circles of light moved inside Rana's eyelids like fireflies. She kept her eyes closed but tried to move her body to a sitting position.

"Oh, *khanoom* is up!" Young Banu had more ring to her voice than Rana's headache could tolerate.

"Please close the drapes," Rana pleaded.

The hooks jingled as they slid on the metal pole.

Rana opened her eyes and squinted at the remaining light. "Where's my baby?" she asked, conscious of the silence around her, wondering who had fed the infant.

"She's with Dayeh, ma'am."

Rana checked the clock on her nightstand. "Noon, already? I can't believe I slept this late."

A wide-eyed Banu shook her head. "Oh, you slept for two days, ma'am. The doctor came and went several times. You were burning with fever."

Rana shook her head. "Two days?"

Banu nodded frantically. "I'll get you something to eat. You'll need your nourishment."

Nourishment. What kind of milk had they given her newborn? Banu was gone before she had a chance to ask questions. And where were the girls? Marjan, now in third grade, could be at school, but little Vida should have returned from her half-day nursery school.

Banu returned, pushing the door with an elbow and carrying a large tray.

"How *is* the baby?" Rana asked.

"Oh, beautiful as the moon she is," Banu said while setting the tray on the nightstand. "Such thick eyelashes on a baby! *MashAllah,* I must burn more incense for her."

Rana touched her deflated tummy and felt as if all the weight missing from her middle had gone to her sore breasts.

"Is the Major home?" Rana hoped her anxiety wouldn't show.

"No, ma'am," Banu said, straightening the bedcovers to secure the tray. "He called last night. I heard Dayeh tell him you were resting."

So he had stayed out all night. Rana would not allow herself to admit where her husband had been. Or with whom.

She surveyed the food: Hot bread, soft-boiled eggs, and a bowl of *kachi*—the saffron pudding her old nanny thought essential for a new mother's strength. Rana took a spoonful, but the smell of rosewater made her feel sick again. She swallowed with difficulty and pushed the tray away. "Take this, dear, and just bring me some water."

Moments later, Dayeh strolled in without bothering to knock. She carried the baby wrapped in a blanket and presented her with pride, as if she herself had a part in her creation. She chanted in her shaky old voice, "I have a daughter, *shah*—the king—doesn't have, she has a face *mah*—the moon—doesn't have!"

With newfound energy, Rana stretched out both arms to receive the infant and placed her own cheek on the warmth of the tiny head. When the initial thrill had passed, she placed the baby on the bed and studied her features, now less swollen and more defined. It was time to absorb the details and familiarize herself with her newest daughter: soft cheeks, flared nostrils, and that tiny button on the upper lip. She leaned closer and inhaled. Oh, how she had missed that milky scent, how she adored her helpless little ones, that soft fuzz of hair, the wrinkled neck. She kissed the top of the baby's head and noticed Dayeh had decorated the baby's gown with all sorts of trinkets: A silver prayer charm in the shape of the holy Koran, a blue glass eye, the word Allah engraved in a silver hand, all joined together with a safety pin and secured on the band that held the baby's swaddling clothes together. When it came to keeping the evil eye away, Dayeh took no chances.

The old nanny beamed a smile and said, "Praise be to Allah, your fever seems to have broken." She touched Rana's forehead who was staring at the infant. "Pretty little thing, isn't she?" the nanny said and squinted. "I think she resembles you. Sure looks nothing like *them*."

Rana smiled. The woman made no secret of her hostilities toward Farhad and his entire family, and the only reason Rana tolerated such insults was that Dayeh had practically been a mother to her since she was a little girl.

"I just hope she has a happy life written on her forehead," Rana said with a deep sigh.

"Oh, dear child, happiness is a garden, but one has to plant the seed and endure the cold winter."

Rana thought about that, but did not respond.

"You have a name?" the nanny asked.

Rana shook her head.

"Well, you better come up with something, or she'll grow to be an old woman called Baby." She cackled at her own joke.

"I'll leave that choice to her father."

Dayeh turned her back. "As if *he* cares."

"*Dayeh*! Of course he cares. He just needs time to adjust."

The old nanny busied herself with the curtains, folding the pleats one by one and tied the stack with a silk cord. "Sounds like you've forgiven him already."

Rana lay back and closed her eyes. *Forgive?* Her old nanny's words couldn't be further from the truth. Which of his treacheries should she forgive? Women absolved their men for infidelity all the time, but how big would her heart need to be before she could forgive Farhad for practically moving in with his mistress? She felt a fire within, flames that no amount of sighs or tears could smother. She wasn't ready to discuss this openly, not even with Dayeh. After all, the nanny was an employee, and Rana's husband the head of this family. Besides, she didn't wish to add more to a subject that had already become the talk around town.

The baby cried and Dayeh rushed over, picked her up, and started to pace. "I don't know what goes on inside that pretty head of yours, child, but I don't like the way you put up with your husband's absences."

Rana swallowed hard and wished she could go back to a deep sleep, one that she would not awaken from for days. She could not recall being so weak with her other two, or ever, for that matter. Conscious of the silence around her, she asked, "Where are the girls?"

Dayeh continued to pace while rocking the baby. "At their aunt's. The Major sent them over to his sister's and said they're to stay there for a few days."

Rana wondered how the girls coped with Badri's house full of boys and hoped the cousins were getting along.

The baby continued to fuss.

"I think she needs a change," Dayeh said, sniffing around the baby.

"Let me do it," Rana said with enthusiasm.

Her nanny stopped pacing and her worried eyes stared at her. "Don't you move, child. That fever nearly had you killed and I don't think you're strong enough. It'll only take me—"

"Please?"

Dayeh studied her with concern, then nodded and returned the baby reluctantly. "Watch her while I get clean diapers."

Rana put the baby on the bed and smiled at the swaddling clothes Dayeh had designed. Multiple layers of cloth were secured around the baby with a yard of embroidered band, making her look like a mummy. Rana loosened the band and one by one unraveled the damp layers. The folds of fabric had left pink lines on the baby's skin. "No wonder you were so unhappy," Rana said, caressing her soft skin.

The baby cooed, her tiny legs kicking the air.

Rana stared at the little girl's nudity. "Ah, what would it have taken God to put a little appendage between your legs and end my problem?"

Just then, Dayeh returned and took over. She removed the wet diapers and spread new layers of clean cloth under the baby. After wiping her, she dusted the baby with so much talcum powder it made her cough. Rana held the tiny feet and lifted the infant's legs so the tiny backside could also be powdered. She stretched them again, then let go with a start as though she'd been electrocuted.

"Oh, my..." she whispered in horror.

"Let me do this," Dayeh said, sounding resigned.

Unable to respond, Rana held the tiny legs again and pulled them straight down, side-by-side, while staring at the baby's right leg. Noticeably shorter, the tiny toes barely reached the left ankle. Rana pulled back and covered her mouth with both hands, unable to breathe, and feeling her old nanny's arm around her, she buried her face into her shoulder.

"The midwife gave her to me so quickly, I'm sure she didn't

notice," Dayeh said, as if this small fact would change everything. When Rana didn't utter a word, she added, "I haven't told a soul." She put a hand under Rana's chin, turned her face up, and staring into her eyes cautioned, "And neither should you."

Rana turned her face. "Oh, my God," she whispered.

She felt Dayeh's hand rub her neck and shoulder the way it had many times before, her voice pouring out her blind devotion. "God will help to even them out as she grows."

Rana pushed Dayeh's hand away. "Oh, will He?" The tears that had gathered for some time now found her cheeks. "Did you stop to think just who created her this way?" Her voice broke amid sobs. "Is this my punishment or is it some kind of sick test?" She looked at the ceiling as if God would be somewhere on the roof, eavesdropping. "It wasn't bad enough to give me another girl, this one had to be crippled, too?"

"Please, child, stop your blasphemy!"

"Oh, I see. He is getting back at me for ... that night ...?" Unable to express her frustration she screamed, "What? He gives my poor child a life of misery just to prove that life and death aren't up to anyone but Him?" She threw her hands in the air. "So you think He won't turn his back on me?" She pointed to the baby, "Hasn't He already?"

Dayeh whispered prayers of forgiveness, wrapped the diapers loosely around the baby and lifted her.

"God is all forgiving, child. He'd never punish in this way. You were just upset that night, my child. You didn't know what you were doing."

Before Dayeh turned to leave, Rana reached over and pulled the prayer seal off the baby's clothes. "You won't be needing *that*, my love," she cried out. "God wasn't there when you were conceived, He obviously wasn't there when you took form, and He sure as hell won't be around to help you with that leg."

The baby started to cry again, and Dayeh rushed out cradling the baby without bothering to close the door.

For a long while Rana clutched the prayer seal in her fist, thought of her bleak future, and wept. Not only had she failed to give her husband an heir to carry his name, now with a less than perfect child, she had given him ample reason to reject her. No one would blame him. She pictured her sister-in-law parading with her sons at family gatherings. But this was no longer a question of gender. Soon the news of her baby's deformity would spread. She pictured the curiosity in the eyes of visitors, the criticism, and the pity. Her heart broke as she recalled the tiny deformed limb, and she had no idea how it would affect the life of her helpless little one. But she stopped there. Unable to send her imagination beyond the misery, she became conscious of her own lack of knowledge. What if the growth of the baby's leg was stumped permanently? How would this affect a growing child's functions? Would she walk? Would the condition worsen in the years to come? In some strange way, Rana identified with that incomplete leg, as though this was her legacy, a way to make sure the baby would inherit some of her mother's insufficiency. Her heart went to this newborn in a way that she had not experienced with her other two.

Dayeh's sad lullaby echoed in the hallway. Rana watched her nanny's shadow on the wall outside her door as it rocked the baby back and forth, back and forth.

⁓

With darkness all around her, Rana wasn't sure if it had been the sound of a car that woke her. She was covered in sweat. Extending her arm, she touched the empty space beside her before the door squeaked open.

"Farhad?" her sleepy voice called his name, but in the light that spilled in from the hallway, she recognized Dayeh's plump outline.

"It's me, child." She came closer and touched Rana's forehead. "No fever. Thank God. It's feeding time and the doctor suggested you should try breastfeeding. I'll go wake the baby."

"No, Dayeh, let her rest. Just bring her to me when she's awake." Before Dayeh had left she added, "Did I hear the Major's car?"

The old nanny hesitated for a few seconds. "You did. It's turned out to be a cold night and he came for his overcoat." She paused before adding, "But he's gone again."

Grateful for the darkness, Rana kept her poise and acted as if she had no idea where her husband might be going. Somewhere, a woman with no face awaited him. Rana would have to deal with that at some point, but not tonight, not while she lacked the energy to plan a future.

"I'll be back soon, then," Dayeh said and closed the door.

The words she had once heard from her sister-in-law now came back. "A true lady learns to adjust." Unsure of how much more adjusting she could handle, Rana sat up and leaned against the headboard. Just then, she heard the car again, now from farther away. She left her bed, and went to the window without turning on the light. Tiny crystals frosted the windowpane. A pale moon painted the snow blue, giving the trees oversized shadows. Moments later the taillights of the army Jeep spilled red over the driveway. Rana felt a chill as the car disappeared behind the gate, and the world around her turned colder.

She knew then the name she would give her daughter—the name of the darkest, coldest, and longest night.

Yalda.

Chapter

· *Two* ·

WHEN RANA HEARD THE CAR DOOR, she wasn't sure how to face her husband, but then came the giggles and the sound of her daughters chirping below the window. He was not alone. She looked out and found her sister-in-law's blue Mercedes in the driveway right behind the army Jeep, and the girls were now racing toward the steps.

Major Moradi greeted his wife with a formal nod and a "Glad to see you on your feet."

Rana did not respond as her attention went to her daughters, but she saw him from the corner of her eye as he helped Badri out of her fur coat before approaching the small table holding his pile of mail.

Marjan and Vida rushed to fill their mother's open arms, but no sooner had Dayeh walked in with the baby than they tore away and seemed to forget all else. "Ooo! How tiny." Marjan screamed with joy and they both hovered over the infant.

Badri pushed a bunch of white chrysanthemums into Rana's hand as if to avoid a hug. "I didn't have a chance to visit sooner," she said and rolled her eyes. "My oh my, girls demand attention!" Her smile showed no joy.

Dayeh walked across the hallway and offered the infant to Major Moradi, but Rana noticed he only glanced at the newborn and gently stroked her little head before returning to his letters.

Rana returned to the sofa and lowered herself into the makeshift bed. "I don't know how to thank you, dear," she said to Badri, and hoped it sounded sincere enough. With her own family in Tehran, if she wanted her daughters to enjoy an extended family, she'd need to stay on good terms with her sister-in-law. She called the maid peeking through the open doorway. "Banu *jan*, be a dear and put these in a nice vase for me." She handed her the cellophane-wrapped bunch that reminded her of funerals.

After Banu had left, Badri raised an eyebrow and said, "I love how you talk to your maids." Her tone disagreed. "Then again, given that you spend so much time with them, I suppose they become your friends." She faced her brother. "Farhad, it must be refreshing to leave all those army boys behind and come to such a calm, *feminine,* household."

Rana winced, but once again she swallowed her words. Major Moradi looked at his sister from over the newspaper he had started to read but didn't comment. The silent agreement between the brother and sister wasn't new to Rana, but now she sensed more, a message, as though they had discussed the matter behind her back and now insinuated that she hadn't tried hard enough to have a boy.

"Thank you for taking care of the children," Rana said with common courtesy. "I would have wanted them back earlier, but the infection had spread, and no matter what the doctor prescribed, my fever wouldn't break. Dayeh didn't think I could handle the noise."

"Oh, they sure are loud, but they needed their mom." Badri said and as she waved a hand in the air, her sleeve slipped back to reveal a new emerald bracelet. "I suppose some women need to take it easy, which makes me grateful for being the strong type." Skipping the topic of Rana's infection, she sniffed loudly as if to pull half the air in the room. "I remember accompanying my husband to social functions just days after each boy was born."

Rana turned back to her daughters, who seemed mesmerized by what must have looked to them like a living doll. Marjan wanted to pick up the baby while Vida stood back and watched, her face already taking on the unsure expression of the middle child. "Come here, you two," Rana called out to them. "I haven't hugged you nearly enough." But the girls didn't seem to hear her as they followed Dayeh and the baby out the door.

"How long before dinner's served?" Major Moradi said from behind his newspaper.

"I have no idea," Rana responded. She thought how calm he was and wanted to confront him. But each time she thought of doing so, fear of what he might say stopped her.

He walked to the coffee table, slammed part of the paper on top of it and exchanged another glance with his sister before picking up a different section to read.

How much did Badri know about the other woman?

Rana pulled the blanket over her shoulders and looked out into the yard. The sun had melted most of last night's snow, and here and there, she noticed the pale green of an early spring. "We need to register her," she said, without turning her face to him and thought of the name that had come to her the night before. "Do you have a name in mind?"

Moradi shrugged without taking his eyes off the page. "Whatever you want."

Rana stole a look at Badri, but she seemed busy examining her nails. Minutes later, the brother and sister started talking about the news around town, and the subject of baby's name was left behind.

After dinner, when the girls were sent to bed, Badri prepared to leave.

"Let me get my hat," Moradi said and walked to the hallway closet. "I was supposed to be somewhere earlier on, but you visit so rarely that I didn't want to miss it."

Badri kissed the air on each side of Rana's face. Farhad put on his army hat and opened the door for his sister. Before following Badri into the hallway, he turned his face in the general direction of the family room and said, "Don't wait up."

The following week when Rana called Tehran to speak to her parents, Dr. and Mrs. Ameli. Her mother chatted as usual, but it didn't take her father long to sense trouble.

"Are you feeling all right?" he asked immediately.

"Yes, Papa. I'm fine."

"Something is wrong." Now it sounded more of a statement than a question.

Rana hesitated. She had never brought her problems to him before, but this was different and she reminded herself that he was a doctor. "I can't talk about it on the phone. Do you think you could come to Shiraz? Just for a few days?"

During the seven years since her marriage to a man from Shiraz, her parents had visited only twice. All other reunions took place in Tehran, and considering that Moradi's presence in the capital was a frequent job requirement, the trips worked out for everyone. But with both girls now attending school, it was harder to travel.

There was a long pause. "Of course we will." Her father's voice reflected deep concern. "I'll call back when I've reserved our flights."

Mrs. Ameli grabbed the phone from her husband. "May death strike me, what happened? Who died?"

Rana smiled sadly at her mother's dramatic reaction. "Nobody died, Mother. I've been missing you and it will make me so happy to see you again."

"You don't have an infection, do you? I knew you should have had the baby in a hospital, these days a delivery at home ..."

Rana wondered how her mother would have reacted to the high fever that nearly took her life. "I'm fine, Maman. This has nothing to do with my health."

"Oh, God, don't tell me it's your husband. He's not quitting his job, is he?"

Rana knew her mother was working her way into one of those scenes where she became the center of attention regardless of who faced the actual crisis. It would be best to tell her about the problem before the woman's imagination had the best of her.

"No, Maman, it has nothing to do with Farhad, or me."

The breathing on the other side of the line seemed to stop briefly.

"It's the baby. Something's wrong with her little leg." She heard her mother gasp. "She is otherwise quite healthy, but her legs just don't seem to match. I—I think something happened while she was inside of me, but I want the last word to come from *Baba*."

"Your father is an eye doctor, dear. What would *he* know about a baby's leg?"

Rana recalled her visit to Dr. Fard and the deep concern in the old pediatrician's eyes as he spoke about a possible need for corrective surgery. She wasn't ready to accept that, much less ready to share it with her mother.

"A doctor is a doctor," she said and tried a chuckle. "But please keep this to yourself."

"What did Farhad say?" Not waiting for a response she added, "Oh, and that sister-in-law of yours. I'll bet she had a few things to say."

Rana bit her lip. "Please don't worry, Maman. We'll talk more once you're here."

—

They arrived on Friday, Major Moradi's day off, perhaps to make it more convenient for their son-in-law to meet the plane. Instead, Rana went to the airport, accompanied by two eager little girls.

"Farhad apologizes," Rana said right away. "He's away on business for the day."

The drive home was noisy. Vida and Marjan clung to their grandfather and demanded answers to all the questions they had stored up for a year. Is that ice cream place open in winter? Have they added a new merry-go-round in Shahrdari Park? When will the public swimming pools reopen?

In the excitement that followed grandparents' arrival Yalda's problem did not come up, but Rana felt its dark shadow lurking in every glance and in the pause between casual conversations. She noticed that as soon as the baby was presented to her parents, despite the adoring comments, they both stared at the swaddling clothes as if to see through them.

Soon Dayeh served an elaborate lunch. The aroma of saffron rice and seared lamb filled the dining room.

"You shouldn't have gone to so much trouble," Mrs. Ameli said.

"Oh Maman, you know how Dayeh loves to fuss over you."

"I do everything for you, over my eyes," the old nanny said, using an old expression to show her willingness to be of service. "I can't forget who my true masters are." A nostalgic look fell on Dayeh's face to show how she missed the Amelis and the time she had cared for Rana as a baby.

Dr. Ameli chuckled. "You better not let your current employer hear such things."

Vida and Marjan took seats on either side of their grandfather. They made no secret about favoring him over their bossy grandmother.

After lunch, they sat in the family room and Banu brought the tea. Dr. Ameli put Vida on his lap. "Now *you* tell Papa-joon what you've been up to since he last saw you."

"We've had a baby," she reported.

Everyone laughed.

"You mean that little thing sleeping upstairs is yours?"

Marjan made a face to indicate she was too old for that game.

Vida nodded several times. "She came from Maman's belly."

"That's amazing," the old doctor said.

Marjan rolled her eyes. "He already knows that, silly."

Mrs. Ameli laughed at the way her husband carried on.

Rana found it hard to share the laughter. The mention of 'that little thing upstairs' made her even more conscious of the main reason for this visit. She realized the urgency of a talk before her husband returned. Farhad still did not know about the baby's leg. True that he hadn't been around much, but he needed to be told. Maybe her father would agree to break the news to him. All morning the girls had been so excited that they stuck to grandpa, leaving no chance for a private moment to ask him for such a favor.

Dr. Ameli stood. "Some of us old people need a nap," he said, but before leaving, he turned to Rana. "When the baby's up, bring her to my room, won't you?"

Rana smiled with gratitude. "I think she's awake. I could do that right away."

Moments later, with Yalda in her arms, she joined her father in the guest bedroom where he had spread a clean towel over his bed. "You can put her here," he said.

Rana knelt down by the bed, put the baby on the towel, and started to undress her. Dr. Ameli sat at the edge of the bed and began his examination as if this were a routine check up. The touch of his cold fingers made the newborn cry. When he stretched the baby's legs side-by-side, Rana thought the difference in their length already seemed more pronounced. She tried to read her father's face, but the old doctor was absorbed in his work. He took time to listen to the baby's heart and lungs, bent and flexed the joints of both feet, and checked the reflexes by gently tapping the knees. When finished, he asked Rana to put the infant's clothes back on.

"She's a healthy little thing," he said with a reassuring smile. "Everything is just fine. As for the leg, I think it's a random anomaly, nothing genetic, and we may never know what disturbed its development." He adjusted his glasses and ran his fingers through his mound of gray hair. "You didn't have any accidents, a fall, or anything like that. Did you?"

Rana's mind filled with memories of that horrific night, but too afraid to confess to her father, she shook her head.

"What does the pediatrician think?"

"Dr. Fard mentioned something similar," she said. "At this point, all I want to know is if it can be fixed, and how serious is the procedure."

Her father stood up and wrapped one arm around her shoulders. "He is a far better judge than I am, but I wouldn't let anyone touch her for years. You should look into surgical correction when she's much older." He looked into Rana's eyes. "How is Farhad taking it?"

Rana didn't reply.

"He does know, doesn't he?"

She cast her eyes down.

"You mean you've kept it all to yourself this entire time?" His voice echoed deep horror. "Didn't the pediatrician mention it to him?"

"Farhad hasn't been around much," she said and tried to sound calm. "He never spoke to Dr. Fard."

"It's been ten whole days, my dear! What made you hide such a thing from your husband?"

Rana didn't know how to respond. She wished she could be the little girl who used to bury her face in her father's chest and cry.

"He is no different from the rest of people out there, Papa. Don't look at yourself. Most people consider handicapped to be some kind of freak. I don't need their pity and won't wish for my baby to be an outcast from the start."

"No one is crazy enough to do that to a baby," he said, but his raised voice did not sound convincing.

"He hasn't been the same lately." Rana took in a deep breath before adding, "A third girl was bad enough news, any more and I was afraid he'd leave me."

"Bad news?" Dr. Ameli exhaled his frustration. "How could you say that? I can't even imagine what my life would have been without my four daughters." He paused for a few seconds and lowered his voice to its normal tone. "I've never heard such nonsense. Men don't leave their wives because there's something wrong with a baby. Stop acting so guilty, it isn't as if *you* caused this."

Rana felt her heart sink.

He hesitated before asking, "Would you like *me* to tell him?"

She nodded several times, amazed at her father's perception, at his aptitude for offering comfort when it was most needed. "I know it wasn't a choice, but the truth remains that I have failed to give him the son he wanted so badly."

"Is that so?" Dr. Ameli said and chuckled. "The last I checked my textbooks, it was the man's chromosomes that made boys. Are you telling me Shiraz's society disagrees with science?" He laughed again. Rana felt his arms tightening around her and realized this was the first time anyone had held her since the baby's birth.

———

Major Moradi made sure he returned long after everyone had gone to bed. He went into the living room and did not need a light to find the bar located at the far end. A drink would relax him. He used to go out with his friends after a tiring assignment, but it had been a while since he'd done that.

The day the new baby was born, finding it hard to accept his shattered dream, he had walked aimlessly for a while before going to a bar. For months he had watched his wife grow bigger and imagined his little boy inside her. Maybe things would never be right between them, but she would now give him the male heir he had promised his late father. He had pictured the little guy so many times that by now his son had become a reality. So when Dayeh told him it was another girl, she might as well have given him the news of the boy's death. He just had to get away from the house, go somewhere to be alone, and drown his silent tears in a drink.

Later, he called his best friend Nader and was told a few of the men were at his apartment. When he joined them and announced the news, he tried hard to mask his grief. At first, his colleagues poked fun at him and teased him about his growing "hen house," but when he didn't share their laughter the jokes stopped. That had been more than a week ago. By now, such gatherings were charged with unspoken words and heavy glances, as if the boys had talked about him behind his back.

On his return from Jahrom, he had stopped by a phone booth and made the call he had tried to avoid for days. Parisa's lively voice filled his ears with a pleasure he had thought he would never feel again.

"*Allo?*"

He held the receiver closer to his ear as if to draw strength from it.

"*Allo?*"

He hung up and went back to his car. He needed to be with Parisa more than she could imagine, but somehow found it wrong to be with her while dealing with a grief that she could not understand. He had gone to Jahrom instead and tried to come to terms with his disappointment away from everyone. Now, standing in the dark, he wished he could have bottled that cheerful voice saying '*allo*' so he could drink it and soothe his nerves. He took a deep breath and savored the calm, the darkness, and the sound of whisky escaping the bottle's neck as it poured into his glass.

"Need company?" a man's voice startled him.

Farhad turned around and in the dim light coming from the hallway recognized the slim figure of his father-in-law in pajamas. "Hello, doctor," he said and his hand searched for the light switch on the wall. "Hope I didn't wake you." He turned on the light.

The old doctor smiled and turned his face away. "No, you didn't. And you can turn that thing off." He covered his eyes with the palm of one hand. "I was up, but by now everyone else must be dreaming of *seven kings.*"

Farhad turned off the light and took another glass. "Soda?" he asked.

"No, water's fine."

In the column of light coming from the hallway, Dr. Ameli found his way to the couch.

Farhad carried the drinks and sat next to him. "I'm sorry I couldn't be here when you arrived," he said and meant it.

"Work is work," the old doctor said. "How was your trip to Jahrom?"

"The same as always. I spent most of my time at the base."

"Rana tells me you were in Tehran last week. Sorry we didn't get to see you."

"Yes. Again, I was mostly in the outskirts."

They sipped their drinks in silence for a few minutes.

"The girls are so grown up," the doctor said. "And, that baby. Oh, she's precious."

Another silence fell between them while the only audible sound came from a small humming refrigerator.

"Son," Dr. Ameli put a hand on Major Moradi's knee. "I hope you don't mind me calling you that. I've always thought of you as my son, especially since your father's passing."

Farhad nodded and for a second wished this nice man could have been just a friend, someone he could talk to. He stared ahead into the semi-dark space and said nothing.

"I know you're disappointed to get another girl," the old doctor said. "It's only natural to want what you don't have." He nodded several times, and as if to support his own opinion, added, "All my friends who had only boys used to wish for girls."

Farhad took a gulp of his drink and remained silent.

"Parenthood is such a privilege that gender should make no difference, but if you ask me, I believe girls are a lot more attentive."

"Is that so?"

Dr. Ameli didn't seem to notice his sarcasm because he added, "My mother used to say that a girl is her parents' walking cane for old age. When she said such things after Rana was born, I considered it her way of consoling me, but now I see there's a lot of truth in that."

Farhad's mind filled with thoughts he could not put into words. The image of the tiny army hat in his closet wouldn't leave him. He had ordered that funny thing just in case this time he'd be lucky. Oh, how he had planned to show off the baby around the base, covering the tiny head with that hat, pinning his single medal on the baby's clothes. In his mind's eye, the baby boy smiled and put his tiny fist to his temple in a salute. For months the vision had made him smile, but now it hurt so much that he could not push it away fast enough. He took another sip of whisky and blinked in fear of getting misty-eyed.

"I examined Yalda this afternoon," the old doctor said casually. "There seems to be a little problem."

Farhad looked at him. "Problem?"

"Oh, nothing serious," Dr. Ameli said and put his glass down. "At least, not at the moment."

Farhad waited for more.

"Rana doesn't think you're ready to hear this, but she may be underestimating your strength." He took in a deep breath and added, "There is a problem with the baby's legs."

Major Moradi shot the old man a sharp look, which he knew couldn't be missed, even in the dim light.

"There seems to be a difference in their length," Dr. Ameli went on. "Not a common problem, and not too serious. Nonetheless, it is a problem and will definitely need attention down the line."

Farhad got up. "That's great," he said and began to pace the floor. "That's just great," he said again before another long silence. No questions came, and no further explanation was offered. After a few minutes, he sat down again, now feeling numb, as if something had hit him in the head.

Dr. Ameli opened his mouth and looked as if he was going to offer more words of comfort, but Major Moradi raised a hand. "Doctor, I don't want to seem ungrateful and really appreciate that you care, but this is my problem and right now I need a moment alone." He went back to the bar to refresh his drink. When he returned, the old doctor was gone.

⁓

Dayeh went downstairs to ask the Amelis to go ahead and enjoy their breakfast without Rana as the baby had kept her up most of the night, and she might sleep late. Vida and Marjan were already done with theirs and rushed to check the baby. The Major accompanied his in-laws, but after the initial greetings, no one seemed willing to engage in a conversation. In the kitchen, Dayeh poured cardamom tea in tall glasses that had a gold rim and set them in ornate china saucers and let Banu take the tray in. She then served a fresh boiled egg to each guest before returning to the kitchen.

"Something's the matter in there," Banu said, nodding to the family room.

"You mind your own business."

Banu raised an eyebrow. "*Khanoom* said she wants to sleep, but the last I checked, she was up and if I'm not mistaken, she was crying."

Dayeh, now warming a bottle for the baby, stopped her work and shot the young maid a harsh look.

Banu looked away. "Can't blame me for caring."

"I know your kind of care. Caring enough to snoop around and blab. If anything is the matter with Rana Khanoom, it's neither my business, nor yours." She shook the bottle to drop milk on her wrist. Satisfied with the temperature, she spread a clean towel over her shoulder and headed for the nursery. To her horror, Vida had managed to lift the baby out of the bassinette.

"You give her to me. Right now," the old nanny shouted before rushing over to grab the infant. "She's no toy, and don't you ever let me catch either of you lifting her."

"Told you so," Marjan said to her sister.

Dayeh sat in the single armchair and offered the bottle to the baby's eager mouth. The girls knelt on either side to watch.

The crash of something in the family room below, followed by loud voices, startled Dayeh so much that she nearly dropped the baby. She turned to look at the girls and noticed they were equally frightened. "Stay right here, you two. I'll be right back." She rushed out, still holding the infant and the bottle. At the bottom of the stairs, she bumped into Banu, who stood short of the entrance to the living room, listening. Dayeh gave her the baby.

"Take her to the nursery," she commanded, giving the girl's shoulder a shove. "And make sure the children stay with you."

No sooner had she entered than she sensed a change in the room. The shattered fragments of a cup under Mrs. Ameli's feet explained the crashing sound. Rana's mother was sitting at the table with her face buried in her hands. Her husband stood next to her, bending down, stroking her hair, and offering what must have been words of comfort. Dayeh looked for Major Moradi and found him at the window with his back to the guests. Rana held her bathrobe around her with one hand and was trying to pick up parts of the broken cup with the other. The old nanny could not imagine what had happened, but the yelling had been a man's voice, and she knew Dr. Ameli never raised his voice.

Rana put the pieces of china in the trashcan and said to her husband's back, "You couldn't wait to start a scene, could you?"

The Major turned and glared at her. "A scene?" He sneered. "Oh, you'd know all about scenes, wouldn't you." When Rana did not answer, he pointed to Dr. Ameli with his chin and said, "Amazing how your courage has returned now that *Papa* is here!"

Rana turned her back to him and slowly lowered herself into a chair. Despite the warm sun that spilled in through the French doors, Dayeh felt cold.

Dr. Ameli cleared his throat uncomfortably and said, "Perhaps we shouldn't be here when you discuss this." He took his wife's elbow to help her get up.

Major Moradi raised a hand. "Oh, no! I think you need to hear this." He shot Rana another look. "In fact, that may be the reason you were invited. This whole problem has nothing to do with the baby, or the weird leg. It's more about what's left of our marriage."

Mrs. Ameli gave out a cry, "Oh, my."

Dayeh turned around to leave, but Rana yelled at her, "Stay right there, Dayeh. Maybe you can tell them how warmly the Major greeted his newborn daughter." She gave an angry laugh.

Dayeh could feel the weight of Moradi's stare.

"Yes, go ahead, wise one," he said. "Better yet, why not tell them how the loving mother tried to kill her unborn baby?"

Mrs. Ameli's eyes darted back and forth between her daughter and the Major. The old nanny uttered prayers under her breath.

Dr. Ameli walked across the room to Rana, lifted her face with both hands, and tried to make eye contact. "What is your husband talking about?" And when Rana did not respond, he added, "It isn't true, is it?"

Rana turned her face away. "Don't, Papa. Please don't ask." Her face flushed, and she broke into sobs.

The old doctor stood next to Rana but his inquisitive eyes were now pinned on Dayeh.

Dayeh stood in the middle of the room, unable to leave, reluctant to speak. It was one thing to lock secrets in her chest and to keep quiet despite her contempt for the Major, but quite another to be the one whose words would be the final verdict that would condemn Rana.

"Tell them," Major Moradi shouted.

Dayeh needed time to rearrange her words. "There's really not much to tell."

Moradi marched to the bookshelf and grabbed the Koran,

which had been there ever since the couple's wedding. He kissed the leather binding and caressed its embossed letters, before holding it out to her. "Put your hand on God's words and swear you'll tell the truth, and may the Koran break your back if you tell any more lies."

Dayeh dropped her head and stared at her hands.

"Oh, God," Mrs. Ameli said. "It is true, isn't it?" she asked no one in particular.

Dr. Ameli took his arm off Rana's shoulder. "What did you do?" His voice now a mere whisper. "And why?"

"That's what I'd like to know, too," the Major said. "Your daughter will not answer my questions, nor will this old witch admit to what she knows. I had to hear it from the doctors." He pointed a finger at Dayeh. "She's good at taking *my* money, but her loyalty lies elsewhere."

Dr. Ameli's questioning eyes turned back to Rana, then as if changing his mind, he walked straight to Dayeh.

"I appreciate your devotion to my daughter," he said in his soothing voice. "But silence doesn't always solve the problem. I think it's best to tell us what happened." His caring tone presented a huge contrast to the harshness in Moradi's. He stooped a little and stared into the old nanny's eyes. "Dayeh-jan, you must know this is no longer about Rana alone. To help the baby, we'll need to know what went wrong. And I mean details. Did my daughter do anything to harm her child?"

Dayeh wished he wouldn't put her in such a spot. How much had been said before she entered the room? She knew Rana enough to imagine her persistence in keeping everything to herself. But someone, and she suspected it would be the Major, had brought up the unmentionable. Swearing on the holy Koran would leave her no choice but to tell what she knew, unless she was prepared to burn in hell. After a long pause, she decided that even God would forgive her for working around the truth a little. No, she couldn't tell any lies, but there was no reason to tell them every detail. She looked at Dr. Ameli as if to address him exclusively and said, "It was an accident, sir. Miss Rana should have called one of us to help her move the dresser, but instead—"

"Stop your filthy lies!" the Major interrupted. "She knew exactly what she was doing." He turned to Rana. "Don't you stand there playing innocent with me. I think your parents need to know just what kind of hideous acts their little angel is capable of."

The mere thought of that horrible night filled Dayeh's mind with images of blood: Blood on Rana's blue nightgown, down her legs, and on the Persian rug. As much as she wanted to blame Banu for what had happened, deep down Dayeh knew the responsibility lay with the Major. The day Banu chatted with the neighbor's maid and went straight to Rana with the news of a woman named Parisa, Dayeh found out too late to prevent the damage. To learn of another woman in that man's life did not surprise Dayeh one bit. That was how some men dealt with their desires. She recalled a cold winter day, when her own husband had brought home a young woman. Dayeh and the new wife lived together for years until they were widowed. She wouldn't put anything past some men, and the major was no saint. But the last person who needed to hear that was his pregnant wife. Dayeh blamed herself for not having seen it coming. Rana's reaction had sounded an alarm. Without a word, she sat for hours staring at the rug, her frail body folded, and unlike other times, she made no excuses for her husband's actions. Knowing Rana would talk only when she felt like it, Dayeh had tended to her needs without a word.

"Don't just stand there!" Moradi said and poked a finger at her shoulder.

But how could she speak of a secret Rana had trusted her with? Her mind flew back to the night when Rana had called her in for a private conversation. One look at the dark circles around Rana's sunken eyes and Dayeh had known she had not slept all night.

"I'm not going to bring another child into this world, not after what I've just learned."

Dayeh still remembered the deep pain in Rana's brown eyes and wished for a way to transfer all that sorrow into her own heart. "Dear child, most men do such stupid things, but I'm sure the new baby will bring him to his senses."

"I don't want to use a baby to mend a frayed tie that is bound to come undone." And the old nanny knew that would be as close as she would ever come to mentioning the other woman. "Do you know of anyone who could help me end this?" Rana had asked, holding the new roundness of her belly as if it were a crystal ball through which she could see her dark future.

Feeling the weight of everyone's stares, Dayeh blinked hard and tried to push the image away. She had no choice now but to share at least part of what she knew. She looked at Rana, who stood there, her eyes closed, her skin as pale as it had been that night Dayeh had found her on the floor of her bedroom.

The old nanny bent down to kiss the Koran and recited a prayer. She put her hand on its cover and looked at Rana as if to ask her permission, but Rana had turned her face toward the window. Dayeh wasn't sure what she saw in that pale profile, but something about it made her decide she had no right to mention the woman who had been at the core of all this disaster. That was something that the Amelis should hear from their own daughter.

"God only knows how the devil crept under Miss Rana's skin, but one night, she called me into her room and said she wanted to talk in private. With the Major being away so much of the time, I figured she just needed company." She noticed the look Dr. Ameli gave the Major and was pleased that her reference to the husband's recent behavior had done its job. Major Moradi seemed to have found new interest in his shiny shoes.

A few seconds of deep silence followed. "You can imagine what a scare it gave me to hear her say that she no longer wanted to keep the baby. I didn't know how to respond. It wasn't my place to ask her the reason, so all I could do was to plead with her not to say such things. I told her, don't you fear Allah's rage, child? I reminded her that the loving girl I'd raised couldn't possibly do such a dreadful thing. But she waved a hand to dismiss me and said, 'That's for me to decide, isn't it?'" Dayeh shook her head side to side in disbelief. "Rana-*khanoom* got angry and said, 'All I'm asking you is to help me find someone who'd do it.' As God is my witness, in all the years that I've cared for her, she's never spoken to me that way. I was flabbergasted. Unable to say more, I just sat there and silently prayed. When she didn't say another word, I figured we were done talking and prepared to leave the room."

Dayeh hoped she had said enough and once again, she turned to the door, but Major Moradi wouldn't leave her alone. "And?" he said to her back.

Dayeh wrapped the fingers of one hand around the other and massaged her arthritic knuckles. Unsure of how much more he would pressure her, she faced him. "Why don't you ask Miss Rana herself? I really don't remember the details."

"Speak!' he said. "Your rotten memory is fine when you want it to be."

Dr. Ameli, who must have sensed Dayeh's agony, said, "Sit down, dear, and take your time. Tell us what you remember."

Oh, what an angel of a man, Dayeh thought and she knelt on the floor, pulled her floral skirt over her loose cotton pants and tucked it under her knees. "I waited there a few more minutes. It didn't take long to get past my humiliation. Someone had to talk her out of it, make her vent, and console her. I told her of the ways of Allah and how life or death is never in our hands. I mentioned all the reasons I could think of to change her mind, but she was so upset that I'm not sure she heard a word of it. Finally, I told her that no one would be willing to do it at such a late stage, and that of all the people, I'd be the last one to take such a chance."

"You did, did you?" the Major said. "So who the hell helped her to make such a mess of things? And who covered it up so well that I had to find out about it only days before today?"

Dayeh did not respond. It must have been that nosey Banu who told him. Who else? She shot the Major a look for even thinking she'd have anything to do with Rana's wrongdoing. She clasped her hands together and held on tight as if to stop herself from throwing a punch.

Once more, Dr. Ameli's calm voice broke the silence. "Go on, Dayeh," he said, disregarding the Major's outburst. "What happened after that?"

"In the evening, Miss Rana didn't touch her dinner. I brewed a nice chamomile tea for her with fresh lemon juice and crystal sugar. There's nothing better than a good medicinal tea and crystal sugar to calm the nerves, you know. When she went to her bedroom, I took my prayer rug and prayed behind her door. I named the twelve Imams on my prayer beads three full circles and begged Allah to give her a good night's sleep and help her to change her mind. At night, once again, the Major didn't come home." Dayeh hesitated to make sure everyone got the hint and noticing the horrified look on Mrs. Ameli's face, she added, "He does that often, stays elsewhere for the night without calling." She noticed the Major had turned his back to everyone and was staring at the dark TV screen. "The next morning, when Miss Rana didn't touch her breakfast, my worries worsened. She was acting strange and left the table without even asking about the girls." She turned to Mrs. Ameli. "You know how she fusses over those two, packing their snacks, checking their uniforms, combing their hair. But not that day. She stayed in her room, didn't come down for lunch, and didn't even open the door for Vida who went to her as soon as she was back from school. I told the girls their mother wasn't feeling well, that she needed her rest."

She stopped for a moment to study Rana's reaction to this breach of confidence. Rana's expression was calm, resigned even, and she now seemed to listen with interest, as if she, too, were learning this for the first time. Turning her head around, Dayeh's eyes found Dr. Ameli's, and she hoped he understood that what she was about to tell was for his understanding only.

"That night, I shouldn't have bothered fussing with a meal because the Major called to say he wouldn't be home and Miss Rana barely touched her plate. After she had gone back upstairs, Banu helped me a little then went to Rana-*khanoom*'s room. I should have known that girl would be sure to say the wrong things. I should have gone with her, but I was so busy that the thought didn't even cross my mind. When she came back down, I could tell from her flushed face that something was up, but she went to bed before I could question her. Oh, let me tell you, that girl can sleep like a polar bear!"

She forced a smile and looked around to see if her light-hearted comment had amused anyone. It hadn't.

"I was just finishing my night's prayer when I heard a crashing sound upstairs-- a sound so terrifying and sudden that I thought the whole roof had come down. God only knows how my old feet climbed those stairs two at a time. I burst into Miss Rana's bedroom. There lay her antique dresser on the floor with the mirror shattered and shards of glass scattered everywhere. It cut my breath off to think it had fallen on Miss Rana, but thank God I found her keeled over in the corner. There was so much blood, you'd think someone had slaughtered a lamb on that carpet."

Dayeh closed her eyes and tried to push the horrifying image away. "My knees folded under me. I cried out Banu's name, but my screams must have awakened the entire neighborhood because it didn't take long for them to storm the house. Things happened fast. Paralyzed, I heard the doorbell, voices, cries and even a siren. I didn't move and wouldn't let go of my Rana's hand. After being tossed around in the back of an ambulance and a swerving ride down the city streets, there I was, standing in the middle of a hospital room with doctors and nurses bustling about."

"Did anyone call her husband?" Dr. Ameli asked.

Dayeh sensed an accusing tone in his voice and looked at the Major for a reaction. But the man continued to stare at the television. His face seemed pale. Was he afraid? He needn't worry, she thought. She wasn't about to spill out everything. Not yet. "We couldn't. It was too late at night and I only know his number at the office. But, I'll have you know, doctor, not once did I let go of my girl's hand and she, too, clung to me the way she used to when she was just a little thing." The remembrance brought the old nanny to tears, but she wiped the corner of her eyes and went on. "It wasn't until a young doctor came in with a syringe and put her to sleep that I got off my feet. As God is my witness, I've never had such a fright in all my life. That one night alone made me age ten years." She covered her face in both hands, and as her tears finally poured down her cheeks, she broke into the sobs she had held back for months.

"Enough of your crocodile tears," the Major said. "Tell them what happened next."

Dayeh lifted her head. *So that's how he thanks me for keeping his filthy secret!* She looked him straight in the eyes, no longer caring if contempt reflected in her face. She wiped her cheek with the corner of her big, white scarf and without responding to him, turned to face Dr. Ameli again. "There's nothing more to tell you, dear sir. In the morning, Miss Rana's doctor came in again and spoke to her for some time. That good man spent an hour trying to calm her, telling her of all the childless women around the world who would give their life just to have one baby. Before leaving, he told her that he had to tell the Major because the hospital needed the husband's permission to discharge her. But he assured her that where he was concerned this was an accident. He told us that, thank God, the baby was unharmed."

Major Moradi glared at her and shook his head. "Unharmed, indeed!" he said under his breath.

Rana's face now turned as white as the wall behind her. She was staring at her father, and by the look on Dr. Ameli's face, he was still struggling to believe what had just been said. Surely he did not pay any mind to the Major's accusations, but the way he looked at his daughter no longer indicated support. It reminded Dayeh of the times when any of his girls did something wrong. He never lost his temper, nor would there be threats of punishment; instead, Dr. Ameli's kind expression would be replaced with deep disappointment.

When Rana spoke, there was newfound strength in her voice. "That's all true. I didn't want another baby," she said. "I figured, if the man wants another child, let his *other* woman give him one."

The entire room froze in silence.

"Oh my..." Mrs. Ameli said again.

"I had maintained my silence long enough." She turned to her parents. "You did not raise me to make a scene and for many months I kept on hoping Farhad would come to his senses before there would be a need to confront him. But when Banu informed me that his mistress is pregnant, I had to do what I could to prevent being tied to him any more than I already was."

This time, Mrs. Ameli gave out a faint cry, and before she could be caught, her body collapsed onto the floor. Her fall pushed a chair out of balance; it hit the leg of the table, and fell on its side.

Dayeh, familiar with Mrs. Ameli's fainting episodes, grabbed a glass of water from the table and rushed over to sprinkle some on the woman's face.

Dr. Ameli knelt on the floor, held his wife in his arms, and for the first time raised his voice. "Someone get my bag!"

Rana ran to the guest room in search of his medical bag while Dayeh picked up a newspaper and started to fan the lady's damp face.

Mrs. Ameli had barely opened her eyes when the front door slammed shut, and in the sudden silence that followed, Dayeh realized the Major had left.

To Dayeh, the idea of a man having multiple women was not reason enough to faint, not for her generation, anyway. Her own husband had brought home a younger wife when she couldn't bear him any children. Even Mrs. Ameli's grandfather was known to have kept three wives. But this was different. None of the younger members in the Ameli family had experienced such shame. Learned people who had a respectful reputation rarely did such things any more. The rules of upper society had changed. Besides, Rana had three children and Dayeh worried about their future. She had prayed day and night that the Major's scandalous life was nothing but gossip—a shameless lie. *Damn that Banu and her loose mouth!* The way he had stormed out of the house without an explanation had to be his way of making it clear that this was no gossip. He had done the unmentionable.

During the next few days, the guests kept mostly to their own room, mealtimes became rather sullen, and no one discussed the matter. It was as though by keeping quiet about it, the problem would resolve itself. In the evenings, Rana took the baby and sat in the living room while her parents pretended to watch television, engaged in small talk, and everyone waited for the Major to return, without once mentioning his abrupt departure. Dayeh was not surprised to be cornered in the hallway by Mrs. Ameli and asked what she knew about the Major's woman.

"It's really all talk, Ma'am," she said, trying to sound calm. "Banu constantly hangs around other maids in the neighborhood and they talk nonsense." She turned away and pretended to tidy the objects on the hallway table. "I personally never heard a thing," she lied.

Later, from the way Banu avoided her, the old nanny suspected Mrs. Ameli had bribed the girl into spitting out all the filthy details, and no doubt, the information would be shared with Dr. Ameli. She hoped they had also talked some sense into the maid about keeping family matters private. What if Banu ever found out about the baby's birth defect? The news of a crippled baby would be sure to blast through the neighborhood and poor Miss Rana needed no more reason to be pitied.

Except for a few times when Dayeh saw Rana came out of her father's room, looking as though she had been crying, life went on as usual and there was no more mention of the problem. Soon the time came for the Amelis to go back to Tehran.

"We couldn't possibly stay longer," Mrs. Ameli said to no one in particular. "My poor husband has to go back to work, and I just left everything to rush here. Oh, there's such a long list of things to do."

That was the most ridiculous claim Dayeh had ever heard. She could just imagine the long list because the woman did nothing but talk on the phone, fuss over her looks, and get on with her socializing. Something in Mrs. Ameli's tone told Dayeh the comment was meant for Rana, as if she was telling her daughter that she no longer cared to be involved in her problems. Over the recent years, Dayeh had heard many such hints, and they were always meant to distance herself from the girl. Whenever the good doctor became too protective of his daughter, Dayeh could swear there was a hint of resentment in his wife's comments, but she somehow managed to dismiss the thought. How could a mother be jealous of her own child?

"That's true, Maman," Rana responded sweetly. "You've done more than your share, and I wouldn't want to bother you with my problems more than I already have."

Her father turned off the television. "Nonsense," he said. "You're our daughter and that makes your problem ours." He put an arm around his wife adding, "But your mother is right. We can't stay here forever." He cleared his throat. "Why don't you come with us?"

Dayeh did not miss Mrs. Ameli's glare at the man.

"How could she just drop everything?" Mrs. Ameli said, but her husband didn't seem to have heard her.

"You need to get away from this place for a while," he went on, "Come to Tehran, stay in your old room, and spend some time with your sisters."

"But, what about her children?" her mother said, this time louder. "And Farhad? What will he think when he returns?" She shook her head and slapped the back of his hand playfully. "Don't you remember *our* quarrels when we were young?" She giggled seductively, then her face turned serious again. "Don't you dare come between these two. A woman's place is with her husband."

Having heard it all before, Dayeh was furious that Mrs. Ameli would take that man's side, expecting poor Rana to overlook his irresponsible behavior. With a husband like the doctor, how could Mrs. Ameli possibly understand what Rana went through? Could such advice from her mother be the reason that girl had tolerated everything so far? Each time there was a problem with anyone's marriage, Mrs. Ameli had said the same things. She had stated over and over that a marriage entailed problems, that men needed time alone. Now Dayeh realized how those comments had been aimed at the lady's own daughters. That was the kind of wife Mrs. Ameli wanted Rana to be and the fact that, even under such dire circumstances, she had not changed her mind came as a shock.

Mother or not, Dayeh was now certain. That woman didn't want Rana back. She enjoyed her life with her husband, the two of them together, going out to dinner, the movies, and trips. She had to smile at the thought that perhaps Mrs. Ameli's motherhood came with an expiration date. She seemed to view motherhood like a job with a time limit, one that she could stop at some point, even retire from. She had stopped worrying about her children after sending each off with a husband, and at this point, she was more concerned about her waistline and thinning hair than her youngest daughter's dilemma.

Banu's arrival to inform Rana the baby needed to be fed put an end to the discussion.

The day before the scheduled departure, Major Moradi called and asked to speak to Dr. Ameli. Although Dayeh didn't know the content of the good doctor's conversation, he seemed disturbed for the remainder of the day. In the evening, he advised Rana to pack her things for a trip to Tehran for a while, and the way he suggested it left no room for a discussion.

"What will she do about the girls' school?" Mrs. Ameli asked.

"Exactly," Rana added. "They have their exams, and I couldn't possibly let them miss school now."

"That can be arranged," her father said.

After further discussion, Dr Ameli proposed that Marjan and Vida could stay with their aunt while their mother was away.

"Stay with Badri? I wouldn't even think about it!" Rana said. "She's too strict with them, too disciplinary. They'd be absolutely miserable."

Dayeh thought the words had come out of her own mouth.

"You'd be surprised how much nicer she may be when they are

her responsibility," Dr. Ameli said in his soothing voice. "You may even be back before the end of the school year, and if worse comes to worst, they can come to Tehran as soon as school is out."

Mrs. Ameli, unable to mask her frustration, turned to her husband. "When are you going to realize that Rana is no longer a baby? I'm sure she's quite capable of handling the situation."

"You're absolutely right, dear. She *can* handle it, but I think you and I will both be more at peace to know she's not lonely." He turned to Rana. "At Badri *khanoom*'s they'll be among family and I'll bet their father will make sure they're not lonely."

Rana gave in and asked Dayeh to do the baby's laundry and to start packing.

"While you're at it," Dr. Ameli said, "Why don't you pack your own things? We could use your help in Tehran."

Dayeh beamed a hearty smile. The Amelis had a young woman who came in daily to do their housework. So Dayeh would be free to give Rana and the baby the attention they needed. Banu was instructed to call her mother to come stay with her and watch the house.

The next day, Dr. Ameli made a private call to the Major's sister and obtained her agreement to stop by and pick up the girls. Once the decision was made, Rana spent a good hour in her daughters' room, and although no one knew how she had broken the news to them, at dinner they acted unusually calm.

Badri stopped by in the evening right before their departure. The encounter was brief and formal. She acted distant and impassive, as though she had come to pick up her nieces for a casual overnight stay. In a way, Dayeh was grateful for that because it helped to give the temporary separation from their mother a civil appearance.

While Rana went upstairs to get the girls, Dr. Ameli's final words to Badri were clear and concise. "Unless your brother shows genuine remorse and comes forward with proper apologies, there

39

will be no need for him to call or to make any attempts to visit." Dayeh sensed many unsaid words in the way he stared at the woman. After a few seconds he added, "Meanwhile, my daughter will live in her rightful home, with her parents."

Badri continued to swing her purse while staring at the curtains with no comment.

As soon as the door closed behind Badri, Dayeh wagged a finger up in the air. "I don't trust that woman. Not one bit." But Dr. Ameli's glare silenced her, and no one else uttered a word.

During the packing, Dayeh noticed that Rana had stopped referring to her husband by name. Instead, she now called him "the Major" as if she, too, were in the army. She had also started to act like a stranger in her own house. She referred to her bedroom as "the bigger bedroom" and her closet became "that closet." As for her personal belongings, she seemed uninterested and planned to leave them behind.

"Should I pack your silver hand-mirror, Ma'am?" Banu asked.

"No, I'm only taking what baby Yalda and I absolutely need. I want everything in the Major's house to remain intact."

Dayeh didn't approve of such a tone, but considerate of Rana's vulnerability, she kept her thoughts to herself. What did Rana's mother know about the troubled thoughts that must be going through her daughter's mind? Sometimes the old nanny was the only one who really understood Rana. Day after day, she cleaned that room, made the crumpled half of the bed and turned its damp pillow over. To watch her mistress in agony sent deep pain into her heart. The bitter reality was evident everywhere: in the guilty expression on Banu's face; in the deep concern that wouldn't leave the old doctor's eyes; and even in that silly, cheerful disposition Mrs. Ameli put on. All Dayeh could do to help was make sure the loose-mouthed maid blabbed no more. The Amelis never mentioned Parisa, and treated the scandalous affair as a passing fling. Maybe that wasn't so bad under the circumstances.

Nobody knew if the Major was still in town, but now that he had left the house, his whereabouts mattered little.

"That's men for you," Dayeh said while she sat in Rana's bedroom, folding laundry. "Their brains are in their pants."

Rana shot her a dark look. "He is still my husband, Dayeh, not to mention the father of my children. I'd respect that if I were you."

The old nanny just shook her head in disapproval. She had done her best to make sure the rumors of Parisa now being the Major's legal wife did not reach the Amelis. They had already been through enough and she would do what she could to save them further anguish. But married or not, the reality of another woman was so harsh that, in comparison, the baby's malformed limb seemed to have lost its significance.

Chapter

• *Three* •

HER OLD ROOM TOOK RANA back to the day she'd left her parents' home as a new bride. She put the palms of her hands on both cheeks where her father's hands had held her years ago in this same room. "This house will always be your home," he had whispered. "As you share your future with your husband and take your place in society, I want you to remember that you will forever be my little girl." And he had kissed her forehead. He may have said those words only to show his love and support, but now Rana wondered if he'd also had a premonition.

The room hadn't changed much, except now a bassinette and a changing table stood in a corner. Rana's Agatha Christie collection sat on a shelf by itself and on the second shelf were the poetry books of Hafez, Khayam and Rumi, which she had left behind only because the Major also had these volumes.

She dropped her carry-on bag and walked over to the wall covered with old photographs: her graduation pictures, volleyball team, and enlarged wedding portrait. She stared at the bride's shy smile and at the young officer holding her hand. They looked like strangers from someone else's album, out of place in a room filled with fond memories of her childhood. She took the large frame off the wall and put it face down on her desk.

"Just you wait and see. He'll crawl back, begging," her mother had said on the flight to Tehran. Maybe she said that because Rana was crying, but those tears were for Marjan and Vida being left behind. Rana felt so detached from her husband that such remarks had no longer offered comfort.

Funny how others continued to hope for everything to go back to normal. For Rana, the mere existence of Parisa in her husband's life was as much a closure as a divorce would have been. The news of his marriage had turned a wrongdoing into an irreversible loss. A death. The humiliation it brought her made it impossible to share the news. Keeping that a secret helped her to maintain some of her pride. Ever since the news, Rana had lived her life from one moment to the next. She tried to find solace in all the advantages of the Major's absence from her daily life. No longer would she have to order his favorite meal, or wait for him to come home from a card game. Late at night she did not wake up to his tobacco breath and drunken desires. How could she love him and why was she so despondent?

She sat at the edge of her bed and ran her fingers over the floral pattern of the bedspread. Oh, how many nights she had dreamed of the day she would leave this room behind. In her daydreams of living with the handsome young officer, she had imagined herself in a house filled with a different kind of happiness. The room offered the peace she had forgotten about. She needed the serenity of old memories.

That morning's scene as her little girls climbed into Badri's car played back and clutched at her heart. Marjan wouldn't look at her. She was so much like her mother, sensitive yet seemingly tolerant.

She despised her cousins. Making her stay with them was punishment for a crime she had no part in. Vida was excited to be sleeping over at her aunt's. She had leaned out the side window and waved frantically, "*Khodahafez*, Maman!" Go with God? The name of God was thrown around so easily, but where was He?

If it weren't for the upcoming tests, Rana would have let the girls miss school and come with her until she figured things out. Now she only hoped that their studies would keep them busy enough not to miss her too much. During the entire past week before she'd left and while the Major stayed away, Vida had asked for her father on a daily basis, but Marjan's knowing eyes asked no questions and not once had she mentioned him.

Rana knew her dizziness was due to all the blood she had recently lost. Lying back on the squeaky bed, she stared at the thin wire mobile still attached to the light fixture. In the warm breeze of the space heater, four little butterflies moved around the lamp in a lazy circle, flapping their wings, following each other around and around. She thought they symbolized her suspended life. A lonely, helpless creature chasing her offspring around a vicious circle that led to nowhere. Thoughts of poor little Yalda filled her eyes with tears. What was to become of the tiny butterfly with a broken wing? She felt a stab inside her.

—

A knock on the door woke Rana. In the darkness, it took her a few seconds to register her whereabouts, though it was hard to tell if it was dawn or dusk.

"Are you okay, dear?" her father called from behind the door.

"Yes, Papa. Come in."

The door opened and her father turned on the light.

"What a nap!" he said smiling. "I'm afraid you'll be up all night."

Rana rubbed her eyes. "That granddaughter of yours will make sure I'm on night shift."

"Isn't that the truth?" he said and chuckled. He came closer and bent over her bed the way he used to check a patient. "Is my little girl feeling happier now that she's all rested?"

Rana's smile vanished. She sat at the edge of her bed, dangled her feet down, and while her toes searched for slippers she said, "Speaking of little girls, someone needs feeding!" She looked at him and added, "Each time I wake up, it's shocking to realize that my life isn't just a bad dream."

He pulled a chair over and sat by her bed. "The beginning of most problems is often their worst. But over the years, I've seen what a wonderful remedy time can be." He held her hand, patting the back of it. "Coming here was the best thing you could do. When you distance yourself from a crisis and give your head a chance to clear, the solution often presents itself."

Rana nodded politely.

"If I were you, I'd concentrate on my recovery. Good wisdom indeed comes from a healthy body. Try to think more about the future, and of course, your wonderful children. That's what really matters, if you ask me. Parenthood does that. Before you know it, your children become the focal point and your happiness will be in theirs."

Rana put her head on his shoulder, leaned on him, and felt an understanding that went beyond words.

⁓

Downstairs, her mother was on the family room floor playing with the baby. Bottles, pacifiers, and plastic toys were scattered around them. "I'd forgotten how one tiny person can mess up the whole house," she said looking around and extending her hand, asking for help to get up.

"Don't you dare mention 'old',"Dr. Ameli said. "Not for another decade, anyway."

Rana held her mother's hand. "Did Yalda sleep at all?" she asked.

"I'm afraid I didn't let her." She stood up. "Oh, my poor old knees," she said, but then reported, "We played games, sang songs, and had too much fun to bother with a nap."

"She can play and sing?" Rana mocked.

"She certainly can," her mother said with a chuckle and turned to the baby who now had a whole fist in her mouth. "Can't we?"

Yalda started to fuss and Rana picked her up. "Oh, Maman, you're the only one I know who speaks newborn-language. Remember your long talks with Marjan before she had learned her first word?"

"It's all in the tone, dear! A tone can have a thousand meanings, no matter what the age may be."

Rana loved this side of her mother; the caring, fun mom. Why couldn't she always be this nice?

Dayeh brought a fresh bottle for Yalda and reached out to take her, but Rana cuddled the infant and went to the sofa. "Let me give her that. I've had no time with her today."

Dayeh frowned. "But, child, you haven't eaten all day."

"Let her do it, Dayeh," her mother said with authority. "We can all pitch in and help, but in the end, a child is the mother's responsibility."

Rana felt a sting and wondered if the recent incidents had made her a bit cynical.

Sanam, the Amelis' housekeeper scurried in and out of the room to set the table, and each time she opened the door, the aroma of pomegranate soup, Rana's favorite, wafted from the kitchen. "Are my sisters ever going to show up?" Rana asked her mother.

"Oh, not today, and that's all my fault. I figured you needed at least a half-a-day to get settled."

"Apparently I did," Rana said. After a few seconds, she cautiously asked, "How much do they know?"

"They know what they need to know. I explained about your severe hemorrhage at childbirth and the complications that followed. I also mentioned your father's decision to keep you here until you regain your strength." She looked around at the Italian furniture, velvet curtains, and a terrace that overlooked the Jacuzzi and added, "Even though there's enough room here, Mandana offered to take care of Vida and Marjan, but I told her they're staying with their aunt in Shiraz. That's all." She went to the samovar in the corner and picked up a glass for tea.

"You mean, you didn't tell them about Yalda's leg?"

Mrs. Ameli shook her head. "When Mandana said you wouldn't come to the phone, I figured you didn't want to discuss certain issues."

Rana nodded.

Not having enough milk, Rana offered the bottle to Yalda and as the baby sucked eagerly, Rana leaned back and tried to absorb the warmth of her parent's home and its distinct contrast to her own. She became conscious of the emptiness she had endured over the past few days. The silence in the Major's house had resembled a battlefield before ambush. It had been in that cold stillness that one day the young maid hissed, "I heard the woman was a childless widow, but she is now with child." Her hushed tone made it clear to whom she had referred. This was a whole new territory, which Rana wasn't ready to enter. If the woman had his child he would no longer be hers alone. Married or not, he would forever be tied to another woman. Stopping the girl did little to prevent gossip. Deep down she wanted to hear it all. If Banu's news held any truth, it would explain the major's attitude, his absences, his moods.

True that her marriage had not started with love, but Farhad was the only man she had ever been intimate with. For many years he was an attentive husband, a passionate lover, and a good father to their children. To picture him father a child with another woman put her in a state of shock. It had been hard enough to adapt to his infidelity and the horrifying notion that each time he left on a business trip, he could in fact be in town, with a widow named Parisa. Rana imagined her to be a typical home-wrecker: a vulgar woman dressed like a whore, her maroon lipstick smearing his face. In a painful way, the ugly image helped. Thinking that the man got what he deserved helped to restore some of her bruised ego, but it wasn't enough. There were times when she had the urge to confront him, but fear stopped her. What if he admitted to all of it? What if there was no remorse? What would she do if he wanted to have nothing more to do with her or the children?

Shame prevented Rana from sharing this with others. She dreaded pity and knew that nothing anyone said could soothe her pain. Besides, others might react in a way that would tell Farhad she knows. Before Yalda was born, from time to time Rana tried to guess how her mother might reason through such a situation. She could just hear her saying that regardless of the Major's indiscretion, she must hold on to her marriage. Such assumptions pushed her to cling to the hope that if she bore him a son, her husband would come to his senses. Now Banu had told her more than she cared to know. The mere thought that this woman's baby could be a boy put her heart on flames.

Rana wiped a drop of milk from the corner of the baby's mouth and shifted her position. By now the news of their separation must have spread throughout Shiraz. She smiled bitterly. *So much for keeping up appearances.*

No matter how calm her parents acted, Rana knew they had their own hard time with the news. With no history of a divorce in their immediate family, their daughter's separation had to be a disgrace. If her husband hadn't provoked her, none of this would have come up. She would have sent her parents back with concerns only for the baby. Her marital problem was not their responsibility, and it already made her heart ache to think she had put her father in the middle of all this.

The bottle had emptied, and it now made a whistling sound while Yalda continued to suck air. Rana lifted the baby and propping her against her shoulder, she began to massage her soft back. Now that the fever had broken, she enjoyed caring for her newborn the way she had done for her other two.

"Dinner is ready," Dayeh walked in to announce. She reached for the baby.

Rana reluctantly gave Yalda to the old nanny. From the first day she had held this baby, Rana had felt a strong connection, so strong that she chose not to mention it to anyone. Guilt had nothing to do with it. Each time someone took her away there was a tug, a sense of being torn, as though it were the two of them against the world.

Dayeh had set a beautiful table. A centerpiece of red geraniums sat between the silver candlesticks that held two tall candles. Warm squares of flat bread, wrapped in an embroidered lining in a silver basket sat next to a lovely tray of fresh basil, tarragon, and mint with radishes shaped into blossoms.

This dining room had always been a favorite place of Rana's. From ordinary days and late breakfasts on Fridays, down to birthday parties, family dinners, and Norooz celebrations, the mahogany table had been a witness to joyful gatherings. Most of their family pictures were taken here. The room was a mirror, reflecting good segments of Rana's life. Now, with only the three of them present, it looked too large, empty even.

The sweet-and-sour taste of the pomegranate soup was as familiar as the rooms of her childhood. Rana turned to her mother. "This is Heaven in a bowl!" She laughed. "I have tried following your recipe, Maman, but my soup never turns out this good. What's your secret?"

Her father laughed. "Oh, don't be naïve, she'll never give away her secret."

They both laughed, but the stern look on Mrs. Ameli's face told them the joke was lost on her. "I don't have secrets," she said and raised her eyebrows. "Cooking is not a science to teach. It's more of a natural instinct." She took a sip of her soup then added, "If recipes were all it took, everyone who bought a cook book would be a chef."

"Look what else your mom made for you," Dayeh announced, carrying a platter of herb quiche, *koo-koo*.

"That's not fair," Rana said. "You should have warned me. Now I'm all full of *Osh*." She patted her tummy.

"You'll have to try some," Dayeh said, and she placed a large wedge in Rana's plate before she could be stopped. "We're going to put some meat on your bones."

How strange it felt to participate in a family dinner and discuss *koo-koo* when her whole world had fallen apart. The dish was also a favorite of Vida's. Rana tried to imagine what kinds of food Badri would serve the girls. That woman was such a health nut that her food was bland. Remembering how Vida would have loved this dinner took Rana's appetite away.

Her father took a forkful of *koo-koo*, put it on a piece of flat bread and topped it with fresh yogurt. Rana enjoyed the way he fussed over every bite and designed his little combinations. He took his time chewing, savoring the taste. "Yum! Your mother may be a gorgeous woman, but the truth be told, *this* is what I married her for."

"Grandma, may she rest in peace, was right," Rana said, "The way to a man's heart *is* through his stomach!"

They all laughed. Rana smiled sadly to herself. What did it feel like to have a husband who came home from work not because the day had ended but to spend time with his wife?

Her father assembled another perfect bite and offered it to Rana. "A morsel of love."

She took it with a smile and remembered years of her father's "morsels of love" and how they had tricked her when she refused to eat. But tonight for the first time, that gesture sounded like an excuse to avoid other topics. Ever since the Major had blamed her for the baby's deformity, Rana thought she saw a new look deep in her father's eyes, as if a suspicion cast its dark shadow on his mind. As for her own thoughts, what had started as a notion had taken a real shape, one that grew and grew until it filled her mind and made it hard to breathe. The question never left her. Her doctor had forbidden her to lift heavy things. All she had meant to do was lift the dresser enough to lose the fetus. Could the trauma of the dresser falling on her be the cause of Yalda's deformed leg? If so, then she not only deserved her misfortune, but also could expect much more to come.

Unable to focus on the moment, she pushed her chair back. "May I be excused?" she said and her voice broke.

Her father got up to accompany her, but Mrs. Ameli grabbed his sleeve. "Let her be, honey," she said and stroked the back of his hand. "She needs time alone."

One look into his eyes and Rana knew he was not convinced, but perhaps out of respect for his wife, he leaned back in his chair.

Rana left the table and rushed out of the room.

The darkness outside, unchanged by the single garden lamp, masked many familiar corners. Rana closed the curtain. Naturally organized, she wanted to sort her thoughts. But first, she had to unpack.

She opened her suitcase, took out a few blouses, and went to the closet to look for free hangers. Inside the closet, the smell of old paper, leather shoes, and dust blended into the faint scent of youth. Except for a few extra boxes sitting on a top shelf, nothing there had moved in years. During their rushed visits, the couple had stayed in the guest bedroom, which had a larger bed. Rana realized that until now, she had never fully returned to her old room. Nothing in that closet had much value, but it offered the sense of security which only comes with possession, something that in all the years of marriage she had never experienced. The Major's money had bought everything they needed, but deep down she'd never considered them hers. The house, the car, even the jewelry were insured in his name. She had referred to them as hers, but had known all along that they came from him. When something was damaged, she felt accountable. If she spent more than the household budget, she sensed a need to explain. Her lips half opened to a bitter smile in realizing that somewhere deep in her heart, she had seen this day, the day when she would come back to repossess what truly belonged to her.

Rana decided to leave her unpacking to Dayeh. She closed the closet door, sat on the bed, and pushed herself back. Stretching her legs, she cleared her lungs in a deep exhale. What would she do with her life now?

A divorce?

The thought was growing stronger each day, but she still didn't like it. Had her marriage been a complete failure? Were the past nine years a total loss?

Rana had tried not to think that far ahead, not even while she packed to leave. But now, alone and surrounded by memories of better days, she began to rediscover the meaning of calm, something that had been missing for years.

She had married the Major not for love or money, but because it had been the right thing to do at the time. She had finished high school. Her older sisters were married and her turn had come. A beautiful girl ready to settle down, with suitors calling often. When the Moradi family made an appointment to introduce their son, Rana had laughed about the whole idea. They came one night, and although she didn't see them, her parents were impressed enough to promise they'd discuss it with their daughter.

Rana smiled at the memory of the night her best friend Minoo had helped her to make the final decision.

"It's time for a list," Minoo had said.

She had taken out a paper and wrote down the positive and negative aspects of marrying Farhad Moradi. The tall, handsome young officer came with the promise of independence, her own home, and a new social status. He would move her to the beautiful city of Shiraz, away from her rival sisters and into a romantic place known for its pleasant weather, rich poetry, and the best wine. When it came to disadvantages, the girls found enough excuses to dismiss them.

"So what if he doesn't have a sense of humor?" Minoo had said. "That'll come later." And regarding the distance of a thousand miles, Minoo dismissed it with the fact that it would only be a two-hour flight. "Everyone will love to visit you. I know *I* will. And, you can come back any time you want, that is, if you should ever miss Tehran's unbearable pollution!"

They joked about it for hours, and finally when advantages of marriage far outweighed the disadvantages, they concluded that marrying the man was the right thing to do.

Rana reached into the drawer of her nightstand and took out a paper and pencil. She wrote in big letters at the top. Divorce. Underneath, she made two columns.

Chapter

· *Four* ·

T HE TRIP THAT HAD BEEN PLANNED to last only a couple of weeks dragged on much longer. Over the first week or so, Rana only saw her sisters and her best friend Minoo. Other relatives and friends called to ask about a convenient time to visit, but a variety of excuses reluctantly invented by Mrs. Ameli kept them away.

"You can't hide from people," Mrs. Ameli said on more than one occasion. "They all want to see the baby and Yalda won't be a newborn forever."

The Amelis decided to throw a dinner party in honor of their new grandchild, but such an event meant a lot of hard work for Dayeh. She also feared it might start a whole circle of new gossip. "I guess your mother has to show off her new china and silver at some point," she said to Rana. "I can't see why she won't let them come in smaller groups for tea. That would be easier for you, too. But no. She had to go and invite the whole town."

"Don't fret, Dayeh," Rana said. "She's not expecting you to do all the work. They've hired a cook and plenty of extra help."

Dayeh waved a hand in the air. "Help? With Sanam going home at night, I'm the only one who knows where things are. I can just hear those helpers saying, 'Dayeh, this' and 'Dayeh, that' all night. I'm telling you, the party's got nothing to do with you or the baby. It's all about your mother." She turned away to put a stack of magazines on the table and mumbled, "Everything's got to be about her, if not, she'll just have one of her fainting scenes."

"Now you're being mean! If I didn't know the two of you any better, I'd think my mother was your *havoo*!"

The word had popped out of nowhere, but the way Rana said it sounded as though she wanted to spit it out and get rid of it for good. That there was actually a word for second wife somehow legitimized its concept. Despite the ban, polygamy for men was very much alive, and the word *havoo* was thrown around daily. This was the first time that she had uttered it.

A heavy silence fell. Rana had meant it as a joke, but no words could describe the line of thoughts it provoked. Vague images of the Major's new wife filled the silence.

It took a minute before Rana regained her calm expression and gave a nervous laugh. "Come on, Dayeh! A party will be good for all of us. You know, a little distraction."

Dayeh did not respond.

—

On the day of the party, a heavy-set man and two of his helpers in white aprons showed up after breakfast, filling the kitchen with the clanking of dishes as the three rushed about. Even though they brought an extra burner, Dayeh couldn't imagine how they'd function in that tiny kitchen. Once or twice she went in to warm up bottles for the baby, but for most of the day she did her best to stay away.

"I can't watch the way they work," she said under her breath and turned to Rana for support. "That fat guy picks up everything by hand. Who knows when the last time was that he washed his hands." She kept busy in the dining room, taking out stacks of Mrs. Ameli's better china, wiping each piece to make sure there were no watermarks, and doing the same with the silverware.

"Could I at least make the salad?" Rana asked her mother after she had put Yalda down for a nap.

"Yes, dear, if it helps to keep you busy."

Typical! That woman wasn't about to make anyone feel needed. With all the work being done by others, her only personal contribution was arranging a showy pink carnation centerpiece, knowing it would receive complimentary remarks from her guests.

Hours before the party, Dayeh heard the doorbell followed by Mandana's loud hello. Although Rana's sisters had stopped by several times, no one had asked any questions, so Dayeh figured the Amelis must have filled them in on the details of Rana's dilemma. Except for long conversations with her father, Rana didn't talk much. Living away had created a distance between her and the rest of the Amelis.

Rana came down the stairs in her yellow, cotton suit. "Do you think this is dressy enough?" she asked Dayeh.

Mrs. Ameli jumped in before Dayeh had a chance to tell her how lovely she looked. "A bit too summery, if you ask me," she said, wrinkling her nose. "But I guess it's okay if you're not too cold."

"Just okay?" Mandana said to her mother. "What are you talking about, Maman? She looks stunning!" Her eyes searched the room. "Where's our little guest of honor?"

Dayeh motioned to the upper floor. "Napping."

Mandana lowered her voice. "I'll just take a peek." Ane she went to the stairs.

As soon as she was out of sight, Mrs. Ameli turned to Rana, "People are going to ask questions, you know."

Rana smiled bitterly. "Bet they already have some answers, too."

"It would be best to save face. As my late mother—may she rest in peace - used to say, 'show pink, happy cheeks, even if it's from a good slap!' Don't tell them anything that could get them talking. Think of *us*. We have to live in this city."

Dayeh turned her back and made loud clanking noises as she took out trays and serving platters from the cupboard. *Think of us?* What about thinking of her daughter for once? If it weren't for Rana's best friend, Minoo, the poor girl would have lost her mind over the past couple of weeks. But good old Minoo came often and sometimes Dayeh insisted on taking the baby so the two could enjoy a walk or go out for lunch.

"I wish Vida and Marjan were here. They would have loved a big party." Something in her voice made Dayeh turn around. The sad look was back in Rana's face. Dayeh knew how much Rana missed her girls. It was evident in the way she held her baby tight, in the sad lullabies she sang at night and how she sometimes gazed into the thin air. But knowing Rana, she'd never say a word about what went on inside her.

Dayeh couldn't begin to imagine what Vida and Marjan were doing or how they adapted to living with that horrible woman. Badri's house constantly changed décor, and Dayeh had no idea how to picture what her guest bedroom was like or how the girls looked, for that matter. Which clothes had Banu packed for them? And who did their hair in the morning? Marjan had just learned to braid her own hair, but little Vida would only allow her old nanny to comb those curls and she hated having her bangs cut, no matter who did it. *Three weeks and four days?* Out of the many times that Rana called Shiraz, they had only come to the phone five times, and even then the conversations were formal. Dayeh had a feeling that was because Rana knew if she spoke in more intimate terms it would only make the girls miss her more. When several other attempts turned unsuccessful, it left Dayeh no doubt that Badri had instructed her maid to dodge the calls. On the last call when Rana finally caught up with them, Dayeh waited until she was done, then asked if she could talk to them.

"I miss you, Dayeh *joon*," Marjan said, and she sounded cautious. "When will you come back?"

"May I die for you, child. I'll be home before you can blink."

Marjan's silence worried her and soon Vida had the phone.

At first, the younger girl showed less restraint, but when Dayeh asked her what kind of a present she'd want from Tehran, she started to cry and said, "I want to go home." Her crying became muffled as Marjan took the phone from her. "She's just being a baby."

"Am not!" Vida shouted in the background and cried harder. But then Marjan was off, too, and Badri's voice came through. "They need to take their baths now," she said without addressing her by name. "So I'll say a quick goodbye on their behalf. Be sure to extend my regards to the Amelis." And the line went dead.

How did others treat Marjan and Vida when their mother wasn't around? Did Badri have any patience at all? The day they left, Rana said her trip would last a couple of weeks. Now it was hard to tell when, if ever, she planned on going back.

Major Moradi had not called.

When no one showed much of a reaction to Rana's sudden departure and even Badri did not contact her, Dr. Ameli had called to talk to his son-in-law. Dayeh figured the good father wanted to patch things up between the couple. He was told the Major was out. A few days later, Dayeh heard him on the phone. "Could you please tell the Major to call the Amelis' residence?" But as far as she could tell, the call was never returned.

Rana's sisters continued to come by now and then, but their visits were brief and soon they returned to their own families and jobs. After a few restless nights, Rana and the baby moved to the guest suite. The relocation not only offered more privacy, but also offered enough distance from the grandparents so the baby's crying wouldn't disrupt their sleep. Best of all, Dayeh settled down in her old room adjacent to the suite and sometimes kept the baby with her the entire night, giving Rana a full night of rest.

Temporary as the arrangements were, that did not stop Mrs. Ameli from hinting. "Oh, what can I say?" Dayeh once heard her saying on the phone. "I guess you're never done caring for your children." Dayeh had no idea who she was calling, but something in Mrs. Ameli's voice told her she was referring to the recent events. Whenever she heard such frustrating comments on the inconvenience their stay had caused, she wished they could go back to Shiraz. But each evening, Dr. Ameli's warm company made her think that maybe, under the circumstances, his presence was exactly what Rana needed.

"Oh, how wonderful it feels to return to a full house again," Dr. Ameli's voice spilled its warmth into the hallway.

Dayeh rushed toward the kitchen to bring his tea, but she could still hear their voices.

"I showed my new granddaughter's picture to a patient today, and she said those must be the most beautiful eyes a baby ever had."

Rana laughed. "And I bet you agreed."

"Nope! I said she should have seen her mother when *she* was a baby!"

⁓

In preparation for Yalda to be shown at the party, Dayeh once more designed her makeshift swaddling though this time she secured the layers of cloth with a satin sash. She counted on the fact that guests would only blame her for the outdated swaddling method. One look at her gray hair and wrinkled face and they'd be sure to forgive her. With this baby, even Rana didn't object to the swaddling, and Dayeh had a feeling it might be because she couldn't bear to look at Yalda's legs. However, she noticed Rana staring at them each time she changed the baby's diapers, as if hoping for a miracle. Once or twice, the old nanny thought she even heard Rana sigh, but neither of them talked about it. The way everyone looked at the baby, their hesitant smiles and their silence made the subject of the shorter leg hang like a cloud. It was as if they all hoped that if they didn't mention it the problem would go away. The bundling covered the baby from waist down, like a little mermaid. A ruffled gown with its long skirt pulled down completed the effect.

When Dr. Ameli saw the baby, he said, "Aha! Now we'll show them whose picture they should put on those cans of formula!" He reached for his camera.

Rana stared, as if her eyes could see through the layers of cloth. Her face had the same sad expression as when she studied the baby's naked body. She turned to her father. "What will I tell them?" Her voice had no ring, her eyes pleading.

Dr. Ameli stopped his photo session. "No one is going to ask questions, my dear." He put the camera down, and holding her chin between his thumb and forefinger, raised her head. "I won't let them corner you. Leave it to *papa* to deal with the mob."

Dayeh poured tea for everyone.

"You're being too hard on yourself," Dr. Ameli went on. "There's nothing to be ashamed of." He studied the baby again and smiled. "Think about all the blessings in your life, and you'll find more than enough reasons to hold your head high." He went to the bar and poured a drink. "Here," he said and offered her the glass. "Forget the tea. One sip of this stuff will be enough to calm you down."

When the Ameli girls were small, if they were out of cold medicine, their father had put a few drops of cognac in their tea.

Rana smiled. "Oh, Papa, you and your medicines."

⁓

Conversations and laughter filled the living room. Guests were taken in by Yalda's angelic face. Best of all, as though the baby also enjoyed the crowd, she did not fuss at all for a long while. When she finally began to cry, Dayeh took her back to the nursery. Exhausted from all the attention, she fell asleep before her bottle of milk was finished.

By the time dinner was served, the happy crowd in the dining room had already diverted their attention from Rana and the baby. When the dessert was served, Dayeh noticed Rana sneaking out, perhaps to check on Yalda, and she followed to help.

Rana pulled up the covers on her sleeping baby and tucked them in. The silence was shattered by the phone's loud ring. Rana quickly picked up the receiver.

"*Allo?*"

One look at her pale face and Dayeh knew who the caller was.

"That's absurd!" she shouted. "My father would never --" She stopped, which made Dayeh think she had been cut off. Moments later Rana said, "He'd never interfere." Her voice had risen more than usual, and from the way she held the receiver away from her ear, so had the Major's. Dayeh could hear him from across the room, though the words were unclear.

"How could you even talk this way about someone who has always stood by you?"

The baby woke up and began to squirm in her bassinet. Rana saw Dayeh and motioned to the baby. She held on to the receiver with both hands and her next words came through clenched teeth.

"Good name? Go and ask the people of Shiraz what kind of a name you've made for yourself."

The baby was now crying and Dayeh began to rock her.

"I believe you've done enough already," Rana said, lowering her voice, as if to make sure the guests wouldn't hear her.

This time, the Major had plenty to say because for a couple of minutes all Rana did was frown and listen. Finally, she said, "I don't want to talk about that, at least, not right now. Just send the papers and I'll gladly sign. You have your freedom, so if what you say is true, maybe my father isn't so wrong thinking I deserve freedom, too."

There came the Major's voice again, but this time only for a brief response.

"You'll have to," she said. "It's the least you can do for me."

He went on and on before Rana cut him off. "Trust me, I *have* grown up." Despite the strength in her voice, Dayeh noticed Rana take a tissue to wipe her eyes.

No longer hearing the Major's voice, Dayeh figured he must have switched to a softer tone. Silence fell for a minute before Rana responded, "Listen, Farhad. This isn't the barracks, and you can no longer tell me how to live my life." Was it rage that made her voice strong?

Whatever he said, Rana's response shocked Dayeh. "You sure don't need me, and having evaluated the advantages of this marriage against its shortcomings, I'm not so sure I need you either." She slammed down the receiver, took the baby, and paced the entire length of the room.

When no explanation followed, Dayeh excused herself and went to serve more tea.

—

After the last guests had left, Rana helped Dayeh to bring back some order to the living room while Mrs. Ameli took her high-heeled shoes off and soaked her feet in a basin of salt-water. Rana gathered the baby gifts and stacked them in the guestroom closet. She then counted her mother's fine silverware and began to place the pieces in their felt-lined drawer.

Dr. Ameli loosened his tie and leaned against the doorframe. "I know an old guy who's so tired, he may fall asleep standing up," he said and gave a mock bow. "So if you ladies don't mind…"

"Farhad called," Rana said and kept her eyes on the silverware. "He said your lawyer contacted him."

Dr. Ameli seemed baffled. "I didn't ask him to do that."

"I didn't think you would."

Dr. Ameli thought for a few seconds. "Maybe it was his son who called. They practice together. It sounds like something an inexperienced lawyer might do." His words sounded as if he was thinking aloud. "I only told my friend to look into the possibilities, your options, etc."

Rana gave an angry laugh. "Well, whoever's idea that was, Farhad called to inform you that he won't do it."

"Won't do what?" her father asked.

"He will not give me a divorce."

Mrs. Ameli gasped, and Dayeh lowered herself onto the near-est chair. She had feared this might be what the phone conversa-tion had been about, but now that it was out in the open she had a hard time believing it.

Dr. Ameli took a deep breath. "And who asked for one?"

Rana stared back in equal surprise. "According to Farhad, you did."

He laughed bitterly. "I wish I could. But I don't have that right. Do I?" A few more seconds went by. "What else did he have to say?"

Rana just shook her head.

"Well then," he said and sounded relieved. "Maybe the man has more sense than we give him credit for." He lowered himself onto the sofa and leaned back. "When Farhad refused to return my calls, I asked my old friend, Mr. Eskandary, to contact him and find out how he felt about the situation and to demand that he clarify his intentions. Who knows? Maybe whatever the lawyer said has brought your husband to his senses. Maybe stating that he doesn't want a divorce is his way of working toward a reconciliation." Dr. Ameli sounded as if he was doing his best to convince himself.

Anger rose within Rana and her burning words poured out in a tone that no one had ever heard her use before. She tossed the last pieces of silverware into the drawer, slammed it shut, and turned to face her father. "Or *maybe* the women in his family have taught him that good wives are the ones who can put up and shut up. And, *maybe* with a new wife and a baby on the way, it's too damned inconvenient, too costly, to deal with a divorce."

"Oh, my," Mrs. Ameli cried out. She wrapped a towel around her wet feet and leaned back on the sofa.

"*Astaghforellah*," Dayeh said under her breath, asking for God's forgiveness.

Rana tucked a lock of hair behind her ear and straightened her back. "I haven't had time to make any decisions, but the idea of a divorce is beginning to sound better and better. Maybe the Major is right in saying I should grow up. Why not call Mr. Eskandary myself?"

Dr. Ameli, unable to close his mouth, stared back in utter silence.

Chapter

· *Five* ·

T HE LAW OFFICES OF ESKANDARY & Eskandary had such
old furniture, Rana was sure it must have not changed in
decades. The door opened and a gray head peeked in. "I
am most embarrassed to have kept you waiting." The small man
walked in and embraced Rana's father, who had risen from his chair
to greet him. The two men kissed on both cheeks, then the lawyer
turned to Rana.

"And who may this vision of beauty be?"

Rana took his extended hand.

"The last time I saw you, you were this big," the old lawyer said,
holding the palm of his hand at knee level.

Rana smiled back.

"This place never seems to change, my friend," her father said
good-naturedly. "Don't you ever get tired of antiques?"

Mr. Eskandary shrugged. "Not as long as I'm turning into
one myself," he said and chuckled. "The day I decide to step down,
Firooz can do whatever suits his young taste." He smiled and looked
around as though to refresh his mind on what the furniture looked
like. "As it is, I think the decor provides a perfect background for my
old face."

Rana's father nodded in acknowledgement of his friend's wit.

Rana had come to this meeting with a few questions. Following their long discussions, her father had concluded that it would be best to have a representative. "Should you decide to go through with a divorce, it will save you a lot of unpleasantness to have Eskandary act on your behalf when possible," he had said. "I would like to be present on the initial visit, make the introduction, and then leave you to it."

The worn leather chairs weren't half as comfortable as they looked and their sloped seats made it hard to stay in them. Rana leaned back and while the lawyer opened and closed a few files, she tried to distract herself with little details around the office. Mr. Eskandary had a busy desk, but there seemed to be a system to the clutter. A stack of files sat on one side, an open phonebook on the other. Between a stapler and the telephone, the angel of justice stood blindfolded. Rana sadly smiled at the thought that if they asked her, she'd say the angel signified how blind the law was when it came to women's rights. Despite the fact that women had even found seats in the parliament, a woman continued to receive half the rights a man had: she needed a man's permission to travel, and the law gave men the right to marry, divorce, and keep sole custody of their children.

She listened to the sound of shuffling papers as Mr. Eskandary reviewed his file. Morning sun filtered through a single window. A thin layer of dust covered the desk, except for a clean rectangle where a file had been. The floral wallpaper was so faded that Rana thought it must be the original.

Mr. Eskandary, apparently satisfied with what he found in the folder, rang for tea and picked up the top pages of the document.

"As much as I regret having to do this for a friend, we have no choice but to deal with this unpleasant matter." The old lawyer looked at Rana with the subtle affection only a wrinkled face can offer. "This must be awfully hard on you, but in light of the latest development, your father and I are glad you agreed to having this meeting. Please pardon me if some questions sound unkind, but I need all the facts."

Rana nodded.

"Your father has briefed me on some of what is going on, but I will need the details from you." He scratched his chin. "How long has it been since you've known about…?" he said.

Rana's mind filled with images of the day Banu had snuck into her room to share the neighborhood gossip.

"Five months," she said.

Her father looked up in shock.

Rana felt a knot in her throat and wished she could vanish for a moment and be alone. It wasn't in her nature to share her secrets with someone she barely knew, much less to cry in the presence of these men she respected so much.

"Have you ever met this other… ah…person?"

Each time she tried to picture Parisa, despite the vulgar visions that came with such stories, Rana couldn't form a solid image. She shook her head.

"This next question is harder, but you understand that, as your lawyer, I need to know everything about the case, and I mean *everything*." He cleared his throat. "Has the Major ever abused you?"

Before Rana could respond her father jumped in. "She just told us it's been going on for five months. Isn't months of mental torture, especially in her condition, abuse enough?" His words hung in the air unanswered. It was out of character for him to interrupt, let alone lose his temper. He must have realized this because he quickly added, "I'm sorry. Please go on."

Rana looked down and her response came as more of a whisper, "No."

For the next minute or so, no one said a word while Mr. Eskandary wrote down his notes.

"One always hopes for a simple, uncomplicated divorce," he said in his soothing voice. "I never call it friendly—as some of my esteemed colleagues would prefer to—because I've never witnessed one." He clasped his hands and put his elbows on the desk. "Some divorces are less traumatic than others, but *friendly*?" He shook his head. "That's just a figure of speech. However, there's no need to make it worse by taking matters to court, especially when we know that our current law will not be of much help to you."

"I understand," Rana's father said, "But what if he continues his stubbornness? It doesn't sound as if he's leaving us a choice."

Eskandary nodded. "Experience tells me that he will not change. Unfortunately the law leans too much in a man's favor, and believe me, he's counting on that." He kept his eyes on Rana, as if to make sure she followed. "I've given this matter serious thought. Your father is a dear friend indeed, and I look at this problem as if it concerns my own daughter. So what I'm about to suggest isn't so much a legal solution but rather my confidential advice, off the record." He put the palm of his hand over his heart and added, "From father to daughter."

There was a knock on the door, and a young man walked in, carrying a tray of tea.

"Leave them here," Mr. Eskandary said and stacked a few files to make room on the desktop. "And hold all my calls."

The man nodded. When he had gone, Eskandary continued. "As I said, this is strictly between us, and I don't need to mention that if any of it gets out, I'll be in serious trouble."

Rana looked up from her lap and noticed that now her father and the old attorney were staring at each other. Neither said a word.

"Let us review all the facts. Under the current law, he has the right to do as he wishes. Not only does he hold all the rights to a divorce, but should you succeed in obtaining one through the superior court, the law gives the father full custody of all children."

Rana did not know much about the law, but what he said was common knowledge. She had hoped that with all the modern changes attributed to the new queen, and the recent accomplishments of the ladies' organizations, something would have been done about women's rights, something that could help her case.

"As long as you live here, your chances are slim," Eskandary went on. "So I would suggest finding a way to go abroad."

"Without a divorce?" Rana asked.

"Precisely."

"But, what could that possibly accomplish?"

"Your freedom," he said and raised his index finger. "Once you are safely out of here, you can act on becoming a resident in another country." He reached over and placed a glass of tea before each of them and passed the bowl of sugar cubes around. "It's been done, you know. There are countries where the laws of divorce are more to a woman's advantage."

Rana thought about that for a moment and was overcome by a feeling of disbelief. "This sounds much too drastic," she said as soon as she could find her voice. "People get divorced all the time. There has to be a less complicated way."

Mr. Eskandary shook his head. "Most divorces are either initiated by the husband or based on mutual agreement. Granted, there are cases that are settled in court, but most of those are far more serious than yours," he said and immediately explained his meaning. "Don't get me wrong. I do understand the seriousness of your case. But I'm looking at this strictly from the legal standpoint."

"Surely we must have laws against a man who abandons his wife and children," her father said.

The lawyer nodded. "Indeed, we do. But Major Moradi hasn't done that, has he?"

Rana moved to the edge of her seat. "How do you define abandonment?"

"I'm not sure I know what you mean."

"Just because I have a roof over my head and food on my plate, am I to assume I've been taken care of? What about his other—" Tears would not let her finish.

"I understand, dear," the old attorney said. "But the law isn't clear on that. As long as you are provided for and there's no evidence of abuse or endangerment, the law assumes him to be a good husband."

"What about his second marriage?" her father said. "I thought it was illegal nowadays to have more than one wife."

Mr. Eskandary looked down at his hands and did not respond.

"Well, isn't it?"

The attorney continued to tap the paper with his pen and remained silent without looking up.

"I don't understand," Rana said.

The old lawyer sighed. "First, you must remember this is still a Muslim country. That means, no matter how much you and I may disagree with multiple marriages, and despite all the clauses that are attached, most folks consider it a man's right to take more than one wife. Still, the law would have been on your side, except I think your husband must have known that." He looked up at Dr. Ameli and then at Rana. "He never registered his second marriage."

"What?" Rana interrupted. She might not understand all the fancy legal terms, but knew exactly what he was saying. "I know for a fact that they are married, that he bought her a house." She hesitated then added in a whisper, "They are even about to have a child."

Dead silence followed her last sentence. Rana was too embarrassed to look at the men, but she could feel her father's surprised stare.

The lawyer waited for her to calm down before he added, "I have investigated the situation, and you're right. Major Moradi sounds like a devout Muslim, at least more so than most of his peers."

"I'm not sure what this means," Dr. Ameli said.

"Such a man would not live in sin, nor would he want to have a child out of wedlock. But my informer in Shiraz tells me that they simply had a religious ceremony, which explains why there's no record of such a marriage." He paused as if to let that information sink in before adding, "In the eyes of God, he has married two of the four wives a Muslim man is allowed, but where the law is concerned, he has but one legal wife." He looked at Rana. "You."

Rana wasn't prepared for this turn of events. She knew nothing about the law, but with each added word the attorney only made this matter sound more complicated.

Dr. Ameli broke the silence. "What about the house he bought? If the rumor holds any truth, that would make the woman his paid mistress. Could Rana file for divorce on the ground that he has been unfaithful to her and taken a different home with another woman?"

The old attorney did not appear to be fazed by this. He was quiet for a few seconds and finally said, "I've checked into that. The house belongs to *her*." He waved a hand in the air. "Some of the money came from the sale of her old home, and her grandmother left her a handsome inheritance as well." His face took on a more serious look. "In short, it doesn't look as if she'd need his money."

Rana resented the lawyer's respectful tone. If that woman was so high and mighty, why would she steal *her* husband?

Her father's voice broke the awkward moment. "I still don't know what's to be gained by Rana running away."

The lawyer finished the last sip of his tea. "Her rights," he finally said. "I've dealt with men like Major Moradi. Under normal circumstances, they can be civil, even admirable. But this is war and he's not trained to lose wars." He took another look at his notes. "Consider it an educated guess, but Moradi will never agree to a divorce. More than that, experience tells me that if he as much as suspects your intentions of staying abroad, he will deny you his consent for traveling." He gave Rana an embarrassed look as if to apologize for the law. "You do know that you will need his written permission in order to leave the country."

She nodded.

"He has several reasons for wanting to stay married to you. First of all, respect." He counted each reason by bending one of his fingers and holding it down with the other hand. "Men often tend to stay married to the mother of their children because that gains them social respect." He bent another finger. "Even if he did not care for you at all, which at this point we're not certain of, he will do what he can to prevent you from marrying another. And third, he knows that a divorce will cost him dearly." He opened his hand again and leaned back. "I've seen men play all kinds of tricks to weasel out of that. And if you should pressure him, he won't hesitate to use emotional weapons." He paused before adding, "Your daughters, for instance."

"He wouldn't dare!"

"Let's be realistic," the old lawyer said with sympathy and he leaned over the desk. "Don't forget, my dear, this is war."

"I will die before I give up my children." Rana said and buried her face in both hands.

Dr. Ameli put his hand on her shoulder. "We're just talking, my dear. Let's hear what Mr. Eskandary has to say."

The meeting lasted several hours, and by the time they left, Rana had cried all the tears that she had tamed for weeks. The more Mr. Eskandary spoke, the more sense his suggestion made. At the conclusion, Rana agreed to think about it and they set another appointment for the following week.

"No need to remind you of confidentiality," Mr. Eskandary said again. "Secrecy is of vital importance in such a sensitive case." He hesitated as if to search for the right words before lowering his voice. "In fact, I don't even see a need for Mrs. Ameli to be bothered with any of this."

"Yes. Yes, of course," her father assured him. "My wife couldn't handle the pressure. It would be best if she doesn't know."

Rana shook Mr. Eskandary's hand. "Thank you," she said and found it ironic to be thanking the man who had just taken away her last hope.

The restaurant at the Intercontinental Hotel wasn't half as busy as Dr Ameli had thought it would be. With the number of tourists from around the world and thousands of Americans the Shah lured with a variety of well-paid jobs, hotels that catered to the Western taste enjoyed a booming business. The Intercontinental was one of the first to offer a buffet brunch that consisted of both Persian and European cuisine. Unaccustomed to a "brunch," most Iranians went there for lunch. Rana used to like their food, and Dr. Ameli recalled the few occasions when Rana had helped at the office and he had taken her there as a treat. Now her mood was somber and she looked as if the thought of food could make her sick. They were shown to a less crowded area at the far end of the large room. Soon a waiter came to take their orders for drink. Dr. Ameli asked for a glass of wine, but Rana said water was fine.

"What am I going to do, Papa?" Rana said and sounded relieved to pose the question that must have been on her mind during the long ride from the lawyer's office.

Dr. Ameli unfolded his linen napkin and spread it neatly on his lap. Indeed, what would she do? Days and days of that agonizing question had failed to offer him a reasonable answer. "I don't know," he said. "All I can say is that I fully trust Eskandary. He'll find a way."

Rana bunched her napkin in her fist. "That's what I'm worried about," she said. "He's a really nice man, but I'm not sure about his *plan*."

Dr. Ameli felt a pressure in his chest. Funny how medicine attributed all emotions to portions of the brain, denying any such connection to the heart, because each time something bothered him, he felt the pain right where his heart was. Lately, the mere thought of what his daughter had to go through gave him that pain and it had only become fiercer.

He looked at her and nodded reassuringly. "I'm certain that as you get to know him better, you'll also learn to trust him." He nodded again. "Believe me, you will." He thought for a moment. "Let's focus on a plan to get you and the baby to Europe."

Rana stared at him in shock. "Leave Marjan and Vida behind?"

How alike they were. The week before, when Eskandary had proposed the plan in private, that exact question had come to his mind, too. It had taken him days to agree. He hoped that time would also help Rana to reach some level of acceptance. He now regretted not having prepared her.

"Well, he didn't exactly suggest leaving them, did he?" Looking at Rana, he knew she was waiting for more. "You can take them along. Or you could leave them here and we shall send them to you down the line, when you're settled." He hoped his words did not sound as unsure as he felt.

"Exactly!" Rana exclaimed. "It's that *line* that I worry about. How long will that be, assuming it has an end?"

Dr. Ameli shared some of that concern, so he decided not to even attempt to come up with an answer.

"Could you just put yourself in my place for a moment, Papa? We're not Europeans who send their babies away to school. A child needs her family. I can't keep just one and hope for the best with the other two. Could you ever pick and choose among *your* children?"

There was that pain again. "No, I couldn't," he said in all honesty. Then realizing that such confessions would not help Rana at this point, he added, "And neither will you." He leaned closer across the table. "You're getting this all wrong, my dear. Nobody is asking you to give up your children. It will only be a temporary separation, only until we figure out a way to send them to you. Think about it. I may play dumb, but I understand what you're going through. I've seen how uncomfortable you are even now, being here with us. But we're all doing what we have to do to make sure this problem is resolved."

"Why can't I just move back to Tehran, get my own place, and live with my children?"

She had either seen too many movies and read too many novels, or didn't want to face the reality of how this society worked.

"Let's look at the situation objectively, Rana. People frown on a young woman getting her own apartment, and you wouldn't want to give up your dignity." He gave her a few seconds to understand. "In our society, a single woman is easy gossip. So, if you want to be independent, you're going to have to find a place where people are more open-minded."

He was right. That kind of woman was also the type who stole another's husband. She could never live with entire neighborhoods talking about her. "Where am I going to go, Papa? How will we survive?"

He hesitated a moment before answering. "New as this proposition may sound to you, I've known about it for a few days. Eskandary discussed his plan with me a week ago. So, I've had time to think it over."

"You *knew* this?" And she sounded outraged.

"Well, to be honest, I had hoped he might come up with a better plan. But I also needed time to figure out a way to go about it, just in case."

Her hazel eyes now stared back in harsh realization. He also saw there something he had never seen before, a doubt, even distrust. Unused to such misgivings, he diverted his attention to the napkin on his lap and needlessly smoothed it. "Your aunt Malak lives alone in America. I've seen her house. It's big enough," he said and looked at other tables, pretending to not notice the angry look she shot him. "Of course, I'll have to check with her and make sure."

"*America?* Why not Mars, Papa?" She gave a nervous laugh. "Oh, let me guess. You don't know anyone there who'd take pity on your daughter and offer shelter."

"Stop it," he said softly and shot her a hurt look. "We're only talking at this point."

"No, Papa, we're not just talking. We're informing Rana of a convenient plan her father and his lawyer friend have come up with, a plot to toss her across the universe!"

Rana's voice rose with those last words and a blonde couple, who were about to take the next table, turned to look.

Dr. Ameli had never seen such an outburst from Rana. Had motherhood strengthened her character, or was it years of life with a military man that had hardened her so? He felt a sharp blade inside him, turning with each word she said, with each painful glance she gave him. Ever since the lawyer suggested this plan, Dr. Ameli was tormented with all kinds of new thoughts. If Rana moved abroad, he would not see her for long periods of time, he would have to travel across the globe to visit his grandchildren, and even assuming they'd remain connected, he was sure to miss many precious milestones in their lives. Such agonizing prophecies kept him up at night. But as daylight had pushed the darkness away, it had also wiped away his doubts. He needed to be strong for the both of them. "I'm sorry you see it that way," he said softly, lovingly.

"Would you just listen to yourself? How can you ask me to move across the globe, tear my children away from everyone they know, and go live with an aunt I haven't seen in years? Even if I could do it, how am I going to finance all this?"

"You don't have to worry about that," he said and welcomed the change of subject. "We'll just pretend you were never married and I'll take care of your educational expenses."

"Education?" she said with an angry laugh. "I barely got through high school. All I have left of that is basic literacy." She shrugged. "Sorry, Papa. It's too late for that."

"It's never too late for an education," he said and smiled light-heartedly. "How else are you going to pay me back?"

Rana frowned and turned her face away. "That's very generous, but it's out of the question. I can't take your money."

"If you don't want to make the effort, then maybe you're pre-pared to live with the situation as is." He waved a hand in the air. "Go ahead and stay in that awful marriage for the rest of your life if you want, but first stop for a moment and think about what that means. This isn't just about you." He grabbed her hand in both of his and pleaded, "What will happen to your daughters?" He low-ered his voice to a near whisper. "Will they have to hang their heads in shame because their father is a bigamist?"

Rana sat straight. So far, all references to the Major's lifestyle had been vague. Absorbed in her own misery, it looked as if Rana had never thought about how the shame of Moradi's transgression might affect their children. Dr. Ameli regretted being the one who drew her attention to this, but someone had to. He continued with a lowered voice while maintaining the harsh tone. "What kind of a miserable mother and how much of a part-time father will they have?" He fought back his reluctance and threw the last stone. "And what happens to you if this woman bears him a son?"

In the long silence that fell, he listened to the hum of conversations and the clanking of dishes nearby. *I should never have agreed to this marriage.* That nagging thought never left him alone. He should have seen the signs and done something about it much earlier in the game. Now all he had was regret, even guilt. When he spoke again it was as if his words were the tears he had been unable to shed. "Don't you ever go thinking this is easy for your old father."

He took a sip of water while Rana bent her head and stared at her clasped hands. He watched the top of her head, that shiny brown hair parted in the middle, and thought of when she was a little girl. Oh, how hard she made it for him not to pick a favorite! His other three always had an answer for the troubles they got into. But not Rana. If he ever found the heart to scold her, she just hung her head in shame. Where did the time go when all she needed to make things right was a good hug?

"I can't imagine anyone refusing my money when I'm gone. So why not make good use of it while I'm around?" He stopped because he could tell she was about to cry.

Their server came back with the drinks and they remained silent until he had gone.

"I'm getting older, Rana-jan," he said and thought his voice sounded as broken as he felt. "I won't be around forever." He blew the air out of his lungs. "God only knows how I wish this had never happened. But the wrong is done and nothing I can do will make it right."

"He'll never let us leave."

"Oh? And who's asking his permission?" He gave a sad smile.

Rana dabbed her eyes and returned his smile.

"We do have ridiculous laws," he went on. "Requiring the husband's consent for an exit permit is one of them. But there are ways to get around that."

"Run away?"

"Not exactly," he said. "But let's assume things cool down. Then who is to say you couldn't take the baby to America for a pre-arranged medical consultation?"

Rana stared at him, her mouth half open.

"Especially if such a recommendation should come from her pediatrician and my good friend, Dr. Fard."

Rana seemed intrigued.

"The good doctor would do it if I asked him nicely," he went on. "And I believe that may take care of your husband's suspicions. What father would stand in the way of his child's health?" He chuckled before adding, "It's a deceptive plan, I know. But a small price for your freedom, don't you think?"

"What about Vida and Marjan? Surely you don't expect me to leave them behind."

"Of course not. It'll be a nice summer holiday for them, too." He smiled knowingly.

Rana shook her head. "You don't know Farhad the way I do, Papa. If he suspects anything, he'll make sure I live to regret it. If he hates one thing, it's losing a battle."

"That's true, but it's also true that the only way to defeat such a strong-willed man is an ambush. I agree that if you suggest it right away, he will do all he can to stop you." He cleared his throat before adding, "But not if you let some time pass and allow things to go back to normal."

"No," Rana said and shook her head frantically. "You're not suggesting I go back to Shiraz and play the good little wife."

He wished he could say she didn't have to do anything she

didn't want to. Did his little girl know that pushing her back to that man was the hardest thing he would ever have to do? But this was no time to be sentimental. He recalled an incident back in his youth, when he had watched the rescue of a fawn from a trap set for foxes. Hunters knew that, if the animal was touched by human hands, its mother would neither accept him back nor breast feed him. So they had to use metal prongs to take him out of the trap and the poor thing cried as they set it free. Rana reminded him of that gazelle. To cut the ties would cause pain, but the alternative was far worse.

"Trust me, this is the only practical plan. Ridiculous as the law is, you can't leave the country without that damn piece of paper. And as you said yourself, if he becomes suspicious, he'll never grant you permission."

Rana shrugged. "Forget divorce. Can't I just leave him?"

"We've been over this before. Life out there is harsh for a single mother." He pointed a finger to the window. "If we are going to do this right, it's imperative that you go back to your husband. The sooner, the better."

Rana shook her head. "Vida and Marjan will be miserable without their father. Marjan may adapt, but Vida is so attached to her father that I'm not so sure she could handle the separation."

"Oh, you'll be surprised. The way kids handle hardships is mind-boggling."

For a while neither of them spoke.

"I can't believe how optimistic you sound," Rana said at last and sounded tired. "I know my husband, and I promise you, he won't let them go. Yalda needs medical care, not Vida nor Marjan. So, what makes you think he'll send those two abroad?" Horror crept into her eyes. "The minute I turn my back, he will move in with this ... this ... woman!"

"Stop your silly imaginings. None of that is going to happen."

He then changed his tone to a more loving one, "If worse comes to worst, your mother and I will offer to keep the girls. Bet he'd prefer that over taking them to *her*." His voice dropped and now it sounded as if he was talking to himself. "There hasn't been a day since we left Shiraz that I haven't thought about them," he said. "A child deserves better, especially those two. The way I see it, he'll fight you all he can. But once he knows you're not coming back, he will send them to you, even if only to make your life abroad more difficult."

Rana buried her face in her napkin and shook her head side to side.

"Who knows why things happen?" he went on. "This could be the beginning of something better for all of you, the darkness before daybreak."

Their server came back and refreshed their drinks.

Rana took another sip of water. "I think I need to talk to someone who could be impartial, a complete stranger, perhaps a professional."

"Isn't Eskandary professional enough?"

"That's not what I mean. I need someone who can help me understand my own emotions. You know? Help me clear my head."

"You mean a psychiatrist?" He couldn't mask his surprise. Most people thought only crazy people needed analysts, and although he understood the need, it was hard to believe the suggestion had come from Rana.

She nodded.

He shook his head. "Not here. I mean, they're out there, but I don't know how good they are." He scratched his chin. "We hardly have enough doctors at the Chehrazi hospital to deal with the mentally deranged, let alone consulting normal people."

"So what are my options?"

"That's one more reason for you to go abroad. Even if I found you a good doctor here, the minute you're spotted around such a practice, people are going to label you insane."

"I'll be lucky to handle the daily life in my English, but discuss my emotional problems? Ha!"

"That can be fixed, too. You can always study, you know? Why not start with improving your English?"

Rana didn't say a word.

"You will have months to focus on such basic tasks. With so many Americans in Shiraz, that shouldn't be a problem."

"You mean taking adult classes?" she said as if she had not taken him seriously.

"Not exactly." He folded his napkin neatly and left it on the table. "You're welcome to borrow my Lingaphone tapes and books. But also try to make new friends, or at least get back in touch with those American ladies at the officer's club. It may do you good, get your mind off things, and teach you more about life in America."

They visited the buffet and filled their plates, but neither seemed hungry and they did not talk during the forced bites they took. As they left the restaurant, the loving father did not put his arm around his daughter's shoulders, nor did he offer his elbow. Rana needed to learn to walk alone. Through Tehran's crazy traffic, they rode in utter silence, each submerged in their own dark thoughts.

—

Rana sat on her bed and ran her father's plan in her mind. Now that she had calmed down, she realized how difficult this must have been for him. For a man who often said a family should stay together, the mere idea of sending her away must be agonizing.

Rana realized this was too big a decision to put on paper and to weigh the options, especially when one of the items on the "disadvantage" column was to abandon her daughters.

She tried to picture staying in Shiraz, but the image that came to her was far too gloomy. Would the Major even bother to come home occasionally, now that his secret was out? Would there be enough love in him for the girls, if he fathered a son? And what about other people? Would Moradi's friends in Shiraz even care who his legal wife was? Wouldn't they open their arms to his new woman? Rana had never been jealous; then again, what else could cause the bitter taste that came to her with the thought of those two together? She wouldn't give self-pity a chance, but with so many bad sides to this situation, it was hard not to.

She tried hard to take herself out of the equation. At this moment, what mattered the most was Yalda. Rana had brought her into this world and might even be responsible for her problem. The least a mother could do was to give her a chance at a normal life. The thought of Yalda's tiny legs stabbed at her heart. Would Yalda walk without help? What if the discrepancy in her legs became worse? In a society that did their best to keep the crippled out of sight, how would people treat a young girl who limped?

Rana recalled an old classmate who had only one hand. Once, when they were little, the girl had raised her dangling empty sleeve and had shown Rana the stump. Her arm ended just below the right elbow and had a mole where the skin gathered. She had allowed Rana to touch it. The soft flesh over the stump had felt the same as her grandma's double chin. The image was seared in her mind. Then in their junior year the girl had come to school with an artificial hand concealed under a white glove. The adult size prosthesis was too big for her frame and though she seemed proud, others stared at it with pity. Classmates often shared their treats with the girl, as if to hand out a portion of their own good fortune. No, this society wouldn't let Yalda forget her difference. She would grow up to feel inadequate. Rana had to prevent that.

A bright moon moved inside the window frame, spilling its silver light. No wonder the moon—*mah*—was a metaphor for beauty. Rana softly whispered the words of Dayeh's chant, "I have a daughter *shah* doesn't have. She has a face *mah* doesn't have."

———

"I'm sorry, Mrs. Moradi," the high-pitched voice of Badri's maid blasted through the receiver. "The young ladies are out. Would you like to speak to Badri *Khanoom*?"

Rana hesitated for a few seconds. "Yes, please."

The maid's slippers shuffled away and soon she heard the approach of Badri's spike heels on the marble floor.

"*Allo?*"

"Hello, Badri-*joon*."

"Oh, hello. What a surprise," Badri said, pretending she had no idea who was calling.

"How are you?" Rana asked politely.

"I'm okay. I mean tired, but okay." She hesitated before adding, "I can't imagine how those mothers of four manage to survive, but I shouldn't complain. After all, my nieces aren't going to be here forever."

Rana had prepared for the woman's sting and tried to sound courteous. "It must be hard. Thank you for doing this."

"I'd do anything for my brother."

"How are my girls?"

"Fine. Constantly inviting their friends over, going to school, you know…"

"Does Vida still wake up at night?"

"No. Not since I told her she's too old for that. All she needed was a little discipline."

Rana's heart sank. Vida's frequent nightmares woke her up and she used to crawl into her mother's bed in the middle of the night. The image was so vivid she could almost feel the tiny cold feet touching her. Rana had spoken to the pediatrician about it and was told to cuddle her, comfort her and take her back to her own bed with a soothing story. What did Badri mean by "discipline?"

"I happen to miss the girls every time. When would be a good time to call them?"

Badri did not respond right away. After a few seconds she lowered her voice. "I think it's best to leave them alone for now."

"What are you talking about?"

"No need to shout, dear. I'm not the one who abandoned them."

"Abandon? I've not abandoned anyone."

"No?"

"No!"

"Call it what you want, dear, but they're just getting used to life without you. Your calls only confuse them. Each time they talk to you, I have to deal with Vida's moods for days. Surely, you don't want to make them *more* miserable."

Rana swallowed her anger and used an equally fake tone. "You're right. It's not worth upsetting them." When Badri did not respond she added, "They've been good for all this time, I guess one more week won't matter." She could not believe her own words. For an entire week, she had debated if, or when, she would return to Shiraz. Now, unbeknownst to herself, she sounded as if a decision had been made.

"One more week of what?"

"Of being a guest at your house. We will be back next week. I don't know the exact time because my father has the tickets. I really called to see if they wanted anything special from Tehran."

Words were pouring out at their own will. Rana had a hard time with lies, even little white ones. When did she become so good at this?

Badri was silent and Rana hoped it was from shock.

"Also, would you need anything from here?" she asked sweetly. "Just name it. It's the least I can do in return for all the trouble my absence may have caused." She smiled at how easy it was to beat Badri at her own game. Living with her parents again, and in particular watching her mother through the eyes of a married woman, had been most educational. Her mother manipulated others in exactly the same way as Badri did. How unfair it was that women who put their own interests above everyone else's often had it easier than the nurturing ones.

"You're coming back?" Badri's voice screeched. "I mean, so soon?"

"Not soon enough, dear. I miss my home and my own family." Rana smiled at how innocent and sincere those words sounded. Playing a role didn't seem half as hard as she had imagined. It was about time the Moradis finally had a taste of their own medicine.

Chapter

· Six ·

ONLY AFTER THE PLANE HAD TOUCHED DOWN at the Shiraz airport did Rana appreciate the weight of her mission. It had been one thing to plot and plan, but quite another to act the part. Theoretically speaking, it sounded sensible to go back and act as the wife returning from a long trip, but suddenly the idea that she was not the only woman in Farhad Moradi's life was too much to bear. Returning to a city that sheltered her husband and his other woman, she wasn't sure he would remain prudent about his double life. How far could she go with acting? Mr. Eskandary and her father were the only others who knew about her new role. Her father had made her promise not to discuss the plan with anyone, not even Dayeh.

"A word that passes through thirty-two teeth will soon pass through thirty-two cities," he had reasoned. "You know I'd trust your mother with my life, but she can't handle secrets."

With Dayeh carrying Yalda and trailing behind, Rana made her way through the crowded terminal as if this were part of a strange dream. She remembered the many times her husband had been there, carrying a bunch of roses wrapped in cellophane. Her eyes scanned the area in search of a tall figure in khaki uniform, but managed to push the image away as quickly as it had come to her. They left the transit area and she asked the young porter who carried their suitcases to find them a taxi.

They were soon on their way in the back seat of a rather small cab. The lumpy seat felt warm from the previous passenger and the cabin smelled like an ashtray. Rana smiled at how the driver carried his items of endearment. Prayer beads hung from the rear-view mirror, while pictures of his children, a large calligraphy of *Allah,* and a peacock feather in a small vase were all taped to the dashboard. Outside, a ring of stone mountains circled the city, and Rana marveled at their magnificent colors ranging from purple to orange. Shiraz's deep blue sky was a welcome change from the smoggy gray of Tehran's.

"Oh, how I love this city," she said mostly to herself as they drove to town.

The driver eyed her in his mirror. "Shiraz does that to people, *kakoo,*" he replied in his deep local accent.

"You said it," Dayeh joined in. "One breath of this air, and I'm young again." And she giggled.

Located further south than Tehran, Shiraz enjoyed a warmer climate. The roses along Zand Boulevard were already in full bloom and the spring air was heavy with the fragrance of honeysuckle and jasmine. The mere sight of tall Cypress trees took Rana back to the first time she had set eyes on them. What a contrast this was to Tehran's arid streets, few dust-covered shade trees and abundance of tall buildings. By now she felt her roots in this city, as if it had been a part of her entire life. The driver had a point. *Shiraz did that to people.*

Each time they returned from a trip, Marjan used to point out the familiar surroundings with cheer. "That's my school, and this is the Gas circle," she would shout as though discovering a new land. Both girls had a deep Shirazi accent, dragging their words the southern way and Rana loved hearing it. Soon those chirps would fill her senses. She took a deep breath, hoping to lift the heavy weight of memories from her chest. The town she loved would soon cease to be hers. Then again, had it ever belonged to her?

They neared the familiar neighborhood with its rows of sculpted iron doors in all colors and honeysuckle draped over brick walls. A sudden anxiety rose within her. She had mentioned the day of her arrival to Badri, but not wanting to be met at the airport, she had withheld the time. What if her husband was home?

The taxi stopped in front of their house and Rana searched her overstuffed purse for her keys. Banu wouldn't be back for another day and she figured even if the Major was home, it would be awkward to ring the bell and have him answer it. Only after the heavy gate opened and she didn't find his car in the driveway did she relax. The driver put their suitcases in the garden and left. Rana took the baby and walked to the building while Dayeh shut the gate.

The garden never had many flowers, but now it looked utterly bare. The gravel driveway was covered with a layer of dead leaves and Rana saw no tire-tracks. The small patch of lawn had started to turn brown and the few remaining geraniums seemed neglected and sad.

"I don't believe a single soul has been here since we left," she said to Dayeh.

"Could be," Dayeh said while dragging one of the suitcases. "Badri-khanoom has a key. You'd think she would have brought Banu to do a few things around the house while we were gone."

"The place smells like a grave."

Dayeh chuckled. "Oh, the things you come up with, Miss Rana! How would you know what a grave—God forbid—smells like?"

Rana did not laugh.

The hallway felt warm and gave out the musty odor of a bath-house. Dayeh went into the family room, pushed the curtains aside and opened a window. "Oo, it's good to be home," she said as she roamed around, looking relieved, touching furniture and seeming to enjoy her reunion with familiar objects. Rana wished she could share the enthusiasm, but she was as cautious as she had been at her parent's home, even worse, as if she were trespassing.

"Would you look at these filthy windows?" Dayeh exclaimed. "It must have rained a lot. I hope that girl shows up soon to help me clean." She took the smaller suitcase and disappeared into the nursery.

Rana turned to her baby, who had just opened her eyes. "Well, Yalda *khanoom*," she whispered. "This is where you were born. You may call it home, though I don't know for how long." She smiled at how she had picked up her mother's habit of a one-way conversation with the infant. "Better get ready to play with your big sisters—you do remember you have two, don't you?" She hesitated before adding, "And, a father, who ..." she stopped mid-sentence. No, she couldn't finish it with, "*who loves you very much.*"

The baby closed her eyes again. Rana kissed the softness at the top of her head and put the sleeping infant on the couch. The scene from the last time she had seen her husband came back to her. It was here where it all began, where she agreed to go to Tehran with her parents. When she had asked Dayeh to pack that small suitcase, neither of them had any idea when, if ever, they might return. As if the past few months had been a time tunnel, she now felt older, more tired, and far less emotional. She wrapped her arms around herself and embraced the vision of her daughters. Except for those two, there was nothing here worthy of a return.

Rana dialed Badri's number. No one answered and she wondered if Badri had mixed up the dates. Standing inside the empty house, her mind filled with her daughter's voices. She'd call again after she had unpacked and taken a shower.

Half an hour later, Rana twisted a towel around her wet hair, wiped the fogged bathroom mirror with the palm of her hand, and peered at her reddened face covered in beads of moisture. Nothing could ever relax her as much as a good, steaming shower did. She switched the fan on, squeezed her damp toes into her bathroom slippers and opened the door. She had taken but one step into the bedroom when she gasped at the sight of her estranged husband, sitting on the edge of their bed, staring in her direction.

Rana's entire body tensed. Was the slight parting of his lips a semblance of a smile? She wasn't sure because he didn't look happy at all. In fact, his eyes darkened with deep sorrow, the kind she had only seen the day his father had died.

"Hello, Rana." His voice was lowered to a mere whisper, and Rana remembered how her friend Minoo thought it sexy and theatrical.

She grabbed the front of her bathrobe and held it closed, while tying the belt into a hard knot. What would she do if he came any closer? Heat rose in her cheeks and the question of why he was there hung in the air.

He stood, but before he could take a step, there was a commotion in the hallway, the door burst open, and their little girls ran inside.

"Mom-eee!" Vida cried out and ran into her mother's arms. Rana got down to her knees and inhaled the smell of baby shampoo from her daughter's soft hair. Kissing any and every part of her face that came in touch with her lips, Rana let her tears roll down into Vida's hair without bothering to wipe them. She felt Marjan's shy hand on her back and turned to embrace her with one arm while still holding on to Vida with the other. Silent tears now changed into uncontrollable sobs as she let go of all the emotions she had locked inside.

"Let me look at you," she said at last and leaned back a little, wiping her eyes. "I can't believe you two have grown so much in such a short time!"

"One month and nineteen days," Farhad's deep voice now filled the room. "That's not so short."

Rana didn't know why she turned to face him and quickly turned away again. This wasn't supposed to happen. Badri had said she would bring the girls back. He wasn't expected. The huge gap between them had been there for months, and she had no intention of closing it. What in the world made him think she wanted to see him at all?

She let go of Vida's hand and Marjan took her chance to wrap both arms around her. Rana held her tight, and feeling her delicate shoulder bones, she wondered if the girl had eaten much during her stay at Badri's. She squeezed her as if to push the sorrow out of her little body and realized how much she needed her big girl. She loved her children equally, but in a way, separation from this one had been even harder.

Vida took hold of Rana's sleeve and tried to pull her toward the door. "Come, Maman, see what we got."

"What do you have, honey?"

Marjan gave her the familiar, knowing look. "It's a surprise!" she said.

"Yes. A big supplies, Mommy!" Vida said, going back to baby talk the way she always did when overexcited.

Out in the hallway, Dayeh held a shoebox with holes around it.

"We sure needed one more of these!" she said and shook her head. "As if there weren't enough alley cats to keep me awake at night."

"It's not a cat," Vida said and pouted. "It's a peeshee."

Rana laughed.

Marjan explained, "Papa got her a kitten because she stopped being a cry baby."

Rana could not believe her ears. A man who emphasized order and practicality, Moradi had been dead set against the idea of any pet, even a goldfish. "Those creatures belong in the wild," he always said. "To be inside a house is a sure way to shorten their lives." Once, when Marjan had caught a butterfly and brought it home in a jar, he had opened the lid, and ignoring her cries, let it fly away. "If God meant for that thing to live in a jar, He wouldn't have given it wings!" he had said. So what brought about the change of heart - *if the man had one?*

Vida opened the shoebox and took out a rounded ball of white fur. The kitten had its eyes closed, but as Vida lifted its chin and scratched under it, he opened his green eyes and looked around sleepily.

"What did we decide?" the Major said in a soft tone that Rana had not heard in a long time. He approached Vida and gently took the kitten from her and placed it back in the shoebox. "Let's keep him there for now," he said in the same soft tone. "He may come out once we've set out a litter box for him."

Rana could not believe the gentle soul before her. Had the man changed, or did he have a plan of his own? Was he, too, acting a part?

Throughout the evening, despite her resentments, Rana tried to behave as if nothing had happened. The household resumed its normal routine now that the lady of the house had returned. Still unsure if her act was convincing enough, she made an effort not to say or do anything that might make the children sense the tension she felt. God only knew what Badri had filled their brains with and it was up to Rana to undo the damage.

"Did you see little Yalda?" Rana asked the girls and made sure her back was to Moradi.

"She's asleep," Vida said.

"I saw her," Marjan said. "She's so much bigger."

Moradi was quiet.

Once they were past the initial excitement, both girls seemed to keep a cautious distance. They seldom touched their mother, as if afraid that she might disappear again. But after a few hours even Marjan acted more relaxed.

Banu showed up earlier than expected and was immediately sent out to buy the necessary ingredients for dinner. Rana gave the girls a few mechanical toys and china dolls she had bought in Tehran. As they began to play and Major Moradi sat down to watch the news, she finally had a chance to go upstairs and get dressed.

Soon after dark, the family gathered for a simple meal of macaroni and ground lamb that Dayeh had quickly put together. Rana took her seat across from her husband and did her best to avoid looking at him. On a few occasions, she felt the heat of his lingering gaze. He made no attempt to initiate a conversation, and if any of his comments were intended for her, they came addressed to the children.

"Marjan, don't you think Mommy looks all better?" or, "Vida, tell your Mom how many times you went on that high slide in the park."

The triangular conversation reminded Rana of a fairytale she had once heard about the newlyweds who had a fight and were not on speaking terms. As a young girl, she had found the story comical and laughed at the way the couple addressed the candelabra each time one needed to say something to the other. But now she saw no humor in it and could imagine just how lonely the young bride in that story must have felt. As for herself, only once did she use the girls as a vessel to send her husband a message.

"Well Marjan, I hope you don't mind company because Mommy

needs to sleep in *your* room so she'll be close to the baby just in case she should wake up in the middle of the night."

Major Moradi cleared his throat and took a sip of water from his glass, but he did not say a word.

Marjan beamed a smile. "Does this mean you will read me stories all night?"

Rana chuckled. "Not *all* night. Mommy needs to sleep, too, you know!"

Major Moradi said nothing and Rana felt a small gratitude for his silence. Had he been any more communicative, she wasn't sure she could have masked her fury. For the rest of dinnertime, he appeared to be inexplicably absorbed in the simple meal on his plate.

After dinner, Dayeh served tea and Rana invited Vida and Marjan to help her give Yalda a bath. They welcomed the offer with enthusiasm, and while Major Moradi repositioned himself in front of the television, Rana and her daughters climbed the stairs.

An hour later, with the baby fed, bathed, and asleep, the girls took a shower, changed into their nightgowns and went down to say good night to their father. They were back before Rana had finished brushing her teeth.

"Papa-joon wasn't there," Vida said.

"Oh?" Rana responded, surprised at the hurt feeling inside her. Apparently, the man had wasted no time. He didn't even respect her enough to pretend and be there at least for the first night before he resumed his evening excursions. She imagined him somewhere else, but where? All she could picture was a house that had no shape, and her husband's arms around a woman who had no face. In her imaginary scene, he drank vodka, spoke incessantly, and was acting more joyful than ever before. Ha! What had she expected? Did she really think that with a warm bed awaiting him, he might stay here?

Rana was shocked to realize that she had hoped for more attention from him, had been prepared to reject him, and had even thought of words to hurt him back. After all, each time he went away on an assignment, he showed extreme passion upon his return. Did he feel any attraction to her at all? She refused to admit that she had enjoyed his heavy glances during dinner. Was it possible to still need love from a man she despised? No, all she needed to push that thought away was to remind herself where he had gone. The thought made her hate the man enough to want nothing to do with him. Nothing at all.

Dayeh came back carrying a bedroll for Marjan, and while spreading it on the floor, she said to Rana, "The master asked me to tell you that he went to bed early. He'll be going to Jahrom in the morning."

Rana wondered if Dayeh was trying to cover up for Major Moradi. But when their eyes met she knew it was true. She couldn't miss the hint of a smile that lit the old nanny's face. How amused Dayeh had seemed by the Major's new attitude, perhaps even pleased with it. Certain that Moradi's words to Dayeh were nothing but a poor excuse to go away, she went to the window, cupped her hands around her eyes, and peered into the garden. It took her a few seconds to adjust to the muted light of the moon behind clouds, but there it was, the Major's Jeep parked in the driveway.

Chapter

· *Seven* ·

RANA HAD FORGOTTEN just how noisy the officer's club could be during the bi-annual dance. A brass band played loud western music in honor of foreign guests, but the tango beat was lost in the moaning of clarinet and the sad Spanish song sounded even sadder in Persian key. Two soldiers, formally dressed and armed with huge rifles, stood guard at the entrance and saluted the Major as he and Rana approached. Strands of colorful lights hung over the courtyard and women in long gowns strolled alongside men in crisp khaki uniforms. Ten years into these gatherings and Rana still had a hard time differentiating the officers' ranks. A few groups had already occupied the tables near the pool while the rest mingled and socialized.

Rana had selected a turquoise evening gown, one of the few items of clothing that hung loosely around her and camouflaged her post-baby waistline. Her mound of brown hair was pinned up with a jeweled clip and she had even bothered with a little makeup. She wasn't used to such fuss with her appearance, but tonight she had to look her best and win everyone over. Major Moradi walked a step behind her, but he didn't hold her arm the way he normally would. For the past few weeks, they had barely spoken, and when they did, it had either been pretence for the children's sake or brief and to the point. Not once did he attempt to touch her, which had been a relief at first and then turned into an inexplicable ache.

Rana greeted a few couples with a nod and a smile, wondering all along if behind their polite salutations lay gossip. For the entire month since her return, the unspoken words about her husband's furtive life hung in the air that circulated the house, as if their problem was a heavy pollution that could be ignored but not denied. Banu and Dayeh no longer referred to Moradi as "your husband." They called him either *Agha*—the master—or Major Moradi. Only the children acted normal around him, although once or twice Rana saw the inquisitive look in Marjan's darkened eyes. Moradi's invitation to attend the semi-annual gathering had sounded halfhearted; then again, anything they did lately had been cast in formality.

Under different circumstances Rana would have refused to attend a party, but now she had an agenda. Maybe an appearance at the officer's club was precisely what she needed to put her in touch with a few Americans. Nearly a year had passed since she was last seen in public with him. How many of those officers knew about Moradi's other woman? Or worse, she wondered if the news of her baby's deformity had gotten around.

At Pahlavi University, the primary language for teaching was English. As a result, Shiraz was fast turning into a bilingual town, second only to Abadan, where the oil refineries had brought in waves of foreign experts over the recent decades. As Rana meandered between tables, she could hear the Americans everywhere, but they spoke too fast to understand. Then she heard Kathy Parker.

"Oh, my *Gawd*, is that Rana Moradi?" The woman's plump and friendly face beamed as she approached. "What a pleasant surprise! I heard you'd gone to Tehran."

Kathy spoke slowly and as if mindful of Rana's poor English, made an effort to enunciate every word. Her speech was so animated that Rana had no trouble understanding her, even when she used new words. Kathy's husband, Frank, worked closely with Major Moradi and Rana had always admired the ease with which he and his wife conducted themselves.

"I come back one week," she said, conscious of her deep accent, and unsure of what else she could add to that. "I must to thank for flowers," she finally said, embarrassed that she had failed to thank the woman months earlier when a dozen roses had arrived right after Yalda's birth.

"You're welcome," Kathy said and beamed a huge smile, revealing a row of perfectly white teeth. "Don't worry, your good husband has thanked us enough. He told us you had a harder time with this one." She stood back and took another look at Rana. "But you sure look radiant tonight. Did you bring us a picture?"

Rana shook her head. Americans carried what looked like a mini album in their wallets, a custom that she found both peculiar and endearing. But now she wasn't sure what to make of the question and wondered if Kathy knew about the baby's deformed leg.

Kathy took Rana's arm and pulled her toward a circle of American women in bright colored, sequined dresses. Rana had forgotten how tall some of these women were. They stood up and extended long arms to shake her hand, but one was so overweight, she just smiled broadly without leaving her chair. Rana was reminded of a book Marjan had brought home and felt as if she, too, had shrunken and entered Alice's Wonderland.

"Girls, you remember Mrs. Farhad Moradi, don't you?"

Most of the women were new to her; the turnover in the army was quick and Rana had not gone to the club in almost a year. She shook hands with each one and heard their names, confident that she could not possibly remember half of them. Kathy's was an easy one, but names such as Gwendolyn and Anneliese were a mouth-ful. Rana found a smile to be the best substitute for the words she didn't know. She glanced over the crowd and spotted her husband across the long swimming pool. He held his hat in one hand, a glass of wine in the other, and seemed to be deeply engaged in a conver-sation with an old general. Not too long ago, he would have been proud to take her around and introduce her to all the new people. How quickly things had changed. The detachment she felt was as if they were parallel lines, together yet forever separated.

Rana turned her attention back to the crowd. People were hud-dled in groups. Women bending towards each other to make sure they were heard over the blast of music. How many of Moradi's col-leagues or their wives were aware of the other woman? Had any of them met her? Or worse, did they take the initiative to invite her to their homes just to please Moradi? And if so, how did she fare in comparison?

The shiver she felt had to be from the night air. She had to stop the questions from pushing her thoughts forward. But each ques-tion seemed to generate a dozen new ones. She couldn't even be sure that she and Parisa had never come face-to-face. For all she knew, her husband could have met the woman anywhere, even here!

A server holding a tray politely bowed before her. Rana took a glass of chilled wine and accepted the small napkin from his gloved hand. Wine was exactly what her father would have recommended to calm her nerves. She glanced across the pool at three older gentle-men who stood where her husband had been a minute ago. The band was now playing a familiar waltz and she realized that was the only tune performed close to perfection.

A few guests entered the dance floor and all heads turned to watch. There used to be a time when Rana and her husband would be among the first to dance. He was a good dance partner and Rana remembered how easily the two had coordinated their steps on the eve of their wedding. How wonderful it had felt to relax and let him lead.

"Would you like to sit down?" one of the ladies asked, pulling a chair over for her.

Rana smiled back. "Yes, thank you." And she took the chair, leaned back, and scanned the area. As if sifted by an invisible hand, men and women were once again separated. Men were drawn to the bar area, where clouds of cigarette smoke rose to the lights above it, while women took the seats on the other side and filled it with the sound of chatter. She spotted Mrs. Rezai, a retired general's wife, who was surrounded by a circle of giggling women and wondered if she was entertaining them with her usual anecdotes. General Rezai would no doubt be somewhere with the men, smoking his stinky cigars. Three tables away, Farah Milani was leaning close to the woman next to her, and the way she shielded her lips with the palm of one hand could only indicate gossip.

Rana took another sip of wine. With the baby now on formula, she didn't have to worry about what she put in her body. It had been a while since she last touched wine and she could already feel her muscles relax.

"So, how's the little one doing?" Kathy asked, and she pulled her chair closer. "I bet she's as pretty as the rest of the Moradi women."

Rana hesitated, but this time her pause had nothing to do with language. The phrase, "Moradi women" had acquired a new, rather strange, ring. Rana pictured her husband walking into one of these functions with both her and that Parisa woman at his side, and she smiled sadly as she tried to imagine which of them would be on his right.

"Fine. Very well," she finally said. *Oh, stop your silliness!* Rana blinked her tears away, emptied the rest of her glass in one big gulp, and felt its warmth rise to her cheeks.

"There isn't a day when Claire doesn't come home with a new

comment on how everyone admires Marjan's looks, her gorgeous eyes," Kathy went on. She patted the back of Rana's hand. "Too bad you don't come to our luncheons, honey. It's a nice break from the daily routine because while we socialize the children can play."

Rana nodded her approval, and as another server came around, she placed her empty glass on his tray and took a fresh glass of wine.

"I like to go to this lunch," she said.

Kathy sounded unsure she had heard her right. "You would? Really?"

"Yes. I like."

"Great! Next Wednesday there's a pot-luck at my house."

"Pot …ah, what?"

Kathy gave a hearty laugh. "Pot-luck. It just means everyone will pitch in and bring something to eat. But you don't have to. Be my guest."

"No, I will bring my pot-luck."

Someone giggled. Kathy leaned to put an arm around Rana's shoulders. "Don't you just love her English?" she said to the other women. "It sure beats my Farsi."

"May I borrow my wife for a dance?" Major Moradi's voice rose behind Rana.

Kathy beamed another smile. "You most certainly may."

Why is he doing this? Rana could not possibly refuse him in front of all these women. As she stood, she felt a little giddy and had to reach for his arm. It was hard to walk over the grass in high heels, and this forced her to continue leaning on him. He didn't say a word until they had reached the dance floor and faced each other.

"Look at me, Rana," he commanded in a low voice. "Everyone's watching and you must look straight at me. Pretend we're talking."

Rana laughed, but it came out sadder than she felt. "Let's just dance," she said, afraid that with the effect of wine, one more word would make her cry and then nothing could stop her. So, saving face was what coming to this party had been all about. She shouldn't have fussed so much over her looks, but then again, hadn't she done that only because such pretence suited her plan, too?

Moradi put his hand on the small of her back and held her tighter, making Rana feel so weightless that for a second she thought her feet were off the ground. Twirling to the smooth tune, she stared at the colorful strands of light in the background and watched them turn into luminous rainbows against the backdrop of the dark sky.

Farhad Moradi had never put his wife to bed before. In fact, without Dayeh's assistance, he wouldn't have found Rana's nightgown. The old nanny had rushed to his aid the minute he walked in and now that they had tucked her in, he wasn't sure if he should stay or go to Parisa's.

Ever since their return from Tehran, he had sensed a change of heart in Dayeh, as if the old witch had finally forgiven him. Rana, too, seemed mellower, which led Moradi to believe his life had finally stabilized. Now if only he could clear his conscience, all would be well.

Rana was never good at holding her liquor and if she drank wine, it knocked her out. On the ride back, she seemed drowsy and finally had fallen asleep on his shoulder and from time to time said a few words that didn't make any sense. Once he thought she said Parisa's name, but that might have been his imagination. Whatever it was, the thought of Parisa came rushing back and what had started to feel like the renewal of an old affection for Rana was quickly replaced with a strong urge to go to the woman he truly loved.

With Rana safely in her bed, Dayeh finished tidying up and said good night. Moradi stood in the middle of the room and stared at his wife's calm face and tried to ignore the heavy burden of blame. *Poor Rana,* he thought. She deserved better than this. Then again, so did he.

His arranged marriage to the lovely daughter of Dr. Ameli had been based purely on the discretion of older family members. His mother had been confident of her choice and assured him that love would come with time. "Son, at nearly thirty, you're past having crushes and silly infatuations," she had said one evening on the topic of marriage. When he said he'd rather wait until he found love, she responded, "Some men are wiser, more practical. If you were the type to fall in love, you'd have done so already. Besides, a marriage based on solid wisdom lasts longer while love tends to fade as quickly as it comes."

He trusted his mother's judgment. Indeed, it might have worked.

But then he met Parisa.

In the soft light of the bedside lamp, Rana's pale face looked so fragile, so helpless, that he regretted the pain he had caused her. Nothing he had done was with the intention of hurting her. They had a good marriage and she had never given him a reason to dislike her. But his mother had been wrong. He didn't love Rana, not the way he did Parisa. Over the years of marriage, instead of growing closer, he and Rana had grown apart. Their emotional detachment had been slow, unnoticeable, like an old seam coming undone, one stitch at a time.

Moradi had wanted to explain himself on several occasions, even tonight when they danced, but that would have misled her. He was sorry, but not enough to go back, not sorry enough to regret having met Parisa. Parisa was worth risking everything, even the love of his daughters and certainly this fixed marriage. His sister Badri had assured him that no matter whom he loved, his daughters would always be his. "Don't you ever forget, they'll carry *our* family name," she said.

Loveless as this marriage was, Moradi had to maintain his family. It was a matter of pride, honor, even principle. He wasn't blind. He'd seen how some officers eyed Rana tonight. What was it like to have one's wife be with another man? How could her father ask him to let her go? The mere thought of divorcing Rana brought to mind images of her in bed with another man, laughing at him the way he laughed at Parisa's fool of an ex-husband. He sometimes went as far as picturing her with a new family, kids who would be siblings to *his* children. To picture these possibilities made his blood boil. No, he was not about to give Rana such freedom. The divorce her father-in-law had suggested was out of the question.

Sometimes he looked at Rana and thought she'd be the type who could live a life of isolation, raising her daughters alone, never needing another man. Earlier tonight, when he spotted her across the pool, she had seemed so fragile, so lonely and so out-of-place among those Americans. She needed him. He was her only link to this society.

Then again, the Amelis never gave him credit. To them he was the son of a farmer while Rana's father was not only a doctor, but also a graduate of some fancy university in Switzerland. Oh, how he resented the way his mother-in-law belittled the lifestyle of small town people! He recalled the looks exchanged between that woman and her other daughters when his mother spoke in her deep Shirazi accent. Rana never even tried to intervene. True that she didn't join the mocking, but she never gave the impression that she disagreed with her family's sentiments, either.

If they were driven apart, her arrogant family shared some of the blame. After so many years of not being good enough, he was giving the Amelis as good as he had gotten. Too bad Rana had to suffer so, but this was *his* life and he deserved all the wonderful feelings that only Parisa could nurture. Life could be sweet, and he wasn't about to let a silly thing like guilt ruin his one chance for happiness.

Rana turned in her sleep, and as she faced the bright light of the bedside lamp, she shielded her eyes with the back of one hand.

Moradi reached over, turned off the light, and picked up his keys.

Chapter

· *Eight* ·

A S MORADI DROVE ALONG the sleepy streets of Shiraz, he smiled sadly at the thought that deep into the night only stray dogs and drunken men were outside. Parisa had to be asleep; then again, she didn't seem to mind the odd hours he dropped in. Hard to believe that the first time they met, she had been a married woman. They had both felt the rush at first glance, and he instantly knew there would be more. It was as if a voice within assured him that their lives would be intertwined.

It had been during one of those boring business dinners in Tehran when she walked through the door and sent his head spinning. Moradi's new lieutenant entered the room accompanied by a stunning woman. The bald and rather unattractive man grinned at everyone as if to confirm that this vision was indeed his woman. The lieutenant had just been assigned to Moradi's new project to substitute in his absence. They had briefly met two days before and he knew little else about the man.

The woman walked with the grace of a queen, oblivious to the stout man at her side. Her slender figure was taller than the average Iranian woman and in fact, she towered over her husband. Her silky dark hair fell to her shoulders, framing features that Moradi thought belonged in the movies. She wore a burgundy dress of Chinese style, with a simple collar and tiny buttons running diagonally to one side. The side slit of her skirt revealed a pair of shapely legs. She didn't look around, nor did she make any effort to exchange casual pleasantries with other guests. When her husband introduced Moradi, she lifted her eyes to meet his, pulling him into a black hole before diverting her attention elsewhere.

For most of the evening, he stayed near the bar, nursing his whisky, unable to take his eyes off her. She glanced at him a couple of times, but it was a distant look, as if she was looking beyond him. She bent her head to one side, letting the downfall of silky hair drape over half her face, and passively eyed the crowd. The way she sat away from other women told Moradi that, for some reason, she would not be welcomed among them. The mystery surrounding her regal presence and the sorrow in her dark eyes intrigued him. He wished he could be nearer, hear her voice, and learn her story. Her mystical presence made him forget everyone else. The pathetic new officer couldn't have presented more contrast to this classy lady. *Talk about the red apple falling into the lap of the lazy!*

"Quite a looker, no?" another officer from Tehran whispered in Moradi's ear, nodding in the direction of the woman. "I hear she can be *pursued*, too."

Moradi glared at him. "Pursued?"

The officer chuckled and tapped him on the shoulder. "You know, purr..sued!" He lit a cigarette and leaned closer. "That's what her husband did. I heard she was a high-class *professional* before he bought her out." And he winked before walking away.

Not all of Tehranis were as traditional as Rana's family. Moradi had heard about a few wild societies, couples in the upper class who had adopted the European "wife swapping" to a point where at some late night parties one couldn't tell who was married to whom.

But such women looked the part. Their bleached hair, exposed cleavages and exaggerated makeup were sure signs. This lady with her graceful manner didn't fit the profile. The officer's negative propaganda had to be fabricated by jealous wives.

Throughout the evening, only once did he have the chance to speak to Parisa. He walked over to her and gesturing to the empty glass in her hand, asked, "Can I get you another one?"

She gave him a faint smile and shook her head. "No, thank you."

His admiring eyes studied her. "I must say, you don't look like the rest of these ladies." When she did not respond, he added, "It's a pleasure to know you."

She looked away. "You don't know me."

Moradi didn't find this offensive. Something in her hushed voice gave the words a heavier meaning, as if she was telling him that no one understood who she really was. The unkind words of his colleague rang in his ear, "She can be pursued!" Yet this woman seemed out of reach. Something about her created a distance. The rumors about her couldn't possibly bear any truth.

Restrained as she seemed, Moradi felt a connection. But just then an old general beckoned him from across the room and he reluctantly excused himself. By the time the old man finished talking, the couple had already left.

—

What brought him to Café Naderi the following week was no doubt sheer destiny. On his way back from a meeting, he parked the army Jeep and went in to get away from the sizzling July sun and enjoy some refreshment. As soon as his eyes had adjusted to the cool shade of the café, he spotted her at a table, alone and oblivious to her surroundings, reading a book. Now in a casual outfit, a white cotton blouse and blue jeans, she looked years younger. He approached her table without giving it a second thought.

"This place is sure crowded," he said. "Would you mind sharing your table?"

She closed her book and gave him a mocking smile. "Why, Major Moradi, I'd expect a charming man such as you to come up with a more creative pick-up line!"

Embarrassed, he chuckled before clearing his throat and said, "Okay then, how about 'could you please tell me what time it is'?"

When she laughed, he drew new warmth from the spark in her eyes. She seemed relaxed, unconcerned about possible onlookers, and not worried about who might say what behind her back.

Nodding to a chair, she said, "On second thought, I'd settle for your original attempt."

Simple as that, there she was, his long lost fantasy, the focus of his dreams and soon to be the center of his entire universe. They talked a little before she went back to her book.

"Must be an awfully interesting book," Moradi said.

She did not look up. "It is."

He sat back and watched her read. Her dark hair parted on the side framed her delicate face. She bit her lower lip while reading. Her expression suggested she was really absorbed in her book and not pretending. Moradi finished his drink, took his keys as well as her indelible image with him and left the café.

The next day at Café Naderi, Major Moradi was not surprised to find her at the same table. This time, she did not have her book and once again allowed him to sit at her table.

"My name is Farhad," Major Moradi said.

"I know," she said and then caught the hint. "Mine is Parisa."

Pari-sa, he thought. Fairy-like. How befitting! She couldn't be so perfect.

Now driving through the empty streets of Shiraz's late night, he neared Parisa's neighborhood. He remembered the day they changed their meeting place. Parisa had shown no surprise at his suggestion and agreed that at the Naderi Café they ran the risk of being spotted. Still, they both acted as though her husband didn't even exist. Parisa never seemed bothered by the gold band on his second finger.

A man of reason, Moradi had never done anything so rash in his entire life. His knowledge of romance up to that point had been a few hopeless crushes in his youth. His pre-marital experience with women consisted of a few visits to the houses of pleasure and one time of being seduced by a neighbor's wife, which left him feeling used. None of those women touched his heart, nor had he respected them afterwards. Then he got married. Rana's serenity had impressed him and she certainly fitted the profile of a good wife. He was proud to have her as his life's partner and for years went through a programmed life with the same passion he gave his other duties. Soon they were a family with all its simple joys, responsibilities and troubles. And, now this!

Moradi stopped at a red light and thought of the new meaning Parisa had given to all the amorous clichés he had laughed at before meeting her. He could see why so much of the world's art, music and poems focused on love. On his first night with Parisa, he had awakened at dawn, stared at her sleepy face in the moonlight, and sensed the fine line between love and madness.

Then he thought of how sad he had felt to look at Rana just minutes ago. All that was left in him for her was compassion with heavy guilt smeared on it. He couldn't touch her any more, not now that he knew the meaning of truly intimate touch. He had never felt for Rana the extreme physical attraction he experienced toward Parisa. The flame of this forbidden love was a passion that he didn't even know he had in him. No one had appreciated him the way Parisa did, and no woman made him feel as grand as he felt with her.

The light changed and he drove on. He couldn't talk to anyone about Parisa. Even when his best friend Nader brought up the subject he cut him off. She was a secret treasure he had stumbled upon and it was best not to share the information. How could any man let her go? Moradi never dared to discuss her previous marriage. Following her divorce, with no children and still a few relatives in this town, Parisa moved to her small townhouse in Shiraz. He offered to help, but she raised her head with dignity and responded, "Money is the evil in all relationships. I won't let it come between us." And she meant it. She may not care what people said behind her back, but had enough rules of her own to live by. When he bought her an expensive pearl ring, she gave it back. "Please, Farhad. Don't make me feel cheap!" And that was the only time he saw her tears.

Over the past months, he had mentioned Parisa to two people: his best friend, Nader, and his sister Badri. Nader said he was crazy to cheat on Rana. Badri understood. The city had its own whispers.

Parisa never spoke about the future. Once, when he mentioned his family's long tradition of lasting marriages, she had smiled wisely and said, "Please don't explain what I've never questioned." But why didn't she? It had always been he who brought up the future, as if the repetition was needed to convince him. What would his life be like if he had met Parisa sooner? Parisa seemed content with living her life one day at a time. Not once did she acknowledge the disrespectful glances of the neighbors, or complain about their whispers. His love for her had grown to a point where it hurt not to be with her and the mere thought of losing her made him crazy. But when he finally gathered enough courage to propose marriage, she seemed shocked. "Marry?" she had said and laughed bitterly. "For what?"

He held her tight and said, "To make sure nothing can ever come between us."

"Nothing can." And she sounded sure. "We can't legitimize what can't be justified."

"You say that today, but what about years from now?" he had argued. 'Lots of people have *multiple* marriages, it's legal, you know. At least, it is in the eyes of Allah."

He remembered the look in her eyes shaming him for the thought. "It is one thing for an uneducated man of the back alleys to take advantage of the Islamic law, but quite another for a man of your status to go backwards and practice his outdated right."

Moradi wasn't sure if it was the effect of wine or the guilt he felt toward Rana, but for the first time, he saw a point in what Parisa had said. Only one of his tens of friends had two wives, but even he had been too embarrassed to publicly announce it. He remembered Parisa's soft hand on his cheek as she said, "My dear, dear man. We *are* united. We're tied together far beyond the common law. What difference does it make if it's on paper or not? We don't need a document to tell us whom to love." She held his hand in both of hers. "Of all people, *I* should know what a worthless promise marriage is."

That was the only time Parisa had referred to her previous marriage and the expression on her face told him he should stop pushing.

Coming from a devout Muslim family, Moradi brought up the topic weeks later. "I fear that living in sin is bound to haunt us at some point."

"All right," she said. "Your God seems to be really bothered by this. So why don't we go to the mosque and have the religious ceremony just so you'll have nothing to fear?"

His initial reaction had been pure shock. "Absolutely not!" he exclaimed. "That's those mullahs way to make prostitution religiously acceptable. I don't want people to think of you as my mistress. I love you, for heaven's sake!"

"I know you do," she had said, wrapping her arms around him.

"And I love you more, but to most people a second wife is the same as a mistress. To them I'm nothing but a home wrecker, *the havoo*, so to speak." Her voice dropped as she added, "The only forgiveness we both need is your wife's and I doubt if marrying you will accomplish *that*."

Moradi smiled sadly at the remembrance of a quiet religious ceremony. No documents to keep, just a prayer. And that was how their relationship had remained. Clean in the eyes of Allah, yet somehow suspended. She was his, and yet not.

He wondered if Rana would be okay or if she would wake up and be sick. It would have been better to stay the night, but Rana gave him little reason to hang around. He took every chance to escape to Parisa's, knowing all along that he was in the wrong. Oh, how he resented Rana for being so damn patient. She went on in her holy way, managed the house, took care of the children and never asked him where he spent his nights. Only Badri offered a semblance of understanding. "Had she paid as much attention to your needs as she does to her housekeeping, you'd never have a reason to look at another woman." Maybe his sister was right, but the logic didn't have enough power to clear his conscience.

Moradi parked the car in the alley and fumbled for his key to Parisa's. The wooden door squeaked open and he went in without turning on the light.

"Is that you, Farhad?" Parisa called out from the kitchen. Her voice did not sound sleepy at all.

He saw her standing at the kitchen doorway. "What are you doing up so late?" The faint light behind her passed through a thin nightgown, revealing her figure that was beginning to show roundness in the middle. He was filled with the desire to hold her and forget all else.

"I couldn't sleep. I kept wondering how the evening went, and if any of your colleagues gave you a hard time about me."

Moradi held her tight and kissed her passionately. Her damp hair smelled of rose blossoms and her cheeks were cold. "Who cares what they say?" he gently stroked her belly. "I didn't want to be there in the first place. This is where I belong. With my true family."

"I'm glad you went. You can't hide forever. It's important that they see you as the active officer they've come to know." She turned off the kitchen light and leaned on him as they strolled down the dark hallway.

Later, he told her about Rana's drinking and how he almost had to carry her home. "She's miserable," he said. "I know she is, but she'd die before admitting it."

Parisa was silent and he wondered if she had fallen asleep.

Damn this small town. In Tehran people got divorced every second of every day, but in Shiraz divorce wasn't too far from such disgraceful acts as stealing, cheating, and embezzlement.

He stared at Parisa's calm expression, the cleft on her chin, the defined jaw line. Would she have agreed to their Islamic matrimony at the mosque if she had not been expecting his baby? He adored the unborn baby for putting an end to their sinful arrangement. But how long would she stay with him in the absence of a legal binding? He couldn't bear the thought of losing Parisa. Wasn't her main reason for refusing to marry him because, in case things didn't work out, she would have an easier ending their relationship?

Moradi rolled on his back and stared at the pre-dawn sky outside the window. Badri had assured him this baby would be a boy. "She comes from a boy-bearing family as you and I do. And, if this is a boy, you ought to get her to accept your name legally." Badri had always known how to get to him. "What will you call your boy? Would she use her maiden name or just give him a first name?"

"Who told you it's a boy, anyway?" Parisa had said and laughed at his silly concern. "But don't worry, we can register the baby under your last name."

Moradi felt a special connection with this baby. Now that Rana's third had been a girl, here was a good chance at finally having the boy he'd always wanted. How ironic that he couldn't publicly celebrate his son's birth. Wasn't that just how life was?

The contrasts in this dual life overwhelmed him. Sometimes his existence seemed so uninhibited and yet restrained, as if he lived the life of a caged bird. The world out there offered more than he was allowed to have. He was reminded of a verse he had heard in an old song.

> *I'm not asking you to free me from the confine*
> *Take my cage to a garden and enchant this heart of mine.*

He shut his eyes and tried to submerge into the darkness of sleep, but with each breath, he felt the bars of his cage closing in a little more.

Chapter

· *Nine* ·

RANA WONDERED IF ANYONE ELSE WAS HOME. A bright sun spread its warmth over her bed and the house was much too quiet. She checked the time on her alarm clock and figured Dayeh must have sent the girls to school. She reached for her robe and went to the window. The Jeep was not there. She thought Farhad must have gone to work while she was asleep.

In the kitchen, she found Dayeh sitting down, one arm cradling Yalda and the other hand holding her bottle. "Good morning," she said cheerfully.

"Good morning, sleepy maman!"

Rana bent down and kissed first the top of her baby's head and then Dayeh's. She poured herself a cup of tea and sat at the table. When Dayeh didn't speak, Rana said playfully, "So, are you going to tell me what happened here last night or do I have to pull it out of you?"

Dayeh shrugged. "What's there to tell? You know very well that every time you touch that poison, you pass out," she said in the authoritative manner saved to discipline a child. "There's a reason Islam forbids drinking."

Rana smiled at the realization that she was being scolded. She knew that for the next twenty-four hours, her old nanny would consider her tainted and would make sure to separate her dishes from the rest of the family's.

"So, was it you who put me to bed?"

Dayeh gave her a knowing look. "Not me, dear. Your husband did that."

"Oh?" Rana said and tried to read the woman's face for signs of what else might have happened. Before she could ask any more questions, the phone rang. It was her father. He went through the routine of asking after every member of the family.

"Farhad and I went to the officer's dance last night. In fact, I just woke up." Rana said a bit too cheerfully.

Her father hesitated for a few seconds. "Is he there? Is that why you're talking funny?"

"No, but Dayeh is here."

This had been their code. Any time someone's presence prevented her from speaking about their plan, she mentioned it early in the conversation. This was the first time in her life that she had kept a secret from Dayeh, but her father had absolutely forbidden discussing the plan with anyone. "Not even your friend Minoo," he had said. "Why take a chance?"

Her father's voice interrupted her thoughts. "Can you send her away?"

"Sure," Rana maintained her cheerful tone. "But since Maman is asleep, maybe I could call back in about half an hour and tell both of you about last night's party."

Lies, lies and more lies! She hoped her father understood what she meant.

Dayeh made a face. "Half an hour? Ha! If I know your mother, she'll sleep till noon."

Rana exchanged a few more trivial sentences with her father before hanging up. When she had finished her tea, she said, "I'd love a good, hot bath, but my hair needs washing to get rid of last night's hairspray, and I'm all out of shampoo." The bottle was finished and Rana reached for the baby and taking her in her arms, she kissed Yalda's cheek several times. She sat down again and used her usual loving tone. "Won't you be a dear and go to the corner store for me, please?"

Dayeh put the empty bottle down and shook her head. "You were never known for being patient." She took some money out of a jar on the counter. "I'll be right back."

As soon as Rana heard the front door being locked, she dialed her father's office. He picked up on the first ring.

"It's me, Papa."

"Good. I wanted to know if my friend sent *that man* around?"

"The telephone guy?" She chuckled. "Yes. And I must say, Papa, you are cautious enough for both of us. But he assured me the lines weren't tampered with."

"Good. Have him check it periodically. You never know."

For a man who didn't have a mystery about him, her father certainly knew what to do.

He cleared his throat. "I just spoke to Dr. Fard. He is planning to call your husband and discuss the issue. He will pose it as a suggestion based on a recent physical exam, as though you know nothing about this."

"I thought *I* was supposed to bring it up."

"Trust me, it'll work better this way. Men like to make big decisions. If sending the baby to America is his idea, he may even encourage you to go."

"And what will we do about Vida and Marjan?"

"I'll make a birthday gift of a ticket for Marjan and it'll be your job to make a case of how left out Vida may feel."

"What makes you think he'll buy that?"

"He probably won't. But his sister will," he said and chuckled. By now everyone knew how Badri had reacted to the girls' extended stay at her house.

"Where will we be going?" she asked.

"Dr. Fard has already spoken to a specialist in Chicago."

"*Chicago?* Doesn't your aunt live in New York?"

"She does, but unfortunately the only specialist Dr. Fard personally knows is in Chicago. He says the Children's Memorial Hospital there is the best place to take her."

"A hospital?"

"Don't worry, she'll be an outpatient. The place sounds like that Mayo Clinic everyone brags about. They do a lot of consultations and are known for their complete check ups." When Rana did not respond, he added, "You don't *have to* go there if you're not comfortable. But we needed the appointment to set the stage for your trip."

More silence followed and her father explained, "Mr. Eskandary also believes that an official appointment with a known institution will make it easier to get visas. Once you're in the United States, you can go anywhere you want."

Rana wasn't prepared for this to happen so soon. What had started as a mere idea was fast turning into a reality. To her, the United States was a vast land with cities full of horrid skyscrapers, not to mention deserts and canyons where cowboys and Indians fought. The idea of living there made her cringe. She was no longer sure she wanted a divorce. Last night had made her realize how much she had cared for her husband. He may have asked her to go just to save face, but she had felt a strange connection, and when they danced it felt good to be held in his arms. Maybe that's as much as she should expect. She had to put Vida and Marjan's happiness before her own pride. He had been a good father, so what gave her the right to take them away?

"Are you still there, Rana?" Her father sounded concerned.

"Yes, I'm here."

"I want you to call Dr. Fard and make one more appointment before we break this to Farhad. You can also give him an idea of a good time to reach your husband."

"Yes, Papa," she said, aware that she could not go back on her word, not after her father had gone to so much trouble to plan everything. And she owed it to Yalda to go through with a consultation.

"Let me know how things go. And, please, beware of the walls that have mice."

"I know. I've been very careful."

"How's your English coming along?"

Rana exhaled at the change of subject. "You won't believe how quickly I'm learning," she said in a more cheerful tone. "Thanks to Kathy, I can read simple storybooks."

"That's great."

"Kathy has been a true friend and now that I understand her language better, I really enjoy her company. Sometimes she takes me to the American Club to watch a movie as well."

"Good. That's really good. Keep it up." There was a slight hesitation before he asked, "How are things between the two of you? He's not mistreating you, is he?"

Rana didn't know how to respond. Her husband's attitude had changed a little, but not enough to validate altering her usual report. She could not possibly admit how she harbored a secret hope, not while her silly notions had no solid ground. Farhad had given her no sign that he cared enough. When he hung around and spent time with the children, she became optimistic, but the minute he went out the door, Rana knew better than to hope.

"Everything is fine," she said at last. "I don't think he suspects a thing."

"Good. How about the others?"

"No one knows. Not even Dayeh." She smiled before saying, "In fact, I think she's beginning to forgive Farhad."

He laughed. "*That* I've got to see with my own eyes."

Rana heard the key in the front door. "I think Dayeh is back. I'll say goodbye."

"Goodbye. I leave you in God's hands, my dear."

As soon as she hung up, Banu walked in. "Good morning, ma'am. Sorry I'm late, the traffic was really bad and my bus ..."

Rana didn't listen to the rest. The sad tone of her father's words stayed with her. *"I leave you in God's hands."* Those were the words he used exclusively before a trip that might separate them for a long time.

—

The pediatrician's office was as crowded as ever. Rana covered the sleeping baby's face with the thin blanket and hoped it offered some protection against the germs floating in the waiting room. Kids ran around dragging plastic toys while sneezing, coughing, or drooling on them. A little boy stared at her and wiped his nose with the back of one hand. Two mothers were engaged in a loud conversation and a man sat in the corner, reading a book.

Finally a nurse called out, "Moradi?"

Rana got to her feet and followed the nurse down a hallway that smelled of rubbing alcohol. The nurse opened the door to the tiny familiar room and placed Yalda's chart on the side table. "Remove everything except diapers. The doctor will be in soon." She left and closed the door behind her.

The room was too cold to undress a baby. Rana took a tissue from the box on the table, wiped the plastic cover of the examination table and put the baby down. Today Yalda didn't have her swaddling wrap. Instead, she was dressed in pink flannel pants and a fuzzy sweater. The pants were loose and comfortable. She stared at the baby's left leg, where only the toes were visible from under the pants, a contrast to the whole foot showing on the right. Lately whenever she looked at Yalda, that leg seemed to be all Rana saw and each time she did, a cold hand clutched at her heart. She removed the baby's clothes without waking her. The worry that her babies might catch something in the pediatrician's office wasn't new, but Rana was even more concerned with this one, as if the slight deformity made her more prone to illness.

Why did doctors keep you waiting so long when you already had an appointment? She studied the same old objects on the counter: A box of latex gloves, the jar full of cotton swabs and tongue depressors. On the opposite wall hung the picture of a brown dog. It had been there for years. Nothing seemed to change about this place, except that the babies grew older and the doctor grew old.

Finally, Dr. Fard came in, all smiles, all good comments and reassuring as usual. Yalda fussed a little while Dr. Fard listened to her heart, tapped on her knees, bent her legs and flexed her feet. He measured the baby's height before focusing on her legs. He stretched each leg as much as the baby would let him, motioned to Rana to hold them and measured the length from knee to heel several times. Finally satisfied, he updated the chart.

"She's a strong little thing," he said at last, and stroked Yalda's cheek with the back of his finger. "Good news is that both legs are growing, and they are doing so at a similar rate."

This did not sound clear enough to Rana. "Does that mean the difference will stay the same?"

Dr. Fard nodded. "That's the bad news. However, the fact that the affected leg continues to grow confirms my initial diagnosis that there's nothing else wrong with it, and that the discrepancy is the result of some local interference rather than a systemic problem or other paralytic deformities."

His words took Rana back to the scene of that horrible night and her attempt at ending her pregnancy. She saw herself tugging at the heavy dresser, saw the tilt, and the sound of that loud crash replayed in her mind. She could almost feel the sharp pain in her belly, as if the strain against that heavy weight had made an artery snap. She saw her blood running, and heard someone screaming.

"Are you with me, Mrs. Moradi?" Dr. Fard sounded worried.

Rana smiled apologetically. "Yes, yes. Please go on."

"As I was saying, the difference of three-and-a-quarter centimeters is more noticeable on a small baby, but should it stay the same, it will be far less pronounced in an adult. In addition, should it remain the same, there's a much better chance for surgical lengthening."

The man spoke with such calm it was clear he had no idea how his words clawed and scratched at Rana's heart. She imagined an operating room, a surgeon cutting her baby's leg and stretching its flesh like an elastic band. God, that must hurt!

"Dr. Fard?" Rana said, but wasn't sure how to pose her question. "There's something I've been meaning to ask, but you must promise you'll be honest with me."

He nodded. His eyes reflected attention as well as concern.

"Did I cause this?"

There! She had finally said the words that had burned her for months.

"Whatever gave you that silly idea?"

"I didn't exactly have an accident," she admitted. "I actually caused it, hoping to lose the baby." She then proceeded to tell him about how she was cautioned by other women that lifting heavy objects could cause a miscarriage and about that horrible night and how the dresser had fallen, hitting her side. Taking his nods for a confirmation, she could hardly believe his next words.

"My dear child, if every bleeding, fall, and trauma could cause such deformities, with so many wife-beaters around, this country wouldn't see too many normal children." He studied her and as if sensing her uncertainty added, "Nature protects the fetus in a miraculous way. Your foolish attempt could have ended the pregnancy, but a discrepancy in the length of a limb?" He shook his head. "I can assure you it had nothing to do with you."

Rana grabbed his hand and was kissing it before the old doctor could stop her.

He pulled his hand away and gave her a hug. "Welcome to true parenthood." He said. "What we do best is take the blame each time something goes wrong with our children."

Rana put her painful thoughts of recent months into a sigh.

Dr. Fard filled in a requisition for x-rays and handed it to her. "I shall follow up on my discussions with your father and plan to call your husband as soon as the radiologist gives me the report. What's the best time to call him?"

Rana gave him a few options. This was the first time the pediatrician had made the slightest reference to her father's plan and Rana felt a new bond with him.

"Doctor, if the condition is under control, I mean, if there's no urgency, then what would make my husband consent to a trip abroad?"

"Oh, but he doesn't know that, does he?" A mischievous smile spread his lips. "Trust me, he doesn't share your confidence in my knowledge. It'll be easy to convince him of the need for a second opinion."

Rana smiled at him through her tears. Her father had prepared his old friend well. Still, she could not overlook the possibility that the call might raise Farhad's suspicion.

Chapter

· *Ten* ·

T HE IRANIAN OFFICERS' WIVES seemed friendly enough, but their friendship remained at a social level. Kathy found it hard to be close to them. For one thing, their lifestyles seemed too flashy. She didn't share their obsession with fashion, jewelry, or heavy makeup. Besides, when they spoke Farsi—which they did often—it left her out altogether. Just when she began to feel comfortable around them, they'd switch languages. By now Kathy had learned enough Farsi for a basic communication, but chitchat was out of the question.

Rana was the exception. She made an effort to speak English, no matter how hard she had to try. Also, she had less of a social life, and coming from Tehran, she shared some of Kathy's feelings in being an outsider. Their daughters Claire and Marjan had hit it off at school and by now had become best friends. This gave the two mothers ample reason to get together. Lately, Kathy had a feeling that her friend needed to talk about something, but when Rana continued to keep her usual distance, she concluded the idea must have come from hearing the recent bizarre gossips about Major Moradi. Who knew if there was any truth to that? Some women were so jealous that they'd say anything!

Earlier that day, Kathy had called and asked Rana if she would like to help her bake something for the upcoming tea at the officer's club.

"Of course I will," Rana said.

Kathy smiled at the way Rana pronounced the word, "will." That there was no 'W' in Persian explained why most Iranians used a 'v' instead. Rana, despite her impressive progress in English, was no exception.

"Bring the girls, too," Kathy suggested. "I'm sure Claire would love to show off the new swing Frank put together. They can play outside while we work."

The whiff of the apple pie she had just baked sent her back into her mother's kitchen. The last thing she had imagined was that someday she'd use those recipes to bake for a bunch of strangers in a country she knew little about. Rana was the only Iranian friend who enjoyed baking; the rest ordered their desserts from a good bakery.

Kathy felt guilty about regretting to be here. Thanks to the army, they lived in a large house, had a live-in maid as well as a personal driver. She wouldn't dream of such luxuries at home and was particularly grateful for the driver. With the variety of vehicles that filled the streets of Shiraz, the low rate of accidents was a miracle. Motorcycles careened between cars while carrying four and five passengers at a time and donkeys pulled wooden carts loaded with melons. Traffic came from all directions, careless teenagers swerved their bikes between cars, and pedestrians zigzagged through it all.

She heard the doorbell and called Claire down before rushing to open the door. There stood a smiling Rana holding Marjan's hand.

They greeted each other and kissed on both cheeks. Marjan

handed her a bouquet of pink gladiolas. "From our garden," she explained.

Kathy thanked her and peeked into the alley. "No Vida?"

"No. She has a cold," Rana explained. "I didn't want her to pass it to Claire."

"Sorry to hear that," Kathy said, grateful for such consideration.

As soon as Claire heard them, she ran down the stairs two at a time. Before Kathy had a chance to offer refreshments, the girls had gone outside.

Kathy watched them through the kitchen window as Claire stood back and let Marjan have the first go on the makeshift swing. With no playgrounds nearby, her husband had attached an old tire to a rope and hung it on the branch of the big mulberry tree in the backyard.

Kathy offered an apron to Rana. "Don't mind this old thing, it really is clean."

Rana took the apron and smiled. "This is lovely."

"Ooh! Listen to the way you manage your "th" now," Kathy said and gave Rana a pat on the shoulder. "I can't believe how quickly you learn."

"I have a good teacher," Rana said and chuckled. "Remember? You were the one who taught me to pronounce it as an 's' the way a baby would say it!"

They both laughed.

It had only been a few months since Rana's return from Tehran and her improvement in English was remarkable. Even at the club, she no longer needed Kathy to whisper in the middle of a film and translate. Also, the books she borrowed were now returned quicker. Lately, Rana could even hold conversations with Claire and everyone knew how fast that kid could talk.

"Don't be so modest," Kathy said. "You have a gift for language. What does Farhad say about it?"

Rana turned her attention to the window, as if to watch the girls.

Recently, the mere mention of her husband's name put Rana in a somber mood. Kathy wondered if any of the town gossip was true. With a lovely wife like Rana, why would he have a fling? So far Kathy had managed to dismiss the talks, but the sorrow in Rana's expression was hard to ignore.

"Do you want to sift the flour while I separate the eggs?" she said cheerfully, hoping to get rid of the awkwardness she had just created.

"Sure," Rana said absentmindedly.

Kathy took a recipe card from a box and started to line up the ingredients.

"We'll need three cups of flour for the banana bread," she said, then on second thought, she pushed the items aside and took two glasses from the cupboard. "Where are my manners? We don't have your good tea, but let's see what kind of lemonade Claire has made." She poured a glass for Rana and another for herself. *"Beh Salamatee,"* she said and clinked her glass, showing off one of the few Persian expressions she had learned.

"Will we make pie?" Rana asked.

Kathy shook her head. "Already baked two of those. We're going to bake two loaves of banana bread and a batch of chocolate chip cookies."

"Will you teach me pie?"

"Of course. We'll even make an extra one today, just for you to take home."

Rana touched her almost-flat tummy. "Oh, no, I must watch my weight."

Kathy chuckled. "So that's how you maintain your perfect shape!" She shook her head and laughed. "Not me. I love food too much to diet."

Appearances were too important to these women, even Rana. Most ladies seemed to "vatch their veights" and considering their designer outfits, they couldn't afford not to.

"Marjan wants to diet, but my husband said no."

And there it was, that dark look had returned to Rana's eyes and Kathy could no longer stand it. She reached across the counter and put her hand on Rana's. "I hope you don't mind me asking, but is something the matter?"

Rana laughed nervously. "No. Why?"

Kathy stared at her friend. She wanted to assure her that she could talk whenever she needed to, but the way Rana looked away blocked the words. She placed the empty glasses in the sink and called out to the girls, "Come in, you two, and have some lemonade before we start working on the cookies."

It took the winded and giggly girls no time to burst into the kitchen.

"That swing is unbelievable," Marjan exclaimed as she climbed the kitchen stool. "I wish we had a big tree, too."

"You're welcome to share Claire's any time you want," Kathy said.

"Mom, did you see Marjan?" Claire asked. "She didn't even need a push, she stands on the swing, pumps her legs and makes it go higher than the moon."

"Marjan?" Rana glared at her daughter.

Marjan blushed and continued to drink her lemonade.

Rana turned to Kathy. "Badri's boys have a swing in their yard. Unfortunately, they use it like a monkey would." She shot Marjan another angry look. "I've told her not to teach their dangerous tricks to Claire."

"Don't worry," Kathy said. "Claire's pretty careful, she wouldn't do anything silly." She turned to Claire. "Would you?"

Both girls pursed their lips as if trying not to laugh. They finished their lemonade and were out in a flash.

Kathy lined up a few recipe cards. Soon they were measuring and mixing the batter and the only interruption of silence came from the girls playing outside.

Kathy marveled at the way Claire had adapted to her new environment. Two years into their assignment to Shiraz, she now spoke Persian fluently and blended in with local kids at the American Community School. No matter what kind of food she made at home, her daughter favored Persian food and had even developed a taste for rosewater ice cream, which to Kathy tasted like perfume. There she was with her best friend, screaming, running, and from where Kathy stood the only difference between the two was in the color of their hair.

"Your house is beautiful," Rana said.

"Why, thank you."

"I love how you decor."

"*Decorate*," Kathy corrected her.

"Yes, décor-rate." Rana smiled apologetically.

The few Iranian homes Kathy had seen flashed before her eyes: magnificent Persian rugs, marble floors and glamorous antiques. Some houses seemed cluttered with lamps, ashtrays, and candlesticks, but they all reflected a lavish lifestyle. The most expensive item in Kathy's was a hand-woven rug, which had cost them a good chunk. The rest they had bought second hand and mostly from the previous American occupants returning to the States.

"I'd hardly call our modest belongings much of a decoration."

"But you make something simple so elegant." Rana pointed to the carved copper colander from Esfahan, where Kathy now kept her onions and potatoes. "And I love how you put the donkey beads on your coffee table."

Kathy laughed. "I still can't believe the name of those beads. Okay, so they're not worth much, but *donkey* beads?"

"Villagers put them around the donkey's neck."

"I see," Kathy said and sounded surprised. "Well, not real turquoise, but they sure are too good for a donkey." She floured the greased pans and set them aside. "Speaking of turquoise, I love that new pendant you're wearing."

Rana's hand went to her neck chain. "This?" She shook her head. "It isn't new. It was a gift from Farhad when I had Marjan."

"That's so nice. All I got for having Claire was flowers." She chuckled. "So, what did he get you *this* time?"

Rana didn't respond and from the way she became absorbed in her sifting, Kathy knew she wasn't mistaken about the source of her sorrow. She switched on the mixer and hoped the noise would drown her friend's sad thoughts. The next few minutes passed without a word and soon the batter was ready. She let Rana spoon it into the pans.

Only after the pans were in the oven and she had set the timer did Kathy study Rana again. Her calm expression seemed to have returned. "How about some coffee?" Kathy said.

"Good. Let me make it."

Kathy mixed the cookie batter and placed it in the fridge while Rana brewed fresh coffee. They took a break and sat at the table.

As if reading her mind, Rana said. "Don't worry about me, Kathy *joon*. I'm really okay. It's just that three kids are a lot of work."

Kathy put a hand on her shoulder. "Should you ever need to talk, you know where to find me."

Rana nodded.

Kathy had just started to pour the coffee when they both heard a sudden crash followed by a scream. There was nothing playful about that scream and it stopped too abruptly. Kathy turned so fast that her hand knocked against a jar, sending sugar all over the place. She looked out the window, but couldn't see either of the children. She also saw how the rope no longer made a loop; now only one end was attached to the branch while the other coiled on the ground under the tire that now hung vertically. She dashed out to the backyard, where she found Claire kneeling in the fresh dirt where Frank had planted lawn seeds and Marjan now lay flat on her back.

The kitchen door slammed as Rana followed and each mother ran to her own child. Seeing Claire as she sat up to rub her scraped knee, Kathy rushed to Marjan. "Are you okay?"

Marjan's face had lost all color and she did not open her eyes.

Rana dropped down beside her, but instead of helping, she started to cry hysterically, screaming words in her own language.

Kathy didn't understand what she was saying, but the wild expression on Rana's face told her that something far deeper bothered her, that Rana had lost it and wouldn't be of much help. She'd have to attend to Marjan herself. Kathy pushed the lock of hair away from the child's forehead to reveal a cut. She rushed back to the kitchen and returned with her first aid kit and a bag of ice.

This time Marjan's eyes were open, but she didn't talk or cry. Kathy tried to check her pupils, but they were hard to see in those deep brown eyes.

Rana dropped down beside her and kept on repeating the same phrase, of which Kathy only understood *khoda* to mean God.

"Claire, what's she saying?"

"Not sure, Mom. I think it means 'not this one, too'."

"She'll be okay," Kathy said to Rana, trying to sound convincing. She moved swiftly and felt grateful for her brief volunteer job at the Red Cross. She wrapped the ice in a towel and gently pressed it to Marjan's forehead.

"We both got on," Claire spoke amid sobs. "She pumped us higher and higher, and that's when it snapped."

Rana was holding onto Marjan's shoes and seemed to be trembling. Marjan's pale lips parted and she said something that must have been, "Maman," but Kathy wasn't sure Rana heard that.

"She's here, honey," Kathy said and started to wipe the girl's forehead with an alcohol sponge. The cut didn't look too bad, but the area had already started to bruise. She took a piece of gauze from the box and taped it over the cut before placing the ice bag on it.

Marjan acted extremely calm and once she even seemed to force a faint smile.

"You're such a brave girl," Kathy said. "If I did this to Claire, she'd have a fit."

But Marjan's eyes looked to the side. Kathy followed the direction of her gaze and found Rana, bending over and still sobbing.

"She's okay, Rana," she called out to her friend. "The cut seems to be only skin-deep. I don't think it needs any stitches or anything."

Rana continued crying and mumbling the same words. Kathy had never seen her so out of control and realized she'd never heard anyone sob that way, either. She thought of the words Claire had translated. Could her friend have lost another child to a previous accident?

After attending to Marjan, Kathy placed a Band Aid over Claire's knee and then went to Rana. "Come on, dear. Let's get her inside." But before Rana had stood, Kathy picked up Marjan and carried her into the family room. How little she weighed compared to Claire. She put the child on the couch. Rana and Claire followed.

"Thank God, it's no big deal, honey," Kathy said. "Kids do such crazy things all the time, you can't let yourself get all worked up about it." She led Rana to a chair and offered her a glass of water. Rana seemed calmer, though she continued to shed silent tears.

Kathy had no doubt that there was a lot more to those tears. What was it that tormented her friend so? She offered her the box of tissues.

Rana finally regained her composure and wiped her face. "I'm so sorry. I don't know what made me cry so hard."

"It happens," Kathy said. "Sometimes I lose it, too." She chuckled at the vision that came to her. "Last week, Frank refused to change the TV channel, but that was right after a week of his new assignments, his many absences from dinner, and whatnot. Oh, you should have seen the way I went off on him, you'd think he had declared war." She reached over to the coffee table and opened a box of imported chocolates. "The best remedy for sadness, yet!" she said and offered it to Rana. She then gave some to Marjan plus a children's aspirin for her headache. They decided it would be best if the girls watched TV while she and Rana finished baking. By the time Rana prepared to leave, the kids seemed fine.

"Can Claire spend the night at our house?" Marjan asked.

Rana shook her head, "No, not tonight."

"Why not?" Marjan insisted. "My head is all better."

Rana proceeded to wipe the counter, even though it had already been cleaned.

"Will Papa be sleeping at home tonight?"

Rana blushed, but didn't respond.

Only after they left did it occur to Kathy how odd that question had been. The child had not asked if her father was in town, or if he'd come home late. No, the question would imply that while the Major was in town, he might spend the night elsewhere. It also indicated that he'd done this on more than one occasion. Could the rumors about the Major's other woman hold any truth?

Rana's hysterical reaction to a simple fall was bad enough. But combined with Marjan's question, it pointed to something big. Rana's melancholic silence was like a barbed wire that isolated her, making an approach impossible.

Kathy's mind went to the many stories of abuse, rape, even bigamy. What did she know about Middle Eastern men? Could violence have anything to do with how obedient some wives were? Major Moradi acted like a gentleman, and one who adored his wife. If so, what could possibly be the cause of that deep sorrow in Rana's eyes, or the deep secret that followed her like a shadow? These questions had nothing to do with curiosity. Kathy sensed danger and could tell her friend was in some kind of dilemma. If she were to help Rana, she had to find out what troubled her.

Chapter

· *Eleven* ·

ON THE RARE OCCASIONS when everyone was out of the house, Rana cherished her time alone with Yalda. No longer obligated to divide her attention between her children, or pretend to be happy when she wasn't, she could fuss over her new baby to her heart's content. She took her time feeding Yalda, sang to her, and admired the developing beauty of her face.

Dayeh had planned to take the girls to the Bazaar, but that morning Marjan complained of a headache and said she wanted to stay home. Rana wondered how severe the headache must be. The girls loved their little trips to Bazaar-e-Vakeel and all the useless junk it offered: Tiny pots and pans for their dolls, plastic pails to play in the mud, and flashy rhinestone bracelets and rings. When Vida and Dayeh had left, she checked Marjan's temperature and gave her a baby aspirin before sending her back to bed. The poor child's forehead had a bump the size of an egg. No wonder her head hurt.

Major Moradi had been away on assignment for the past few days. Banu, taking advantage of the sunny day, had moved her washbasin and kettles of boiled water outside to do loads of laundry. Rana finished giving the baby a bath and took her down to the family room.

Minutes later, Banu brought her some tea and busied herself around the room. She appeared in no rush to leave. By now, Rana had seen this kind of lingering enough to figure the girl had something to report, but she knew better than to ask. Best to keep silent and let the girl say what was on her mind.

After a few minutes, Banu walked over to her and sat on the floor near the couch. Staring at the rug, she said, "Khanoom, now that Dayeh isn't here to snap at me, I've come to plead for your forgiveness. You must know how sorry I am for being the one who told you about that awful woman the Major keeps."

The girl sure didn't mince her words. As much as Rana resented receiving such news, being kept in the dark was no better. In fact, there were times when millions of questions popped into her head and pride prevented her from using Banu as her informer. She was certain of the talks behind her back. Dayeh's lips were sealed, so it had to be Banu who'd bring her the latest.

"Dayeh thinks it's none of my business," Banu went on, "but, *khanoom*, how could I keep quiet when it involved your happiness?" She wiped her eyes with the corner of her scarf. "I remember how my mother's days became black when my father took another wife. Oh, Miss Rana, that woman cried not just tears, but blood! And, I'll never forget how my stepmother abused me after my mother— may she rest in peace—died." Banu was now rambling on and at this point, her tragic story made her cry even harder.

"*Stepmother.*" Rana could feel her own tears gathering, but she took a deep breath and blinked them away.

"Everybody in the neighborhood speaks of you with much respect," Banu went on. "Over and over, I hear them say how gracious you've been through this shameful ordeal, how you have kept your head high. That awful woman sure doesn't deserve to walk the face of this earth. May she never see one bright day in her life, may God strike her with crippling ailments." She made a fist and beat her chest.

"That's enough," Rana said. "How could you curse anyone, especially someone you don't know?" She thought for a minute and added, "Or, maybe you *do* know her."

Banu's eyes widened. "Know her?" She shook her head violently. "As the creator is my witness, I saw her just once and only from a distance."

"Oh?"

Rana was dying to know what this enemy looked like, but it would be beneath her to ask direct questions. Luckily, the girl had a habit of talking with or without questions.

"I was at the butcher's to pick up the lamb Dayeh needed for dinner," Banu went on. "I saw the Major's Jeep stop at the curb and he got out to open the door for a woman. I'd never seen her, but sure as the daylight, it was *her*." She made a face. "I'm telling you, ma'am, she's got nothing over you. She's a dry stick, you know, with no meat on her and long scrawny legs. Her eyes big as a cow's and a head of black hair that wasn't even curled." She snickered. "Worst of all, she had this plain outfit, not at all as pretty as some of yours, ma'am. Ooo, she made a sour face, kind of miserable, may Allah give her more misery."

The description didn't help at all. Banu's report on the woman's looks was hardly the worst it could be. The image coming to Rana was a tall woman with dark eyes and hair that she left natural. That was neither vulgar nor cheap. For months, she had imagined her rival to be a common streetwalker, but the girl's portrayal contrasted that. It had been much easier to hate a fat woman who wore layers of greasy makeup. How effortless it had been to despise the woman's crude laughter in her nightmares. It would be much harder to hate a nondescript woman who, if anything, sounded sad.

Rana shook the image away and forced a smile. "You have nothing to be sorry about, dear," she said. "Try not to take offense at what Dayeh says. She is like a mother to me, and asking you to keep quiet is her way of protecting me. I was bound to hear about this. I wish none of it were true, but I'd rather know what goes on behind my back. And she knew this would be the closest she could come to asking the girl to be her informer.

Banu nodded violently. "Exactly what I said to Dayeh, Ma'am. She said to keep my mouth shut, but I didn't want you to hear it some place else. Would it be any better if some stranger told you?" She moved closer and grabbed Rana's hand and brought it to her mouth, but Rana pulled her hand away before the girl had kissed it. Banu cried again and said, "As God is my witness, it nearly killed me to hear of your husband buying a house across from the Khalili Garden for somebody else! Why must he go and have a child with another when you have blessed him with the best of them?"

Rana felt a chill down her back. So it was official. He did have another family, another home and of all the places, it would be in her favorite spot in the entire city. She felt weightless, as if being pushed off a cliff, suspended midair. Banu's words had taken away her irrational hope that there may not be much merit to the neighborhood gossip. Pride would not allow her to ask the girl the many questions that haunted her. How old was the woman? Was her house bigger or better than this one? How far along was she in her pregnancy?

"I must ask you to forget the whole thing."

"Yes, ma'am."

"I mean it. Should anyone talk to you about the Major again, just walk away."

"Yes, ma'am."

"Now go back to your work."

Alone with Yalda, Rana held the infant on her lap, and marveled at the tiny features that refined with each passing day. The child's brown eyes no longer looked beyond her and she cooed as if to respond to each loving remark her mother made. Lately she

146

had started her belly laughs and made sounds as if talking in long sentences. As she grew, Rana felt a tight connection to this one, as if she saw herself being reborn.

In a strange way, they were so alike; they shared the inability to take certain steps in life and neither of them knew how dark tomorrow could be. Sometimes, Rana felt so bitter that she even wondered which was worse. Was it any better to be emotionally crippled? How much of an advantage was there in having two healthy legs that couldn't go far enough? Sad as she felt for her infant, she hoped that Yalda's physical problem would cause her less pain than what her mother endured.

Banu had given her a fuzzy image of Parisa. "Across from the Khalili Garden," the girl had said. That ought to be easy enough to find. She knew that area well and there weren't too many houses across the way.

Khalili's was a small private garden built by a wealthy man who left it open for the public to enjoy. Rana had memorized the last verse of a poem displayed at its entrance as it clearly reflected the man's allocation.

> "If not for the joy of sharing, then why
> would a wise man believe
> The futile value of a castle that someday he shall have to leave?"

The garden's proximity to the Nemazee Hospital attracted many of its employees and students at lunch break. Rana often took her daughters there after a checkup. There they ran among flowers and watched the noisy young students in their white lab coats. But later in the afternoon, with only few visitors around, Rana loved to take a walk alone or read a book there. The garden was her private sanctuary. Its well-groomed flowerbeds, gravel paths, and inviting benches along the walkways provided a most relaxing environment.

A long time ago, her father had advised, "The best way to put your fears and worries behind is to face them." He had said this when a classmate had bullied Rana and made her cry. "Don't be afraid. Go look her straight in the eyes and you'll see she's nothing but another kid!"

Her father's direct approach had helped her to overcome many silly fears of childhood. He would make her look at the bike that she had just fallen off, or stare at the needle the doctor was about to stick into her arm. Despite the horror she had felt, facing the source of her fears had helped each and every time.

Rana needed to find Parisa and see the enemy's face. It was time to pay the Khalili Garden a visit.

———

Dayeh knew her way around the Vakeel Bazaar, enjoyed her frequent trips there, and moved down the long passage with ease. But Vida was bound to slow her down. Their taxi passed the Cyprus trees around Nemazee hospital and continued down Zand Boulevard. Despite having three lanes on either side, at no time did the traffic ease on this main street of Shiraz.

"You're going to be patient," she said, staring at Vida. "Your shopping will have to wait while I visit a friend."

The driver pulled to the curb and stopped across from the Bazaar's main entrance.

"What friend?" Vida asked.

Dayeh paid the driver and helped the child out of the car. "You don't know her," she responded. "She's old and quite sick and I don't want you near her."

Ever since their return from Tehran, Dayeh had sensed Rana might be keeping a secret. She hid in her room and whispered on the phone, went out more than ever before and in general something about her seemed different. Unable to find out, she counted on the old soothsayer to give her some insight. She held the edges of her chador between her teeth, and grabbing Vida's hand, looked this way and that before rushing across the street. Cars protested with blasting horns. Breathless, she stopped at the sidewalk to finish what she was saying. "If you promise to be good, I'll buy you some *faloodeh* to enjoy while I visit my friend."

"I love *faloodeh*," Vida said.

Dayeh's mouth watered at the mention of the treat and she could almost taste the sweetness of those rice noodles in crushed ice that smelled of rose water. She pushed her way through the crowd of pedestrians, beggars, and peddlers and looked down to make sure she didn't step on anything. She ignored Vida's protest that she was holding her wrist too tightly. They passed the main entrance, turned into a branch and approached a corner store to buy the frozen, sugary noodles she had promised. The store was dimly lit and smelled of rosewater and herbs. An old man in a green turban sat behind the counter, busy weighing something on his brass scales. Vida seemed to enjoy having all of Dayeh's attention and she waited patiently while the old nanny made her purchase. Though it was a modest store, Dayeh knew it had the best *faloodeh* in all of Shiraz. She could almost taste its rosewater and fresh lemon juice.

Dayeh carried the plastic cup of frozen noodles, led the way to the end of a cul-de-sac, and pushed a door that opened to a small courtyard. She gave Vida her treat and pointed to the single tree in the corner. "You be a good girl and wait there for me." And, nodding to a small wooden door, she added, "I'll be over there watching you, so don't you move from here."

Happy with the treat, Vida settled down in the shade while Dayeh knocked on the narrow door. Soon it opened a crack and a familiar head wearing a scarf that only partially covered her white hair peeked out. Every time Dayeh saw Bibi Moneer she wondered, how the old woman, with her back so badly bent and her feet so swollen, could live all by herself? Bibi Moneer had told her of a dream that had brought her here years ago. In her dream, she had been promised a cure for her ailments on the condition that she lived in the shadow of the shrine of Shah Cheragh. She had no hope of a cure, but felt Shiraz was where she belonged.

Dayeh removed her shoes and entered the single room. A felt mat covered part of the cement floor and the single small window failed to fallow in enough sunlight to get rid of the dampness and musty odor. Bibi Moneer's bright floral dress and her green scarf presented a contrast to her dull surroundings. Dayeh thought it strange that such an old woman selected colorful outfits over the more suitable dark ones.

Before the woman could close the door, Dayeh put the palm of her hand against it. "No, leave that open." She nodded to where Vida was sitting. "I'll need to watch her."

"Why won't she come in?"

"There are matters I don't want her to overhear," Dayeh whispered.

"Then you'll have to pay a little extra," she said and squinting her eyes, she added, "Leaving the door open could give me a chill. I can't afford to catch a cold."

"A cold? This time of the year?"

"I'm old. I can catch cold even when a summer breeze hits me hard," she said, and the way she pursed her lips made her face look like a wrinkled sac whose string was pulled shut.

"I had already planned to give you three *tomans* extra. But not because you asked. Consider it my way of helping you out with your medications."

The woman now gave Dayeh a toothless smile and thanked her profusely. "Oh, you good woman. May gold pour on your path as you find your way to heaven."

At this point, Dayeh wasn't even concerned with heaven, or gold for that matter. Believing in the old woman's mystic powers, all she hoped for was that somewhere in her books of prayer and magic, the old woman might find an answer to Rana's dark secret and maybe even a resolve for her dilemma. Beside a Koran and a tiny prayer booklet, Bibi Moneer possessed an ancient book of secret codes that had all the answers to the unknown. She never let that book out of her sight. She obviously kept it under her pillow at night because whenever Dayeh happened to go there in the morning, that was where she retrieved it from.

Over the years, Dayeh had come to believe in the healing power of the prayers in that book. Bibi copied special verses off her book, blessed, and sewed them in decorative beaded cloths. Worn on an armband or around the neck, these sealed prayers could ward off evil spirits and shield one against all harm. Bibi Moneer was not only a diviner, but she also could cast spells. Her potions cured infertility, brought men success, and could even make one's worst enemies go away. Dayeh had known her for years, but only of late did she come to see her on a regular basis.

Months ago, she had promised that Rana would have a boy this time, but when another baby girl was born, she explained that the potion must have been used at the wrong time of the night, not to mention on the wrong night.

"Come in and sit down," Bibi said and went back to take her place. "How are things in your household?"

"Oh, much the same," Dayeh responded. "Still trying to get over the disappointment. But I must say, that little girl is turning more beautiful every single day." And she put emphasis on the word 'girl'.

The old woman must have caught the hint because she cleared her throat and said, "Are you really sure it was a full moon when you gave her the potion?"

Months had passed and Dayeh could not remember the details. She shook her head. "It looked full. But I can't be sure." She thought of that night. Indeed the moon had looked a full circle when, as instructed, she had brewed tea and placed the piece of paper with the prayer on it inside the teapot before pouring it in Rana's cup. She must have done something wrong because Bibi's predictions worked more than half the time.

"I've told you before, you must take extreme caution," Bibi Moneer said. "If my instructions aren't followed 'hair-by-hair' the prayers won't work."

They sat down on the felt mat. Bibi's checkered bedroll was spread over the cement on the other half of the room. Dayeh noticed a single burner with a black teakettle steaming on top and didn't hesitate to accept the glass of hot tea soon offered her.

After she had finished her tea, Bibi Moneer reached over and, taking her book, she paged through and read a few verses. The book's pages had yellowed and a few leaves came loose. She then tilted her head to the side and peered into Dayeh's eyes as if trying to enter her mind. She finally put down the book and wagged a finger at her. "Life is only in God's hands. You must never wish for anyone's death!"

Startled, Dayeh pulled back a little and stared at her, wide-eyed.

The woman put the palms of her hands together. "I am a God fearing woman. I came here all the way from Yazd to live in the shadow of this saint," she said and motioned in the general direction of the shrine. "I think I've made it clear that I can only help when the outcome promises to be good. You must never approach me with sinful thoughts, for I can't help you with such dark intentions."

"I can't imagine what you're talking about," Dayeh said and sounded hurt. "I'm no less of a Muslim than you are, and I've never wished for anyone to die. Never, ever!"

Indeed, she had not. True that she couldn't forgive what Parisa had done to her Rana, but *death*? Such a wish was too evil, even for that woman. What had Bibi Moneer foreseen? Doubts began to seep into her mind, spreading like a dark stain. Had she resented Parisa enough to wish her dead? Now she wasn't sure. Still, that had definitely not been her reason for coming here today. On this visit she wanted to find out what was on Rana's mind, why she no longer confided in her, and what secret she could possibly be keeping.

Bibi closed her beady eyes and rocked slowly as if she had gone into a trance. Minutes passed in utter silence. "I see a road." She finally said, but stopped again. In the silence that followed, only the buzzing of a few flies could be heard.

Dayeh glanced out and saw Vida gathering pebbles. She had finished eating and was now playing in the hot midday sun.

A minute or two went by before Bibi opened her eyes. "Are you thinking of making a drastic change in your life?"

Dayeh shook her head.

The old fortuneteller nodded. "Good! Glad it's not you. Because someone is stepping on a road that will lead to misfortune."

A road? Dayeh didn't know what to make of that. Could her nightlong prayers be answered and it was Parisa who would finally go away? Or was it the Major, leaving Rana and shaming the family with a divorce? She tried to shake away such dreadful thoughts. What if the prediction meant a combination of both? What if the Major and that woman went somewhere far and took the children, too?

"Is this traveller a man or a woman?"

Flies gathered on the bowl of sugar cubes and Bibi picked up a straw fan and shooed them. She mumbled a few prayers and closed her eyes again. "I don't know," she said. "I'm not even sure it's a journey." Then as if changing her mind, she added, "Actually, the road I see feels more like a decision and the only thing I can sense clearly is tears. Lots of tears."

The loving nanny shuddered. She had seen more than enough tears already.

"Can't you do something? I mean, couldn't you stop this from happening?" Dayeh pleaded.

Bibi Moneer opened her eyes and stared at her through the gray film that old age had pulled over her pupils. She threw her head back. "*Na!*" She picked up her prayer beads, twirled it around her fingers while whispering verses in Arabic. Dayeh had not heard this prayer before and although she didn't know the exact meaning of any Arabic prayers, this one sounded even more strange to her.

Finally, Bibi Moneer stood up to indicate the session was over. "This time I can't help you." She shook her head. "The avalanche has already left the mountain, it can only roll down and get bigger and I doubt anyone can stop it." She raised her palms, the rosary dangling from her left hand. "All any of us can do is pray."

Dayeh got up, pushed some folded money into the woman's rough hand. Feeling disoriented from the shock, she struggled to put her shoes back on and called Vida over.

"I will pray for you," the old woman said before they parted. Then as if a new thought had come to her, she pointed a finger at Vida, who had come closer and was now staring at them. Her voice turned into a mere whisper as she added, "And, I will pray for her, as well!"

Chapter

· *Twelve* ·

A RUSTLING NOISE WOKE RANA. She realized she must have dozed off on the family room couch next to her sleeping baby. A thin, shiny film had formed on top of her tea and when she picked it up, it felt much too cold to drink. She looked around to see where the sound had come from and found her husband at the far end of the room, half hidden behind his newspaper.

"When did you come home?"

He lowered the paper and removed his reading glasses. "Not too long ago." He looked around. "I wonder if any more of that tea is left."

As if he had called a genie, the door opened momentarily and Banu walked in with two steaming glasses on a small silver tray.

"Eavesdropping *again*?" the Major said, glaring at the girl.

"No, sir. *Khanoom* hadn't touched her tea, and I knew she'd be up by now."

"Thank you, Banu," Rana said, taking one of the two glasses from the tray. "Would you take Yalda to her room?"

Banu put the tray down and picked up the baby. Rana noticed the girl's trembling hands when she cuddled the baby and scurried past the Major, as though fearing he might strike her.

"Have you spoken to Dr. Fard lately?" Moradi asked.

Rana knew right away where this conversation was going and despite her preparations for this talk, she felt the blood rush to her face. "Why?" She was surprised at her own calm voice.

"He called a couple of days ago to discuss the baby."

Rana noticed yet another peculiarity in the way he spoke about Yalda. Not once had he called her by name and still had not registered the birth.

Moradi cleared his throat and went on, "He thinks we should take her abroad for a second opinion."

Rana held her breath. *We?* She prayed he wasn't thinking of going. That would mess up the entire plan. She tried to remain calm but his words echoed. *A couple of days ago?* He had been on a job assignment till now. Or had he?

Moradi checked his watch then removed it and started fiddling with the knob.

"I had to think about it." His words had a condescending tone as if to imply he was the only one capable of thinking. "He says in America they may be able to do something about *that leg*, and recommends seeing a specialist and looking into ways to fix it."

Rana shuddered at his phrasing. It sounded as if he was talking about a repair job, a leaking faucet or a crack in the driveway. He put his watch back on and said, "I'm wondering how much such a trip would cost."

Even without looking, Rana could sense the curiosity in his stare. She shrugged. "Probably more than we can afford." And she hoped her opposition would only make him more determined to follow through. "Especially if it involves seeing a specialist." While saying the words, she couldn't help but wonder which cost more, a trip abroad or having a dual life?

He shrugged. "I think the doctors in America ought to be better than the ones they send here. Look at Nemazee Hospital. The place is practically run by Americans. But if these guys were any good, they'd find jobs back in their own country."

"I don't think that's true," she said. Years of good care at Nemazee had gained Rana's trust, but she realized that might be the wrong argument. She forced a smile. "Anyway, a consultation won't hurt and a trip may be good for us," she said calmly and couldn't believe her own voice.

Moradi shook his head, "My work won't allow me a prolonged absence. Not this year, anyway."

Rana's exhale of relief came out sounding like a sigh. So he wasn't planning to go, but was it really work that kept him here? *Why does it still matter?* She studied him across the room and wondered how two people, who once acted as one, could be so torn apart?

Moradi went on, "I don't think you can manage such a trip alone, especially not while dragging a baby along." When Rana didn't respond, he continued, "The fact that your English has improved helps, but in a strange country, language isn't the only problem."

Rana wondered how he could know that. He had never been abroad.

"Where will you stay?" he went on. "A woman alone? We don't know any men in America to help you in case there's a problem."

Rana did her best to appear calm. He mustn't detect the rising rage within her.

"Why don't you talk to Papa about this?' she said. "He's a doctor and has been abroad. He may have good suggestions."

"I've thought of that." He frowned and swallowed, as if the idea gave him heartburn.

Somehow his pause carried more weight than Rana cared for. She doubted the two had spoken since her return from Tehran. The unpleasant memories of the past few months came back and with that, the foggy image of that woman became more visible. Moradi claimed he was away on an assignment, but for all she knew he could have been right here in Shiraz, with his Parisa. Images of the two together filled her mind and she struggled to push them away and remain calm.

"I'm in no position to ask for a favor," Moradi said at last. "But *you* could."

Rana just stared at him.

"He favors you, so maybe if you asked, he'd agree to accompany you." This was the first time he had made a remark about to recent change in his relationship to her father. Rana realized that his mellowed tone was the closest he could come to showing remorse.

Moradi cleared his throat uncomfortably. "I also think it would be best for me to move out of this house."

Rana stared at him. The announcement was so unexpected that for a second she thought she must have misunderstood him.

He looked away. "I'm on assignments most of the time anyway. And, we're not—"

The door burst open and Banu staggered in, "Ma'am! Marjan khanoom is very sick." The girl's face had turned crimson and the way she panted made it clear she had run all the way down. Rana dropped the cup she was holding, flew out the door and ran up the steps two at a time.

A sour odor filled Marjan's room. She was lying on the carpet, where she had vomited, her cheek touching the mess.

Rana screamed. *"Bemeeram"* - may I die!" and dropped on the floor next to her daughter, lifting her head and resting it on her lap.

"What happened to you, my love?"

Marjan did not respond. Her eyes were closed and bits of food were stuck to her hair.

Rana touched her forehead. It felt a little warm, but not enough to explain her unconscious state.

"I'll rush her to the hospital myself," Moradi said from behind and before Rana knew it, he had picked up the child and was out the door. Rana followed, unaware of being in her slippers, or that she was leaving her baby with a careless maid. All she could think about was the fall Marjan had taken the day before and prayed this had nothing to do with it.

Moradi put Marjan on the backseat. "You sit with her," he shouted before jumping behind the wheel.

—

Rana didn't know how her husband managed to fill out Marjan's registration forms. Now that the paramedics had wheeled her in for x-rays, the parents were told to wait in a small room.

On the way to the hospital, Rana had tried to tell her husband about Marjan's fall from the swing, but she wasn't sure her words could be understood amid her uncontrollable sobs. With each bit of information, he had grunted, hit the steering wheel or glared at her through the rearview mirror, but he did not utter a word and didn't need to.

After they had taken Marjan away and as soon as the two were alone, he started to pace the small area. "Why didn't somebody bring her here yesterday?" he asked in an accusing tone.

Rana stared at him from behind a shield of tears. "She was *fine* yesterday."

"Fine?" His face was flushed and he pointed to the hallway. "You call that fine?"

"She wasn't like this," Rana said and sounded defensive. "Nobody takes a kid to the hospital for every little bump!"

"You call that black egg on her forehead a 'little bump'?"

"Kathy iced it down. We did what we thought was needed. Kids fall all the time. Claire was hurt too."

"You should have known better," he said.

Rana covered both ears with the palms of her hands. This

wasn't going anywhere. Worried sick for her child, the last thing she needed was to feel guilty.

Moradi found a magazine, sat with his back to her and started reading. She was grateful he had finally shut up.

Marjan's pale face amid white sheets wouldn't leave Rana. When they put her on the gurney and took her away, she felt a painful tug, as if they were taking her heart out of her chest. She realized how this child in her serene way had been a little adult, her quiet presence a comfort, her sad eyes understanding her mother's pain. Funny how some children were never a child. Marjan's old soul had always been evident. Those dark eyes had forever understood. Rana thought of all the unspoken words and realized what a special place her oldest daughter had in her heart. She prayed silently, even made bargains with God. "If you save my daughter, I promise to help many poor children ..."

Now and then the sound of footsteps outside broke the room's silence, a phone rang in the distance, or the speakers made a muted announcement. For a long time no one came in. When the door finally squeaked open, a nurse in a blue uniform peeked in. "Moradi?" she said, facing the Major as if Rana didn't exist. They both jumped out of their seats. "The doctor would like to see you now."

Rana dashed past her before she could be stopped. The young nurse soon caught up and opened the door to a room down the hallway. Moradi followed.

A middle-aged woman in a white lab coat greeted them. "I'm Dr. Mehrzad." She shook hands with them and offered them seats. "I have spent the past two hours in the operating room with your daughter."

"Operating roo...?" Rana's voice broke.

Moradi raised a hand to stop her. "Let the doctor speak."

But Dr. Mehrzad seemed in no rush to say more. She nodded with understanding and said to Rana, "It's alright. I'm a mother, too. You have every right to be upset."

A few seconds passed and this time, it was Moradi who showed no patience. "Well?" he said and they both stared at the doctor's weathered face.

Dr. Mehrzad looked at Rana, then the Major and shook her head. "I'm afraid the news isn't good."

No one responded as they both continued to stare at her.

"I've done everything I could," the doctor said.

"Are you a pediatrician?" Moradi asked and did not seem to care how rude he sounded. He said the words as if to mean such a report would only be valid if it came from a children's specialist.

The doctor's calm expression did not change. "No, sir. I'm a neurosurgeon."

Rana gasped.

"Your daughter suffered a seizure. X-rays showed a fracture of the skull, which had led to a large subdural hematoma." She hesitated as if just realizing that they would not understand such medical terms. "It means some blood had gathered around the brain. So they called me in."

A heavy silence fell. With each passing minute, the gravity of the situation intensified and Rana could hear her heart racing. The doctor maintained her calm tone, but Rana knew her bucket of patience was full, that each word was another drop that it could no longer take.

"Such incidents are not uncommon," Dr. Mehrzad said, "but we usually expect to see them following a more severe trauma. Falling off a swing is not a major accident, but she must have hit her head really hard on that tree."

"What can be done now? That's what I'd like to know." The

Major's voice maintained its authoritative tone, as if ordering action.

"We have successfully drained the hematoma and relieved the pressure on her brain."

"And?"

The doctor shook her head. "Unfortunately, she's still in a coma."

Rana could not hold her scream. This time, Moradi walked over to her, but before he could touch her arm, Rana stood and pulled away. This put her near the doctor, who caught her just as her knees folded. Rana felt the woman's arms around her, holding the weight she could no longer support.

—

Rana opened her eyes to the fuzzy image of Dr. Mehrzad. She stared at the unfamiliar ceiling and as her mind darted back to Marjan, she begged to be taken to her daughter.

The doctor put a hand on her shoulder. "I think you should rest a little longer."

"I want to see my Marjan," she begged and sat up, still dizzy.

"You do understand, she won't even know you're there."

Rana nodded sadly.

The doctor walked with Rana and she pushed a button to open the doors to a restricted area. They entered a cold room and the doctor drew back a canvas curtain. Marjan lay on a narrow cot, a white blanket tucked tightly around her, her head propped on two large pillows. The vision of all the mornings when she had found her child sleeping face down, her pillows tossed to the floor again, rushed back to Rana. How resigned she seemed now. If it weren't for the bandage around her head, or the tubes in her nose, one could assume the child was peacefully asleep. Her long eyelashes cast a fan-shaped shadow over her pale cheeks.

Moradi stood on the other side of the bed, holding Marjan's hand. "Maman and Baba are here, *azizam*—my darling." When Marjan's expression did not change, he gently touched her cheek. "Do you hear me, *baba-jan*?"

The only sound in the room came from a beeping machine. Dr. Mehrzad helped Rana into the chair near the bed.

"What's the use of staying?" Moradi said. "She doesn't even know we're here."

Rana didn't look at him. "But *we* know."

Rana continued to pray, but as the clock on the wall ticked, her faith lost power. Dr. Mehrzad checked in a couple of times. On one of those quick visits, she stayed to talk. "We had to make an opening in her skull to drain the fluid."

Rana wished she hadn't explained. How did they make an opening? If her skull was already fractured, did they have to open the crack line? Drill it? She wanted to know all the little details, but then again, she'd rather not. *Is my little girl in pain?*

On her last stop, the doctor sounded despondent. "I hate to tell you, but things don't look good. I can't give you false hopes. She's been in a coma too long. In such cases, most patients don't make it, and those who do, will never be the same."

Rana dismissed that bit of news without bothering to respond. She was beginning to hate the nice woman. *What do doctors know?* She sat as close to Marjan as the bed would allow her and stared at her, hoping against hope, praying hard.

Moradi was in and out of the room. Maybe to eat, have tea, or to smoke a cigarette. But he happened to be there when the machine's beeping turned into one long, sharp note, a hushed siren that would stay with Rana for years to come. She watched him put his face in both hands and envied him for being able to weep. Moving closer, Rana kissed her little girl's face, then put her mouth to the child's ear and whispered the slow song she used to sing to her years ago.

> "*Baroon barooneh …raining, it's raining,*
> *the grounds are soaked*
> *But things will soon get better,*
> *Winter will leave, spring is behind it …*"

When the machine was finally silenced, the tune of Rana's song spilled a morbid resonance through the room.

> *Oh raindrops, please pour gently*
> *You're making the orange blossoms lose their petals …*

Marjan's face was losing more color, her hand was turning cold, and Rana sang louder.

> *Oh, merciful God, amid this winter,*
> *Either take me, or don't take her away,*

Then like a broken record, she stayed on that line, *either take me, or don't take her away. Don't take her away. Don't …*"

She finally stopped her song, patted the back of Marjan's hand and tucked it under the covers before pulling them up to the child's chin. She sat back in her chair, this time a little farther, and waited.

Dr. Mehrzad approached the Major. "I'm really worried about your wife."

Moradi nodded. "This isn't like her at all."

"It's a huge shock for both of you and I wish there were words of comfort to offer. But she needs to react, to let it all out."

What did they expect? How does one react? Someone should send a message to her father in Tehran. Then again, what for?

Hours later the orderlies came to wheel her little girl away. Rana bent over the bed for one last kiss, but that icy cheek wasn't Marjan's.

She heard Moradi's silent tears change into sobs. Everyone in the room sobbed with him.

Everyone except Rana.

———

One can age years in a matter of days. Rana could feel that. With Marjan's loss, what was left of Rana's youth was now behind her. There was no looking back. Unable to fill the void her little girl had left behind, Rana felt old and lonely. In a way, she became conscious of how in the recent months her first born had been a source of comfort, her serenity a sign that she was her mother's wise little friend. Rana recalled the nights when she had cried silent tears and as if knowing by instinct, Marjan had crawled into her mother's bed, her little body offering warmth, her cuddle helping to hold the pieces together.

Rana's grief was beyond the traditional mourning. *Let him respond to people's expressions of sympathy. Let him cry for the daughter he would have preferred to be a son.* They grieved for the same child, but not in the same way, not together.

"Where's Marjan?" little Vida would ask.

Rana listened to Dayeh's sad voice explaining to the child that her big sister had flown into the sky and was now above the clouds, with God. Dayeh knew nothing. There was no God. Marjan's soul had left her body and entered her mother's heart. She would forever feel her daughter within her, she would draw comfort from having absorbed her. *She's back inside me.* Rana was convinced of that.

Throughout the following days, even when that small casket was lowered into the cold earth, Rana remained dry-eyed. No one would know why she now carried a much bigger purse. No one would see Marjan's favorite doll tucked at the bottom of her baggy purse, nor would they find it in Rana's bed every night. Others could cry all they wanted, but not Rana, not as long as she could hang on to a piece of Marjan. Tears would only confirm her loss. They were an invitation to others to share her grief. But how? No one could understand, no one, except Marjan herself. She would have known what went on in her mother's heart. Her old soul would have shared the depth of her sorrow. Like an invisible fairy, Marjan's spirit hung around Rana. Curling up to Emily-the-doll, she denied the pain of separation, the agony of being torn apart. Rana would forever be near her wise child, her oldest, and the one who now made her feel so old.

—

Dr. Ameli and Mandana came for the funeral, but they could only stay for two days. Her mother was taken ill, perhaps due to grief. Dr. Ameli said he didn't think she could handle the burial. After going back, Dr. Ameli called several times a day and if the call was from home, his wife also came to the phone. Rana didn't talk much. What was left to say? She took the pills her father had prescribed as they helped her to sleep and reduced the need to talk.

Moradi insisted Vida stay at Badri's again. This time Rana didn't mind. The two girls had been so attached that the name Vida-Marjan sounded like that of one child, not two. It would take a long time to separate them. Rana wanted both of them there, or neither.

Moradi was happy to take Vida away. He wanted her close by and no longer pretended he wanted to stay at home. Did he really blame Rana or was that his way of justifying his absence? Dayeh was reminded of her own father and how each time he wanted to stay away, he picked on something.

Regardless of how quiet Marjan had been, the house was empty without her, a dark abyss that nothing and no one could fill.

Dayeh took care of Yalda, though Rana seemed to find a semblance of comfort in cuddling the baby. Sometimes the only way for her to sleep peacefully was to have the baby next to her. Rana wasn't sure how much time had elapsed. Then one evening when her husband was home, her father's call from Tehran reminded her of their abandoned plan. All these weeks later, Dr. Ameli still spoke to her as he had done on the day they lost Marjan, his voice a near whisper, as if fearing to awaken her. "How is my precious daughter?"

"Fine, Papa," she said, trying to sound casual and relaxed. "How are you and Maman?"

Moradi sat at the dining table, balancing his checkbooks or something. He looked up, but didn't seem curious and soon went back to his work.

"I know it's hard for you to give this matter a thought, but we need to work on your trip. Have you and Farhad discussed it at all?"

Rana wasn't sure if Moradi was listening.

"Yalda is fine, too," she said out loud. "We had a healthy check up, but her doctor has spoken to Farhad and they both think we need to see a specialist abroad."

"That's my girl," Dr. Ameli said. "I knew I could count on you. Is he sitting there?"

"Yes, Papa. But unfortunately, Farhad's work won't allow him to go on such a trip."

Major Moradi glanced at her again.

"Good girl, Rana-jan," her father said softly.

"I wanted to talk to you about this, but it's hard to fall back into my usual routine." She stopped. How matter-of-factly she sounded, how calm, as though they were talking about someone else. She paused before adding, "I can't do this alone, Papa, and I hope you realize I'm begging for your help."

"Well done…" Dr. Ameli said. "Has he suspected anything?"

"No. In fact it's the opposite. Farhad thinks with you being a doctor and all, that would be a huge favor to him." She glanced over at her husband, who was at full attention and nodding his approval. Encouraged, Rana added, "He would have called you himself, but considers such a request too much to ask."

"Ha! I'm touched."

"Papa, please, if not for me, do it for Yalda."

"You don't have to beg, Rana. It's the least I could do for you."

"Really?" Rana's voice rose with emotion.

Moradi looked at her with a new twinkle in his eyes and Rana thought she even saw a faint smile.

"Oh, but don't tell Farhad, yet," her father said. "Just let him know that I'm going to think about it."

Two long days went by without any calls from Tehran. Moradi came by both evenings and Rana knew he wanted to be there in case her father called. They didn't talk much. The only time her husband made a hint was when he paid the radiology bill. "The way these doctors charge for a single picture …" He did not finish his sentence. He had used the same tone when the emergency room bill had arrived. "What the hell am I paying for? You'd think they'd saved my child's life!" His grief for Marjan was all anger.

When Dr. Ameli finally called, Rana was not surprised to see her husband rush to pick up the phone.

"Hello? Yes, this is Farhad," he said and sounded sheepish.

The exchange of greetings was brief and then all Rana could hear was her father's muffled voice while her husband scratched behind his ear and listened. When he finally spoke, it sounded as though he were cutting in. "But what about her school?"

Rana's father spoke another minute or so in response.

Looking even more pensive, Moradi turned his back to Rana. "I understand, but …"

More muffled words came from the other side, to which Moradi only nodded. "Of course. I wouldn't possibly question that." His face was flushed and Rana knew that whatever her father was saying had caused him deep embarrassment. "As you wish," he said, and Rana thought he even bent his head a little, giving a bow. "She's right here."

Rana grabbed the receiver and hoped her apprehension wouldn't show. Moradi stood there for a minute, staring at her, but then walked back to the dining table.

"Sorry for taking so long to call back, honey," her father said. "I wanted to do this when your mother wasn't around. She gets too excited about such matters."

Dr. Ameli's word choice indicated he thought Farhad may still be on the line.

"I know," Rana said.

"I've just had a long chat with your good husband. I'd be willing to go on this trip, but have suggested Vida should also go. I had meant to do this before … " His voice broke and Rana braced herself against the pain of remembering how Marjan had been part of this trip.

For a few seconds, neither of them could talk and when her father spoke again, he sounded resigned. "A trip will be good for Vida. Especially now." He tried a chuckle. "It'll give her a chance to practice her other language, too."

Marjan never had the chance to visit a place where people only spoke her "other language." Rana's father spoke of tomorrows while Rana continued to struggle amid her yesterdays.

"I've also told him this'll be Grandpa's treat," he said, "a belated birthday present."

There will never be another birthday for Marjan.

Rana cleared her throat. "No, Papa, that's too big a gift."

"Oh, don't be too quick to disagree with your old father. I've made up my mind. I really want to do this for my granddaughter."

Rana closed her eyes and instead of Vida, she pictured Marjan visiting a museum, carrying the book Grandpa would buy, listening to him explain things with patience.

"Vida's lucky to have such a generous grandpa," she said.

Moradi's eyes were on his paper again, but his expression told Rana that he had heard every word she said. There was no doubt left in her. She needed to pack her daughters and go as far away as she could, away from this place, from him, and from every corner that was empty of Marjan's presence.

The thought helped Rana to notice the trembling inside her. She hoped her voice did not betray her as she mentioned the aunt in New York. "Oh, you're right. Aunt Malak is there. I'd forgotten all about her."

Moradi bunched his newspaper and looked up in surprise.

Under any other circumstance, Rana would have felt horrible about being so deceitful, but not now. Not if that was what it took to save her and her daughters from an imminent public humiliation. *I wonder if it wouldn't be best for me to move out of this house,"* Moradi had said. Just like that. Treating her like his property, maintaining her.

The only good that had come out of this darkness, was that once again, Rana had her thoughts in order. With memories of Marjan safely stored in a separate compartment, she now had to think of her other daughters. To live so far away would be lonely, but she had to break out of the prison that her life had become.

Chapter

· *Thirteen* ·

O N HIS WAY BACK FROM THE OFFICE, Dr. Ameli stopped by Eskandary's to pick up the documents that had just arrived. As he drove, he found himself reminiscing about some of his trips abroad and regretted the fact that on this trip his wife would not be with him. She loved going to foreign countries, and although he did not exactly share the feeling, some of her enthusiasm rubbed off on him. They took sightseeing tours during the day, tried different restaurants at night and he didn't even mind sitting on a bench at department stores, waiting for her to show up with multiple shopping bags in all colors. "Oh, wait till you see what great bargains I found," she would say in breathless exhilaration.

This time was different. To begin with, she seemed to be in complete denial of the loss of their granddaughter. She often spoke about Marjan as if she were still alive and sometimes he wondered if she had not forgotten the entire matter. Besides, the whole idea of accompanying Rana had been a last minute agreement. When he mentioned that most of his time would be spent on medical appointments and consultations, his wife gladly agreed to stay behind.

Stuck in traffic, he recalled the busy streets in America. They had traveled there only once on a tour, organized by the Association of Iranian Physicians. At the time, they had only their first child, Soraya, who stayed with Dayeh in Tehran. On that trip they met a couple from Shiraz, a pediatrician and his wife, whose friendship had lasted to this day. How ironic that the same friend would now help him to banish his youngest daughter back to that country. Then again, that was no more ironic than having his best friend, an honest lawyer, show him ways to get around the law.

Eskandari greeted him with a warm embrace. Had the old lawyer been a psychiatrist, he would have been just as great at his job. He understood, sympathized, and always went that extra mile, but this time Dr. Ameli knew that the lawyer had gone out of his way to help him.

"I have the documents," Eskandary said, pulling a few items out of a manila envelope. "But please make sure you hide the actual birth certificate somewhere safe." He looked into his friend's eyes and continued, "For you, I would do ten times more, but should this fall into the wrong hands, it will end my career." He tapped on the small burgundy booklet with the golden emblem of lion and sun on its cover.

Dr. Ameli took it and looked inside. A photograph of the baby was attached. His heart raced as he read on.

Name: Yalda Last name: Ameli Date of ...

He skipped a line.

Father's name: Mehdi Ameli

That had been the name of a distant relative, a young man whom Dr. Ameli barely knew. He had heard the sad news when the young man was killed in a bus accident shortly after Yalda's birth. To obtain the man's birth certificate had been the easy part. The fact that Moradi had not cared enough to register the baby's birth helped. But this was Eskandary's ultimate gift to his friend. Somehow the lawyer had managed to produce a birth certificate for the baby that showed no trace of Moradi.

The two other booklets were the passports. Vida's showed a picture of her alone, and it was under Moradi's name. That would also be what her exit permit would indicate. Rana's had two photos attached and it said Rana Ameli and baby Yalda. How clever that was. Iran's law for women to use their maiden name had come to their rescue. If Moradi ever saw the documents, he wouldn't suspect a thing. But seeing Yalda's birth certificate would be the end.

"Don't worry," he assured his old friend. "I will guard it with my life."

Eskandary handed him another envelope. "Oh, and here is..." he said and stopped, as if to search for the right words. It took him a minute to finish his sentence. "... the other passport."

Ameli knew exactly what was in that envelope. He would not - could not - open it. He didn't have the heart to look at Marjan's soulful eyes in that photograph, how serious she had looked, how grownup. He could feel the tears pushing behind his eyes, the pain building up in his rib cage. He blinked hard and pushed the envelope back. "Would you mind hanging on to that for now?"

The lawyer nodded without a word, put the envelope in his drawer, and he rang for tea.

The same young man Dr. Ameli had seen on his previous visit brought their tea.

"What about visas?"

"It's all in there.," Eskandary assured him. "They have a transit through Heathrow and a three months visa to the US. Once there, Rana can apply for a permanent visa, better known as Green Card."

The word 'permanent' gave Ameli a jolt. "I wish I could arrange for them to live somewhere closer, London, for example."

"We've already been over that, my friend. She could live in

Lodon, among other places, but after years and years, she'd still be a foreigner. America is different. Over the years, it has opened it has embraced citizens from all nationalities and is among the few countries to offer such a chance."

Dr. Ameli remained silent.

"Don't worry, my friend. America will be the best place for her," Eskandary said, as though sensing his friend's doubts. "No more self-pity, a positive outlook and that 'can–do' attitude will be precisely what Rana-jan needs to build herself a new life."

Ameli nodded sadly. "I just can't bear the separation. For all I know, the next time we meet, my grandchildren won't even know me."

Eskandary chuckled. "Oh, they will! When it comes to love, children have incredible memories, just like little puppies." And he laughed good-naturedly. "Americans have the highest regards for family. The kids will grow up wanting to learn more about you."

"I know so little about that country," Ameli said, and the way he emphasized the word 'that' were as if he was referring to outer space. "I only remember museums, tall buildings, and lots of taxis."

"That was a whole different experience," Eskandary said. "America's abundance of everything is attractive to the tourist. But to live there can go either way. It can be heaven if one is financially secure, and hell if not."

"Speaking of finance, I want to make sure she won't have to wait for money to arrive by mail. What about arranging some kind of a trust?"

"Absolutely. There's no restriction on the amount of money one brings into the country. In fact, the more the better." He raised his index finger. "Good credit is as important to those people as good name is to us. Here, they help when they know you. Over there, help is available only if you can afford it."

Eskandary opened a different drawer and started rummaging through. "The other day, a friend stopped by. He's a long-term resident in America and we had a chat about money matters. He answered some basic questions and I took notes for you." He kept searching and finally pulled out a sheet. "Aha!" He adjusted his glasses and studied the note. "He told me plenty, but the bottom line is this. A savings account over there isn't the same as here. Their banks pay minimal interest, and what little they do pay is subject to tax. But I still think at the moment that may be the best way for her to be safe."

Safe? Ameli's mind flew ahead and he could just picture those three, alone, and lost in a faraway land. How safe would Rana feel? He could provide her with comfort, but safety could not be bought. "Oh, I don't know," he said out loud as if exhaling the words.

Eskandary smiled. "What don't you know, my friend?"

"None of this makes sense," Ameli said and shook his head. "Despicable as it may be to live with a bigamist, I'm not sure a single mother living in exile is any better."

The old lawyer nodded in empathy. "It's only natural to have doubts. However, one may consider such hardship a small price to pay in exchange for freedom."

Dr. Ameli could sense how somewhere among those shrewd "however"s and "buts" his friend was trying to help him overcome his broken heart.

Eskandary studied him with deep concern. "You look tired. Have you been sleeping enough?"

Ameli smiled. "I'm fine." But he wasn't, and knew he had not convinced his friend, either.

Eskandary opened the window and reached into a small box and produced a pack of Kent cigarettes and a tiny book of matches. "As long as we're putting so much pressure on you, we might as well break the office rule and enjoy one of these," he said with a coy smile.

Ameli had lost count of the years since he quit, but he still enjoyed a puff now and then. Whenever his wife objected that cigarettes were poison for his heart, he said an occasional cigarette calmed his nerves. "I'd rather die a little sooner and in peace than be old and grumpy."

The lawyer lit two cigarettes and offered one to him. Oh, that smell of a freshly lit match and his first puff were enough to bring back the desire to be a smoker again.

The two sat back in silence for a while.

Eskandary gave him two more copies of the birth certificate. "Rana will need an official translation of this for long term use."

Long term. He stared at the familiar lion-and-sun. Having grown up under a flag with that lion in its center, the mere sight of it used to make him feel secure. But now something about the way that lion held his sword in the air gave him a shudder. It was as though the little beast had raised it with the intention to sever the cord that tied him to Rana. He placed the documents back on the table. "I don't know!" he repeated.

The lawyer slid a paper across the desk. "Would you mind signing the receipt for me?"

Ameli nodded and took the pen offered him.

"You should go ahead and confirm your flights," Eskandary said. "Have you decided on a tentative date yet?"

"I'm hoping for next month, but will need to double check with a colleague who'll cover my emergencies," Ameli said. He felt like someone standing at the edge, ready to dive, unsure if what he saw below was not just a mirage. His next words came out of nowhere. "What kind of assurance do we have that she'll get her divorce?"

The lawyer tapped his pen on the pad of paper and Ameli knew this to be his way of dealing with doubts. "All I can tell you is that I've seen it done multiple times. It will be a long process. First she will have to deal with the obstacles we talked about: establishing residency, enrollment in school, and settling down in general. Once she reaches that stage, she will be ready to find herself a lawyer and file for divorce."

"What if Farhad goes after her? She can't possibly claim abandonment, as you've suggested. He'll drag her right back here."

Eskandary raised the palm of one hand. "Wait a minute," he said and smiled incredulously. "It's not that simple. For one thing, he'll have a hard time tracking her in a country he knows nothing about. But even if he should find her, she'll be in the free world and with her own set of rights. He can't just 'drag her' anywhere."

Ameli wished some of that confidence would rub off on him.

The lawyer said, "Once she is out of this country's jurisdiction, I can't imagine what the man could possibly do about it." He thought for a few seconds. "But until then, my concern is what he may do here."

"Here?" Ameli smiled sadly. "With the kids gone and Rana making absolutely no financial claim, what could he possibly do?"

The lawyer did not seem convinced. "He is a shrewd man. He might go after anyone Rana cares about." And he looked straight at him. "You, for one."

"Now you're getting paranoid," Ameli said and chuckled. "What could he possibly do to me? He may be shrewd, but he's not a criminal."

"No, I'm not suggesting he'll commit—God forbid—any crime. But what if he should decide to pursue the matter from a legal standpoint? Our original plan would not incriminate you in any way, but now you're an accomplice. After all, it's because of *you* that he's letting the children go, and it's your money that subsidizes the entire plan. Any lawyer could easily prove you as the master mind behind the entire scheme."

"Nothing Farhad can do is going to hurt half as much as what he's doing to Rana. And, I still doubt he'd stoop so low. I've been like a father to him."

Dr. Ameli hoped his remarks masked the anxiety he felt. He had seen his son-in-law's mean side. Each time he thought about Moradi's possible reaction, a memory from his childhood came to his mind. Once, their gardener had spotted the children throwing rocks at a garden snake and cautioned them. "One can kill those things, but don't ever wound a snake. A wounded snake will not rest until he has found his attacker and retaliated." He remembered the many nights when he lay awake and imagined a snake coiled under his bed. Days weren't any better, either. The slightest rustling in the grass brought him images of a crawling presence. He never saw one, but now the images were back. Unable to sleep at night, he sometimes listened to his wife's calm breathing and tried to imagine what his son-in-law might do if and when he found out.

Eskandary left his chair, circled the desk, and put a heavy hand on his arm. "No matter what happens, don't you ever doubt what a great father you've been."

Ameli nodded and gave his friend's hand a pat. He picked up the passports, stuffed them into his breast pocket and would not look at Eskandary. As he rushed out with a quick 'thank you', he was grateful for the man's silence. One more word of compassion and he knew he would have broken into sobs.

Out on the street, he passed his parked car, and turning away from traffic, walked along a side street. Dusk had fallen and the evening breeze cooled his flushed face, dried his tears, and soothed some of his pain. He walked and walked, feeling a heat where those passports lay in his pocket, as if they had ignited a fire and would burn a hole into his heart.

—

Moradi stopped by the house at dawn to pick up some of Vida's school supplies before going to the barracks. He grabbed the bag Dayeh had packed, and rushed to his car. He had just put the Jeep in reverse when he heard Dayeh's voice outside the driver's side. "Excuse me, Major," she said while tapping on the glass.

He lowered the window. "What is it?"

She hesitated as if unsure how to word her question. "How long will Miss Rana and the young ladies be gone on their trip, sir?"

Considering the old woman's close relationship with Rana, he found it odd that she didn't know.

"I'd imagine a few weeks. Why?"

"Oh, nothing, sir. That's what Miss Rana said, too. Just making sure I had heard her right." Then as if still skeptical, she said, "Will that be long enough for the doctors to fix the baby's …umm… problem?"

He let go of the brake and started to back up. "Who knows?" And he was gone before the old woman made him late for work.

Lately, a few changes around the household puzzled him. It had started when Rana came back from Tehran acting as if their previous unpleasant encounters were figments of his imagination. He figured her parents must have talked some sense into her. The new Rana seemed more content, befriended American officers' wives and her English had improved so quickly that she now read books. When they lost Marjan, though he knew her enough to imagine how badly her heart had broken, she didn't grieve. In fact, he couldn't recall her crying at all. Had the shock helped her to finally grow up and mature? Was that why she had stopped making long, annoying phone calls to her mother? On the last bill he noticed most of her calls to Tehran were no more than a few minutes long.

Even the old nanny's behavior had changed. He no longer overheard her chatting with Rana in the bedroom, and on one occasion when Rana was on the phone, he walked into the house and could swear the old witch was in the hallway, spying. As for Banu, he was just waiting for an excuse to get rid of her and her big mouth.

Badri also commented on how Rana fussed over the new baby. "The way she handles this one you'd think she'd never had a baby before." At first he thought that might be because of her baby's malformed leg, but there was more. Since Marjan's death, Rana spent most of her time in the nursery. For a while, he didn't really care because in a way that gave him the freedom to be away. But when she sent Vida back to her sister-in-law, Badri accused her of picking favorites. "You know what, Farhad? I think she doesn't like the fact that Vida is so much like you." She chuckled. "She really is, except she needs to learn a little order."

She had a point. When Moradi visited his sister, her organized household impressed him. The boys had more gadgets and toys than he ever remembered having, but their rooms were neat and at dinnertime they engaged in conversations. True that they were older, but they spoke of bikes and guns and fist fights, subjects that he could relate to. He could never understand the girls' baby talk, or why they cried so much. Vida's sweet nature amused him. Marjan had been different. He missed her terribly and grieved her loss, but she could never mask her resentment, and in a strange way, her absence made the house a bit easier to walk into. He had felt scrutinized under her accusing stare; it was as though she knew too much and questioned his devotion.

Suddenly, he felt ashamed of the way he was judging his dead daughter. Had Rana been a better mother, the child would still be alive. He turned on the radio and tried to shake his negative thoughts. Soft flute and dulcimer music played. As he relaxed, he thought of how his life had divided into two opposite zones. The difference between life at home and time with Parisa was the same as between work and leisure. Rana tied him with chains of responsibility and in the end, left him with a sense of inadequacy. Parisa strived to please him and her mere presence was enough to forget the strenuous hours of work. She made no demands and let him be himself.

Thoughts of Parisa, and the son they would soon have, made him dizzy with anticipation. With all the love he felt for her, he knew this one would be a boy! Despite her frequent hints that he shouldn't build up his hopes, he'd already picked a name. They would call him Morad-Ali. Morad, for being his biggest wish, and Ali for that saint of all Muslim saints. "We can call him Ali, so it won't sound funny next to my last name."

His thoughts branched, grew and spread visions before him, and as if they had bridged the way, he soon reached the barracks. He returned the salute of the parking attendant, left his car for him to park, and headed toward the office building. The sun had already come up and it now spread over the red clay grounds that were sprinkled with water, raising a smell of dampness. The base had already brought in the day and somewhere behind the walls of the courtyard, soldiers were marching. The beat of their heavy boots echoed in the distance and the morning breeze carried muffled calls of their commander. In the hallway, Moradi saluted a couple of lieutenants and asked a soldier to bring his tea.

One look at the piles of folders, memos, and mail on his desk reminded him of the long lost order his office had once enjoyed. Working in and out of town, checking in at the house in case someone dropped by to offer condolences and rushing to Parisa's had left no time for tidying his desk and putting the files in order. The windows must have just been washed and now the dazzling sunlight spread over the layer of dust on the file cabinet. He noticed the black telephone had started to fade into a grayish yellow and realized how the entire place lacked color. The brick walls, tile floor, and simple furnishings were a clear reminder of the bare minimum an army man must endure.

Before Moradi had a chance to settle in, his phone rang.

"*Allo*, Farhad."

He recognized his mother-in-law's voice. This number was for emergencies only, and each time a personal call came through, somewhere inside him an alarm went off. She sounded sad and he even thought she might be crying. It shocked him to realize that he had never seen that woman in tears.

"What seems to be the trouble?"

She sobbed and for a minute, made no attempt to respond. "It's my husband," she finally said, and the way she went on crying made him think the good doctor had died. For a moment he forgot their differences and prayed it wasn't so.

"Please calm down and tell me what happened. Is Dr. Ameli all right?"

She cried a little more before clearing her voice. "He's in the emergency room," she said. "I've just come home to get a few things so I can stay with him. They're going to keep him there for a few days."

"I'm so sorry to hear this. What happened?"

"His heart ..." And she sobbed harder.

Moradi did his best to be patient while Mrs. Ameli sniffed and blew her nose. She then told him that the day before, two pedestrians had found her half-conscious husband on the sidewalk behind his lawyer's office. "They called an ambulance and the hospital called me."

Moradi gave off a sigh before asking, "What can I do to help?"

"Would you believe it? No sooner had he opened his eyes than he called for Rana." She cried some more. "Please, have her call me at the hospital. I'll be going now, but should be back in the evening."

"Why don't you call her?" he asked.

"I did. She was in the shower and I didn't want to tell her maid." She sniffed more. "After what she's been through, it's best if you tell her in person. You know? Be there for her?"

"I certainly will, Mrs. Ameli," he said. "I have an important meeting, but I'll go home the minute I can." He wanted to offer her words of comfort, but realized how distant he felt. He did not identify with Mrs. Ameli's pain. This news worried him only with regard to the old man himself. "Please give the doctor my wishes for a complete recovery."

For many minutes after the call, he sat there unable to focus on his work. He worried for the old man, but why did *he* have to be the bearer of bad news? Rana wasn't yet over Marjan's death, how would she react to another trauma?

There was a knock on the door and a soldier brought in tea. He dismissed the boy with a wave of one hand while his other hand picked up the receiver to dial Parisa's number. It took her a while to pick up, and she sounded as if she'd gone back to sleep. He lowered his voice, not to be overheard in the hallway. "Sorry to wake you up, but I'm afraid I won't be joining you for lunch. Something urgent has come up."

He told her the news briefly and concluded, "I'm sure the old man will be okay, but under the circumstances, I think I'll have to stay at the house again."

She said she didn't mind, but he wasn't convinced. Parisa had no reason to be jealous, yet each time he cancelled a plan, something in her voice made him feel awkward.

It was hard to imagine Dr. Ameli, that strong caregiver, in need of medical care. When the man had agreed to accompany his daughter and further insisted on taking Vida along, Moradi had considered it a blessing. He craved that freedom and wanted to give Parisa his full attention when their son was born. *Now what?*

Unable to work, he sipped his tea and thought about his life. It reminded him of his father and a strange metaphor he had once used. During a drought when Shiraz's farmers suffered losses, Moradi's father joined the business of a friend, a rug-merchant in the bazaar, to make ends meet. Running from one job to the other, he once had said, "My life has become that of a bigamist, stealing time from one place to be in another." A pre-teen at the time, Farhad hadn't grasped the full meaning. Now he knew.

When he had first started seeing Parisa, he refused to think of it as an affair. She was more of a reward for whatever good he may have done. Even when he wanted to marry her, he knew that those snobs in upper society would see it as plain bigamy. To take more than one wife was often seen as a sign of greed and lust, but his was an ethereal experience. The physical attraction was only a fraction of his many emotions. He had found a missing part of himself, experienced being whole. That feeling alone made everyone else's opinion immaterial. The more he looked for ways to see himself as an exception, the more he found them. Now for the first time he allowed doubt to penetrate his mind. *Am I just another man with two wives?*

Could his grief for Marjan push a wedge between Parisa and him? He was reluctant to talk to her about his lost daughter, whom she had never met. His pain was his alone and the only person he shared it with was his sister. He spent many evenings at Badri's. Was he giving Vida the time he had stolen from Marjan? Poor Vida looked so lost without her big sister. Occasionally he took her to the officer's club for a treat. Once he even took her to Parisa's. But despite the fact that Vida seemed to take to her, it had felt so awkward that he decided not to do it again. Everywhere he looked, the doors closed on him and now Dr. Ameli's heart attack!

Ever since Marjan's tragedy, Rana had remained dry-eyed, but her expression cried, her whole body cried. She ate less and was fast wasting away. She moved around the house like a ghost dressed in black, and the only one she smiled for was her baby. Lately she had started to prepare for her trip, but even then her movements lacked enthusiasm. He would find her in Marjan's room, staring at the objects of childhood, in no hurry to get past her grief.

That mother of hers didn't even show up for the funeral, did nothing to help her grieving daughter, but she didn't hesitate to call with more bad news. How was he going to tell Rana about her father?

—

Major Moradi picked up his mail from the hallway table and reluctantly went to the family room. He found Rana sitting on the sofa, staring at the television set that wasn't on. She looked at him without responding to his greeting. From there he could see the kitchen table set for lunch and decided the news about Dr. Ameli could wait until after they had eaten.

Rana must have been busy with another one of her nostalgic projects. Family albums lay open on the coffee table and loose pictures were scattered over the couch. Some photographs were trimmed around the edges and pieces of the trimming made a mess on the floor. He brushed a few pictures aside to make room and sat down.

"What's all this?" he asked.

"Oh," she responded without looking at him. "Just gathering favorite pictures."

He glanced at an album he had not seen before and figured that was where she planned to put her new selection. The project would probably leave some gaps in the old albums that he had so painstakingly organized, but he no longer cared what she did with them.

It wasn't until after the table had been cleared that he sat down with his glass of tea and said, "Won't you join me?"

Rana shook her head. "I've had enough tea today."

"Then just sit down for a minute. I need to tell you something." He glanced at Dayeh, who was about to leave. "You, too," he said. "I think you both should hear this."

Dayeh's questioning eyes were on him, but Rana busied herself with the pictures again. Did she think he was going to talk about their personal problems in front of the old nanny?

"Your mother called this morning."

Rana's eyes shot up. "My mother called *you*?"

Moradi smiled inwardly at how Rana always asked a question just to buy time.

"Your father is rather unwell." He said it reassuringly to suggest he was fine now.

"What do you mean, 'unwell'?"

"He had a minor heart attack."

Dayeh slapped her face. "Dear *Imam Hossein*!"

Rana continued to stare at him, wide-eyed.

"She wanted you to know because he asked for you as soon as he regained consciousness."

Rana stood, as if to go somewhere, but then sat down. "He was *unconscious*?"

"He's stable now. Those are your mother's exact words, 'he's stable'."

Dayeh put a fist to her chest, "Oh, that saint of a man, that father of all fathers," she said the words quickly and in a monotonous voice. "Save him, *ya Allah*, save him!"

Despite her sudden pallor and the glistening of tears, Rana maintained her poise. The woman he used to know would be screaming, tearing at her hair, and rushing to the phone to call Tehran. After a few minutes of silence, she took a deep breath, stood up again, and her lips quivered as she commanded, "If you don't mind, I would rather be alone and call my mother."

Her tone was so controlled that he thought she must be in shock. He looked at Dayeh, but the old woman did not seem the least bit surprised. In fact, she gave him a look as if to say that such dignity was expected from her lady. He heard the baby crying, and the old nanny left the room, still whimpering and making her usual bargains with *Allah*. "Dear God, just bring the good doctor back to his feet and I promise to read an entire round of Koran." Her voice faded down the hallway and Moradi knew she would carry on for hours.

Before leaving the room, Farhad glanced at his wife and almost could not identify the proud woman sitting near the telephone. Had Mrs. Ameli known how well Rana could handle such crisis, she would have called her directly. Rana worshipped her father and from the way she pursed her lips and pressed her eyelids shut, he could almost hear the scream locked inside her. Indeed, life had made a new woman out of her. The way she kept her distance allowed him to see her in a new light. The woman, who had leaned on him in all their times of trouble, no longer needed him. He had pitied the tenuous Rana, felt guilt for breaking her heart, but the last thing he'd imagined was that she'd be the stronger. Had their positions reversed?

Forget the drunken night he had come home with a broken heart over the loss of his father. Forget the brief intimacy that brought an unplanned baby to this world. He had not felt close to Rana in more than a year. Maybe that distance was the reason he was so shocked by this sudden pain at their estrangement.

Chapter

· *Fourteen* ·

DURING THE NEXT TWENTY-FOUR HOURS, the phone calls to and from Tehran became more and more reassuring. With Vida out of the way at Badri's house, Rana prepared to go to her father, but just before she had booked her flight, he called from his hospital room. "I knew you wouldn't trust anyone's report," he said, and his attempt at a chuckle made him cough.

"You're absolutely right. I was just looking at flights." Rana blinked her tears away.

"Don't you dare do anything so silly," he said.

"You sure gave us all a good scare."

"It wasn't half as bad as you think. It's wonderful to feel loved."

"Oh, Papa, as if you needed to test us!"

He told her they would keep him at the hospital a few more days, but the cardiologist had prohibited traveling for weeks. "I have your passports," he continued. "But I didn't think they'd be safe here, so I've sent them to the office, just in case."

In case of what? Was her father holding back? Would he tell her if there was any bad news?

"Are you absolutely sure you don't need me to come?"

"Absolutely. I'm in the best of hands here and there isn't a thing you could do to help." He coughed again. "I'll be much happier knowing Vida won't have to do extra time at her aunt's boot camp on my account."

He had no idea how she hated sending her there. The image of Vida at Badri's clutched at Rana's heart, but the more that child stayed away, the less reason there would be for Farhad to stop by the house. Then again, was that the real reason?

She had a hard time tearing apart that funny combined name. Everywhere she looked she saw her Vida-Marjan. But she had to separate them, and as she tried, it was hard to believe what she had done to her little girl. She pictured Vida's days alone in that house and with an aunt who forbade waking up in the middle of the night. Did children grieve? How could she be so self-absorbed? For once, Badri's words made sense. She did have another daughter and it was time to give Vida the attention she deserved.

As soon as her father hung up, Rana dialed Badri's. The maid told her no one was home and all the children were at school.

"Please tell her I called to report that I am feeling much better and would like Vida to come home."

Rana sat by the window and looked out at the driveway. Would Vida get up late at night and stagger in the dark hallways of Badri's house, looking for her sister? Visions of the day Badri had dropped off her two daughters filled her mind. A car would soon pull up, but this time only one child would emerge. Her throat constricted. Her heart raced. She felt sick to her stomach. Never again would Rana look into her beautiful Marjan's eyes, nor would she hear her loving voice. Her arms ached to wrap around that slim body, but it wasn't going to happen. She had to face the reality. The loss of Marjan was no one's fault, not hers, not Vida's, not even God's. There was not going to be a Vida-Marjan ever again and she had to accept that from now on, it would be Vida alone and she needed her.

"Oh, dear God!" Rana called out to the one patch of cloud in the sky as if God had been hiding behind it. As reality shattered the weak dam of denial, her tears finally burst forth. Rana leaned her forehead against the window and sobbed and sobbed.

The baby woke up and her sound brought Rana back to the real time. How long had she been standing by the window? She wiped her tears and went to Yalda's crib. The infant stopped whimpering as soon as she was picked up. "We will be okay, won't we?" Rana whispered into the baby's ear. "Vida will soon be home. Grandpa will recover, and we will all travel together." More tears slid between her cheek and the baby's. Rana whispered, "Pray with me, my angel. Pray."

—

The delay in their schedule turned out to be a blessing of sorts. Even though it meant that Rana had to carry on with her charade for a few more weeks, it gave her time to review what else to pack for such a long journey. What kind of clothes would Vida need, and how much of a seasonal change should they expect? Beside the new album, which of Marjan's things could she take along?

Late at night, she let her guard down and lay awake thinking. She had never felt she belonged in Shiraz, or even to this house, but the truth remained that this was the closest she had come to having a nest. Despite a surge of bitter emotions for Moradi, she knew that he, too, was hurting for Marjan. As if that child had been the last link, Rana knew that soon her husband would also be a shadow in her past. Her friend, Minoo, used to tell her a woman would never be completely over her first love. Forget love, what about the only man she had been intimate with? After all, the mere habit of having her husband around had to count for something. Too proud to admit she was hurt, she had never confronted him, never asked what made him need another woman. But pride notwithstanding, she ached to know. Why indeed?

The descriptions of Parisa remained vague. If she could just give the woman a face, it might provide a clue as to what Moradi had seen in her. These were her last days in Shiraz, her last chance to find out who Parisa was. As her father had taught her, if she hoped to put the entire matter behind her, she needed to look the enemy straight in the eye.

———

The Khalili Lane, which had once been a part of that family's estate, and where the garden was now located, had not changed since her last visit. Still, Rana looked at it as though this was her first trip. In the past, the taxi had always dropped her off in front of the garden and she had gone in without paying the slightest attention to its surroundings. But today, hiding behind a large scarf and dark sunglasses, she asked the driver to take her to the Namazee Hospital and walked the short distance. She studied the alley with care and paid close attention to the houses located across from the garden. The wrought iron gate would allow her to see the two houses across the garden.

For a moment, Rana closed her eyes and thought of the last time she had been there. In her mind, she saw her little girls running down the gravel path. The memory of Vida's giggles and Marjan's firm commands to her little sister filled her with deep sorrow. When she opened her eyes, all she saw was the brick wall surrounding the garden. For the first time, the sense of security had changed into a feeling of entrapment.

This was the earliest she had ever been there. No visitors had arrived yet and two men were busy watering the flowers; one had a black hose in his hand and the other hauled large watering cans into the gazebo. The wet flowerbeds glistened under the morning sun, and even from behind her dark glasses Rana could see the vivid colors of geraniums, petunias and marigolds. The smell of freshly cut grass mixed with the scent of lilacs. Rays of sunlight broke into a tiny rainbow where water sprayed out of the hose. Rana returned the gardener's greeting and headed toward the gazebo.

From the bench on the gazebo, Rana had a clear view of the two houses across the way without being seen. Her little sanctuary had turned into the enemy territory and the last thing she needed was to be spotted here. She opened the book she had brought along and pretended to read while glancing at the house now and then. Once a woman, who looked more like a maid, came out of the house to the left. The woman carried a plastic shopping basket and used her key to lock the door before walking past the garden. From time to time a bicycle or a few pedestrians passed by. The gardeners finished their work and were soon gone. Finally realizing she could sit there all day and not see anything of interest, Rana left just as other visitors were starting to trickle in.

The next morning, she went back, but this time less nervous and a little less hopeful. There was only one gardener at work. When he stopped his watering and began to make little loops with the hose to put it away, Rana gathered all her courage and asked him in what she hoped would be a casual tone, "Do you know who lives in those houses across the way?"

The man stood straight, stretched his back, and glanced at the alley as if he had never noticed the houses before. He gave an uncertain shrug and said, "The one to the right is empty, and I don't know who owns it. The left one, I think some Tehrani people moved in last year."

Rana felt a surge of excitement. So that had to be Parisa's, and the woman she had seen could be her maid.

"They are so lucky you maintain this lovely view for them to enjoy," she said.

The gardener put the coils of black hose around a tree stump.

"True," he said, "Mr. Khalili's garden is the best in Shiraz!" And he walked away.

———

That evening, when Moradi stopped by long after dinner, Rana noticed a distinct change in him. He had a stubble of a beard and his uniform seemed a little wrinkled. He did not read the paper nor did he open his mail. Dayeh brought him a nice plate, which he barely touched. Even the old nanny eyed him with curiosity.

"How was work?" Rana asked, surprising herself. She had no interest in his work, or in any other aspect of his daily life, but thought the question may encourage him to talk. She couldn't share Marjan's grief, but knew she had to somehow act like a normal wife.

He gave her a vacant look. "Work?" He blinked a couple of times. Something was amiss and if Rana hadn't just called Tehran, she would fear it had to do with her father.

Moradi walked over to the bar. "Work is work," he snapped and Rana knew that would be the end of that topic.

"No need to talk to me as if I'm one of your orderly soldiers."

He started to pour a drink. "Then don't ask."

Rana decided she should let him burn in whatever hell he was in.

Moradi retreated to his chair and turned on the television, but didn't watch it. He kept tapping his left heel on the floor and when Vida tried to climb onto his lap, he pushed her away and growled, "I'm tired."

Vida, not expecting the push, lost her balance and fell to the floor and started to cry.

Rana shot him an angry look and went to the child. "Don't cry, honey. Papa didn't mean to hurt you."

Vida cried harder. "Yes he did. He doesn't love me!"

"Oh, don't you be silly," Rana said and kissed her, "*Mommy* loves you."

"Aha!" Moradi said. "Go right ahead, turn her against me, too. You've already done a great job of it with everyone else."

Rana did not know where all this was coming from. Something was eating him from inside. He got up so abruptly that he tipped a small table and sent an ashtray across the room. She watched him as he went back to the bar and made himself another drink, took his glass, and went upstairs without saying goodnight.

The next day, he left before breakfast.

At lunchtime, Rana took a taxi to the European bistro called One-O-Three, where Kathy had arranged to meet her. More than a month had passed since that horrible accident. Rana had not paid her friend—or any friends—a visit. Most of the women she knew in Shiraz were the mothers she met at school, lucky mothers of Marjan's classmates, mothers who needed to be there as the third grade assembled. She didn't even care to see the parents of Vida's friends, let alone Marjan's. The look of pity in their eyes stabbed at her heart, and so did the softer than normal tone they used when they spoke to her, as if they feared their voices could shatter her. The only friend she spoke to was Minoo, but she lived in Tehran, and phone conversations were hardly enough. Now that she didn't see Kathy, Rana realized what a supportive friend she had been. Maybe if she had lost Marjan some other way, somewhere else, she would draw comfort from seeing her friend, but not now, not when she thought of her more as the lucky mother of Claire than anything else. Kathy called on a regular basis, asking to see her, and at this point, Rana had run out of excuses. Hard as it was to talk to Kathy, Rana realized how much she had missed her friend.

The restaurant was located off the main street. Kathy had said she chose this place for its peaceful atmosphere. The familiar tune of a soft melody played on piano confirmed that. Rana looked around and found Kathy, sitting at a corner booth, waving at her.

As she wove between the tables, she was reminded her of better times when she had enjoyed dinners here. She had learned to brush away such memories as quickly as they came to her. The past was only that, and she was determined not to allow it to rob her of the needed energy to face the future.

Kathy left her seat to give her a hug. "I've really missed you." she said.

"Me, too," Rana responded politely.

When they took their seats, Kathy reached across the table and put a hand on hers. "How are you holding up, honey?"

Rana diverted her attention to the next table. Her best response would have been to admit she wasn't! She still couldn't talk about Marjan, especially not to her. Images of the school bus dropping off Claire at the curb came to her. Had Frank put the swing back up? Something bitter rose in her throat. "I'm fine," she lied and knew her tone was dry.

"Frank has been a mess about the accident." Kathy said, as though having read her mind. "You would think as an army man, he'd be the stronger one, but he was so devastated that, after a few sleepless nights, he asked the owner to chop down that damn tree."

The tree is gone. The swing is gone. But so is my Marjan.

A few seconds passed in silence.

"How long before your trip to the States?" Kathy asked and Rana appreciated the change of subject.

"I don't know," she said and proceeded to tell her about her father's heart attack and their delayed plans.

"Is it okay for him to travel?"

"He thinks so. But I'm afraid he is acting stronger than he feels just so we won't miss our appointment with the specialist." She thought for a moment. "I hear it's going to be hot when we're in

Chicago. But what if we need to stay longer? What kind of weather do they have in autumn, or winter, for that matter?"

"I wouldn't worry about it. You'll be back long before Chicago's famous winter even starts. Mind you, summers in the Midwest can be all four seasons wrapped in one." She smiled. "I mean, you'll definitely get the heat, but there will be intervals of rain, cold, even hail."

"Hell?"

Kathy laughed. "No, not Hell—hail! as in frozen rain," she explained. "We have a saying, 'If you don't like our weather, just wait a minute!'" She chuckled. "It's best to always have umbrellas and sweaters handy, just in case."

"Do they wear boots and gloves in winter?"

"In Chicago? Honey, you bet! Sometimes the entire Midwest turns into the North Pole. Especially with that wind, no amount of winter gear seems enough."

"I had no idea." Rana's suitcases were already full. Maybe she should buy those once they were there.

As the restaurant became more crowded, they spoke a little louder and now there was so much noise that she could hardly hear her friend.

"I hope your husband is all better." Kathy said and sounded as though she thought he was recovering from something.

"He's fine, why?"

"Frank wondered if he'd be going back to work soon."

Rana didn't know how to respond. "I think so," she said absentmindedly.

"Glad to hear that."

Had Moradi missed work? By now he didn't need excuses for his absence from home and he certainly didn't have to skip work to sneak to Parisa's. *Where else could he have been?*

Throughout the visit, they never once mentioned Marjan.

Once, Kathy spoke of how hard "the incident" had been on Claire, but maybe she saw something in Rana's face because she immediately switched to the newly opened Army's food mart. When they had finished their small meal, an appointment was set for Kathy to bring her a couple of new books and show her pictures of Chicago and its surrounding areas.

The next evening, Moradi stopped by again, but once again, he didn't eat and would not say a word. This time, even little Vida sensed something. "Is Papa mad at me?" she whispered to Rana, but loud enough for Moradi to hear.

"Don't be such a pest," he yelled at her.

Rana did not react. What had come over the man? His recent attitude had nothing to do with grief. He seemed to be done with his share of mourning and crying on his sister's shoulder. His life had gone back to its routine and the only visible change was the occasional games he played with Vida. He had visited Vida at his sister's house on a regular basis, and except for the past two evenings, he had given her his full attention. Sometimes the games they played made him laugh. By contrast, Rana wondered if she'd ever laugh again.

She couldn't figure where Moradi's anger came from and didn't care enough to probe, but maybe it would be best to take Vida away before he ruined what was left of good memories. She had heard about angry men and their cruelty, especially army men. She wouldn't let Vida be his victim.

—

Moradi had left a message with Dayeh saying he wouldn't be home for dinner. Rana decided to pay the Khalili Garden another visit, but this time she would go at dusk, shortly before the gates closed. She figured the darkness would make it easier for her to conceal her identity, and there was a good chance that Moradi might show up there closer to evening.

Not too many visitors were left. A few younger couples hid here and there, looking as if they were on secret dates. The gardeners were making their rounds with insecticide sprays and the air smelled medicinal. Perched at her usual spot in the gazebo, Rana wondered what others might think of her sunglasses, but at this point she was too preoccupied to care.

She hadn't been there long when a taxi pulled up to the house. Three people sat in the back seat. As Moradi stepped out of the taxi, Rana could not miss his tall shape, which now looked even taller with his army hat on. The shock of seeing him made her rise from the bench, but she immediately sat down and ducked behind the climbing rose. He stood next to a small woman who, judging by the curve in her back and slow moves, was much older.

Moradi reached into the back seat and helped another woman out of the taxi while the older one went to the other side to remove a rather large bag. It was hard to see their faces, but based on Banu's description, the taller one had to be Parisa. Moradi helped her up the three steps while the other woman rushed to open the door. As they faced the door, in the pale streetlight Rana could see their backs. The way he slid his arm around the woman made it clear she was in need of support to stand. Rana recalled the warmth of his long fingers in the curve of her own back and had the urge to scream, "That's my husband!" But something about the helpless way the woman moved told her she wouldn't want to be her.

Parisa took small baby steps while being supported. She bent her head to the side as if lacking the strength to hold it up. Rana felt cold all over and it had nothing to do with the cool evening breeze. As soon as the door opened, a bright light came on inside the house and for just a second, the tall woman stood against the light in a way that Rana could make out her profile. From a distance, her features were not clear, but the way her long hair flowed to one side, and something in her slow moves conveyed deep sorrow.

The door closed behind them, leaving the alley in the obscure purple hue of dusk. Only then was Rana conscious of something peculiar, something that the mere thought of it froze her heart. Now she knew what had given her that shiver. She crossed her arms over her middle as though making sure her insides stayed in place and her whisper sounded as cold as the wind, "Oh, dear God!"

The woman's body had been slender, too slender for someone who was about to have a baby.

Chapter

· *Fifteen* ·

"WOULD YOU LIKE THE LIGHT ON?" Dayeh asked Rana, who sat on the couch staring out into the garden. Her lovely silhouette blended in with the shadows of the darkening garden, as if she, too, belonged out there among the flowers.

"No," Rana said. "Let it be." She pulled her knees up to her chin. "It's easier to think in the dark," she turned to face her nanny. "But I could use some tea, if the *samovar* isn't too cold."

"Let me check."

Going back to the kitchen, Dayeh was puzzled. Rana had turned peculiar and sometimes acted so distant that Dayeh had to remind herself that was the girl she had raised. Lately, there were too many new developments to adjust to. When Rana told her about her unexpected and rather sudden plan for a trip abroad, Dayeh's first reaction had been pure panic. No sooner had the word "travel" left Rana's mouth than Dayeh recalled the disaster that Bibi Moneer had cautioned her against. A strong believer in Bibi's predictions, Dayeh was sure something dreadful would happen on this journey. But maybe the good doctor's heart attack was what the woman had predicted. Lately she couldn't figure out what was the matter with the Major, either. He had been acting strange. He did come home every single night, but Dayeh heard the squeaking of the parquet floor above as he paced the floor into the latest hours of the night. In the morning, he was gone before prayer time and when she went to do his bed, it was untouched, with only the covers a little scrunched. His pajamas sat in the drawer, neatly folded, unused.

After two additional sessions with the soothsayer when the woman failed to reveal anything new, Dayeh wondered if Bibi Moneer was too old and her power of prophecy was no longer reliable. On her last visit, the woman had made no sense at all. "You were planning to go on a pilgrimage to Mecca," she had said. "But the money you recently lost was quite a lump sum." Dayeh couldn't think of anything that came the least bit close to such a description.

Bibi Moneer went on with her forecast as clearly as if she was watching the events on a television screen. "With the first snowfall, a holy man in a green turban will leave you a good amount of money and that's when you'll make the trip." She played with her rosary and gave Dayeh a coy smile. "You won't forget Bibi's gift when you get that money, will you?" After such gibberish, Dayeh searched for other ways to find out what was going on.

She took a glass of tea to Rana and set it on the side table. "What time will your husband be home?" she asked, more concerned with dinner than his presence.

Rana shrugged.

"Vida will have dinner at her Amerikaee friend's, so I made the lamb stew you like." She chuckled. "Oo, she hates that stuff! If God hadn't created rice, that child would starve."

Rana didn't laugh. Had the remark brought Marjan to her mind? That child had never objected to what was served. Dayeh knew her mistress well. She felt deep guilt. She glanced at the grandfather clock, unable to make out the numbers through tears.

"The Major *is* coming home for dinner, no?"

Rana glared at her. "Why not ask Banu?"

So we're back to that, are we? Dayeh thought

When the Major had turned up every evening, and especially when he did not yell at Vida the way he normally would, Dayeh started to believe the man might have had a change of heart. She hoped that maybe Rana's travel plans and the mere idea of weeks of separation had finally brought him to his senses. But now it sounded as though things were right back to where they started. With Bibi Moneer turning senile on her, Dayeh figured it wasn't such a bad idea to talk to Banu and find out more, but how could she do that and still save face?

"Would you like dinner now?"

Rana shook her head. "You go ahead and eat. I'm not really hungry."

Dayeh opened her mouth to say something, but decided anything she said at this point might only add to the tension. It was bad enough to sit in the dark and think, but the way Rana skipped meals, soon there would be nothing left of her.

Back in the kitchen, Dayeh turned off the burner where the lamb stew was simmering. The aroma of saffron, turmeric and dried lemon filled the air, and the windows were fogged with steam rising from the pot. She took a large ladle and poured some stew into a china bowl, then cut a large onion in half and set it in a small plate. She placed the food on a tray along with a *lavash* bread and two glasses of water and headed down the hall. Before entering her room, she knocked with the toe of her shoe on Banu's door. "Come for dinner."

Dayeh felt too exhausted to eat. It had been a long day. Not only had she done loads of laundry and ironing, but Yalda, about to cut her first tooth, had fussed all day.

Banu entered Dayeh's room, left her slippers at the door and joined her on the rug. As soon as she sat down, she tore a piece off the flat bread and dipped it into the stew, then let it drip all the way to her mouth.

"Where are your manners, girl?" Dayeh said angrily. "Wait till it's ready to eat, and use a spoon for Heaven's sake!"

Banu struggled to chew the big piece of bread and apologized with her mouth full.

Gone were the days at the Ameli's when Dayeh would be invited to the table with the rest of the family. The Major didn't even like it when the servants ate in the kitchen, let alone in the dining room. She took the bread and cut it into bite size pieces and dropped them into the stew. Stirring just enough to soak each piece, she offered half of the raw onion to Banu and took a bite from the other half. The onion was fresh and its sharp taste made her eyes teary. She took a spoonful of the stew to neutralize the effect.

"Heard anything new in the neighborhood?" she asked Banu and tried to sound casual.

The girl eyed her with disbelief and shook her head.

Dayeh put a hand on Banu's shoulder. "You can tell Dayeh anything." She lowered her voice. "It's Rana-khanoon I don't want you to go talking to."

Banu took a spoonful of the stew and looked down without a word.

Deciding that questions would not get her far and that they might even make the girl suspicious, Dayeh changed course. "I wonder what the neighbors think of the Major's recent problem. He sure isn't the same."

"You *know* about that?" Banu said, wide eyed, yet somehow sounding relieved, as if pleased to know the secret was out.

Dayeh gave her an encouraging smile. "It's all over the street, dear."

Banu nodded. "You're right. I don't know what made me think you wouldn't know." She stuffed her mouth again. "I heard it day before yesterday, waiting in line at the bakery," she went on, now hissing as her voice burst with enthusiasm. "I couldn't believe Leila—that's the new maid down the alley, whose mother works for the Major's woman." She took a bite of the onion and followed it with a loud gulp of water. "She has the nerve to feel sorry for what happened. The Major's woman sure had it coming to her." She looked at Dayeh and whispered, "I mean, she had no right marrying Miss Rana's husband to begin with, not to mention growing his seed!"

"*His seed?*" Dayeh glared at her. "Where did you learn to talk that way about your master?" As soon as she had said that, she thought of the reason behind this conversation and switched back to being friendly. "But I see what you mean." Despite extreme curiosity, Dayeh would not say another word because, knowing Banu, she'd go on until she had told everything she knew.

Banu swallowed hard, and raised her voice. "It was a boy you know," she said, as if to announce the most important headline.

Was? At first, Dayeh didn't know what to think, but it only took her a minute to regain her presence of mind. She shuddered at the shocking news, but managed to appear calm. *"Astaghforellah,"* she said under her breath, and couldn't say the rest. Major Moradi had paid dearly for his cruelty, but having experienced two miscarriages herself, followed by infections that left her barren, Dayeh found it hard to rejoice. Divine justice? But the loss of life was still a loss. Any life.

Unable to chew, Dayeh let the piece of bread sit in her mouth while she tried to make sense of the past two days: The Major's restless attitude, his coming home, not eating. Did Rana know about this? And if so, who had told her? Dayeh was tempted to ask, but that might reveal the fact that she was hearing the news for the first time.

"This happens all the time, dear, lots of women lose their babies," she said at last, using her age and experience to regain the upper hand. "And in most cases, there's no rhyme or reason why."

"Oh, but Leila's mother said this one was because of the accident." Banu sounded triumphant at knowing something that Dayeh didn't know. "I bet that's why the Major is acting so weird, I heard he himself was driving!"

"*What?*" This time Dayeh could not mask her surprise.

Banu raised her chin and smiled as if enjoying her informed status. "Near the Khalili garden, a bicycle darted out of the alley right in front of the Major's Jeep, and wham!" She clapped hard, giving Dayeh a jolt. "God was with the Major because neither one was hurt," she said. "I mean, except for the woman losing her baby."

The bowl of stew was finished and Banu took the last piece of bread to wipe it clean. Dayeh wondered how that girl could eat so fast and talk at the same time.

"His car is all ruined," Banu said in closing.

"That explains the taxis."

"Uha." Banu nodded several times like a goat. "But I don't think he'll be coming home tonight. Leila said the woman was due back today from the hospital."

Dayeh picked up a few breadcrumbs from the rug, put them back in the tray, and pulled her aching body up.

"Go to bed now. I want you up early in the morning," she said to end the conversation. There would always be time to chat, but for now she needed Banu out of the way to have a good talk with Rana.

—

Rana let the visions of the obscure scene across the Khalili garden circle her mind. She knew that sitting in the semi-dark room to mull over her half-knowledge would only keep her up all night, but she couldn't stop. A million new questions came to her mind, but how was she to ask Banu or Dayeh without revealing the fact that she'd been spying on her own husband?

She turned on the small lamp next to her, picked up a magazine and began to page through. The pages were blurry and no matter where she looked, she saw only her husband adoringly supporting that woman up the stairs and into their love nest. She recalled Parisa's profile at the door, her body leaning back, standing sideways to reveal a flat tummy. Maybe if she blinked really hard, the images would go away, but they continued to pop out of the magazine pages, danced around the room and circled in her head. Oh, if only she could scream and get it all out! She threw the magazine aside and picked up her book. The printed words marched on the page like a row of little ants.

Rana's mind had become so exhausted that when the bright light came on without Dayeh bothering to ask permission, she covered her eyes in protest. "What are you doing?"

"Taking care of you, is what," Dayeh said with sarcasm. "You'll lose precious eyesight reading like that," she went on with authority. "It's one thing to sit there in the dark and brood over the demon in your husband and quite another to try reading in the dark." She picked up the magazine Rana had tossed to the floor. "Care for more tea?"

Rana shook her head.

Dayeh stood next to the couch for a few seconds before slumping down on the carpet. "Oh, child," she began with a sigh and put her elbow on the coffee table to support her. "Will you talk to me while I've got a few days left, or am I already as good as dead to you?"

Rana gave her a sad smile. Dayeh had become an expert in using that martyr's tone, making her think of the worst just to get an answer. Maybe she had learned this from Rana's mother and her fainting episodes, a drastic approach that ultimately made everyone take notice. True that Rana had strict orders to keep her nanny in the dark, but she could now sense the distance she had unwillingly created. Soon their intimate talks would be impossible.

She frowned. "Don't you dare use such words."

"Why not just say 'shut up Dayeh and watch Rana suffer because she doesn't trust you any more?'"

Rana reached over, put her hand on Dayeh's cheek and gave it a loving stroke. Age had drawn a gray ring around the pupils of her eyes and the deep lines that radiated around her eyelids made it seem as if she squinted all the time. When had she turned so old? Rana remembered the same expression on a much younger face of the woman who tucked her in at nights, whispering soothing words. These shriveled lips bore no resemblance to the young mouth that had sung to a sleepy little Rana. Could one's face collapse under the heavy burden of life? Or was it the tears that, like a river, left a deep groove on their paths? The bitter truth in Dayeh's remark filled Rana's heart with anxiety. Indeed, the time to talk was now or never. She didn't have to tell all, but keeping one secret didn't mean they couldn't remain close.

"Oh, Dayeh-joon, you know I trust you."

"*Know?* And how do I know that when you don't talk to me for months?"

Rana laughed light-heartedly. "We're talking right now, aren't we?"

Dayeh turned her face away and muttered, "Don't you mock me, child." She clasped her arms around her knees and rocked side-to-side as if to draw comfort from the gentle movement. "When you let someone into your heart, you absorb their joy as well as their pain." She gave out a deep sigh. "Lately, my heart has been tormented by what goes on inside you, and it kills me not to know the cause of it."

Rana felt a shiver, but she would not allow herself to become too emotional. This was how Dayeh would remember her for years to come. Rana had to assure her that she was fine. She watched the tears slide down her old nanny's sunken cheeks and through deep wrinkles until they finally disappeared into the white scarf around her neck. She longed to hold that arched torso in her arms, but did not dare for fear she, too, might cry.

"Let me tell you," the old nanny finally said. "Sorrows can kill if we don't vent them. Dark secrets to the heart are like flame to a candle, they make you melt silently. But words are the fan that blows out that flame." As if pleased with her poetic analogy, she raised her eyebrows and nodded, "That's why you need to talk, child. That's why!"

Rana looked out into the garden without a word.

"You think I know nothing?" Dayeh went on. "Let me tell you, child. In a small town, gossip circles like the whirlwind, and it reaches the common man first. It's no longer a secret that the cursed shrew carried your husband's illegitimate child."

She paused, sniffed hard, and using the corner of her scarf wiped her face.

Rana just sat there, hoping her face showed no emotion.

"You know?" Dayeh went on, "Losing that baby serves them both right because *it* happened to be a boy." She gave out a nervous chuckle.

Rana stared at her nanny. "I didn't know," she whispered.

"I'd be the last to want to bring you any of this, but I've seen how you hang your head about having no sons. It's about time your husband realized that maybe God doesn't want to give him a son."

The sadness Rana felt surprised even her. If this was war, the enemy had ended up far less than victorious. She recalled the day she lost Marjan and her eyes welled with tears at the remembrance. Oh, how long it had taken her to stop denying the bitter reality. What others considered coping, or worse, "getting over it" was nothing but painful silence. By now Marjan's life supplemented her own. Rana knew the unbearable agony of the first few months following the loss of a child. "Oh, that poor Parisa," she whispered.

Dayeh stared at her in bewilderment, unable to respond.

Rana shook her head side to side and repeated, "Poor, poor Parisa!"

Chapter

· *Sixteen* ·

THE NIGHT BEFORE they were to leave for Tehran, Dayeh was sure morning would never come. She tossed and turned in her bedroll, counted the twelve Imams on her prayer beads, and said seven times the first *surah* of the Koran. But sleep would not come. Dr. Ameli had specified she must accompany Rana to Tehran, but what about later on? She had no idea what was expected of her while Rana and her children were abroad. She hated house sitting in Shiraz, with Banu being the only other person left. Maybe the Amelis would ask her to stay in Tehran a while longer. What did Bibi Moneer know? God willing, everyone would return safely within a few weeks. But still, something stirred within her as if her heart itself was boiling over.

The Major was away, but he had said he'd be back late at night, and even asked Dayeh to wake him up in the morning.

"I'll drive to the airport myself," he had said.

Dayeh was furious at such pretence, but tried to keep her peace on this last day and say nothing that might bother Rana.

She thought maybe it was hunger that kept her up and decided to get a bite to eat. She had left a light on in the hallway for the Major, but noticed another light upstairs. Had Vida left it on? She took off her slippers at the bottom of the stairs and crept barefoot up the carpeted steps. The light came from under Rana's door. That poor girl had worked so hard that she must have fallen asleep before she could turn her light off. Dayeh hesitated a moment, then decided to go in and turn it off. She twisted the doorknob with care and now saw Rana sitting on her bed, with her back to the door and talking on the phone.

"No, I haven't told a soul," she said into the receiver.

Dayeh froze in place. Something in the way Rana said those words piqued her curiosity.

"Papa, I can't do that." Rana said. "At least, not the ones Farhad has given me. Besides, don't you think he'd be suspicious if suddenly all my jewelry was gone?"

There was a long pause. Then Rana responded in a voice that was just short of crying. "I don't care what he does, Papa. I promise you, I won't even look behind me." Her voice broke and she sniffed. "My only regret is not saying a proper goodbye to those I really love."

Rana slid to the edge of her bed and ran her big toe on the floor as if in search of her slippers. Dayeh closed the door before Rana turned.

Back in the kitchen, she leaned against the wall to catch her breath. Those last words had set off an alarm. This trip was not a short visit abroad. Rana was leaving without saying a "proper goodbye" and taking some of her jewelry, too?

Bibi Moneer had said someone was about to go on a long road. She had said it would end in disaster. The old witch had been wrong many times. Maybe this, too, was pure gibberish. But where was Rana really going and why was her father helping her?

Dayeh stared at the glass-covered pots of leftovers. But despite her churning stomach, she had lost her appetite. What did that brief conversation mean? Looking back, she realized that this time

Rana hadn't asked her to pack for her. Not only had she packed her own suitcase, but insisted on doing the girls', too. "You won't be there to help me unpack," she had reasoned. "I just want to know where I put everything." At the time, it sounded logical, but now she wondered if there was another reason.

Overcome with anxiety, Dayeh realized that the only clue might come from what was in those suitcases. As quietly as she had gone down, she climbed the stairs back up. Rana's light was now off. Dayeh slipped into Vida's room.

Two of the suitcases sat by the closet. In the darkness, she listened to the little girl's deep breathing and decided it best not to turn on the light. The single bulb hanging in the closet would do. She turned on the closet light and left its door ajar. The latch on the first suitcase opened with a loud click, but Vida did not move.

The suitcase contained mostly baby clothes. She knew many of them but as she checked deeper, she found new ones in much bigger sizes. These had been gifts from friends, and she remembered Rana asking her to put them away till the baby had grown. Back then, she had enjoyed the vision of Yalda growing to be that big, but now the idea that they may plan to stay away that long made her feel betrayed. *"My only regret is not saying a proper goodbye to those I really love,"* Rana had said.

The second suitcase was Vida's, but except for a few items of winter clothing, it contained nothing unusual. Then again, with the changing weather that Rana had mentioned, those jackets and sweaters would come handy. She was about to close the suitcase when out of the top pocket something heavy slid and fell onto the rug with a thud. Dayeh looked up at Vida, who had now turned her back to the light. When the child resumed her deep breathing, Dayeh picked up the fallen object and her heart nearly stopped at the sight of the Koran, the one from Rana's wedding ceremony.

This was the only object to which that girl seemed to be attached. She wouldn't let Banu touch it and had specified it should never leave the mantle.

"Dear God, no!" Dayeh whispered. She clutched the book in her hands and pressed it to her chest as if to calm her racing heart. Now she had no doubt about some kind of trouble ahead.

Dayeh's mind flew back to years before and the ceremonial visit by the late Mr. and Mrs. Moradi a week before the wedding. Mrs. Moradi had shown good taste in the way she presented the Koran, along with a large silver mirror and matching candelabras. A servant carried the items on a tray, lined with a cashmere shawl and covered with rose petals. Everyone had cheered and clapped while Dayeh circled the room carrying a brazier of burning wild rue. Later, Mrs. Ameli served a delicious cake as Rana herself served the tea. "May you be safe in the shadow of this holy book," the groom's father had said the traditional words.

When the Major took his new bride back to Shiraz, that Koran had found its place on the marble mantle, to be used only on special occasions. Each time someone went on a trip, the Koran was held above their heads and they kissed it before leaving the house. Each new baby passed under the Koran the first time they entered that front door. Rana had always carried a smaller Koran in her purse for long trips. This one had never left the house. When a woman took her wedding Koran out of her house, it signified trouble. Was Rana getting a divorce? If so, why would she keep that a secret from her? Dayeh felt both angry and sad at the same time, angry enough to consider going straight to the Major and demanding an answer. But Rana obviously wanted it this way. How could she betray the trust of a lifetime?

She closed the suitcases and turned off the light.

Moradi stood at the front door, checking his watch every few seconds. Vida anxiously knelt on the floor and cuddled her cat one last time before going.

"Maman won't let me put Peeshee in my suitcase."

Moradi smiled at her, but did not argue.

Everyone waited while Banu ran around looking for the Koran. "It was here on that marble shelf just two days ago," she mumbled and now kept on looking behind the books on the bookshelf. "I dusted and put it right back on its stand."

Rana came down the stairs holding her purse in one hand and her case of makeup and jewelry in the other. Dayeh followed, carrying the baby.

"What's all the fuss about?" she asked Banu.

The girl looked as if she was about to cry. "Can't find the big Koran. I swear it was right here." And she pointed to the bookshelf.

Moradi watched his wife and thought she turned pale, but then again, she looked pale lots of times. A deep silence fell for a few seconds.

The old nanny turned to face the maid. "Why didn't you ask *me*?" she said. "I took it upstairs to Miss Rana's room when we were packing, and I read verses to bless their trip."

With a sigh of relief, Banu rushed to the stairs, but before she had climbed, Dayeh grabbed her shirtsleeve. "Don't waste more precious time, girl. Go get mine." And she nodded to her room down the hallway. "A Koran is a Koran, and we're late as it is."

Moradi noticed the exchange of a peculiar look between Rana and her old nanny, but managed to dismiss the thought. Was he becoming obsessed? He had no time for such silly notions, and it was out of character for him to make something out of nothing. Glad to see the maid approaching with a Koran and a glass of water, he prepared to leave.

Vida, proud of knowing the ceremony, passed under the tray three times and kissed the Koran before leaving. Once all the passengers had gone through the ritual, Banu picked up the glass of water, reached for a pot of geranium and topped the water with petals.

Before driving away, Moradi readjusted the rearview mirror of the new Jeep. In it, he saw the maid standing by the stairs, ready to pour the water behind them to grant the passenger's safe and speedy return.

⁓

The emptiness of the house hit Moradi the minute he returned from the airport. Maybe he should have gone straight to Parisa, but he needed to pick up a few things.

The maid came in with a tray. "Thought you'd want your tea before I turn off the samovar, sir."

He nodded and settled in his chair.

The silence was so unbearable that he almost welcomed the mew of Peeshee. The cat circled his legs before settling on the couch and for a split second, he expected Vida to follow. He looked at the dining table, where Marjan used to do her homework. Her absence was as soundless as her presence had been, but like a footprint left in cement, her trace would never be erased from his life. When she was alive, he saw her as a shadow of his conscience, now he would do anything to have her back. Vida was different. To miss her so soon surprised him. Unlike Rana, who seemed to have buried her soul along with her daughter, Vida shared his grief. She had helped her daddy to fill the gap Marjan had left behind. But now even Vida couldn't help him as he grieved his unborn son. Parisa was too crushed to talk about it and there was no one else who'd know the depth of such pain.

Moradi listened to the hollow silence around him. The house would remain void of life for weeks to come. He sipped his tea and surveyed the room. The empty brass stand on the bookshelf, where the old Koran had sat for years, reminded him of all that he had lost. That Koran had become the single object connecting him to his late parents. His father put great emphasis on respect for the holy book. "Always keep it on a high shelf, and never place anything on top of it," he had said. But this Koran had a unique value, as it had been in the family ever since his parents were married. His father had recorded the birth of his sister, Badri, and later his own, inside the front cover. Once, when he mentioned how rare that special edition had become, his father smiled and said, "May you write the names of your sons inside it, as we wrote yours years ago."

When he had daughters, his father inscribed their births in his neat handwriting. While recording Vida's birth, the old man had repeated, "May God grant you a son." He fussed with each letter as if he knew that those notes would become his legacy. "Your mother and I weren't able to have more than two children, but I hope you'll be blessed with many more." Moradi remembered the words as if they were spoken only days before. His father gently blew over the writing to help the ink dry then closed the Koran and kissed its cover. "Each child is a gift," he said. "But only a son grants the family longevity and keeps your name alive."

"Don't worry, Father," he had said jokingly, "We will go on having children until you get your boy!" Now he wondered if the name Moradi was about to die.

He called Banu. "Go to Rana khanoom's room and bring me the Koran."

"Yes, Major."

Moradi leaned back and thought of his mother. No one understood him the way she had. She loved Rana, but her loyalty lay with her son, and he had a feeling she would have accepted Parisa, even liked her. He could use that kind of support these days as he dealt with yet another loss.

His heart felt heavy at the thought of Parisa. She had offered hope against hope, given him a new outlook on life's simple pleasures. At first, he attributed his excitement over her pregnancy to the prospect of finally having a boy. But he would have loved that child, no matter what it turned out to be. If that baby had lived, she could have been a little Parisa, her mere existence could have strengthened their union. As he pictured her alone in that small house, his heart filled with longing. Why was he sitting here sipping tea?

"What's taking you so long, girl?" he shouted.

A breathless Banu came back empty handed. "I'm sorry, sir, but I can't find it."

"Are you stupid?" he grunted. "How could you not find a book as large as that?"

"Can't figure out where Dayeh put it. I even went through all the drawers." She shrugged and threw her hands in the air. "It's not there."

Moradi couldn't be more annoyed. He put his tea back on the table so hard that it made a loud cracking sound. "I'm going to leave now, but you better find that Koran soon, or God knows what I may do to you and that old witch."

Ignoring Banu's crying, Moradi took his keys and left.

On the way to Parisa's, he tried to push away the new anxiety that crept into his heart. Months ago, when he and Rana had exchanged rough words on the phone, he told her there would be no divorce. At the time, he had dismissed what she said as pure anger, but now her words came back to haunt him. "If it's money you worry about, then relax. I don't want a *shahi* from you. You give me my freedom and all I'll want out of that house is the holy book your parents brought me, the one on which we swore to be loyal to one another." At the time, he thought she meant to remind him of his broken promise to God. Besides, that was such a cliché. Women threatened to take their Koran or "one stem of crystal sugar" in return for their freedom. Now he wondered.

The Moradi family took pride in their record of prolonged marriages and, as far has he knew, there had been no divorce. That was why rather than buying a new Koran, his parents had parted with the one from his mother's wedding. They trusted it would stay in the family forever.

The missing Koran had only annoyed him at first, but by the time he reached Parisa's, he knew it was serious. The signs had been there all along: The way Rana's face lost color at the mention of the missing book, the silence, and that strange glance she exchanged with her nanny had been a look of surprise, even bewilderment. *Taken upstairs to bless the packing?* Oh, what a fool they had taken him for!

Then again, wasn't he going a bit ahead of himself? What if Banu did find the book? How silly he would feel about this imaginary conspiracy and his crazy suspicions. No, the recent tragedies and all the stress had made him irrational. He needed to view the situation logically. Where could Rana possibly go with no money, no job, and two kids to care for? Besides, she was still his wife and would remain so until *he* decided otherwise. With the security regulations set by the secret service, all passengers had to send their documents to their respective airline at least twenty-four hours ahead of time, and Rana had gone to Tehran even a day earlier than needed. That left him plenty of time to think this through. If his suspicions were founded, that woman had underestimated him.

Chapter

· *Seventeen* ·

MEHRABAD AIRPORT had never seen a busier day, nor could it possibly have displayed a more diverse crowd. The annual swarm of pilgrims to Mecca had reached its peak. While the European passengers and young Iranian women paraded in the latest fashions, hauling their Christian Dior and Louis Vuitton luggage, there were rows of women on their way to the holy pilgrimage, their long black gowns and white veils giving them the look of oversized penguins.

The constant hum over the loudspeakers made it hard to understand a word. Most messages came across as an insignificant mumble and no one seemed to care.

"We'll be next," Rana's father said as a couple standing before them went through the door leading to the inspection area.

"When will they give back our passports?"

"Iran Air has them," he said and nodded to a room ahead of them. As soon as the guard motioned them in, he picked up his carry-on bag and said, "I'll wait for you in transit."

Rana nodded. With no Dayeh and no other help it was quite a task to hold on to Vida while carrying the baby.

Rana waited anxiously. Over her last days in Shiraz, Moradi had acted casually, as though she was only going as far as Tehran for another short visit and for the past couple of days, he didn't even bother to call. Once, when Vida fussed too much over missing her Peeshee, Rana rang the house in hopes that Banu would reassure her about the cat, but no one picked up. She imagined the girl down the alley with neighbors' maids and knew exactly where he'd be, too.

"I want to sit down," Vida said, shifting her weight from one leg to the other.

"I know, dear. It shouldn't be much longer."

"Where did Grandpa go?"

"I thought he was tired of standing and insisted he go first," Rana said. "He'll meet us on the other side." When she looked up, her father had already gone beyond the glass doors that separated the passengers from the rest. Yalda's head finally rested heavily on her mother's shoulder, a sign that the infant had fallen asleep. They would be next, though Rana had no idea how long that might take.

A porter pushing an elderly woman in a wheelchair approached. "Excuse me, ma'am, would you mind if we go through first?" And he nodded to the woman in the chair.

"Not at all," she said, and stepped aside. Something in that old woman's face resembled Dayeh. She had been such a great help all along. How easy this trip would have been if her nanny could accompany her. But America was on the other side of the world.

Her turn finally came and Rana took her children into a smaller room with three receiving booths, each occupied by someone in a dark blue uniform. The woman sitting inside the booth to her right motioned to her and while approaching, Rana looked around for her father. He must have gone ahead because two Iran Air agents constantly ushered the passengers into the transit area. Rana put the receipt for their documents on the counter.

The heavy-set woman eyed her with what Rana interpreted as sheer curiosity before handing her one passport.

"There should be two," Rana said and gave the woman a polite smile. "My daughter Vida has her own."

The clerk looked at her from above the rim of her glasses. "I'm afraid that's all I have for Moradi."

Leaning against the counter for support, Rana felt her knees shaking. "But I have the receipt for two," she said. "Could you please look again?"

The woman gave her a condescending look. "Ma'am, I know my job. The only document here is for you and baby Ameli. Sometimes, passengers are denied the exit permit. In which case, the passports aren't sent to us."

Rana stared at her for a few long seconds, feeling totally confused. "You can't be serious," she finally said and her voice was surprisingly high, making other passengers turn to look. She lowered her voice. "No one would issue—or deny—an exit permit to a child." The words came out without conviction. "I'm her mother and she's traveling with me!"

"I'm only doing my job, ma'am," the woman said and busied herself with the papers on her desk as if to dismiss her.

"I know you are," Rana said in an apologetic tone. "But there must be some mistake."

The woman looked up again, but this time, Rana noticed she stared over her shoulder at a point beyond her. Instinctively, she turned to see what had distracted the woman, and lost her breath at the sight of the two people who had just left the corner office marked, "Security." From the far end of the room, Moradi approached, accompanied by a heavy-set policeman, and they were headed straight toward her. Fear penetrated every cell of her body. A sinking feeling told her all had ended, but despite her strong intuition, she gave herself a chance to be wrong and took a step toward him, but as their eyes met, she knew.

"Hello, Rana," Moradi's sarcastic tone implied it had been a while since they last met.

"What's going on?" Rana said without bothering with any pleasantries. "What's this lady talking about? What happened to Vida's passport?"

Vida saw her father and ran to him, "Papa, you're going, too?"

He picked her up and held her in his arms before giving Rana a cold smile. "She won't need one. She's not going anywhere!" He reached into his pocket to produce the missing passport. Waving the document in the air, he gave her a piercing look and tucked it back into his pocket.

"Pardon me, Captain," the clerk said to Moradi. "I can't keep people waiting. Do you mind taking your discussion to the side?"

Moradi carried Vida a couple of steps away from the counter.

"What are you doing?" Rana said, still puzzled.

"I'm taking my daughter back," he said, and the fire in his eyes left no doubt that somehow he knew her plan.

"You're making a scene," she said in a hushed voice and rolled her eyes toward the other passengers. "Give me the passport. Papa's already checked in and waiting."

Moradi laughed. "Oh, you're more than welcome to join *Papá*. After all that plotting and planning, God knows you both deserve a nice, long vacation." His words had a perilous tone, and a wicked smile spread across his lips.

Unprepared, Rana realized that she needed to think fast, but felt too confused to do so. "What's the problem?" she asked for the lack of a better response.

"Problem?" he said and laughed. "I've just left your father's house. That good-for-nothing Dayeh of yours wouldn't tell me much, but it was what she *didn't* say that left me no doubt just who stole my father's Koran." He bent down to Rana's level and used an equally lowered voice. "A shameful theft, if you ask me." He gave her another mean smile. "Far beneath even *you*!"

So that book had led him to this, but still, he had no proof. She tried to keep her poise. "You're right about the Koran, it's in my suitcase, to keep us safe during this ordeal, and I was planning to bring it back. That's no reason to deny your daughter a holiday."

"A holiday, ha!" He threw his head back. "You don't really think I'm *that* stupid, do you?"

"I don't know what you mean."

"Oh, but you do." He smiled. "I came to Tehran on a mere hunch, but as luck would have it, I had the good fortune to bump into the young custodian of Mr. Eskandary's office." He nodded several times and broadened his smile. "You'd be amazed at what a couple of large bills can do to a servant's tongue."

Rana had completely forgotten about the young man who served tea at Mr. Eskandary's. So Moradi knew that their passports had gone to the lawyer's office. What else had that stupid young man told him?

"So, this is all because of what some servant told you?" Rana said, forcing a smile. Her pulse was now pounding in her temples, as if her brain was about to explode. How could Rana and her father have overlooked this possibility? Then again, who could have imagined a trusted lawyer's servant eavesdropping? "And you bought such nonsense?" She laughed nervously.

"What about stealing my Koran, is that also *nonsense*?"

"That was a gift to me at my wedding, therefore it is mine to—"

"Like hell it is," he shouted. Then, as if conscious of the onlookers, he lowered his voice. "That holy book belongs to the Moradi family," he said and nodding to Vida he added, "And so does she. I'll be damned if I'm going to lose her."

"You won't lose anything. Too bad the luggage has already gone

through, but don't you worry about your precious family posses-
sions. I'll send it back as soon as I unpack."

Vida seemed scared and Rana wished she could say something
reassuring to her. As if sensing danger, the child's initial joy had
vanished and she now squirmed under Moradi's grip. "Put me
down, Papa!" she begged.

Moradi ignored her and said to Rana, "Just where the hell
you plan to go doesn't interest me one bit, but if you think you can
sneak out of the country and take *my* daughter, you're a bigger fool
than I had thought."

Vida looked up. Her face was flushed and she looked as if she
was about to cry. What kind of an emotional scar would this leave
on her little girl? Vida had always been easy to bribe, but this was
serious.

"Take *your* baby and go wherever the hell you want, do whatever
will fix her problem." He wrapped his arm tightly around Vida's
shoulders. "But this one's coming back home to Shiraz." And he
took another step away. "I'll be damned if I'm going to lose another
child."

Rana felt disembodied and couldn't believe that the stranger
now holding her child hostage had been her man for years.

Moradi turned to walk away and she called after him, "Wait!"
With a few hurried steps she reached him. "Please don't do this,"
she pleaded, and immediately regretted it. His eyes were so cold
that her words froze inside her. She turned to Vida and tried a smile.
"You be a good girl and wait with your father. I'll be back as soon as
I find Grandpa."

She then turned back to him. "I don't know why you're doing
this, but I'm not going to leave my daughter like this. If she's not
going, then no one is. Just give me time to find Papa and tell him
the trip is cancelled."

Moradi shrugged. "Makes no difference to me. We'll be in the lobby."

Rana took her boarding pass, adjusted the baby's position on her shoulder, and rushed to the door at the other end of the room. With each passing moment, she felt more anxious. Would her husband keep his word and wait for her or was he already dragging Vida home? No sooner had she entered a larger area with shops all around than her worried father rushed to her.

"What took you so long?" he asked looking beyond her. "And where's Vida?"

"Farhad came for her."

His face turned pale. "What?"

"He knows, Papa. It's over."

He bit his lip, scanned the area and spotted a row of chairs near the wall. He took her elbow and motioned to them. Rana felt him trembling and deeply regretted the way she had delivered the shocking news. As soon as her father could grab the handle of a chair, he let go of her arm and lowered himself into it.

Breathless, he loosened his tie, undid the top button of his shirt, and gasped for air. "Now tell me."

Rana sat down and tried to sound calm. "Farhad found out about our plan." It surprised even her that the words did not sound half as horrible as she felt, as if the fear of giving her father another heart attack had reminded her of more immediate priorities. "I'm not sure how much he knows," she went on. "But apparently, Mr. Eskandary's manservant knew enough and Farhad bribed him into telling what he knew."

Her father slapped his forehead in disgust. "Curse to the devil!"

"Farhad has seized Vida's passport. It's okay, Papa, we'll have to cancel the whole deal."

He cupped his large hands over hers. "Slow down, dear. Where are they now?"

"Waiting in the lobby."

For as long as Rana had known her father he had never looked so baffled. The lost expression in his eyes could only mean that he, too, was confused by this new twist. "How? I mean, what prompted him to come to Tehran? And how the hell did that servant know?" More than anger, his voice had the tone of resignation, as if the answer no longer mattered.

"I'll tell you later. Please let's go now. I'm not sure how much longer he'll wait."

Her father seemed to be thinking hard as he scratched his forehead, taking his time. He would not even return her look and may have stayed that way much longer if there hadn't been another broken announcement. "Iran Air Flight- num... 973 to London and N.. York is now boarding at gate B1..." the nasal voice came through.

He looked up and squeezed Rana's hands. "That's you, honey. Go on. Take that baby and go to America and do everything as we had planned." He stood, put a hand on her back and gave it a gentle push. "I'll stay behind and deal with him. You go now."

Rana took a step back. "Go?" she exclaimed the word in protest. "And just where do you propose I go after abandoning my child?" She couldn't believe the tone she had taken with her father. She lowered her voice and said, "You know I've never disobeyed you, Papa, but do you have any idea what you're asking me to do? God took my Marjan, but no one can make me abandon any of my children."

"Oh, sweetheart," he said, shaking his head. "Nobody is suggesting you abandon her."

"What then?" she said and glared back.

"You have a return ticket. All I'm suggesting is to go ahead. Not only will you return and prove the man wrong, but also the break will be good for you and it will also give you the final word on what can be done for the baby. It was not easy to make her appointments and I want you to make sure she benefits from them."

Rana stared at the sleeping infant and felt a tug at her heart. Under those garments hid a tiny leg in desperate need of help. Could she deprive Yalda of a chance to be seen by those who might be able to help her? Of all the people involved in this mess, Yalda mattered most and she had no voice here. Dr. Fard had said they would not do anything until Yalda was much older. He was a good doctor, but how much did he know of surgeries? Rana owed it to her little girl to make sure.

Her father's voice broke her chain of thought. "True that you won't be able to stay as planned, but why not go through with the medical consultations?" He thought a little and added, "Going back at this moment won't solve anything. It will only hurt your infant and in a way, it'll prove Farhad right. All he has is the words of a servant. Nothing is documented and he hasn't seen Yalda's birth certificate, either." He motioned to the lobby. "I'll go there and make sure Vida is okay. When you come back in few weeks, you'll prove your husband wrong. Meanwhile, this'll give everyone a chance to think things over."

She shook her head. "Vida is all alone," she said. She swallowed hard and whispered, "Badri will make her life a living hell!"

"Not if I'm alive!"

"Oh, Papa, what could *you* possibly do across the miles?"

"What miles? I'll go to Shiraz if necessary. As long as I have taken time from my work, who's to say your mom and I can't pay our little girl a visit?" He forced a smile. "I don't know what exactly that boy has told Farhad, but it's all talk. He has no proof." He gave her shoulder another gentle push. "Go on, sweetheart. Listen to your old father and do what's right. I will call your Aunt Malak right away and ask her to meet you at the other end."

Yalda started to wiggle and Rana gently rocked her back to sleep.

A second announcement came through, calling London passengers to gate B1.

"Go on, my dear. If you miss this flight it'll be hard to find another good connection to New York." He held her head between both hands and kissed her forehead. "May God keep you safe." He bent down and kissed the top of the baby's head before taking a couple of steps back.

"I can't leave her like this," Rana said, yet the resignation in her tone indicated she had already agreed to do just that. "At least, let me say good bye." And she moved toward the exit.

"There is no time for that," her father said and held her arm. "Stop tormenting yourself, my dear."

"Just leave her?" Rana whispered, more to herself.

Tears dripped down her father's quivering chin. "I will give her many kisses from you," he said and wrapped both arms around the mother and child. "Go on. Go before it's too late."

Rana watched him pull back and walk away and before she could say another word, the door had closed. Alone in a crowd of strangers, she was reminded of her first day of school, when a tall wooden door had closed behind her father. Once again, she stood there with the feeling that her single connection to humanity had just been severed and that by walking away from that door, she would enter a world that offered no guarantee for being rescued.

Approaching her gate, she looked out the window and saw the bus waiting to drive the last passengers to the huge plane sitting in the middle of the hazy runway. Now the sound of jet engines could be heard and she saw a plane take off in the distance. As her eyes followed the soaring jet, her mind raced. There was still time to run. She could go to Shiraz and make sure her daughter wasn't harmed more than she already had been. Or should she go forward, knowing she'd soon be back? Would she see Vida again?

Outside, the summer air felt heavy with the oily fumes of engines. Before boarding the transit bus, Rana stopped to look back at the large windows and imagined her little girl standing somewhere out there, waving good-bye. She brought her fingers to her lips and blew a kiss to the dark windows. "Mommy will be back," she whispered and turning to the bus she nearly missed the steps through a flood of tears. Someone took her arm and helped her up the stairs while another offered her a seat. Yalda woke up and started to cry. Rana pressed her face into the baby's gown and her sobs were drowned in the engine noise as the bus drove away.

"Please secure the baby in that bassinette before doing your own seatbelt," a British hostess instructed Rana while closing the overhead bin with a loud thud.

Rana went through the motions and was sure none of this was real.

As the plane took off and soared, the blurry city lights sank into the darkness below and Damavand became a magnified silhouette in the chain of mountains. Rana felt numb, as if she had left all her emotions in the darkness below. Why did she continue to stare out the window when there was nothing to see? She recalled a verse from an old poem:

They describe in many ways, how a soul leaves one's body to fly
But I witnessed my own soul depart, I saw this with my very eye.

Part Two
Yalda

· *Eighteen* ·

CHICAGO, AUGUST 1997

I TELL MY NAME TO THE WET LEAVES on the sidewalk of Sheridan Road, I shout it to the cars that pass by, churning up rain, but what I really need is to pound it back into my own head. "My name is Yalda Ameli. It is Yalda Ameli." I know what's happening is not a nightmare, but it has all the right elements of one. This time, the storm has damaged more than a few trees in our backyard, it has uprooted my family tree.

A fierce Chicago wind crawls under my skin and the drizzle has glued my shirt to my skin. Did I drop my jacket or have I rushed out of Mom's apartment without it?

A man passes me on a bike and I shout after him, "Moradi is a pretty weird name, isn't it?" He turns his head, but is fast gone. I'll never get used to this. Moradi? What happened to Ameli? It hasn't been the easiest, but I've worn the name proudly. I feel lost without it.

A car honks. I move back to the sidewalk from the middle of the street and shout at the driver. "I am Yalda Ameli." He sticks his middle finger out the window and speeds by.

I repeat my name to the tiny drops of rain dangling from branches, to a young boy who passes by. He's wearing a hooded coat and turns back to stare at this talking lunatic. It's hard to think straight, but there's no doubt that I heard my mother correctly and that she meant what she said.

I'm walking, walking, endlessly walking. I must have gone down every block in north Evanston, talking to myself, shouting my questions and crying like a mad woman. I pass Central Street and am now heading north toward Gilson Park. It is late afternoon and though it has stopped raining, the wind stings.

At the park, I sit under a tree near the shore and try to picture what I don't know. We moved from downtown to Evanston when I was in third grade. I know this park well. Mom used to watch me play here. But all of a sudden it is no longer filled with good memories, nor is it the place where I come to compose letters to my late grandfather. Today the park looks more like a graveyard and even Lake Michigan has turned black. Did Mom bring me here so I wouldn't care about not having a family? Was the love I received from her nothing but a bribe?

Who is my father?

In second grade, I once came home crying because a kid told me I had a weird name, but Mom said some people were just stupid. To this day, if someone raises an eyebrow at my name, I try to think of Mom's response. Now all of a sudden I'm the one who feels stupid.

In all these years, I've never seen Mom cry. So this morning when I walked into her apartment and found her crying, I feared for her life, or my own, and prepared for the worst. I dropped my heavy bag of books and ran to her. "What's the matter, Mom?"

Cupping her face in both hands, she leaned further onto the kitchen table. "Sit down, Yalda. We need to talk." Her muffled voice was heavy. Different.

What was wrong? A million questions raced into my head, but horror wouldn't let me ask. Maybe something had happened to Grandma?

I plopped into the nearest chair.

"I have waited your whole life for the right moment to share what I'm about to tell you," Mom said this formally. She had the look of someone about to admit guilt in court.

I waited patiently, like the lawyer I am about to become, then suddenly had a feeling I didn't want to hear what she was about to say. I studied her white roots in need of coloring, her clipped nails, her trembling clasped hands.

She took in a deep breath and said, "I realize I may have waited too long, but at some point I had to beg for your forgiveness." She sounded sadder than I had ever heard her.

So it had nothing to do with Grandma, or her own health. I exhaled hard. *Forgiveness?* This must be the moment she would reveal the secret I had suspected. I wanted to shout, "Finally!" but needed to stay neutral and let her talk without worrying about how I'd react.

"Don't worry, Mom. I'm a gown up. This is the right time."

She cried harder. "Right time? No, my love, I've done so much wrong that no time will ever be right."

I patted the back of her hand. "Come on, Mom. What can be so bad that you can't tell your own daughter?"

"You had a right to know who you are, Yalda. Now I don't even know where to begin."

"Who I am? The suspense is killing me!"

"Maybe I was right to take you away." She buried her face in her hands. "But I shouldn't have separated you from your sister."

I have a sister? Too stunned to respond, I held my breath. Mom lifted her head and her worried eyes met mine. I saw deep fear in them, as though she expected me to strike her.

"I had a phone call today," she said, but seemed unable to finish her sentence.

I rubbed the back of her cold hand. Whatever this phone call had been, it must have shocked her enough to make her talk nonsense.

"I don't have a sister," I said as calmly as I could.

She looked down at her hands and nodded repeatedly. "You do." Something in her voice rang too true to be dismissed.

Fear paralyzed me. *Has my mother suddenly gone mad?* "What's wrong with you, Mom?"

"I'm not crazy, if that's what you're thinking. You need to know your true identity."

I sat there, numb, confused even, and began to listen to a bizarre story that made no sense, a tale about how she abandoned her other daughter, husband and home, a soap opera I had no desire to hear.

Her husband?

My head was spinning. I have a sister *and* a father? There were no words to react with and no sound came through my throat.

Most people like to talk about their roots, but not my mother. Except for the fact that I was born in Iran and that she was widowed when I was an infant, Mom hasn't shared much. My last name doesn't have a significant story behind it, at least it didn't till now. A single parent in a foreign country, my mother did her best to give me a normal life. I've always been curious about her past, about who my father was and why I have never seen any pictures of him. Knowing that she married a cousin—or so I'd been told—explained why our last names were the same as her father's, but she never answered all of my questions. Her story about burning my father's pictures so she'd forget the tragedy of his loss had always sounded strange. I've taken every chance to drill her about the past, but all she ever told me was that a bad car accident took my father.

The lack of an extended family wasn't unusual for an immigrant, but all along I've had a feeling there was more to Mom's story. What was in her past that made her so reluctant to talk?

I don't know when but at some point the sounds in my head prevented me from hearing her words. She was talking about my sisters. Now there were two? No. One is dead. Suddenly I was enraged and had the unbearable urge to get out of that place, to be as far from my mother as I possibly could. Did I say anything before leaving? Did I slam the door?

I must still be in shock. This isn't like me to walk aimlessly, talk to strangers or shout in public. I'll soon be a lawyer and that alone has taught me enough about order. I had two sisters? I repeat their names, "Vida. Marjan. Which one did she say died? Mom has been married for all these years! She must have told me a lot more, but at this point those are the big facts that stick out. What made her keep this from me? And more importantly, why didn't Grandpa Ameli tell me while he had the chance?

Grandpa was the closest I ever came to knowing a father. He was a physician back in Iran and the best grandfather in the universe. I remember his visits vividly as those were the only times I came to sample having a father. I remember our trips to FAO Schwarz downtown Chicago and coming home with practically half the toys in the store. On two of his trips, grandma accompanied him. She was nice, but our relationship didn't come anywhere close to what I had with Grandpa. He was the only person who spoke at length about my father, or at least the father he invented for me out of kindness. "Mommy will be sad if you ask her such questions, but I'll tell you anything you want to know." Some days, we walked around Gilson Park and he painted the most beautiful pictures for my young mind to keep. He told me my father loved having a brand new baby girl and how proud he would have been to see me all grown up. When I questioned Grandma,, she said she didn't remember. We didn't believe her, not until she was diagnosed with Alzheimer's. When my aunts called, they spoke Farsi to Mom and if I answered the phone, they only asked, "Ha arr yoo?" Mom tried to teach me Farsi, but once I started kindergarten, I forgot the few words I knew. As a teenager, I used to imagine all kinds of dark secrets, and didn't even leave out the horrible possibility of being an illegitimate child.

Just as I was forming more detailed questions to ask my grandfather, he had a heart attack in Iran and died. His loss broke my heart and I am not sure I grieved for him any less than Mom did. I don't think I'll ever stop missing him. Mom was a mess for a year, so I grieved alone. I found a semblance of comfort in continuing to write to him even though he was gone. I still do that and it helps me to unload my problems. Grandma never visited after that and now she doesn't even know any of her family. She lives with one of Mom's sisters. I doubt I'll ever see her again.

Once my awkward teens were behind me, I relaxed about the past and decided to leave the matter for a time when I would be rich enough—brave enough—to travel to Iran, see Grandma, meet my aunts, and visit Grandpa's tomb. All along, I knew that if my mother were to tell me more about the past, it would have to be on her terms.

There's no one in the park today. It's too cold and I feel utterly lonely. Even Paul wouldn't understand how I feel. I don't have my watch, but the darkening sky tells me it's time to go back.

Like a solved riddle, now that I know the truth everything seems too simple, too clear. Mom never went back to Iran, not even for her father's funeral. She didn't have much contact with her sisters, except for a call at Persian New Year and occasionally on her birthdays. Why wasn't she in touch with old friends? Surely there were people in Iran who could have visited. Even here, she knows few people and mostly keeps to herself. Just last month I jokingly asked if she'd met any handsome guys at the clinic. I should have wondered why such an innocent question made her so angry. Anyone with half a mind would have seen beyond her bogus tales, but I grew up with her stories and through repetition, they became my reality.

As I near Mom's neighborhood, I realize that the only remaining truth is her immigrating to the US, where I saw specialists and later received treatment for my weird leg. I feel pain just thinking about it. Surgery after surgery and the long nights when pain kept me awake. As I learn more about a lifetime of deception, her loving support and constant rewards lose their value. For years, the only life I knew was going from town to town, hospital to hospital, all in hopes of being normal. Normal? How many normal people have a father they don't know about? How many of them don't even know their own last name?

Where was my father when they cut open his little girl's leg to install screws in her bones?

I try to invent a face for the man. But how? I hate him, so why should I care that someday I may see him? But as much as I want to deny myself any positive thoughts, the fact remains that, loving or not, there's a father out there, a big sister, and a whole other family. As a child, I used to imagine a crowd around our Thanksgiving table, a Christmas tree with many presents under it, and all the similar scenes I had seen on TV. I invented relatives who could remember Mom's house in Iran, had saved pictures of her wedding, and knew the father I had lost. I even tried to love the ghostly images of the man I didn't know. Why is it so hard to feel anything for him now that I know he exists?

Rush hour traffic interrupts Sheridan Road's calm. It's getting colder and I wish I had my jacket. I pull down the sleeves of my sweater and bunch it in my fist. *What is it like to have a sister?* The only other relative I know is Mom's aunt in New York, who now lives in a convalescent home. As I near my mother's apartment, I feel the resentment rise within me. Whatever her reason might have been for such vicious secrecy, I don't believe she was ever planning to come clean. What was in that phone call that made her change her mind?

—

I find Mom in her kitchen, exactly where I had left her. The faint light coming through the window defines her silhouette. As I turn on the bright fluorescent light, she squints and looks up from the table where she has surrounded herself with crumpled tissues. She wipes her red nose and looks at me. Her eyes are bloodshot, her lips swollen and the sight is more heartbreaking than anything I have prepared for. I've gathered all my strength for an argument, but what could I possibly say to this broken woman who seems so bitterly lonely? Instinctively, I rush over and wrap my arms around her.

"I have no hope for redemption," she says under her breath. "And I can't possibly expect your forgiveness." She is now sobbing.

Her trembling body feels thinner than it looks and as I hold her tighter, I think this must be how it feels when picking up an injured bird. "Please don't cry," I say and sound silly. Her cold hands grasp mine and for some time we both just rock and shed silent tears.

I wait for some time before gently unlatching her fingers from around mine. "Let me make some tea."

She only nods and holds her head in both hands.

As I fill the kettle, I can't help but wonder about all the broken hearts that a good cup of tea must have soothed. *Forgiveness?* Where should I begin? I light a match but forget to use it until the flame reaches my finger. I throw away the curled-up match and light another. My thoughts aren't about whether I can forgive any of this. The woman I'm about to have tea with is no longer just

"Mom". Tonight I'm meeting the real Rana, the fugitive wife, the struggling immigrant, and the lonely woman, who has been hiding behind a graceful smile. She'd better prepare to tell me the real story of my life.

While I search for Mom's special glass and the dried fruits she takes with her tea, I steal glances at her. She is leaning forward, her elbows on the table, her chin resting on two fists. After a couple of minutes, she picks up a few crumpled tissues, throws them in the basket under the table and straightens her back, sitting taller. Always a proud woman. I should know her better than to expect defeat now. When I put her tea on the table, Mom thanks me and wraps her fingers around the hot glass, as if in need of its warmth.

"I'm glad you came back," she says.

Where did she think I might go?

"Why, Mom?" I sound hoarse and the words come out like a soft cry. She must know what I'm asking her.

"Aw," she says, and that simple sound reflects a million inexplicable reasons. She wipes a teardrop with the tip of her fingers. "I could talk all night, but what I have to say won't make much sense to you." She takes a sip of her hot tea and glances over at the refrigerator door, where a magnet holds a faded picture of me on my fourth birthday. "If God can hear me, I pray that you will never have to live through anything close to what I have."

I stare at her hands, the bulging veins and tiny dry wrinkles. I have not looked at my mother this closely for some time. When did she start to age?

"For so many years, you had more than enough to cope with. The last thing you needed on top of all the surgery and rehab was to deal with the ugly truth." She takes a sip of her tea then continues to stare at my picture as if to make that a focal point for her thoughts. "Maybe the reason why mothers can't stop protecting their children is because they never accept the fact that their little ones grow up."

A smile spreads over her lips, but her sad eyes remain unchanged. "To me, you will forever be that tiny thing, the one who detested anyone with a stethoscope around their neck."

"I still do," I say, and try a smile. I think of the stories my mother used to invent, the rewards she promised just to make me see the doctors. And see them. And see them again.

She drinks her tea and the distant look in her eyes tells me she is not going to say more. Give Mom a choice and she'd love to end the discussion here and now.

"I have a lot of questions."

She nods.

"Why not start with telling me a few facts about your life with … *him*?" I don't know how to address the man. That he is a living and breathing person makes it harder to talk about him. *Who is he*? "There must have been some good days, maybe even some form of love. After all, you're still married to him, aren't you?"

She puts down the glass. "Now there's an interesting subject, no?" She attempts to clear the mess she has made, picking up more pieces of tissue, smoothing the wrinkles on her skirt, and centering her tea glass in its saucer. I am not about to take my inquisitive eyes off her. I want to give her the chance to speak at her own pace, but my patience is wearing thin.

"Love is one thing to you and quite another to someone with my background—not to mention my age." She smiles again and for a split second I can see a younger woman. "Impossible as it may be, you need to put yourself in my place—a teenager in a glass jar." She closes her eyes for a few seconds and I know there must be a million visions behind her eyelids, but all I picture is the huge glass jar with a folded body inside it. She is now talking with the same voice that once told me fairy tales.

"I went to school, and I came home. That was my life. Not that the other girls had a whole lot more, but being the youngest of four girls, too many eyes were on me. I would do anything to gain some independence. So I got married."

"Is that why you married your cousin Moradi, or whatever it is?"

She turns to me and her face is flushed. "I didn't marry my cousin."

Now I'm really confused.

"The man I married was an army officer from Shiraz. Major Farhad Moradi." She looks at me hard. "Your father."

Moradi? No matter how many times I repeat the name, it still sounds ridiculous. More-odd-ee. How appropriate! Indeed it's odder than the name I have. I don't want to be a More-odd-ee! What did she do? Dump him? I wonder what would make a woman take her child away, give her a new identity and live a hard and lonely life?

She adopted me! The mere possibility of that makes me want to laugh, but the best I can do is not to cry. "Did you love him?"

She lifts her left hand and stares at her bare ring finger. "I married him when I was twenty-one and we stayed together a bit more than nine years. Then I left."

It is odd to picture my mother being married when she was four years younger than I am. I repeat my question, "Was there any love at all?"

"Honey, we're talking about a Middle Eastern husband. He *owned* me."

"Owned you?" I exclaim. "How can you even say that?"

"I don't mean it literally, but men treating their wives like their property wasn't a big deal to us." She looks at me. "As we say, 'a mass funeral is like a wedding'!"

I am used to her strange paraphrases and sometimes even understand their meaning, but today I'm at my wit's end. "Mass funeral?" I repeat with bitter sarcasm.

"It sounds awful in English, but it means that when everyone shares the same misery, it's not so terrible." A wan smile parts her lips. "At least he treated me right and even seemed proud to show me off." For a brief moment, she has a dreamy look and I wonder if she misses those days.

"Judging by the fact that you're still married to the man, in a way he *did* own you. Why didn't you just divorce him?"

Mom shrugs. "Married, divorced, it doesn't make a bit of a difference, does it?"

"Doesn't it?"

She straightens her back in dignity. "He has his life and I went away to find mine."

"What about … your other daughter?" I say, unsure how else to say this.

"Poor Vida," she says and the name's ending comes out more like a deep sigh. "That wasn't planned." She closes her eyes again and her face shows the pain of remembrance. "You and I were to go back to Iran. In a way, he kept Vida hostage to ensure my return. But then things changed." Her expression now goes from sorrow to resentment. "He turned that child against me just so Vida would accept his other wife as her mother and …"

"Wait a damn minute," I exclaim. "He had *another* wife?" My father isn't just some dead-beat, he's also a *bigamist*? The deep hurt in Mom's expression is answer enough. I suddenly realize that this story, out of the .stone ages as it may sound to me, is more Rana's tragedy than mine. While Mom seems to dive deep into another dark well of unspoken memories, I realize I must hold back my shock and do my best not to interrupt her.

"I wanted to go back. I might have. I mean, if for nothing else, just to bring Vida here."

A long silence follows. I close my eyes and see a little girl standing on the curb, waiting for her mother to turn around and take her hand. A motherless childhood. How would I feel if it had been me she had left behind? The image makes me feel one with that girl and my anger is back before I can stop myself. "But you didn't go back to her, did you?" My voice has an accusing tone and I can hear the defense lawyer in my head shouting, *"Objection, your Honor! Mrs. Moradi is not on trial here."*

Oh, but she is! Putting myself in Vida's place leaves me little sympathy for her mother. No matter how I look at it, Vida is the real victim. Rana is on trial not just for what she has done to me, but also for having abandoned my sister. In fact, she has robbed us both.

"I couldn't," she says, and leans closer to stare into my eyes. "I could not—would not—take a chance. Yes, it was *my* decision to stay here with you. Somebody had to do it. My baby needed good medical care."

"Oh, no," I say and push away the space between us with the palm of my hand as if to ward her off. "You're not going to pin this on me!" I get up and begin pacing. "If you ended up in a lousy marriage, decided to leave the country and sell out one of your kids in the process, I can try to understand. But don't you go around saying it was all for Yalda. My first operation was done when I was seven. You could have gone back. So don't go telling me you abandoned your daughter just so I could receive treatment all those years later."

Mom is staring at me and I'm not sure if she's shocked or disappointed.

"No," she finally says and looks pensive, as if unsure of how to explain this. I have seen this faraway look on her face whenever she wants to explain something that is too Persian for the American me. "I didn't *abandon* Vida. You could say it was she who discarded me."

"Come on, Mom. Little girls don't discard their mothers. Did you ever try to reach out to her?"

She shakes her head. "I tried. Each time I got her on the phone, she just cried and cried. I knew she missed me as much as I missed her. I told her how much I loved her. I told her to be patient and promised I'd go back to bring her here. It didn't take long for Vida to stop crying. Then for a while she didn't come to the phone at all. On her birthday I called, but that was when she asked me not to call her any more. I still kept on calling, asking whoever picked up about how my little girl was doing. Finally, I was told by your aunt Badri to stop calling, that Vida was happy living with her father and … and she had started to call that woman 'Maman'."

She wipes her tears. "After that, even the maid wouldn't tell me much." Her voice breaks and she starts to weep again. "Still, I couldn't give up. I called my father and he sadly confirmed that. He told me about how flexible children can be, especially Vida, who had always been her father's pet. Grandpa tried to make me understand how nicely Vida was adjusting. They sure knew how to train that child." It takes her a minute before she can talk again. "All the gifts I sent for her birthdays or *Norooz* were returned, but that didn't stop me. I refused to believe what Grandpa told me. How could my child forget her own mother if I continued to miss her more and more? When my father told me she no longer needed me, I thought he just said that to put my mind at ease. But I also knew he had a point when he said having two mothers is only going to confuse her. For some time past her eighteenth birthday, I secretly hoped she would practice her rights as an adult and finally contact me. When she didn't, I stopped writing. She never called." She takes in a deep breath. "Not until today."

Resentment takes over and Mom stops crying. She looks drained, but I want her to tell me all of it.

"What made her call today?"

"My first thought was that something bad must have happened to your father. But that wasn't it." Her lips parted in the saddest smile I have ever seen. "My Vida is getting married." The sorrow in her voice is so deep, it's as if this news isn't any better than what she expected.

"I'd think that would make you happy," I say.

"I don't know how to feel. How does a mother walk her child from nursery school to the wedding *sofreh*?"

For a moment I remove myself from her story and try to imagine how she feels, but my shock at all the new findings is too deep to ignore.

"She called out of nowhere, introduced herself and invited me to attend her wedding." She takes in another deep breath.

"What did you say?" I am as excited about this as I remember being at some of the twists and turns of her strange fairytales.

She shrugs. "What could I say? I had no words. This time it was me who cried and cried. I desperately want to believe that her invitation is a sign of maturity, that she has finally seen everything clearly and needs her real mother by her side. But I'm not stupid. She sounds too happy to need me."

For the first time today, I can understand some of what my mother is saying. I've lived my life with one parent. Mom has been alone. But Vida is different. She had a whole clan to make her happy. I can't believe how jealous I feel at the mere thought of it. "Who knows?" I say more to myself. "Deformed or not, even I might have been happier living under my father's roof." As I think more, my anger is back and I make no attempt at removing the sting from my words. "But nobody asks a baby what she wants, do they? Guess I'll never know how it would have been to live with my father's love."

"Love?" She glares at me as though I've uttered a forbidden word. "Do I have to spell it out for you?" She turns her face away. "His love went elsewhere! He never even took a close look at you."

She stops for a moment and her next words come out in a painful whisper. "What do you think made me register you as Ameli? That man didn't even bother to get you a birth certificate!"

This I'm sure is not true. How could a father not love an innocent baby? Mom is being cruel. She's just trying to stir me against him as he has done with Vida. My father, dead or alive, must have loved me. This is so infuriating that I no longer care to discuss it. I put my head in my hands and am now bawling uncontrollably.

A moment passes before I feel my mother's hand on my hair.

"Shhh," she whispers, and begins to softly stroke my hair. "I'm so sorry, sweetheart. I had hoped to never have to tell you any of this. I knew it would break your heart. Do you see now why I had to lie to you?"

She wraps her arms around me. With my cheek against her bosom, I think how wonderful it would be to return to being a fetus, to curl up and hide in the darkness of a womb, to never be born.

She kisses my hair. I want to push her away, but instead I lean deeper into her. My soul shrinks back inside - - a little fatherless child. As I draw comfort from my mother's warmth, I seek relief in the only refuge I have ever known.

—

I have no idea how late it is, but suddenly feel hungry. My mother and I have talked, cried, and finally reached a semblance of composure. I want to cry a little for Marjan, the sister who died a long time ago and the daughter Mom never stopped grieving for. I want to cry a little for Rana, the woman who is left with no one but a daughter who doesn't know her and another who's been kept at a distance. But most of all I want to cry for this clear image of baby Yalda. My childhood, despite being tainted with excruciating pain and doctors and hospitals, has been okay. Mom made sure I'd grow up to remember only the good. She gave me ample rewards after each surgery and was always there for me. For years I've managed to tuck away the bad days. But tonight I'm back to those tiny gray rooms with the fluorescent lights. My leg begins to ache and I wonder if this is just my imagination.

"You must be exhausted," Mom says in the soothing tone she has used over the years. "Why don't you go and take a nice shower while I prepare something to eat?" It's a strange request in the middle of a discussion that could go on forever, but maybe right now she needs to be alone as much as I do. Maybe a shower is just what I need to unwind. She looks worn out. We will have the entire night to talk.

I nod and get up. "Please don't cook, Mom. I'm so hungry, leftovers sound great."

"Okay, I'll warm up the soup."

Upstairs, I run the water and wait for it to get hot before I undress and step into the shower. My body finally folds under the weight of this new sorrow and I sit down on the tile floor, wrap my arms around my shoulders and cry hard. *He didn't want me!* It isn't that my father didn't care what happened to my leg, or that he neglected getting me registered. No. He simply never wanted me. The pouring water washes my hair, my face, my tears and the sound of it drowns my whimper.

There seems to be no end to these tears. For a long time I just sit there and let it all out, but as the water begins to cool, I realize it's been long enough. When I turn the water off, the silence makes my ears buzz. I step out and put on my bathrobe. Mom must have bought me new bathroom slippers because I haven't seen these white ones before. That's my Mom, never saying much, but always buying things to tell me she cares, spoiling me.

"You out?" Mom calls from the kitchen.

She has set a small table with two bowls and a small pot of Osh. I feel cold and welcome the heat my favorite soup sends down my throat. We eat in silence except for when she offers me some bread and cheese. "Eat something solid or hunger will wake you in the middle of the night."

I nod and take a piece of flatbread.

After dinner, I wash the dishes while Mom brews another pot of tea. I feel calm, light even, and am ready to ask more questions. We take our tea to the family room. She brings me a small afghan and wraps it around me then grabs a dishtowel to squeeze the water out of my hair. "I don't know how you young people just leave your hair to dry without catching your death!"

I smile sadly and thank her. As we sip tea, she begins to tell me more without being asked. It's as if releasing the memories is helping her, too. Little by little, she tries to untangle my old web of questions, adding love, and offering solace.

"Dayeh loved you the most," she says and looks into the distance as if she can see her old nanny. "She always chanted an old verse to you:

I have a girl shah—the king - doesn't have

She has a face, mah—the moon - doesn't have!"

I smile at how I've always found the moon to be a strange metaphor for beauty. Mom uses the word 'mah' in reference to the utmost of beauty and the purest of nice. I may never see Dayeh and she won't know how her moon daughter has turned into an ordinary American girl. How is it possible to miss someone I've never even known?

I want to believe there was no way for me to find out any of this, but know that's not true. Somewhere deep inside I have always sensed there were secrets. Maybe as a small child I needed to believe my mother's stories, but doubts grew as did I. Something was never right and I knew it. There were ways. I could have contacted old Aunt Malak in New York. I could have tracked down Mom's American friends who gradually returned from Shiraz.

Oh, what's the point of all this? I didn't do anything and went on pretending, coping and accepting my fate.

"Remember when you saw the psychiatrist?" Mom asks.

How could I forget? As a troubled teen, I had to see the woman so she could help me cope with my medical problems or with the fact that even after surgery I would continue to walk with a minor limp, that I was never a member of a sports team, or that no one asked me out on a date. It was thanks to that woman that I finally agreed to that final operation.

"She told me you weren't ready to know," Mom goes on. "In fact, we both worried that the shock would push you over the edge."

I can see that. I'm not too far from the edge right now.

Mom lets out a deep sigh. "So now that you know, maybe you and I should both go back for Vida's wedding."

I can't believe she's said it. At this very moment, I see that entire country as one man. To me, that land and its whole nation is nothing but the father who wouldn't bother to register his baby girl. "You go ahead, Mom. Not me. I'm not wanted over there, remember?"

Mom opens her mouth to say something, but I stop her by holding my hand up and leave the room.

As I lay on my bed, I am back to another bed that is much too large for me. I count glass jars of gauze, alcohol and cotton swabs. There's the box of latex gloves and the framed pictures of animals. A sharp needle pokes my skin, the fat nurse holds me too tight. Butterfly balloons and the cuddly bears can't make the pain go away. The tiniest details are all there, but somehow the face of little Yalda has always been someone else's. For the first time she is really me, and more importantly, a part of me is still *her*. I'll need to take my time and revisit the dark corner where she's been hiding. I'll have to know her all over again.

The door to the hallway is open and a column of light spills into my room. I allow images of little Yalda to visit me again. There she stands on the bare floor, the poor crooked thing, the baby Yalda of my mother's passport, the infant with and without a father. As she takes her wobbly step, her body shifts and moves sideways before it goes down like a sinking paper boat. The movement allows her shorter leg to touch the ground, but she tilts, slips, and falls.

Chapter

· ℕ*ineteen* ·

GRADUATION COULDN'T HAVE BEEN TIMELIER since it has provided the distraction Mom and I desperately need. I somehow manage to maintain a calm face for her sake, but calm I am not. Mom calls every day, though we both avoid the subject of my father. The fact that we need to talk about that is a mutual understanding, but I've spent most of the past few days at school and with Paul. I haven't been able to tell him what I now know. It's too confusing as it is and I can't share something that still doesn't make sense. If it weren't for Paul, I'm not sure how I would cope with these final days of school and my unfinished work. He has helped me with the final touches on my paper. His peaceful presence and undemanding affection give me a chance to sort my thoughts and to come to terms with my new findings. As changed as I feel, life seems the same. I don't know what I feel. I wouldn't call it sad, yet can't think of another name for it, either. I have never been so puzzled about anything, which may explain my sudden interest in memories that were tucked away.

For a week after that talk with Mom, the last thing I could focus on was law, any law. What a useless subject I've devoted my life to!

Law knows nothing about emotions, it does nothing to protect a helpless infant in Iran, and it sure as hell could never make a father love his unwanted child.

During the past few days, I've been busy with my own investigation into baby Yalda's life. I didn't think my medical history would reveal anything new, still, that's where I began my research. Multiple visits to the hospital and contacting the office of the pediatrician who is still practicing revealed nothing significant. Old files and x-rays meant little to my untrained eyes and the young intern helping me had to explain some of the images. I saw pins and screws where they had broken the bone to do the elongation of my leg and all of a sudden the old pain was back with full force. That was the first time, but I continued to feel it on and off over the next week. One night, I had a nightmare about my leg being drilled and woke up in fright. I stared into the darkness, and although the fear had vanished, the pain was there. I'm sure that's a psychosomatic thing because I have no pain when I'm happy, my minor limp is unnoticeable and all that anyone else can see is a negligible scar on my calf.

While checking my medical records I paid close attention to family history. There was no mention of my father's name anywhere in those files. The only name I saw besides Mom's, was Grandpa's when he took care of a few bills that were not covered by Mom's insurance. What was I looking for?

I am at my small apartment downtown and Paul is here to help me finish the dreaded paper. He knows so much more about Intellectual Property, a topic that seems to constantly change, and I swear I'll never have anything to do with it. A few minutes ago, as I was organizing some documents and explaining my non-existent progress, he asked, "What is going on with you, Yalda?"

The question came out of the blue, but his voice echoed a concern that must have been brewing for days. I knew that was my chance to talk. Maybe that's precisely what I need, to let it all out, to confide in someone outside the family. Instead, I shook my head and said, "Nothing. Why?"

He stared at me with those blue eyes for a few seconds, then diverted his attention back to the stack of papers on the table.

I stood behind him and gave him a tight hug, but he only patted the back of my hand.

Paul understands me enough to know something is wrong. We have lived in the same building for three years, and over the past year, we seem to be living together as he spends all his time here. I love having him around, and if I thought Mom could handle it, I would ask him to move in. Mom pretends she doesn't know about him and I know that's only because she's hoping someday I'll find a nice Iranian-American. I love Paul and don't normally keep secrets from him. But these new discoveries are too bizarre and I'd hate for him to judge my family. Maybe in the dark ages an innocent newborn could be rejected based on gender or it was no big deal for a man to take multiple wives, but not in this day and age. *What kind of a man is my father?*

When a few minutes pass in utter silence, Paul turns around and puts his arm around me. "You would tell me if there was a problem, wouldn't you?" He waits a few seconds then slaps the stack of notes with his free hand. "Damn it, Yalda! Your happiness is far more important than this silly project."

I chuckle. "Well, then, we better finish the silly project because right now that would make me really happy."

He looks at me, his kind eyes urging me to change my mind. When I don't say more, he finds a pen and pulls a file from the stack.

We start to work and I'm suddenly conscious of the fact that with all the craziness around me, Paul may be my only hope for happiness. In the beginning, I thought our physical attraction had a lot to do with being so different. He's tall, fair and casual, while I'm small, dark and too fussy about my clothes. I had seen how other girls eyed him and thought I'd never have a chance. So when I bumped into him at a sports bar, where I'd gone to watch the Bears' game and he offered to buy me a drink, I was speechless. We are both serious with our studies and share a geeky neatness. Whatever it was that attracted us to each other, soon we were a couple.

"Would you like some coffee?" Paul asks a while later.

"Sounds great," I say and feel ready for a break.

Paul makes a good coffee, but what I enjoy the most is his eagerness to do things for me. I can just picture an easy life with him around.

I hear him from the kitchen. "My dad asked again why we don't all go to graduation dinner together. He says the restaurant will be happy to add two more to our table."

I smile to myself. *Why don't we just give Mom a heart attack?* This morning, she asked me, "Would any of your friends like to join us for graduation dinner?" Ignoring the American tradition of having dinner out, she has been cooking up a storm. I imagine she has invited a few Iranian friends and her upstairs neighbor, who has forever wanted to match me with her nephew. When I said my friends already have plans with their own families, she seemed rather relieved.

I raise my voice for Paul to hear, "That's really sweet, but my mother has invited friends over."

These days, something else about Mom is weird; she has been acting rather secretive. I once walked into her apartment and as soon as she heard my voice there was a loud thud, like a door being slammed shut. When I asked her about it she denied having heard anything. I don't know what's on her mind, but the calm won't last and I do sense the approaching storm.

"You didn't review this brief?" Paul asks, waving the pages he's holding.

I shake my head absentmindedly.

"Maybe this isn't the best day to work." He stands near me and holds my face in both hands. "Whatever is on your mind, I'm sure it's important and I want you to know I'll be all ears when you're ready to talk." He kisses me lightly and holds me for a few seconds. I fight my tears and savor the way his voice is soothing my nerves. "Graduation is going to happen with or without these final polishes. Plenty of time to turn your paper in." He starts gathering the papers from the table and neatly stacks them. "The remaining work will be the best excuse for us to spend the day after graduation here."

If I only knew how, this would be the perfect moment to share my problem with him. But I first need to sort my own feelings, learn a few more facts, and know where exactly I stand emotionally.

Mom puts the roses she has bought on the dinner table and everything seems ready for our return from the commencement ceremony. Mom is still fussing, rearranging the stuffed grape leaves, adding a garnish of mint leaves and sliced lemon that resembles a rose bud. She finally puts the platter on a side table, ready to be served with cocktails.

"Okay Mom," I say to her back. "I'll be in my room if you need me."

"Yes, honey, go make yourself beautiful. I want lots of pictures today."

What a relief it will be to get this day over with. I've just finished the paper, my cap and gown is back from the cleaners, and Mom has bought the town's supply of film for her camera. Still, deep down I fear something is going to ruin this.

I'll have to spend a little time with Paul's parents, and by now the Warners must be ready to meet Mom. The mere thought makes my heart sink. They have no clue that my mother is still in denial about this entire relationship. I can just see a chitty-chatty Mrs. Warner approaching Mom to say how pleased she is to meet the mother of Paul's girlfriend and can't even begin to imagine what my mother would have to say to that.

As far as my mother is concerned, there's only one kind of suitable husband for me: an Iranian one. Though considering her own experience, now I'm wondering why.

Back in my room, I dry my long hair and reach for the hot rollers. There has to be a hairstyle that the graduation cap can't mess up. As I prepare for this biggest event—as Mom puts it—my entire life flashes before me.

Paul claims he has been in love with me since day one, and I know I love him, too. Not the giddy kind of love, but a stronger, more secure feeling, the kind that would make it easy to imagine having him around for the rest of my life.

We each live downtown close to the law school. We spend so much time together that if it weren't for fear of Mom's reaction, we'd be better off living together. I convince myself that the reason I don't tell Mom is because I know the Persian in her will consider such a lifestyle a dishonor. True that she'll never be able to forgive me for losing my virginity, but isn't it possible that I'm also unsure where this is going? Maybe I'm just buying time and want to avoid an unnecessary conflict. Over the past three years, I've put the thoughts of Mom and Paul in separate compartments and I don't know if I'll ever be ready to change that.

I glance at her picture on my dresser. In it, a much younger Rana in blue jeans and tee shirt is sitting in a park somewhere, holding baby Yalda on her lap. Who knew we'd be this close and yet so far apart?

That's fine, mother. You have your secrets and I'll have mine.

Satisfied with my hair and makeup, I slip into the canary-yellow suit. Its lightweight cotton and short sleeves make it suitable to wear under the gown. I grab my gown, my cap with its shiny purple tassel, and go downstairs.

Mom is wearing a lovely polka-dot dress and looks so elegant with her hair pinned up. She walks over and puts her arm around my shoulders. "Ah, just look at you!" She kisses my cheek. "I'm proud of you, honey."

Weeks earlier, those words would have meant the world to me. I force a smile. I haven't forgiven her. Not yet, anyway. Night after night I lay in my bed and try to be fair by telling myself that maybe it has been our joint effort to keep me in the dark. Maybe if I had really wanted a way out of this maze, I could have found one. But I also remember how each time I attempted to reach beyond my mother's halo of mystery she somehow managed to pull away. Did I let the information slip for fear the truth would destroy the only pillar I knew? Had I welcomed the ambiguity all these years?

Deep down, there's another irrational fear I don't want to admit. For the past week, I have thought of it enough times that by now it has become a distinct possibility. What if out of nowhere, Major Moradi shows up at my graduation? If I close my eyes I can clearly see the shock on Mom's face. I even go as far as picturing Paul making an attempt to approach him. But I blink hard and the image dissolves.

There, in the darkness of my mother's past lay a monster that for years the little Yalda would not dare awaken. Have I grown up enough and gathered enough courage to face it now?

Chapter

· *Twenty* ·

THE THEATER IS SO CROWDED THAT, for a while, I can't even find Paul. This is a more private graduation ceremony, yet the crowd is bigger than I had pictured. Conversations and cheerful greetings create a loud buzz and camera flashes and cellophane-wrapped flowers are all over the place.

"I should have brought you flowers," Mom says.

I smile at how she always finds something to blame herself for. I put my arm around her. "I saw the roses you put on the table, Mom. It's good you didn't bring any or we wouldn't know what to do with them here."

She smiles back before reaching into her purse for her camera. "Let me take your picture with the crowd in the back."

Someone I don't know spots us and asks Mom if she'd like to be in the picture. As he takes her camera and I stand next to my mother, I wonder if I'm the only graduate here who doesn't have an extended family attending.

I stand on tiptoe and look over the groups around us. Paul is nowhere in sight and in fact, neither are any of our friends. Mom takes a few more pictures and then puts her camera back in her purse. "I'll save the rest for the ceremony." She looks around. "Why don't you go find your friends? I can wait here."

"I don't want to leave you here by yourself."

"Don't be silly. This is your day, honey. Do you want the camera?"

I take it from her and give her shoulder a squeeze. "Thanks, Mom. Be right back!"

I finally spot a few friends near the concession stand and ask if they've seen Paul. When I finally find him, he is in a circle of family and friends and insists on introducing me to each one of them. "This is my uncle from Wisconsin," he says. The balding man next to him offers me a warm handshake. Paul holds my arm and says, "Come meet my cousins."

It's the first time I see my Paul as he must have been as a small boy and it makes me love him more. "Let me take a picture of you two," his mom says and she takes several. We also pose for a few with his family. It feels wonderful to be here and for a second I wish Mom knew them.

When I start to walk back, Paul asks to join me. "I'd love to meet your mom." I hesitate and he must know why because he adds, "I just want to congratulate her." His understanding tone tells me he's not about to make me feel awkward.

We find Mom where I had left her. She looks up and I take a deep breath before speaking. "This is my friend, Paul," I say and hope I'm not being too obvious.

Mom gives him the once over before she extends her hand to him.

Paul holds her hand in both of his. "It's so nice to finally meet you, Mrs. Ameli."

She smiles at him. "Same here. And congratulations."

"Thank you. I actually came over to congratulate you for Yalda's success." He then apologizes for not being able to stay. "Family is waiting," he says with a smile. As he walks away, I notice Mom's eyes are following him.

"Paul was a great help with my last paper," I say, feeling the need to explain.

She looks at me in a way that makes me think she is about to ask something, but she doesn't.

I see Paul again as we line up for the procession. I know Mom will be watching and am grateful for the alphabetical distance between Ameli and Warner. When the announcer calls Yawl-da Ameli, I spring out of my seat, but then freeze for a few seconds. I look over the crowd, as though expecting someone to protest that my real name is Moradi. Then realize I am Yalda Ameli and always will be. I don't need my father here. His absence is no longer a factor in my life, his heart of stone doesn't matter any more, and the fact that he won't ever be a part of my life is immaterial. A loving father existed only in my imagination. I exhale and begin my march to the familiar music. There will be no drama to the mundane ritual of this day.

After the ceremony, all hell breaks loose and it is clear that Paul will not find me before we leave. If you ask me, graduation is a tiresome, overrated show. Its only merit is that it signifies an end to a long ordeal.

Still, I do feel lighter, relieved even.

With bumper-to-bumper traffic on Central Street, no one is moving. Mom must be exhausted from the earlier overflow of emotion. As for me, the change I feel has nothing to do with a diploma. I stare at the small park on the north side of the street and the line of shops across from it. So hard to believe I'm the same person who passed down this street earlier today. It is as though the moment I shed that gown, I also banished the anxiety that had haunted me for years. Are all my fears self-inflicted?

"So how does it feel to be a lady lawyer?" Mom asks, her voice ringing with pride. She turns to me with a beaming smile. "You've got to be a mother to know how this feels."

She's been so radiant this entire day, so pleased with the world around her.

"Thanks Mom, but I think the way you cried and cried, the entire stadium must have known how happy you were!"

She gives me a sideways glance. "I didn't cry *that* much."

I chuckle. "Oh yeah? Then where's that box of Kleenex you brought along?"

Mom stops at the red light and looks at me again. "I could swear you're a different person now." She nods her certainty. "Definitely different. Mature, and a lot more confident."

I smile back and am amazed at how well she knows me. "Or maybe you're just taking a harder look at your 'little girl'."

She sighs and looks out her side window. "My little girls grow up too fast for me to keep track of."

I don't think she meant to change the subject. But this gives me a chance to ask a question that has been on my mind. "So, are you still determined to attend Vida's wedding?"

She thinks for a moment. "Not exactly." She sighs. "I mean, sure, I'll go, but there are days when I'm not too sure about my decision. I guess I'm nervous." She continues to drive and just when I think she won't say another word she adds, "Then again, I think it's time."

I want to ask more, but we have arrived.

She nods toward the curb. "There's your graduation present."

Parked near her driveway is a brand new VW Beetle. The metallic yellow shimmers under the late afternoon sun. Across the windshield there's a wide purple ribbon with the word 'Congratulations' in gold letters.

"Oh, my God," I whisper. "I couldn't possibly accept such a huge gift from you."

She hands me the keys attached to a silver charm. "Not me. It's from your grandpa," she says while parking her car. "He left you the money and specified it must be used for either a wedding gift, or graduation, whichever came first."

That sounds so much like the Grandpa Ameli I know.

"Its door opens with a push of this button," she explains.

All my life, we've gone from one used car to another. With so many mechanical problems, by now the guys at Frankie's Car Shop are like family. True that I had hinted at needing my own car, but this? I look at the lovely curves of the car's front and say, "He left me *that* much?"

"More," Mom says, now standing next to me. "There should be enough left for a plane ticket to Iran, if you'd agree to accompany me." She walks away and enters the building. Her last words have an eerie ring to them. Is she afraid to go alone, or does she want to me to go back for a different reason?

Another look at the Volkswagen and I forget all else.

Wait till Paul sees this, my very own, brand-new car!

I open the car door and slide onto the front seat where the strong smell of leather reminds me of shoe stores. My sweaty fingers leave a mark where I touch the gleaming dashboard. It's hard to tear myself away, but I should join Mom and help.

Soon our guests arrive and for the rest of the evening, we eat, drink, tell jokes and take pictures. The neighbors' gift is a new digital camera. "These things don't need film," he informs me and I thank him and pretend I didn't know.

When everyone is enjoying dessert, I take my camera and walk to the window. There's my little bug, now a deeper shade of yellow under the streetlight. *Will you be safe there?* I take the first of many pictures. I'm a kid owning her very first toy, reluctant to leave it out of sight, wondering if it'll still be there in the morning.

———

For many days Mom acts as if she has given up on me going with her on the trip and I am too busy driving my car all over town to bother with a conversation that can be unpleasant. But tonight we're home with no plans and I have a feeling the subject is bound to come up.

"Yalda-*joon*, will you take down the soup bowls?" Mom calls from her bedroom. She has just finished cooking and has gone to change her clothes.

"No problem," I shout back.

The aroma of sautéed mint flakes, fried onions, and mom's pomegranate soup fills the small apartment and I can imagine the smell wafting down the hallway and into the elevator. She has also made lamb cutlets, though I never understood why she bothers when all I care to eat is this thick soup. As I cut the *lavash* bread into little squares, I hear Mom's footsteps and she walks into the kitchen carrying a shoebox.

"What have you got there?" I ask.

"Oh, some old pictures I thought you'd want to see."

I don't know how to respond to that. Something in her expression tells me these aren't *my* old photos. *Just how old are they?*

"I always knew the day would come when you'd want to see these," she says.

With that simple statement, I am suddenly conscious of how little I know my mother. So she did mean to tell me at some point. That's why she saved the old pictures.

She puts the box on the counter. "But let's first eat."

I jump out of my chair. "Are you kidding me?"

And so it is that I hold a stack of black and whites and stare at faces of strangers. Mom looks so thin and so delicate in her wedding gown. And the groom? Is this handsome man really my father? For all I know these pictures could be clippings from a Hollywood movie.

I look up and Mom is standing by the window, looking out into the street.

"Won't you come and look with me?"

She shakes her head. "I've looked at them so many times, I know them all by heart."

An image flashes before me. Rana, alone, sitting in her room and looking at a past she will never forget. I feel guilty of neglecting something that I should have known.

"Come and sit here anyway. You can tell me who these people are."

"Ask away," she says, without making a move.

"Who's the girl in the ruffled dress?" I ask.

She hesitates and her next words sound as though she is saying them amid silent tears. "That's my Marjan."

She has told me little about the daughter she lost. But all of a sudden, I think maybe the loss of Marjan was the main reason she left everything behind. Maybe leaving the life that reminded her of her misfortunes helped her to deny everything. The more I think this, the more sense it makes. If she immigrated so that she could file for a divorce in the free country, why then did she stay married to him? Why not move on?

Then again, she had these pictures, didn't she? And the way she knows them by heart tells me she has been looking at them often. I stare at my sister's picture. Marjan's hair is long, a bow holding it on the side. She is so beautiful standing next to the mousey little Vida with big eyes.

The tiny little Vida is about to be married! I begin to understand how Mom feels about the news.

"Who are these two in a boat?" I ask, staring at the woman with dark lipstick and curly hair who is holding on to her wide rimmed hat. There's also a man with rolled up sweater sleeves, rowing the boat on a small lake.

"Maman and Papa," she says and turns to me with a smile. "They took that one in London's Hyde Park."

If I squint, I can almost recognize Grandpa, but old Grandma? This is unbelievable. She looks like a movie star of her era.

Mom walks over and sits by me. She finds a picture of my aunts at younger ages. I have seen their pictures on her dresser and know all their names, but this one is from when Mom was a teen, long before she became a mother. As she talks about where the picture was taken, her voice reflects deep nostalgia. She points to an old woman in a photograph. This one I almost know. She is the only other woman who loved me unconditionally. Before Mom has said it, I whisper, "Dayeh," and I bring the picture to my lips for a kiss. Mom squeezes my hand and when I look up, her cheeks glisten with tears.

I flip through many more pictures, unsure of what I expect to find. I've seen such photographs around the antique mall. These aren't all that different, they could have been taken anywhere in the world. The houses look a bit atypical, but they have a certain familiarity about them. The people may be strangers, yet loving them seems so plausible. My mother is in a few snapshots, too, though she's so young that I need her to tell me which one she is. I've seen other pictures of my mom, but this is the first time I see Rana for who she really is. *She saved these for me!* I try to imagine how they made her feel as she secretly viewed them over the years. *How could I be so blind?* Why did I consider her selfish when all she did was devote her life only to me?

The handsome man standing next to the young Mom could have been a loving father, but that's not who he turned out to be.

Searching for his own happiness, he discarded me. Did he find it? *I hope not!* He stands tall in his army uniform, yet to me he is but a small man. I hate him for what he has done to my mother. And to me. If there's one thing I want to do, it is make sure he is sorry.

I notice Mom is holding a small picture in her hand. I take it from her. It's a typical ID photo, obviously taken in a studio. Marjan's expressive eyes stare at me and there's a faint smile on her lips. This could have been a school picture because she's wearing a uniform with a starched, white collar. The corners of the photograph are cracked and I have a feeling this isn't the first time Mom has held it.

"I still feel responsible," Mom says. The sorrow in her voice tells me a mother is never done with her grief. Like a vital organ severed from her body, Marjan's loss has left irreparable damage. There will never be a full recovery. She proceeds to tell me more and the deep sorrow I have always seen in her eyes begins to make sense. "I killed her!" she says. "If only I hadn't taken her to Kathy's that day ..." she says, then stops. She is not crying. As the details of how Marjan died pour out, I see myself standing next to her at the hospital. "I held on to her little hand, sure that if I let go she'd leave me. Your father took breaks to make phone calls, smoke, even to eat. I still hear the machine, still see the green light making its line up and down, reminding me of the fine line that separates life and death."

I wish I had been there for her, that I could have held Rana's hand, tell her she's not alone. Hard to believe she has lived all these years with such deep pain, not to mention an unfounded guilt.

"Listen to me, Mom, you're not God. You are no more responsible for what happened to Marjan than you are about my leg's deformity. Such is life. Things happen, Mom!"

But I know she won't hear me. My mother is the type who welcomes guilt. Maybe this has to do with being the youngest of four, or maybe it's the outcome of living with that horrible man. I don't know. But all of a sudden I feel awful about having blamed her for my isolation.

Neither of us cares about dinner as we willingly dive into another world. Each time we see a picture of Vida or Marjan, I notice Mom holds it a little longer, and as we reach images of my father, she looks away and lets me have my time with them.

With each viewing, I'm one step closer to a true identity, to having a family. I don't know how to feel and wonder if I will ever be ready to share this heavy load with Paul. At this moment I'm not ready to even think about that.

By the time we reach the bottom of the box, I am determined to accompany my mom as she returns to her past. This isn't my journey of choice, but now it's my turn to be there for her.

Mom wants to put the box away, but on second thought turns to me and says, "Do you want to keep any of these?"

Yes, I would love to keep them all, but to me they are but ashes in an urn, while to her they are the remnants of a life filled with love.

I shake my head. "Thanks, but you should keep them. We can always share."

She seems relieved. "They'll be on the top shelf of my closet."

Before going to bed I stop by her room again. "I'm glad we've decided to do this, Mom. It'll be good to reconnect with the people you love."

"Reconnect?" She gives out a deep sigh and as always recites what must be her own translation of a Persian poem:

"If a cord is severed, you may tie it together again.

But the knot in the middle, shall forever remain."

⁓

Over the coming days, there is so much to do that we don't have time for another good chat. Mom has helped me to apply for Iranian travel documents, shop for souvenirs, and prepare for our journey. In some strange way, the decision has brought me closer to her. There's plenty to think about. Going to an Islamic country is an adventure I don't know how to prepare for. I can't begin to imagine how Mom feels about the changes she will find twenty-four years later. She has to be anxious about what and whom she may see, or how her loved ones may view her. The country has gone through a lot in the past decade and Mom has stated on more than one occasion that it's no longer the place she remembers. With the new regime, we are expected to observe the Islamic *hejab*. Luckily Mom knows what that entails. She has explained how I'll have to wear long-sleeve shirts, pants, and no makeup. A woman can't show hair, or wear an outfit that may show her natural body curves. I don't really care because it'll only be for three weeks. I feel more sorry for Vida having to dress like that her whole life. I wonder if the recent hardships have changed people's attitude. Are they going to be as nice as Mom remembers?

As we get closer to our departure date, my anxiety grows. I keep reminding myself that since I have no expectations, it'll be easy to meet these new people. With the exception of Grandma, they are all strangers to me and in her state of mind even she won't know who I am. So what if I don't like anyone? This trip isn't exactly for fun. I have an agenda. I'm going to make damn sure that my mother's pride is restored, that she gains her independence. But more than anything, I want to see that man suffer.

I still haven't told Paul about my father and hope to do that after I get back because by then I should have plenty more to share.

All he knows is that Mom and I are going to Iran on a vacation. Paul follows the news and can say Khomeini's name better than I can. He doesn't approve of a trip at this time and is genuinely concerned for my safety. But I've assured him that over there I'm still seen as a native and should be fine.

Mom and I don't talk about such concerns, but we both sense the other's apprehension. We are comrades going to the same war, each with our own set of duties, each with fears concealed under a brave mask. *What if he wants to keep her there?* Lately, I've learned enough about the Iranian laws to know that a husband holds all rights to his wife's travels. *Will he deny her permission to exit the country?* I can't let such silly worries stop me from this mission, and indeed it has turned into a mission.

I dread unpleasant surprises and sometimes am not sure if it's wise to take my mother back to a place where a real threat lurks over her head—if not both our heads. It isn't as though I'm eager to be reunited with a father I wish I didn't have.

The highlight of this trip for me will be meeting Vida. I do care about her and although we don't know each other, I feel awful about her having missed out on such a great mom. Then again, doesn't that mean I'll have to share Mom? I'm not going to fool myself. Mom is the real reason I'm going on this trip. My mission is clear and no part of it includes giving her up.

Our Iranian passports finally arrive. I open the manila envelope and stare at the burgundy cover. It is in Farsi, with English translations so page one is at the end. There I am with my hair covered under a silly scarf, not smiling, not communicating. Yalda Ameli now has an Islamic passport, but this little document is a lot more than that. This is the key that will finally open the door to whatever is left of Mom's secrets, and if my training is ever going to benefit her, it better be now. I take a deep breath and give my passport and the birth certificate back to Mom for safekeeping.

She looks at me and I don't know what makes her say, "Don't worry, Yalda *joon*. It should be a peaceful journey."

I don't know how to respond. I'm not going to Iran in search of peace; in fact, peace is the furthest from my mind. This journey is all about justice.

Chapter

· *Twenty-One* ·

T HE FLIGHT BETWEEN PARIS AND TEHRAN has been sol-
emn. Most passengers are taking a nap. As we begin our
descent, I wonder if the Air France hostesses could be any
more dramatic in their silence. One by one, they return from the
back of the plane with new attire, long-sleeved shirts and silk head-
scarves, in preparation for landing. I also notice none of them will
return my smiles.

"I don't know what to expect," Mom says, facing the window
for a glimpse of a land she hasn't seen for over two decades. I suddenly realize this will be her first time in Tehran without her parents greeting her and wonder who will meet us. I have only briefly
spoken to Aunt Mandana and even that has been a few words in
greeting. The other aunts are just pictures hidden in a shoebox. I
wonder how we will communicate. And what about their families?
Do any cousins speak English? I run my few Persian words in my
head: *Salam* – hello. *Merci* – thank you. *Noosh-e-jan* – bon appetit!

Mom turns away with a sigh, opens her carry–on, and hands
me a cotton robe in navy blue. "Put this on, honey, and button up."
The command in her action brings back the Chicago winters and

that rough wool scarf she used to push on me. But now Mom looks so sad that I show no resistance. "The idiots cover you head to toe just before doing their ridiculous body search." She sounds angry, and I am surprised to find out this bothers her more than it does me.

I take the robe, slip it on and manage to mask my resentment. Next, I reach for my black scarf and put it on, pulling it down on my forehead as if to hide baldness. The knot in my stomach tells me this may well be the trip to give me a big fat ulcer, but as I look around, the sudden change in everyone else gives me a chuckle. In an instant, all the women have acquired some degree of Islamic look. Their colorful outfits are hidden under plain dark outerwear, giving them a more somber appearance. Even the little girl waiting in line for a last minute use of the bathroom is wearing a black shirt, thick black knee-highs and a white scarf is wrapped around her head and neck. The French hostess who is collecting the last empty cups has wrapped a big scarf around her head and this reminds me of the American woman in Mom's building, who became a devout Muslim after marrying an Arab. I could never stop feeling sorry for her even though Mom insisted she did this of her own free will. Strangely, the Islamic change seems to be exclusive to women— though I do see a man across the isle removing his necktie, which must be another no-no in the new Iran.

"There it is!" Mom exclaims, pointing to a mountain range below and she sounds as if she's expecting me to know it.

I wrap an arm around her and lean over for a closer look, aware that I could never see what she sees. I know from her descriptions that the mountains around Tehran to her mean ski trips of long ago, young fun, and a family that dispersed over the years.

"It's beautiful," I say and am conscious of the inadequacy of my response.

Mom takes a paper out of her purse and crumples it into a ball before stuffing it into the pocket behind the seat in front of her.

That must be the letter I saw her writing last night. At the time, I thought it was for a friend back in the States, but the expression on her face is so sad that I am now more than curious.

A group of passengers chant what must be a prayer.

We finally land and despite the illuminated seatbelt signs, people are already reaching for the overhead bins. It takes a while before we deplane. I follow a lady whose suit I had previously admired; but now she looks haggard in her long black overcoat.

"Oops! I forgot something," I say to Mom and try to push my way back to our seat. There, in the magazine pocket, I find Mom's crumpled note. I put it in my purse and go back to her. There will be plenty of time to read it.

"What was it?" Mom asks.

"I thought I left my wallet, but it was in my bag all along." Lying gives me shame, but what else can I do? I know I've just stolen something that belongs to my mother, but there's no way I can stop it.

None of Mom's descriptions have prepared me for such a modern airport. As we stand in the passport line, I can sense Mom's anxiety from her silence, the way she watches what is going on ahead and how she keeps on pulling her scarf over her forehead.

At first glance what strikes me the most is the dark colors. I hadn't paid attention to how colorful clothes cheer up a crowded room, but the sea of people looks like a rowdy funeral home. People talk too loud, babies cry, and two little girls are giggling and chasing each other around us. The older one, who must be seven or eight, is wearing a white veil, but the other, about five, is the only female whose lovely brown hair is flying about. In her bright pink dress, she moves among the crowd like a bright dot on a black-and-white screen.

Mom presents our passports and when she points to me and says something with the word *Farsi* in it, I gather she's explaining that I don't speak it. We are motioned to go through and I notice the man giving me a head to toe. Mom gives me my passport and whispers, "I guess we'll have to go through the body search separately."

"*Again?*"

"Just do it," she says and sounds impatient. "I'll see you on the other side."

I enter a small cubical that reeks of body odor. A woman in black mumbles something and I clench my teeth as her hands run over every inch of my body. I am sure this is taking less time than it feels and just when I think I can't take it any more, she motions me out where there's air to breathe.

Mom rushes toward an approaching group and before I know it, people surround us. I stand back and watch her as she embraces all the women. This is Mom's moment and I enjoy watching her while she reunites with her past amid tears and laughter. It takes her a while to remember me. "Meet your aunts, honey," she says with a pride I have never seen before. I am hugged, kissed, and spoken to in Persian, of which I'm happy to understand the Yalda–*joon*.

We jam into four cars. Mom and I are with Aunt Soraya and her husband. Much to my delight, they all speak a few words of broken English.

The drive to town is long and astonishing. After I graduated from high school, Mom took me on a trip to Paris and Rome. But this is the Middle East, the Islamic Iran, and nothing I have seen in the news has prepared me for such a modern city. I know from the dry heat that the desert is still somewhere out there. The mountains that surround the city provide a magnificent backdrop to the ordinary high-rise buildings.

"Tehran *something something*," Mom says in Persian as she looks around with equal bewilderment, then quickly switches to English, "I don't remember seeing it so *green*."

I follow the direction of her gaze down the road. Green, it is not. True that there are trees lining the side streets, and there's an abundance of roses in the center division of the road, but a thin layer of dust makes the trees almost the same color as the walls surrounding each and every house. I wonder if it's those high walls that give the place a dry look because I can see more trees peeking from behind them. The air is hazy and smells of gasoline. Traffic is unbelievable and most cars are in need of a good wash. I see no sign of any police as drivers create their own lanes and honk for no apparent reason.

Aunt Soraya plays tour guide and names a few of the structures. She points to a banner with the picture of a turbaned man and says, "You have movie stars, ve have dis!"

After a few more such efforts, I say, "It's okay, Auntie. You don't have to explain. Go ahead and talk to Mom in Persian." Unsure if she understands, I ask Mom to tell her there will be plenty of time to take me sightseeing, that I want them to enjoy their reunion.

"Vhy you no espeak Farsi?" my aunt asks me and I'm grateful as Mom intervenes. The question has bothered me even back in the States, making me feel inadequate, a failure. Sometimes I wish I knew Persian, but when people ask me in an accusing tone, it's so offensive that I am no longer sorry for not knowing it.

They break into a loud conversation using exaggerated hand gestures. We must be in downtown Tehran because the traffic is suddenly out of control. Here, streets are lined with shops and the place turns into a mishmash of a variety of buildings and roundabouts with lawn or statues of somebody or other in the middle.

I look out the window and think about Vida, Dayeh, my aunts, and all the other people who up till now have just been names. I do my best to push away the name 'Moradi' for now. The reality of being here and that the names I have memorized will soon have faces, voices and personalities is more than I can grasp. I take in a deep breath and tell myself, "All in good time, Yalda. All in good time."

———

We are at Aunt Soraya's home and I'm amazed at the resemblance of her taste in decoration to Mom's. Her mahogany china cabinet is adorned with similar objects in pink glass and her sofa is the same Italian style as the one Mom found at a house sale. On the mantle, there's a color photograph of Grandpa and Grandma, of which I've seen a smaller print in Mom's bedroom. There is also a photograph of Aunt Soraya and Uncle Ardeshir's wedding. A charming bride in her knee length dress, she wears her hair up with a tiara in front. Who knew the years could change her so much?

I hear Mom's voice, "Come here, Yalda. Somebody wants to see you!"

My heart drops. There has been too much excitement already. Vida won't be here for another week and I'm not ready for more surprises.

A thought creeps into my mind. *Oh, please, not Moradi!*

Mom holds the door open and in walks a frail old woman, leaning on a walking cane, her floral *chador* wrapped around her waist. She needs no introduction.

"Dayeh!" And I am down on my knees, embracing her bent back.

The summer heat is here, but regardless of that Dayeh is wearing a sweater. The white cotton scarf pinned under her chin forms a halo around her angelic face. She is the only person I meet on this trip whom I know well. Her name was sprinkled all over my childhood and her living ghost followed us. It was her recipes that put the best delicacies on our table and even the fairytales Mom told me were attributed to the old nanny. So now that I meet her, that loving expression is familiar.

She holds my face in both hands and peers into my eyes. I wonder how clearly she sees through her clouded eyes, but she gives me a satisfied, toothless smile. I welcome the coarse fingertips against my skin and don't mind the wet marks as she gives my cheeks hearty kisses. I tighten my arms around her and she hugs my head. Her clothes smell of tobacco and mint. We stay that way for some time before Mom gently separates us.

"That's enough, you two. You don't want to make everyone else jealous."

I wipe my tears with the back of one hand and hold on to Dayeh with the other. She follows me to the couch, but chooses to sit on the rug at my feet. I want her to sit next to me, but know she's comfortable there. All of a sudden language barriers don't matter and words aren't needed. We are so deeply connected that each knows exactly how the other feels.

I'm not surprised when Mom explains that she has just come from her village to see us. It is no surprise because at the moment it feels as if I, too, have traveled this long way only to see her.

Dayeh's trembling hand clutches mine. Unable to tell her how I feel, I let her calloused fingers stroke the back of my hand and know the motion is to the rhythm of her moon daughter chant. In silence, we both hear it. This is the only line that connects me to a loving babyhood.

—

It's late at night and my aunt and her husband have gone to bed. I take out Mom's note and read:

Most passengers are asleep, even Yalda. I have thought of you lately more than ever and as we make our way back to reunite with everyone, it is you I need to talk to. This is much harder than I thought and so I've been sitting with the pen in my hand and the words in my head. They just don't come out, they like staying in the dark.

I have a lot to talk about, but in a world already filled with trouble, no one deserves to share more pain. So I write to you instead. You would know how to transcribe my thoughts, decipher the words. This is my chance to finally tell you how it was on those first days after you left, on long nights when I refused to accept that your bed would forever remain empty, that your ragdoll would never be hugged again. Do you miss her? You named her Emily after an American classmate. Together we sewed many dresses for your Emily and I helped you to braid her long hair. I have taken good care of Emily for you and now I'm bringing her back because we both know it's time to finally bury her, don't you think?

I didn't want to see them take you away. If I denied there was a grave, I would never have to visit it, I wouldn't be forced to imagine your rose-petal skin buried under mounds of dirt. I can finally succumb to seeing your stone, the one with your name, the one with two dates that are only eight years apart. I remember stopping by such stones and wondering how the mother felt seeing it. I still don't know how that feels. Is the cruel God who took you from me now kind enough to give me the strength?

After all these years I have finally admitted that my Marjan is gone. I keep telling others that your sister Yalda is the reason I never went back. But that's not entirely true. If I went back, I would have to visit your grave, to accept your loss and face reality. When I went abroad, I didn't just leave my homeland. I left an entire other life, a life that had my Marjan, my Vida, and a man who had once been mine. "Take it all," I shouted at God. "You can have everything I once loved!" Staying away helped me to pretend you were still with Vida, growing up, becoming a woman. In my mind you grew old and *remained the oldest sister. Oh, child, you are even older than your mother, and certainly wiser than her.*

Mom had not finished the note; then again, she never would. Such thoughts have tormented her for all these years and will remain with her for as long as she lives. I smooth the wrinkles on the paper, fold it neatly and place it in my book. I need to read it over and over. This pain, old as it may be to Rana, is all new to me.

———

Vida! This is the Vida day. My sister's name has echoed in my mind all morning. I woke up, showered, had breakfast and went to my room to change, but all along one thought kept coming back. Today I will know my big sister.

It has been less than a week and I'm already content to be among my aunts and uncles, especially the uncles because they treat me as their own. It's odd to realize that while I am just meeting my family, they have known me all my life. In all their houses there are pictures of Mom and me, and Aunt Mandy even has one from my Junior High graduation. When I ask why they didn't contact the grownup me, they dodge the question or make inadequate excuses such as the language barrier. That's no longer believable as I have no trouble communicating even with Uncle Ardeshir. Maybe they were just being cautious and trying to avoid a slip that might make me suspicious. My father's name is never mentioned and I have yet to see any sign of him. But today Vida is arriving from Shiraz.

From a life where family meant Mom and me, I have taken a big leap and landed in the middle of a clan. It has been easy to put a face to familiar names, but now there are cousins and cousins of cousins whose names I'll never get straight. Almost everyone speaks some English, even though theirs sometimes sounds very Persian and often has their own words mixed in. Even the people on the street know some English. Everybody tells me I should learn Persian, followed by some hint that if I do, they'll have a good husband for me. I smile inwardly. *Paul would love to hear this!* I think of him often and the thought only makes me realize how far apart we are. I haven't called him yet. I don't want to impose and add to my aunt's phone bill by calling States and anyway, there's no way to share what I'm experiencing. It's as though I have flown to another planet.

"We're ready to go, Yalda *joon*," my aunt calls from downstairs.

I open the door a crack and shout, "Be down in a minute."

I am in Mandana's guest room, where I'll be staying for the duration of our trip. From day one I've called her Aunt Mandy and she seems to like my Americanization of her name. The aunties have divided us between them. Mom is staying with her oldest sister Soraya.

Taraneh—Aunt Tara to me—lives somewhere in the northern suburbs with her husband, their son Arash, and Grandma. Mom tells me the family decided that would be best for Grandma because her house is bigger and the mountain air is free of the downtown's smog. Mom went there for a visit the day after we arrived. Today the bride-to-be comes to Tehran and everyone will gather at Aunt Soraya's, including Grandma. "Don't expect her to remember you," Aunt Mandy has cautioned.

It's a Friday, everyone's day off. I think of my Fridays with Mom, when we looked forward to a peaceful dinner and a movie. Life here is different and this sure hasn't been a typical vacation. Just a few days into it and I'm already exhausted. One party after another, and although it's always the same people and the same food, each gathering has its own character. Aunt Soraya being the eldest of the sisters holds a more formal gathering.

Mom and I haven't had a chance to be alone, but I know she's as anxious as I am. How will Vida receive us? The fact that we have not known each other lowers my expectation, but what about Mom? If

Vida has indeed adopted that other woman as her mother, how will she feel toward Mom? I can't even begin to guess what goes on in my mother's mind. How will she feel now that she has a real Persian daughter and is about to have an Iranian son-in-law?

My aunts have done everything they can to make our trip pleasant. I feel sorry for the way they bring up the past. It's as though by doing so, they hope some of their sweet memories may rub off. Aunt Mandy tells me stories of their best summers on the shores of the Caspian Sea. She tells me how they went swimming, dancing and even peach picking. She tells me grownups dressed up and went to the casino while kids made bonfires at the beach and a servant helped them to roast corn-on-the-cob. None of that is easy to picture when all I see is their long robes, dark scarves and a society that leaves little room for fun.

"You look beautiful," Aunt Mandy says.

I chuckle. "In this?" I'm wearing pants and a silk top, but it's all covered under my Islamic garb.

"Even in that," she says and smiles. "You'd look good even in a burlap sac!"

"Thank you." I no longer question her odd expressions.

None of my mom's sisters resembles her and yet there's a family thing going, a similarity in the way they walk, the sideway glances they give me. Aunt Soraya's giggle is exactly like Mom's. I'm most comfortable around Aunt Mandy. Maybe it's the language, or because I'm staying with her, but I also think we have more in common. She teaches English at a high school and is the only relative with whom I can have a normal conversation.

Today, Uncle Jamshid will drive and he offers me the front seat to see more of the city.

"Do you like Iran?" he asks me for the umpteenth time.

That's the first question everybody asks and I have trained myself to guess the level of their English from the depth of their accents. At first, I used to elaborate on the points I liked, until I realized they'd be just as happy with a nod or to hear me say, *Kheili*—a lot.

And I do mean a lot. With each passing day, I am more impressed by its contrasts. The superhighways, tall buildings and subway system are all notable, yet it's no longer a surprise to see a donkey on the street, a dilapidated building in the best section of town or to find an incredible mess on its sidewalks. I figure those must be what they showed on the news abroad, things that had also caught the eyes of the cameramen. Did I really expect this to be a nomadic society riding camels? The huge green signs above the highways are much like ours back home, except I can't read most of them. Such similarities to the US give the place a surreal look. It's as if I'm seeing all this in my sleep because one moment I'm close to home and the next I find myself in the land of Ali Baba. Here the sounds are too loud, the smells too strong and the foods, even the ones Mom has made for me before, look the same but taste different.

"You must be excited to see your sister, no?" Aunt Mandy says.

I nod, but can't find words to add.

"Excited" doesn't begin to describe how I feel. It's as though I'm about to see a ghost, a good ghost. At the same time, I am conscious of the fact that she connects me more than anyone else to my real father. We talk about Vida, but no one has mentioned his name. It's a taboo subject and sometimes I think there must have been frictions between him and my mom's family at some point. That no one asks how I feel about him is just as well because, if they did, I wouldn't have a simple answer. To see Vida may be a reunion, but the word doesn't begin to describe what I have in mind for the now Colonel Moradi.

"Have you talked to her?" my aunt asks.

I shake my head. "Not yet. But she sounds nice."

"Very nice." Uncle Jamshid jumps is. "Vida very nice person!"

Aunt Mandy tells me how Vida makes a point of visiting all the aunts. The more I hear about my sister, the more I like her. I sure couldn't be that nice if I'd been the one left behind.

I look out the side window at this busy city. Tehran has many attractive sights, but overall I can't say it's beautiful. There's no particular pattern to its architecture, it's just been built, and in some areas over expanded. Luxurious modern buildings are adjacent to a shabby old bazaar where the air smells of tobacco and spices. Even under the Islamic robes, one can see how some women are overdressed for this time of day. Here and there I notice a lock of bleached blond hair, red nail polish, or flashy jewelry. They mingle with ease around the bazaar, pass the beggars on the sidewalk, and haggle with store owners. I don't know if it's the way our TV back home has conditioned me, but each time we're out of the house, I expect chaos, even an outbreak of violence. Something about this place both allures and frightens me at the same time.

"That is Khomeini," Uncle Jamshid points to a banner over the street. I've seen the Ayatollah's face in the media, but there are a hundred versions of it around Tehran and they vary based on the artist's impression. The one we just passed seemed angry, definitely not his best.

"Do people miss him?" I ask.

Uncle Jamshid looks at me, but waits for Aunt Mandy to interpret before responding. "Oh," he says and switches to Persian for my aunt to translate.

"In the privacy of our car and with no fear of the SAVAMA I can tell you this. We thought things might change after him; unfortunately it has been much worse. He sure raised a lot of snakes in his sleeve."

I think about that for a while and marvel at the sharpness of some Persian expressions. I want to ask if Khomeini knew about the snakes in his sleeve, or if they grew there unbeknownst to him, but unsure of whose side my uncle is on, I decide it best not to.

I'm not surprised when an entire family loaded on a motorcycle passes by. At the light, a woman wrapped in a black chador drags a child by the hand and zigzags through traffic.

Making this trip was the right thing to do. Even if I don't achieve what I have set out to do, being here is helping me to understand my mother's background better. Each day I seem to chisel a bit more at the wall she has built between me and the life she had put behind us.

I see a couple of planes above and picture Vida in one of them. There are rumors of my father accompanying her on this trip. Knowing that none of my aunts would welcome him, I wonder why he wouldn't fly separately. But for all I know, he could be up there, sitting next to Vida. We are supposed to greet the bride at the airport and I can't even guess what I might do if indeed he is with her.

It's good that Mom has decided to stay home with Grandma while we pick up Vida. I'm happy we will stop by Aunt Soraya's first as I'm dying to finally see Grandma, even though I'm prepared for her not knowing me. I'm also hoping to talk with Mom. Does she feel as I do, or is it worse for her? And how does Vida feel about all this?

"Why so quiet?" Aunt Mandy says.

I smile. This is the first time that anyone has called me quiet. But if I am, it may be because I feel so out of place.

We arrive at Aunt Soraya's shortly before noon. The iron door to the garden is ajar and I see Uncle Ardeshir, holding a striped green hose and watering the lawn. Regardless of our language barrier, my uncle is quite chatty. "*Befarma* - come in, this your house!" he says, and puts the watering hose down. He walks over to us and insists I should enter the hallway before him. "We have not children. I like everybody like is my children." He receives an extra hug from me just for that remark.

As we cross the vast yard that has an abundance of fruit trees and roses, I notice a couple of wooden platforms under a window. Aunt Mandy has told me how years ago people slept outside during hot summer nights, the mountain breeze offering comfort in the absence of central air conditioning.

I nod to the beds and whisper to my aunt, "Do they sleep here?"

Aunt Mandy shakes her head. "Not any more. Ardeshir won't allow it."

"Why not?"

"I think he worries about Soraya being out there in her nightgown." She gives a long sigh. "Ever since the revolution, people don't even use their swimming pools for fear the neighbors might peep." She turns to me with a smile. "But maybe if I repair the mosquito net, Jamshid will assemble our outdoor beds and you and I can give it a try."

Uncle Ardeshir holds my elbow and leads me to the guest room. "You here first. More person not here." He then goes to the staircase and calls out, "Soraya *jan*. You come here."

We hear aunt Soraya's giggle and I understand the word '*Englissee*' before Mom joins her laughter. I gather the two sisters find it funny that he has spoken English to his wife. I link arms with my uncle to show I appreciate that.

The house has a faint smell of mothballs. Heavy velvet curtains block the sun and a ceiling fan is going full-blast. As soon as we are seated, in comes Dayeh, followed by a younger woman who carries a tray of tea. I am grateful to Aunt Soraya for finding Dayeh's whereabouts and even more than that, to the old nanny for making the long journey. She must be in her nineties.

Though an icon of Mom's past, I feel even closer to Dayeh now that she is with us. She studies me through the shield of tears. Ever since our arrival here, I've had more than my share of being stared at. Yet, when Dayeh does it, it's neither rude nor unpleasant. I sense her approval, as if I have turned out precisely how she wanted me to, that I am the harvest of her field.

It's hard to fathom the kind of pressure that would prompt anyone to leave a place where so much affection is gained effortlessly. How did my mother cope with her lonely life in a foreign land?

A commotion in the hallway tells me Grandma and Aunt Tara must have arrived. They enter the living room. Grandma is carrying an elegant walking cane, but I notice she prefers to lean on Aunt Tara. She has aged much more than I expected and seems heavier, too. As always, she smells of a good perfume, but gone are the fancy clothes and stylish hairdo. I go forward and give her a big hug. "Good to see you, Grandma." Her face takes on the expression of a lost child. "It's Yalda, Grandma, I've come all the way from the US to see you." Her eyes glaze over. There's no recognition.

Mom rushes over, helps her into a wingback chair and tucks a cushion behind her. She then greets me with a tighter than normal hug, perhaps hoping to make up for the fact that Grandma doesn't remember me.

Aunt Tara is wearing a sage-green cotton dress and I notice how the matching Hermes scarf she slips off her head is meant to stay on her shoulders as an accessory. Even though she's not the prettiest of the four, her poise and the way she pulls her graying hair into a bun give her the elegance of a ballet teacher.

She embraces me in a tight hug. "Tehran weather is good. It make you more beautiful!" she says, and everyone laughs. By now I'm used to such pleasant exchanges, they call this *ta-arof* and it seems to be a form of social etiquette.

The men come in last and suddenly everyone is talking, but nobody offers a translation.

How good is Vida's English? I wonder.

I check the time and realize that with the long drive from the airport and in Tehran's heavy traffic, it'll be two to three more hours before we will return and Mom will see Vida.

My uncle says something and all at once, everyone stands, which to me indicates they are preparing to leave.

I whisper to Mom, "Do I really have to go? I hate to leave you here."

She strokes my hair and smiles apologetically, "You're the younger sister. It's expected of you." And when I don't move, she gives my back a gentle push.

Aunt Tara grabs my elbow. "You go my car. Mandana see you many time," she says and plants a kiss on my cheek.

Back into our Islamic shrouds, we jam into three cars and hit the busy streets. As we drive to the airport, I picture Mom sitting down with Dayeh and trying to make some conversation with Grandma. She must be even more nervous than I am.

I check my watch again. It will be anther hour before I will finally meet my sister and possibly face my father, too. Ever since Aunt Mandy hinted at that possibility by mentioning that his presence will be needed for the pre-wedding arrangements, anxiety hasn't left me alone. I tell little Yalda that there's nothing in this for her, that the man is probably too old and it's much too late for him to begin playing the father role, but that doesn't stop her from checking the time every few minutes.

We pass the large roundabout and turn into the airport boulevard. A heavyset policeman is standing by his car on the side of the road. For all I know, the handsome Major Moradi could now be as fat as this man. But why should I even care what he looks like? *Will he speak to me?* My heart drops at the thought. I am shocked to realize that after an entire month of preparation, I am still not ready for this. *Is that why Mom didn't come?*

Little Yalda may be excited to see her dad, but it's too late for me. I'm here to greet my sister. Maybe the Colonel had enough sense to take a different flight. And if not, maybe he will slip away before Mom's family spots him. I curl in the corner of the backseat and for the first time admit to my deep fright. With each mile we drive, my anxiety grows another notch.

Chapter

· Twenty-Two ·

W
E ENTER THE LOBBY OF THE AIRPORT and the smell makes me feel I have stepped into a huge ashtray. People push and shove without apologizing, and their chatter makes it hard to hear the announcements that come in all languages. A few kids are chasing each other and screaming, but it doesn't seem to bother anyone else.

My eyes search the crowd, but then I check the time and realize the flight won't land for another half hour. My uncle leads the way to a row of chairs. No one bothers to ask me what I want to do. This is Iran. You follow the leader and do as they plan. Even invitations are never a question and need no response. "We are going to Aunt Soraya's for lunch." End of subject.

"This way," Uncle Ardeshir says with a nod and I notice he won't touch my shoulder the way he does at home. By now I'm familiar with such social limitations. Under the Islamic law, only men who are immediate family can have the slightest physical contact with a woman, and even then, they'll need proof: a birth certificate, marriage license, or what have you. It has taken me a week to finally stop expecting a man's handshake.

What am I doing here?

My feet are so heavy, it's as though little Yalda has wrapped her arms around my ankles, begging me to stay with her. I know it's time to let the child go, but that's not as easy as I had thought.

When it's time, I follow my aunt to the middle of the lobby. Aunt Soraya stops and waits for the rest to catch up. There's a huge monitor on one of the walls, showing the customs area, where overseas passengers wait in line. For a moment, I wish they had a similar screen for domestic flights so that I'd get a glimpse of my sister before facing her. Or is it Moradi who I want to see on a screen?

We pass through the terminal and reach a gate. Even I can read the heart-shaped number five above the black curtain. Two bearded men and a veiled woman are sitting on their plastic chairs, chatting. They each have a picture ID hanging around their neck and I gather they must be waiting to receive—or inspect—the incoming passengers. As more people gather, we form a tight frontline behind the rope. I listen to my thumping heart and wonder if I will recognize my father. Will he recognize me?

For the first time I'm experiencing an incredible adrenalin rush. This can't be fear, though I do understand why Mom had been afraid that Moradi would have detained me as a minor. But what can he possibly do now that I'm an adult? He was never there before, never mattered and didn't play a role in my life. What makes him so important all of a sudden?

Each time the black curtain is lifted, I hold my breath in anticipation. Now the passengers come out two and three at a time. More women are wearing black *chadors* than I've seen around Tehran and I figure that must be how it is in smaller towns.

"Vida!" Aunt Mandy's joyful voice turns my attention to where she is running now.

A young woman in a lightweight raincoat and turquoise-blue

scarf has just come through and she turns to the voice and rushes to embrace my aunt. My tears make it hard to see. Mesmerized, the rest of our group is standing back. It's only when Vida puts her hands on my aunt's shoulders and pulls back that I notice the tall man in a gray suit standing a couple of steps away. In civilian clothes and wearing glasses, with so much gray hair and a white moustache, he looks nothing like the pictures in Mom's shoebox.

The man is staring directly at me. He won't move, paralyzed. I can't understand why I wish this moment would last longer. Aunt Tara touches my back and gives it a push, but my feet are in heavy cement. Aunt Mandy says something in Vida's ear and now it's Vida walking over to me. I hear someone sniff. Vida's uncanny resemblance to Mom, especially the bashful smile, makes it easy to hug her, to kiss that familiar face. She is much taller than me and as she pulls me into her arms, I welcome her soft scent of Jasmine and rest my head on her shoulder. "Yalda *joon*," she whispers and I feel her fingers stroking the back of my head. I have a sister. I have a loving big sister! Engulfed in newfound warmth, I am suddenly at enough ease to face anything. I look over her shoulder and prepare to meet my father.

But he's gone.

I look around where he had stood a minute ago. At his height, it should be easy to spot him in a crowd. I scan the room in all directions, but there's no sign of the man.

"Baba had to leave because a friend is giving him a ride," Vida says. She has read my mind. "I'm sure he'll make some other arrangement to visit you."

Like a stubborn child, I look away and shrug, but I'm furious. *Come on, Yalda, you didn't really expect anything different.* Now I'm not so sure what I expected, but it wasn't this, not being ignored. Pride had not allowed me the enthusiasm to meet him, but I was in no way prepared for not being met.

On the way home, Vida and I are moved to Aunt Mandy's bigger car while Uncle Jamshid takes care of her luggage.

"I asked Bijan—my fiancé—not to come to the airport," Vida explains. "I wanted this to be our time, just me and my little sister."

I smile at hearing the sweetest words I've ever heard and am grateful for having "our time." Vida's English is flawless. The way she annunciates her words gives her accent a British touch and I notice she doesn't skip her 'T's or 'D's as I do. I suppose that may have something to do with post-revolutionary Iran and how they banished all things American. She is talking to my aunt, but her eyes are mostly on me, as if examining this new sister.

"Rana is so anxious to see you, but she had to stay with Maman," my aunt says. "I can't even begin to describe how much she has missed you."

Vida hesitates a moment as if to absorb that, but doesn't respond.

"She still talks about you as 'my little Vida'," I add.

Vida looks up and I'm not sure if the faint smile means she is finding this funny or the thought has made her happy.

"What should I call her?" she asks.

"What do you mean?" I realize it's a stupid question.

She looks at her hands without responding.

"Yes, exactly," my aunt says and she sounds angry. "What *do* you mean?"

Vida looks at me, then at Mandana.

"Well?" my aunt pushes.

"I have another Maman, you know."

My aunt grunts and turns to the window, but I can see Vida's point. Barely five when her mother left her, she grew up with this Parisa woman, even adopted her as her own mother. It must be just as hard for her to make room for Mom as it is for me to accept Colonel Moradi. What will I call him?

I gently lay my hand on Vida's. "You could call her Mom, like I do."

She looks up and smiles. "Yes," she whispers. "That sounds really nice." And she nods with genuine approval. "Mom."

A few minutes pass in silence before my aunt starts talking Persian in long streaks. I'm used to this and figure my sister must be getting a sermon. Whatever it is that my aunt has said, Vida is beaming.

"Congratulations," she says to me. "You must feel quite accomplished having your degree in law."

I laugh. "Thank you, but I'd feel a lot more accomplished if I could find a job."

"What do you mean, 'if'? There must be hundreds of jobs waiting for you."

"I wish. This sounds crazy, but in the US, the more you qualify, the fewer the jobs."

This seems to surprise her even more. "Not here," she says. "The salaries may not be that great, but as soon as you get your degree, there are many jobs. Sometimes you actually get to choose."

"Even for women?"

"Well, yes. That is, if you're willing to comply with the Islamic dress codes."

My aunt laughs. "I can just picture Yalda wearing a veil to the court!"

That gives me a chuckle, but I stop immediately for fear I might offend them.

"Oh, go ahead," Vida says, bumping shoulders. "We all laugh at such absurdity. Even after years of this odd dress code, one sees how crazy it is." She shrugs. "But what can we do?"

For the rest of the way, conversations fluctuate between Persian and English and mostly circle around the wedding. Who's the lucky groom? How did they meet? Aunt Mandy wants to know all the details. As Vida fills in the blanks, I study her with newfound interest. Maybe it's too late to be as close as sisters, but I'm beginning to like this bubbly Vida.

"So what did you think of Baba?" Vida asks in such a casual tone, it could be a reference to anything in Tehran.

I take a deep breath and think of the tall man standing there who had made my heart beat so fast. How he had maintained his dashing looks, how proud and dignified he seemed. But I have no answer for her. She doesn't push.

Somehow the drive back seems shorter and soon we are at Aunt Soraya's alley. Tara's car is already parked in front, the door to the house is open and I can picture her running inside to announce Vida's imminent arrival. Next, Mom rushes out and is crossing the alley. In her haste, she has forgotten her shoes and her scarf. While I follow Vida out of the car, I realize this is the first time I have seen my mother run.

"*Khodaye man ...*" she cries out, and I don't need a translation to know she is calling God's name. Mom does this whenever she is overwhelmed.

Vida stays in place, her arms down. Has she forgotten what Mom looks like? Did Moradi hide her pictures the way Mom did his? A million thoughts go through my head while Mom wraps herself around her missing child. She has her back to me, but from the way she buries her face into Vida's shoulder, I know she must be crying. Her hand slowly reaches to feel Vida's shoulder-length hair. A moment passes and she pulls away to take another look at her daughter's face. I feel my own tears as Mom's hand gently wipes away the tears from Vida's cheek, a move that seems to awaken Vida because finally, her arms rise to hug Mom.

A window across the street opens and an old woman cranes her neck, watching as if enjoying a show from her special box. My aunts have joined the rest of the family in a group, weeping. I'm ashamed of my own dry eyes.

After a slight hesitation, as if energized by Mom's warm embrace, Vida opens her arms, first with a slow move, but then they tighten into a firm embrace. Mom is saying something amid tears, but it comes across as wailing. Vida is too quiet and now gently peels Mom's arms from around her. She closes her eyes and her face is covered in tears. Even Dayeh has come out to watch. She leans on her walking cane with one arm and is hitting her chest with the other, yelling out something that makes Vida look up. No sooner has Vida seen the old nanny than she runs to her and nearly knocks her over with a fierce embrace. Now it's Vida who cries loudly and this finally brings tears even to my eyes.

The commotion brings out a few more neighbors and Uncle Ardeshir encourages us to go inside the house. Everyone is talking at once and a few voices rise higher. Now it is all in Persian and in such a cacophony, I wouldn't understand a word even if I spoke the language.

As they all push their way into the living room, I stay back in the hallway. I plop into the single chair by the phone and listen to the affectionate voices coming from the living room. Love sounds the same in all languages.

A young maid takes a tray of tea inside and as she leaves the door open, I can see Mom sitting on the couch next to Vida. The way she eyes her lost daughter is like a young lover looking at the beloved.

I want to remind myself that my time will come. But it won't be the same. *He wasn't thrilled to see me, was he?* I have no patience for self-pity and need to remind myself that I'm here for my mother. *This isn't about you.*

Chapter

· *Twenty-Three* ·

WEDDING PREPARATIONS ARE A LOT MORE FUN here compared to the States. I remember a couple of years ago, when I was a bridesmaid at my friend Jennifer's wedding. All I had to do was show up for a fitting, pay for my gown, and be at the rehearsal. Here the entire family is involved. Vida has no bridesmaids and there's nothing to rehearse, but we have all been involved in some way and it feels so much more personal.

Mom has been busy with many responsibilities, since Vida has graciously put her in charge of details for the ceremony. She is constantly in and out of the bazaar, buying laces, little silk flowers, ribbons and such. Sometimes I think she's a whole new person, but that may be because I've never seen her this happy before. I wonder if this is the reason she wants me to marry an Iranian, so she could take care of a ceremony she knows best. Maybe now that she is getting it out of her system, she might accept my choice. I had secretly feared that between Moradi and his other wife, there would be no room for Mom in any of this. Thankfully there's more substance to Vida's character than any of us had presumed. I still don't know her well, but if we have anything in common, it has to be our habit of building compartments in our heart. Just as I have separated Mom from Paul, Vida seems to have little trouble separating her two mothers. One mother is back in Shiraz, taking care of invitations and the general plans for the reception while the other's artistic touch is essential in gathering whatever's needed for the *aghd* ceremony. And the father of the bride is still at large.

Analyzing the airport encounter over and over in my mind, I've tried to find the reason why Moradi would not want to speak to me there. I rerun the scene, analyze his expression and read more into it than I should, but no matter how I resent him for leaving so abruptly, it's hard to picture him doing anything else. Maybe it's only my imagination, but there are times when I convince myself that I saw affection in his eyes. Then again, given a chance, he might have preferred to slip away without being seen. *Was he caught off-guard?* Maybe he feels as awkward about this whole reunion as I do. I don't know and I'm doing my best not to condemn him before I have enough evidence. Still, the longer he waits, the less I like him.

Over the past couple of weeks, once or twice we've had suspicious calls at Aunt Mandy's. The first time she was too far from the phone and asked me to pick up. She has taught me to say, "*Gooshi,*" so the caller will hold until she gets to the phone. I look forward to such moments and feel very Persian saying the word. That day when I said the word whoever it was just listened until I hung up. Half an hour later, it happened again. There have been two other such incidents since. I sometimes tell myself that any of these could have been my father, hearing my voice, maybe even wanting to talk to me. I don't know why I do this. Maybe the thought soothes my bruised ego, makes me feel less unwanted. Twice, Aunt Mandy picked up and the line went dead. Both times I let myself believe it was him. He doesn't know my voice, but my accent has to be a dead giveaway. I would never share such notions with anyone, but at night I lie awake and wonder.

Colonel Moradi and his Parisa have kept a safe distance. The woman has enough class to send Mom a basket of flowers along with a card that my aunt translated as, "Welcome home. I look forward to knowing Vida's real mother." I was not there when the flowers arrived, but the basket with the card still attached still sits in Aunt Soraya's hallway. Mom hasn't said a word about it.

Today I met the groom. His name is Bijan, and I was happy to hear him speak English as fluently as Vida does. He has just dropped us off at the dressmaker's, where Vida will have the last fitting before her gown is delivered to the salon.

"You should go with her," Mom advised, and her tone indicated it's another tradition.

On the way here, Bijan pointed out a few buildings and explained their history. I'm surprised that the information is as new to Vida as it is to me. When I asked him about a few skyscrapers near the northern hills, he said, "We don't seem to have enough palaces for the clergy, so they're building their own version of castles there." We all laugh at the absurdity of their high rise castles. At first glance, this balding young man with a mustache and silver-rimmed glasses hadn't impressed me, but he seems every bit as nice as Vida herself. If anything, he has more wit and I enjoy his humor.

Vida asks Bijan to come back for us in a few hours. When he drives away, I ask her, "Why hours? I thought the dress was ready."

"It is, but I'd love to have a proper visit with you." She smiles warmly. "There's a nice tea place next door and we can enjoy our afternoon tea and have a sisterly chat before everything becomes too crazy."

I smile back and think, why not? I should sample the joys of sisterhood. Half an hour later, we are at a most charming teahouse, sitting on wooden platforms under the trees. Vida orders our tea and takes a pack of cigarettes out of her purse.

"Don't tell anyone," she says and offers me one.

I shake my head. "I don't smoke."

This seems to surprise her. Most people here smoke and in fact, tea and cigarettes seem to go hand in hand. So I'm curious why Vida keeps hers a secret.

"Bijan wants me to quit," she says and giggles.

"How did you two meet?"

"We didn't. His Mom just showed up at our door. *Khostegar,* you know?"

"Does that really happen in this day and age?"

She shrugs. "How else is a girl supposed to find a husband in this suffocated society?" She lights her cigarette. "Of course, I wouldn't marry someone I didn't like." She takes a puff from her cigarette. "Maman and Baba approved of him and they invited the family over for dinner. I liked him right from the start and as I saw him more, I began to love him."

I smile at the irony. Love has been far less complicated for her in this closed society compared to mine in the free world. I ask, "Does everybody marry a suitor?"

"No. Some girls take a chance, sneak around, or fall in love. Not me. I guess you could say I'm chicken."

The sun reaches me through the branches and I enjoy its warmth. The aroma of food and tobacco fills the air and a parrot in a cage hanging from the willow tree repeats a Farsi word I don't know. As Vida continues to smoke, her expression turns more serious and I have a feeling she really wants to talk. It takes her a while before she is ready to plunge into the past, but when she does, it's with ease.

"I never kept anything to myself," she says and I know she is referring to her childhood. "That's how I came to terms with what happened and was able to forgive Mom." She takes another drag from her cigarette and the air between us fills with smoke. "Baba Ameli was always watching out for me. I spent summer holidays with them in Tehran and he took me for long walks in the park, where I could talk to him about how I felt. We kept it our secret."

That sounds like my grandfather, making sure his little ones passed safely through hard times.

"What a grandpa we had," I say and it feels good to share him.

She sighs. "What a grandpa."

"How come you never called Mom from his house?"

Her eyes darken. "I hated her!" And she turns her face away. "I hated her because I thought she hated *me*. When Marjan died, I saw how she wished it had been me instead. Marjan was the perfect child, the one who got the good grades, her room was neater, and she never whined. The list went on and on. I was nothing to be proud of."

I can't believe what I'm hearing. How could Vida be so mistaken? Was she brainwashed into believing such nonsense? Over the next hour, my sister tells me how after Marjan's loss, our grieving mother withdrew from everyone. Vida's care was left to Dayeh, or worse, to Aunt Badri.

"Dayeh said Mom needed time to herself, that she needed to grieve. Aunt Badri believed Mom never loved me. But I knew better." Tears fill her lovely eyes. "I watched Mom. She just sat in her room for hours on end, clutching at Marjan's old rag doll, smelling it. She never cried and always seemed to be mad at me. Sometimes she didn't even see me there, or just asked Dayeh to take me away."

My sister wipes her tears. I wipe mine.

"The worst part is, I'm still convinced that if it had been me who died, Mom would have come back for Marjan. That losing her was her reason for leaving me." She buries her face in her napkin and when she lifts her head, black mascara is all over her cheeks.

How alike our lives have been!

My big sister proceeds to tell me how her father gave her double the love, how she slept in Parisa's arms after awakening from nightmares. The more she speaks, the more Moradi begins to sound like a real father. But I still can't talk about him the way Vida speaks of Mom. The fact that she has forgiven Mom makes her words more understandable. I can't forgive Moradi that way.

A man approaches and sets a brass tray on the rug for us. There's an old teapot with a repaired crack on its side, two hourglass shaped tea glasses in floral saucers and a bowl of cumin candies. When he leaves, Vida pours our tea.

"So, what made you forgive her?"

"Maman Parisa's talks."

"Parisa?"

Vida nods. "Some nights, she told me stories about mothers and daughters and when it came to the part where the mother loved her daughter, she added, 'just like your real mom.' And when she told me how much she loved me, she made sure to add, 'but I'll bet Rana loves you even more.'"

Hearing this makes it hard to hate the woman.

For a few minutes, we drink our tea in silence. I know it's my turn to talk. Unable to share my resentment of Moradi, I tell her about my childhood operations and how much I suffered before I could take normal steps. "I'm still not normal. In fact, my right leg is about half an inch shorter, but I've learned how to balance my steps."

"I had no idea it was that bad."

"It's okay now." I pull up the leg of my pants and show her the scar. "This is all that's left of those horrible days."

She gently runs her fingertip over the scar, as if to smooth out the deep hurt.

I take us out of that subject by mentioning Paul. She seems fascinated by our freedom to practically live together.

"Well, I'm not really free to do that. Mom is still in denial and Paul understands my limits." I suddenly miss Paul more than I thought possible. In a perfect world, he would be my date to this wedding and we could be free-spirited tourists sharing the fun of visiting a new place. He needs a vacation as much as I do. Instead, I imagine him eating take-out and watching football.

"So when are you going to tell Mom?" Vida asks.

"No idea."

It's a hot afternoon, but sitting under the tree shade and sipping this simple tea is fast turning into a highlight of my visit. By the time Bijan shows up, Vida and I are ready to return to our crowded family. I am miles away from Chicago's lonely days and it feels great to be going to a house full of relatives. Deep down I wish Moradi would show up and get this awkwardness over with. Still, with the wedding just a day away, it looks as though that's going to be when both Mom and I will finally face him. Maybe he could be a nice father to Vida, but I hate him for being so cold toward me.

⁓

I have not been sitting idly. Never losing sight of what brought me here, I have asked Mom's permission to look into the Iranian divorce law and plan her next move. She seems to have finally come to terms with her separation and for the first time is willing to claim her freedom. Aunt Mandy helped me in contacting a good friend of grandpa's—the same old lawyer, who Mom says was instrumental in what she continues to call her "escape." This is my third visit to Eskandary & Eskandary law firm. Mr. Eskandary senior no longer practices, but his son has taken over and he has been most helpful. He must be in his fifties and says his biggest dream is to visit the United States. My aunt thinks he is extra nice because I'll be able to send him an invitation to facilitate his visa. Whatever the reason may be, he is doing more than I could have imagined.

Mr. Eskandary is short and a bit overweight, and despite the summer heat, he insists on wearing a three-piece suit. He is also one of the few men I've seen wearing a necktie in public. We are investigating the different possibilities to petition on Mom's behalf for her divorce. A ray of sunlight comes through the single small window, but the room is rather dark. I imagine my grandfather sitting in this same chair for the exact reason that has brought me here. I watch Eskandary scan through a folder and wonder if I'll ever understand the Islamic law.

"As we discussed on the phone, Islam allows a man to retain four legal wives," Mr. Easkanday says. "The law only states that he should treat his wives equally. That's where I hoped the hardship your mother has endured would help us."

"Doesn't it?"

"Unfortunately, no. There is no evidence of mistreatment and it was your mother who abandoned her spouse, and not vice-versa."

His English, despite the heavy accent, is clear and strong. In fact, he sometimes uses words that sound too bookish, but maybe that's his lawyerly nature, trying the most impressive vocabulary.

"This fact may astonish you," Mr. Eskandary says, "But he still has inclusive power."

"What do you mean?"

"The law gives the man full control over a wife. For example, in order to leave the country, your mother will require his authorization."

I've known that, but realize there's more to learn. It doesn't help to be reminded how none of my law books are of much help here.

Our day's work is done and as I get up, I tell him I still want to go to court with this.

He extends a hand for me to shake, a sure sign of defiance toward the new regime. "Rest assured, Miss Moradi. If there's a way to obtain your mother's freedom I will find it."

I am tempted to remind him that my last name is Ameli, but decide we both have bigger things to worry about. As I leave his office, it's clear I shouldn't build up too much hope.

—

Aunt Soraya's beautician is all ours for the day. The entire salon is closed to the public so the bride and family can enjoy all kinds of beauty treatments. Disregarding the Islamic ban, lively dance music blasts throughout the place. There's a young girl in charge of serving Turkish coffee and pastries, and if it weren't for the strong odor of hair color and cosmetic products, this could very well be a party.

Aunt Badri has finally materialized. Making a special appearance all the way from Shiraz, she arrived last night and is staying at a hotel. So this is the first time we meet. When she first sees me, she comes close and studies my face closely. "You turned out more of an Ameli, no?" I'm not sure if she means that as a compliment, but decide that's how I'll take it. She doesn't know a good hairdresser in Tehran, so Aunt Tara picked her up on the way here. Apart from that comment, despite her good English she had nothing more to say to me. She did say a few things to Mom and mentioned my name while giving me a few suspicious glances, but they speak Farsi and I am not even sure I want to know what she says. Now sitting under the dryer, she dips her long nose into a fashion magazine and I decide I'm not going to like her.

This is the first time I see Mom with rollers in her hair. Back home, she only blow-dries her hair and either ties it back or wears it in a bun. Vida is behind a striped curtain, getting a facial. I'm the first to be done with my simple chignon, although the way the woman pulled, pushed, and teased my hair was anything but simple. The only English words she could utter were an occasional "Peeleez" and also for each one of my "Ouch"s she had a "So sorry" to offer.

Mom stops reading her Persian magazine and shouts from under the dryer, "How do you like your hair?"

I mouth my words. "Love it!"

She gives me a broad smile and takes out a pencil to do a crossword. It is fascinating to watch people do that in Persian, going right to left, especially since I don't even know the alphabet. Mom seems to have slid back into her old lifestyle with such ease, you'd think the past decades didn't exist, that she was frozen all these years and has just been thawed.

I glance in the mirror and have to admit, the woman has done a good job with my unruly hair. With nothing more to do, time goes by too slowly. There are a couple of French hairstyle magazines, but everything else is in Farsi. *Why didn't I bring a book?* I change seats, drink tea and eat another cream puff. Everyone else's empty Turkish coffee cup is sitting upside down on a napkin, waiting for the owner of the salon to read fortunes. I couldn't swallow the thick contraption; otherwise I would have loved the ritual.

We have brought our eveningwear, shoes, and accessories. The young girl who served pastries is now running around, helping us one by one to get dressed in the side room.

When Mom is done, I'm not too crazy about her coif. It looks a bit too formal, a contrast to her subtle style. But after she is dressed, I see how it complements her blue evening gown with its collar raised behind her graceful neck.

"Your mom has really aged," Aunt Badri whispers, but loud enough for everyone to hear. I am now thankful that the salon's workers don't understand English. She then turns to me. "You must learn to 'esspeak' Farsi." And just then Vida emerges from the corner room looking better than any bride I have ever seen. In a way, she now resembles Mom in that old wedding picture and I wonder if I'm the only one noticing that.

"*MashAllah,*" Mom whispers and I know this is her word for knock on wood. She bites her lower lip, a sure sign that she is fighting tears. Everyone applauds and someone brings in a tray of burning incense. Smoke fills the room and it smells exotically good. Vida

YALDA

is blushing and she seems pleased. A female photographer appears out of nowhere and starts taking pictures. I'm not sure what I had expected, but as beautiful as Vida looks, I'm disappointed that her gown is no different from what a bride back home might wear.

There's a knock on the door and a man announces something. Mom whispers to me, "The groom is waiting downstairs."

"Isn't it bad luck if he sees her?"

She smiles and shakes her head. "The groom is expected to bring flowers and drive his bride to the ceremony. That's our tradition."

What kind of ceremony will Paul and I have if we ever get married?

Although Vida has a veil, the hairdresser carefully drapes a chiffon scarf over her hair, which Mom explains is to ensure Islamic coverage in public. I'll never understand these stupid regulations because in her sleeveless gown, she sure doesn't look so Islamic to me. We each have a similar scarf to see us safely home.

Downstairs, Bijan in his tux is standing next to a silver Mercedes that is covered with many white flowers and resembles a mini float. He hands Vida a bouquet of orchids before helping her into the passenger seat. I notice there's no kissing, not even touching.

The rest of us pack into two other cars and now all three drivers beep in unison. People wave at us from the sidewalk, other cars join our beeping rhythm, and we're off. Tehran traffic is not too bad in the afternoon, so there's a good chance we'll make it in time for the ceremony at a garden in the suburbs.

I think of the shock of last week when I asked Aunt Mandy, "How come they don't have their wedding in town, at one of the many hotels?" She looked at me as though that was the weirdest question. "And risk a raid by the committee?" She went on to explain the social ban on gender mixing, loud music, dancing and serving alcohol. Now I know better. As we drive toward this remote garden, I'm wondering if the committee won't find us, anyway.

We exit the highway and turn onto the gravel road that leads to the garden. Strands of colorful lights illuminate the gate. Drivers begin to sound their horns again and a man standing at the gate begins to clap. Dust rises behind the bride's car and even as we park and get out, remnants of it linger around us. I hold my long skirt up a little as I walk through the dusty lane. There's a blue partition in the middle of the garden, separating the men's section from the women's, and high enough to block the view.

"Why didn't anyone tell me it's not really a mix?" I say to Mom. "All this time I've been fretting that we may get arrested."

"What did you expect?"

"You know, like our family dinners, men and women together, no *hejab*."

"You seem to forgot that the crowd here isn't just family. We dare to mix and next the *Komiteh* will be here to arrest everyone."

I nod, though I'm still confused. I can't understand why we had to come all this way if it didn't guarantee some degree of privacy. Maybe I will never grasp the strange rules of this place, but tonight all I really care about is Mom. I give her my best smile. I'm here to make sure she enjoys every minute of this, that she is protected, and that Moradi and his woman won't do anything to upset her.

Loud music can be heard from the men's section—no doubt an all male band. The sound system on our side is fabulous and a few women have already started dancing, kicking their heels, twirling, swaying their arms. Other guests watch, clap to the rhythm, and encourage the younger girls to join them. A tall woman in a long-sleeved black gown approaches to greet us and she motions to a long table close to the dance floor. The largest orchid arrangement sits in the middle and two of the chairs around it are decorated with white lace. Aunt Mandy and I proceed toward the table, but I notice Mom lags behind. I look back and find her at the entrance, still talking to the tall woman.

"That must be Parisa," Aunt Mandy whispers.

I can't mask my shock and turn around for a better look. She is bending her head to hear mom over the loud music and keeps on nodding. "And Mom talks to her?"

My aunt shakes her head in disapproval. "Tell me about it! And this isn't the first time, either. Did she tell you about coming here yesterday to help her set the *sofreh aghd*?"

I glare back at the woman, fully aware of my own resentment. Yet as I watch, there's an aura of serenity about her that surprises me. Dressed in a simple black gown that frames her tall figure with subtle elegance, she is clearly not trying to fit the mother-of-the-bride mold. I also notice a certain politeness, a respectful little bow to Mom now and then. I'm reminded of what my aunt once said. "There's something about Parisa that makes it difficult to hate her." But I can try.

Mom seems uncomfortable, but not sad, not even upset. I watch the two of them walk toward the building in the far corner of the garden. Aunt Mandy explains that's where we shall have the ceremony. My aunt and I sit down and a server brings us tall glasses of *sekanjebin*. The minty sweet-and-sour drink soothes my dry throat and I use the tall spoon to fish out a few tiny cubes of floating cucumber. The music from the other side of the partition is too loud, making it impossible to talk, so my aunt and I just sit there and watch the guests and their parade of sequined dresses.

"Would you like to go around and meet a few older relatives?" Aunt Mandy asks.

I shake my head and have a feeling she is relieved. What's the use when I know their first comment is going to be about my failure to learn Farsi? For all I know, this may be the first and last Persian wedding I'll ever see, and to be sure it's my only chance to be the bride's sister. I look around, familiarize myself with faces, and absorb the details. By the time Mom comes back for us, the garden is filled with guests.

"How are all these people going to fit in that tiny building?" I ask her.

She chuckles. "They won't, honey. Only the close family is allowed to watch the aghd."

I'm now thinking that with so many regulations, there should be a manual about this for people like me. Mom is acting calm, but I don't think she's herself. Something about her pleasant façade is weird. Before she has turned around, I hold her sleeve and whisper, "Was that our beloved Parisa you were talking to?"

She glares at me. "I'm only going to say this once. I don't know her well, but we are her guests. She could have forbidden my presence here tonight."

I sneer. "It's *your* daughter who's getting married, Mom. Yours alone."

"Is she?" Now my mom sounds angry. "That woman raised my child with all the love she had. She did everything that I failed to do." She is holding my hand a little too tight. "In that sense, she is in a class all her own and the least I can do is show some gratitude." She clenches her teeth. "And I expect the same from you."

Mom turns around and starts walking toward the building. As much as I hate to admit it, I know she is right. I follow in silence, a little kid who has just been repremanded.

My aunts and a few members of the groom's family join us along the way. I whisper to Mandana, "Is the ceremony private enough for male relatives to be inside?"

She shakes her head. "Men are never allowed in the *aghd* room, anyway." Then noticing my surprise she adds, "An old practice."

So at this rate, I may leave the country without really seeing my father.

The small building consists mainly of three connected rooms. I find Mom in the larger room to the right, putting the final touches on the decorations in the middle of the room. There's a rectangle white cloth on the floor and a single bench next to it. I don't know half the items of this spread, except for the silver mirror and two candelabras on either side. Then I recognize the open book sitting on a carved wooden stand. That's the Moradi family's Koran, the one Mom has kept on her mantle all these years. Even though neither of us is religious, for as long as I can remember she has passed me under it before I went on a trip. She must have brought it along, thinking Vida should have something that holds her history.

The combination of old and new items has created an amazing *sofreh*, a sort of alter which is both exotic and elegant. There are flowers everywhere, including two planters of unusually large orchids. The silver mirror is as large as the one on my small dresser. The reflection of candlelight in the mirror enhances the dreamy quality of all this white lace.

"In the old days, it was in this mirror where the bride and groom saw each other's face for the first time," Aunt Mandy tells me. She's still holding a few items that need to go somewhere. "Would you like me to explain the other items?"

I shake my head. "Maybe later. For now, I'm kind of enjoying the mystery." My thoughts fly back to Paul. Stuck in a Muslims surrounding, it's even harder to imagine a possible future for the two of us. At the same time, with each passing day I miss him more. I would never survive here, where I only understand a few words, among people who know nothing about my culture, who seem too close for comfort. I love my relatives and appreciate their undivided attention, but oh what I wouldn't do for a quiet day when I could be alone and invisible.

Loud music followed by everyone clapping announces the bride and groom's arrival. I look up and see Vida, her veil lowered, her soon-to-be husband holding her elbow. I look beyond them, but only see a few cheering women following. Aunt Soraya helps Vida to sit down, rearranges the train of her gown, and makes room on the bench for Bijan. She then reaches for two sugar cones that are wrapped in lace and adorned with tiny pink flowers. Aunt Mandy beckons me to join her and the women who now hold a white lace over the heads of the bride and groom. In the silence that follows, we hear men talking next door, but then they stop and a man begins to recites verses. I know this must be the clergy because his Arabic words lack the melodic tone of Farsi.

Aunt Soraya starts grinding the two cones together and a dust of sugar falls on the white lace like soft snow. I give Aunt Mandy a questioning look and she whispers, "A shower of sweetness over their joint life."

Sweetness indeed. Whether it is Baklava, white candies, or cream puffs -- whatever we back home celebrate with a glass of wine, Persians commemorate with something sweet. They also take every chance to celebrate. From the bride's dress being delivered, to the new shoes we bought, everything required a *shirini*—sweetness.

Aunt Tara picks up a large needle that has a rainbow of silk threads. Everyone laughs as she chants something while putting stitches into the lace we are holding. "She is sewing the tongues of the groom's mother and sister—an old ritual, something to laugh about." Judging by what I've seen of Aunt Badri, I'm now wondering if they neglected to sew her tongue at Mom's wedding.

The clergy says in a louder voice, "*Khanoom* Vida Moradi, blah blah blah?" Vida doesn't respond and Aunt Tara shouts something back that makes everyone laugh again. Aunt Mandana translates, "He asked Vida to say yes, but she's not supposed to, not until the third time."

I see Parisa standing outside, just short of the room's entrance. When Aunt Mandy finds me staring, she whispers, "Women in black shouldn't be in the room. It's bad luck." I want to believe this is a coincidence, but whatever her reason, I'm glad it is Mom who is here, now nodding her permission to Vida. Now that Mom has given her blessing, I notice everyone is looking to the adjoining room. *Both parents' permission is required.* My heart leaps. I look at Mom, whose eyes are also fixated in that direction. Despite the heavy makeup, suddenly she looks too pale. Finally, a man's deep voice is heard as he says something with Vida-*jan* in it.

Throughout the next minutes, while the bride and groom say their *"Baleh"*—yes, the man's voice echoes in my head. "Vida–*jan,*" he had said. Would he ever call my name in that tone? Loud cheers followed by music and clapping drown the voices in my head. Mom reaches into the pouch she's been carrying and showers the couple with tiny white candies and small golden coins. Women close in and one by one, they take turns to kiss Vida, kiss Bijan, and congratulate my mom. I keep an eye on the archway that connects this room to the next, still waiting, waiting for my father to walk through.

—

The *aghd* ceremony has long ended, but there are still several women, holding small jewelry boxes, waiting their turns to offer a bridal gift. Mom's ruby necklace looks beautiful on Vida, but from her forced smile I can tell how tired my sister must be. I knew jewelry was the traditional gift, but didn't expect the items to be so elaborate. I watch Vida reach up to another lady, who is now presenting her with an ornate gold chain. She kisses the woman's cheek and passes the gift over to Aunt Mandy to hold.

"Yalda-joon, could you bring me that velvet sack, please?" Mom calls out over the cacophony of women huddled around the *sofreh.* Amid all this, poor Bijan sits idly, his cheeks covered in all shades of lipstick. I'm surprised that the Islamic law allows the groom to be among women; then again, I suppose in his vulnerable state, he is not considered a threat to their virtue.

I rush to the adjoining room, where I've left my purse. There in the middle of what must be a dining room, is a large table with a few gift-wrapped boxes and a mound of handbags, shawls, and scarves. I lift a paisley shawl from over the other purses and can't help wondering why so many women carry a black purse.

"Hello, Yalda."

His voice is deep and even though I haven't heard enough of it, I know it well. My swift turn knocks something off the table, but neither of us bothers to check. He stands less than three feet away and now seems taller than the man at the airport. His eyes are dark, but they are filled with tenderness. Their warmth hooks me, yet I can't find a name for how I feel.

His smile is lopsided, filled more with sorrow than joy. He leans forward and opens his long arms. I instinctively take a small step back. I am not going to let him come any closer. Touching him would only validate his presence in my life. It's hard enough to be in the same room with the man, and I realize that despite the days and weeks of being here, I'm not ready for this. How much time does one need to accept that the dead is in fact alive? I look at my sweaty palms and remind myself how he has long missed the chance for such an embrace. It is now my turn to reject him and I want him to feel what it's like. No matter how many times I have dreamt of my father's arms around me, I feel compelled to refuse him. Doing so is a touch of ice over my deep sore.

From the corner of my eye I watch him lower his arms in slow motion. I stare at my trembling hands and pray that, with my back to the light, I'm just a dark shadow to him and that he can't see my anguish. A few seconds pass before I slowly circle the table. Hoping to appear casual, I continue to sort the pile of purses through a blur. Under the weight of his stare, and of all that is going on in my head, the thought that he might be checking my imperfect steps is the clearest. For the first time in years, what's left of my limp no longer seems so slight. I won't allow him to feel sorry for me. Does he have any idea what I've endured to come this far?

The fear that I might stumble and fall is back and the timidity that I left behind years ago now creeps back with full force. *Am I sweating?*

"Yalda *jan*, it's wonderful to be reunited ... at last."

Oh, what a voice. I bet this is what attracted his woman to him, this warm, loving, conniving tone and his theatric performance. I prefer the Shirazee "*jan*" over Tehran's "*joon*." How strange it is to enjoy his voice, his rolling "rrr"s and how he annunciates every word. Part of me wants him to go on talking. What a cozy feeling it is to be standing here, facing my father, a living, breathing person who despite the gray hair is still strong and handsome, more so than all the after-school-fathers of my childhood.

In a few small steps, I have distanced myself as far as the small room allows. I turn to the single window, where a blue curtain separates us from the world out there. For a moment, I let my mind paint a variety of endearing pictures. I imagine him in his car waiting in front of my school. He opens the door to his car, helps me up and fastens my seatbelt. He goes around the car and waves to my friend Tanya's father. I picture him clicking his camera as I blow out the candles on my birthday cake. I hear my young giggle as he picks me up for a ride on his broad shoulders. He looks so great in all those visions that I want to hold on to them. But then I turn and flinch at the man across the room. Warm as his eyes may try to be, his mere presence sends a cold sensation through me.

Here is my purse. I open it and take out the green velvet sack Mom has brought along for the bridal jewelry. I toss my purse back among the others and go around the far side of the table. He doesn't move and I have a feeling is no longer looking at me, either. I grab the door's handle, but before leaving, I turn and nod politely.

He looks up, his jaws tight, his eyes dark. No, I'm not going to let his sad expression soften my heart. I'm only here to make sure my mother's future, and mine, will have nothing to do with this man.

"Good to meet you, too, Colonel."

I don't think my voice has ever been colder. The mere mention of his army rank builds a wall of ice between us. His tormented face bears no resemblance to the arrogant man in that picture Mom had shown me. The faint smile has vanished and he suddenly looks old, fragile even. He looks down and I want to believe that he is bending down his head in shame. Then again, maybe he's just studying my feet.

When he looks up, I think I see the sparkle of tears in his eyes and I'm surprised at the sting of regret inside me. Have I pushed him too far? Am I hanging the man without the benefit of a fair trial? For all I know, this could well be my only chance to exchange words of affection with someone whose absence has left a huge void in my life.

Stop it, Yalda!

I am back in the crowded room where many women are talking at once and no one seems to be listening. Mom's eyes find mine and as I pass the velvet sack into her outstretched hand, her fingertips stay on my hand a bit too long. She stares into my eyes before taking the sack then turns back to Vida, but in her hesitant touch she has already told me she knows.

Loud music blasts through the room and Bijan's sister—whose name I'll never be able to pronounce—starts her solo dance in the middle of the crowded room. Women step back and open a circle and everyone, including the bride, claps to the beat.

Of all that I had pictured, that sure was the worst way to meet him.

I join the clapping and marvel at the woman's swift moves in a seductive dance. Someone circles the room with a tray of burning wild rue. I take a deep breath and pull in the pleasant aroma. Mom is finally sitting down with a glass of tea and has removed her shoes. I study her across the room. She takes a sugar cube, dips it in her tea before putting it in her mouth and sipping the tea. Back home, she never did this. Like the rest of us, she poured a package of sweetener in her large mug. Then again, back home she wasn't so animated, either. As much as I hate to admit it, my mother seems to be home for the first time.

Mom looks up and I wonder if her eyes are questioning me. Did she know when she sent me for the pouch that Moradi would be there? I must be crazy to think this. How could she? Fascinating as this ceremony has been, my mind won't leave the adjacent room and I'm not too happy about the way I've handled the situation.

Then again, I was polite. At least I did tame my anger. A Colonel might consider such discipline good enough for now. But will he call again?

I help Aunt Mandy with the cleanup and gather scraps of wrapping paper from the floor. Over and over I revisit the scene in the next room and try to be objective about it. I know Mom's side of their marriage, but what's his? There has to be more to find out. If I am to ensure Mom's freedom, I will need something to nail him.

Chapter

· *Twenty-Four* ·

M R. ESKANDARY'S DARK OFFICE furniture prepares me
for the gloomy job ahead. This must have been how the
place looked when his father practiced law, but now
that it's his alone I can't see why he doesn't make it more cheerful.
It's as though lawyers anticipate unpleasant discussions and set the
mood. In the heavy silence of the room, I glance across the desk at
our lawyer and detect a stern expression on his face.

Mr. Eskandary clears his throat. "I'm afraid I have some bad
news." He wiggles in his chair. "Colonel Moradi has sent back the
documents." He flips through a few pages of the file before him and
adds, "Unsigned."

"Why?" I ask as a reflex.

The young lawyer looks at Mom, then at me. "He demands to
be present at the hearing."

I look at Mom and wonder if she feels my anxiety. If she has any
of her own, she sure has a good way of masking it.

So far, my father has only discussed the matter of a divorce
with Mr. Eskandary. Throughout the proceedings, he agreed with
Mom's suggestion that his lawyer represent him whenever she was

present. This is the first I hear of this, and judging by the expression on Mr. Eskandary's face, it can't be good.

The next minutes go by in silence. I study Mom and wonder why she decided to wear black today. Lately she hasn't worn any bright colors, not even at home. She also seems more distant and I sense a world of cultural differences standing between us. Here, my mother's otherness is more evident to me. It's hard to see her contentment in a place that is so foreign to me. I love listening to her chatter, or to catch the sparkle in her eyes. But the new distance between us scares me. The fact that we share so little makes me feel like an intruder. Sometimes I wonder if she resents having left this place, resents her American life, and I don't even want to consider how she feels about her daughter being so American.

As for me, it's just a journey, a chance to know the family I didn't know I had and become familiar with my mother's background. Sometimes I think I've had just about enough of it. Like a common cold, the melancholic mood of this nation has spread, affecting each one of us. Sometimes the only thing Mom and I seem to share is a charged silence.

I loosen my headscarf and let the breeze from the ceiling fan cool my sweaty neck.

"Good idea," Mom says and she unties her own scarf, fanning her face with its sides.

Mr. Eskandary looks away and ignores our lack of *hejab*, but he stays on the subject. "Trust me, I was surprised to hear this request." And he sounds ashamed for my father's behavior.

A bitter smile parts Mom's lips and she recites a verse, "*Each moment another new harvest arrives from this garden.*" Mr. Eskandary nods his understanding and I wonder if this is another one of her word-for-word translations. For as long as I can remember, my mother has put Persian expressions to English words, disregarding how much of the meaning may be lost in translation. But lately it happens too often and sometimes sounds like a whole new dialect. I have also noticed she has a heavier accent, dragging her words and ending most of her questions with a 'yeees' or a 'nooo'. *"You're going shopping with me, nooo?"*

"In another circumstance this should make no difference," the lawyer says in a calm voice. "It's just that Colonel Moradi's charisma may make it harder for us to convince the judge of his … neglect."

Neglect indeed.

I realize that for a polite lawyer, there would be only a few words to describe my father's indiscretions, especially his bigamy.

"Maybe it would be best if *we* weren't present," I suggest, not knowing what else to say. "I'm obviously not going to be much help before a Persian-speaking judge. And as for Mom, I've said this before, I won't send her in alone."

"I understand. But you're my key witness."

"What witness? I was just a baby, remember? Why not call on my sister to testify?"

Mr. Eskandary looks disturbed. "I did. But Miss Vida has specifically requested to be excluded." He gives me a desperate look. "You're all I've got." He smiles bitterly and points to the street. "Unless I hire one from out there."

"Hire? I'm not sure I know what you mean."

"Madam councilor," he addresses me formally, as he did when we first met. "Please don't forget you're in Iran. There are thousands of jobless people who for a small amount would swear to anything you want them to. You'll see them hanging around the courthouse like hungry flies. But that's not the kind of witness you want, especially not when the judges know them all."

Mom is quiet and I wonder if she is losing hope the way I am.

I think for a moment. "Everything I know is already documented." I nod to the file before him. "Can't you use *that*?"

Mr. Eskandary gives me a sad look.

"We could. But I'm afraid Colonel Moradi's request is very specific. He has insisted that both of you be present."

———

Out on the hot sidewalk, Mom and I are instructed to take the back seat of Mr. Eskandary's car. "Islamic rules," he explains while holding the door for Mom.

The first time I saw his beat up BMW, it surprised me that a successful lawyer could not afford a better car, but now I've been here long enough to know. With a declining economy and a ban on foreign imports, a luxury car, no matter how much of a wreck it may be, is still an indulgence.

With Mom and me safely tucked away, Mr. Eskandary gets behind the wheel and plunges into Tehran's heavy traffic.

"You're a great driver," I comment.

"Thank you, but as we say, all the drivers in Tehran are great because the bad ones are already dead." He chuckles at his own joke.

As he settles into what resembles a normal lane, I try to organize my thoughts. I am definitely not prepared for this court session. Moradi's request has taken away some of my earlier confidence and I feel the kind of jitters that were saved for finals. I try to picture the situation as a game of chess but, no matter how I look at it, I can't guess what the lawyer's plan of action is.

Mr. Eskandary breaks the heavy silence, "You'll see a crowd outside the courthouse, Some may offer to step in as your witness—*shahed*—family, and even be your lawyer."

Mom chuckles. "Only in *the land of flowers and nightingales*."

I don't understand her using such poetic description to criticize or mock the system, but gather that maybe Iranians use poetry even in their insults.

We turn into a side street and stop by a two-story building. Mr. Eskandary inches forward through a crowd that takes little notice of the approaching car. Finally he pulls alongside a whitewashed wall without running over anyone. "Please, ignore the mob and follow me into the building."

A single flag hangs above the narrow doorway and the guard standing outside has his hand on the barrel of his shotgun, watching the crowd. The building looks so ordinary that, had there not been a flag, I would have thought it to be a residence.

"*This* is the Courthouse?" I say, not hiding my ridicule.

Mr. Eskandary eyes me in the rearview mirror. "It is, and it isn't. You won't find the glamorous courthouses of America here; however, this is just a small branch of the main court." He chuckles. "We're not *that* bad."

I think I have offended him and want to say something, but he gets out of the car and opens the back door. "The main courthouse is in the central portion of the city. This one is what we call The Family Support Court." He shakes his head in sorrow. "When you consider that only matters of divorce, domestic violence and so on are brought here, the name becomes an oxymoron."

There's no parking meter. Mr. Eskandary takes out a heavy chain from the glove compartment, wraps it around the steering wheel and locks it with a padlock. "Car theft is so common that we need to take matters into our own hands," he says and then calls a boy standing nearby and gives him some money. I figure he's asking the guy to watch the car.

I adjust my headscarf and follow Mom, who is trying to keep up with Mr. Eskandary's fast pace. Suddenly people swarm around us, "*Khnoom, shahed?*"

Mr. Eskandary looks back and calls out to me. "This way please."

No sooner do they hear a foreign language than the younger guys start yelling, *"Mademoiselle? Hey, Mademoiselle!"*

Mom grabs my hand the way she used to when I was a little girl and pulls me. I willingly follow and try hard not to look around as we pass through.

Mr. Eskandary presents the guard with a document, which is probably our entry permit. We step into a long and poorly lit hallway. Here, too, there are many people, though these pay little attention to us. There are a few benches, but they are occupied and people are also sitting on the mosaic floor, leaning against the wall. A woman holds the edge of her *chador* between her teeth while rocking an infant in her arms. As I pass by, she looks up with suspicion. She has dark, beautiful eyes, but I sense hostility in them, even resentment. Men stare and one says something to Mom, but she doesn't seem to notice as she continues to follow Mr. Eskandary. We stop in front of room 11. I know this number because it's the only one in Persian that resembles ours.

Mr. Eskandary knocks on the wooden door and a guard opens it halfway. They exchange greetings before he steps aside, leaving the door wide open.

The room is no larger than Aunt Mandy's guestroom. Its meager furnishings consist of a long table, where two men are seated facing three short rows of metal chairs. Two of the chairs are already occupied. A turbaned clergy sits behind the table with a young man next to him, sitting erect, hands on his typewriter. The other two have their backs to us, but I have no trouble spotting my father's tall torso. At the sound of our high-heeled shoes on the mosaic floor, he stands and turns to face us. My father's lawyer and the young clerk also stand up in a show of respect; only the clergy remains seated. He glances at us sideways and continues to twirl his prayer beads.

We reach the row of chairs and I notice my father's eyes are on Mom. No, it's more than that. Their eyes are locked. The moment lasts long enough to make me uncomfortable. I don't know what to make of it, so I look away.

Mr. Eskandary is saying something to the clergy, then turns around and pulls up a chair for Mom. My father has finally taken his eyes off Mom. He beckons to the chair next to him, but I pretend to miss that and take a seat on the second row behind Mom. When Mr. Eskandary gives a bow and presents the clergy with a file, it is clear that we are indeed in a courtroom and the turbaned man must be the judge.

I had heard that most men here went to work without bothering to shave, but for some reason expected the judge to be an exception. Aunt Mandy has explained that a necktie is considered a sign of being pro-west and I've noticed how most men don't bother to button their shirts at the top. Still, this man in a brown cloak and black turban seems more suitable for delivering some sermon than presiding over a court of law.

As if sensing my apathy, the cleric gives me a harsh look and turning to the files before him, he mumbles, "*Bissmillahee ...*"

Even I know this to be the formal opening of a session, "in the name of Allah, the kind, the merciful." It's hard not to think of the many death sentences this man must have given in the name of his merciful Allah.

While discussions go back and forth in Persian, I try to figure out which way they are leaning. Our chairs are positioned in a slight curve and I can sense my father watching us. Mom is listening to the defense lawyer, ignoring everyone else in the room. I steal a look at my father and find him equally focused, but once in a while he looks at Mom, his wan smile lacking joy, giving him a vulnerable look. Does he seem affectionate toward her or is it my little girl's eyes, still looking for an unbroken set of parents? Ashamed of such thoughts, I remind myself the reason we are here.

Earlier, Mr. Eskandary mentioned we needed to be on best terms with the Colonel to finalize the divorce and I'm trying hard to convince myself that face-to-face, my father may cooperate.

Then again, Mr. Eskandary also says that divorce in Iran is only possible with proof of wrongdoing. "There has to be a substantial reason, such as addiction, mental disorder, abuse, and so on. In most cases, incriminating evidence or the presence of an eyewitness is required." As it is, our lawyer can't come up with a valid argument. His words echo in my mind, "... it was your mom who left him and not the other way around."

So, despite the superficial fairness of the Iranian law, it still comes down to the husband's consent. "Some justice!" Apparently I have whispered the words loud enough for everyone to turn and stare at me. Mom gives me a flustered look. My father's eyes meet mine briefly, but the look is blank and I'm not sure what to read in it. In no way does he resemble the loving father that Vida has portrayed.

Mr. Eskandary gently shakes his head and mumbles words that must be some form of apology. The defense lawyer clears his throat, but before he says a word, Mom's hand darts up like a student who has something urgent to say.

The judge looks at her from above his glasses. "*Baleh?*"

Mom stands and begins to speak. Her voice is shaky and while talking, she points a finger in my father's direction without looking at him. I don't have to understand the words to sense her rage. She goes on and on and I hear my name, Vida's, even Marjan's, but the way she annunciates the 'R' and the 'A' is different. When finished, she sits down just as abruptly and stares ahead. Silence chills the room and I'm dying for someone to explain what just happened.

When silence continues, Mr. Eskandary finally leans toward me. "I don't know how much of this you understood," he says, "but your mother has just dropped a bomb."

Please don't tell me that after all this, she has changed her mind on getting a divorce.

Eskandary continues, "She waived all our financial demands."

"She *what*?"

Mr. Eskandary motions for me to lower my voice. "Just before her announcement, your father's lawyer had declared that the colonel forgives your mom's wrongdoings and wishes to stay married."

"Forgives?" I mouth the word.

"That was his exact word. He is willing and able to keep both wives, and to secure that possibility, the defense has also produced a letter of consent from the new wife."

I'm trying to be quick and grasp the situation. Mr. Eskandary has told me about the Iranian prenuptial agreement—*Mehrieh*. My mother's comes close to a quarter-million dollars and it is payable any time she wishes, even today.

"Your mother must have seen this coming. She obviously knows that unless he agrees to a divorce, her only way out is to give up his financial support. She came prepared."

For a woman who can barely make ends meet, Mom's pride seems to have gotten the best of her. I clench my teeth and wait for more. The judge leans back, closes his fist around the prayer beads and faces Mom without looking at her. He says something in a surprisingly soothing voice.

Mom responds with equal calm while clutching her purse. She says something of which I understand only one word, "Merci."

Forms and papers are passed around, first to Moradi to sign, then to Mom, and finally the judge. The clerk keeps on typing for another minute before he wraps it up, stacks his pages and follows the judge out a back door. My mother has done it.

Moradi's flustered face tells me he cares as little about money as Mom does. He stands and I notice a slight bend in his back. Has it been there all along? I want to think not. I want it to be a sign of his wounded ego, that he is a soldier defeated at war. The defense lawyer shakes hands with him and judging by his rush he must have another appointment to go to. Moradi picks up his briefcase.

Mom stands. "Guess we're done," she says to me.

"Not quite," I say and am surprised at how authoritative I sound. "I believe we need to talk."

My mother looks up, first at me, then at Moradi. In her eyes, I see apprehension. It's clear she did not expect this. Maybe for her, the divorce is the end. What more could there be to talk about?

I glance at Mr. Eskandary and he quickly stands. "I'll be waiting outside," he says.

When the door has closed behind the lawyer, I motion to the chairs and my parents obediently take their seats. I face my father. "It's about time you offered your ex-wife a formal apology, Colonel, don't you agree?"

"Yalda!" Mom glares at me.

Moradi's face is flushed. He clears his throat, but no words come out.

Mom is looking down at her clasped hands and she too, seems flustered. A few awkward seconds pass. I would do anything to know what is going through their minds. *Come on, army man, I am offering you a chance to redeem yourself.*

Moradi's lips are pressed together, forming a thin line.

Mom finally looks up at where the judge had sat minutes ago and says to no one in particular, "It's too late for such formalities." She shakes her head in sorrow and a lock of her brown hair escapes from under her headscarf. "As I see it, no amount of regret is going to change anything. My life is mine and I have come to terms with it."

I wonder how small Moradi feels at this moment and when he doesn't say a word, I respond, "I know that, Mom. But for once, it would be good to hear your ex-husband ask for your forgiveness."

She looks ahead, beyond the room, perhaps into a day in her distant past.

Moradi exhales hard before speaking. "Parisa has been saying the same for months, that an apology is in order. But how does one apologize for something that spans over decades?" He tries to clear his throat, but the next words still come out scratchy. "I don't need to tell either of you how sorry I am." He sounds desperate, making me think he needs this talk more than anyone else. "I've spent two decades thinking about the pain I have caused you." He is looking at my mother, but the distant look on her face indicates that her mind is far away.

Moradi continues, "I feel shame for the way I dealt with the loss of our Marjan." His voice breaks and he stops a few seconds to swallow hard. "I let you grieve alone."

Mom's expression does not change. She seems unmoved and shows no sign of personal involvement.

"Look at me, Rana," he pleads.

Mom turns to him and blinks hard, then looks away again. "I didn't grieve," she finally says. "At least, not for years. And yes, I did deal with all my losses alone. I still do. One could say I buried my lost daughter just last week and I chose to do that alone, too." She stares back at him. "As for you, I buried you way back then."

Her words give me a shudder. I can't help thinking that in fact she is burying him at this very moment. Does he feel the chill? Just when I think Mom may say more, she picks up her purse, stands and turns to me. "We mustn't keep poor Mr. Eskandary waiting." She walks to the door, but stops just short of it and looks back at him. I have a feeling she wants to express some form of forgiveness, but she changes her mind and leaves.

Moradi doesn't move. He stays seated, facing the wall to his left. His expression bleeds the deep sorrow of a stabbed ego and I'm surprised at how sorry I feel for him. I follow my mother to the car.

On the long ride home no one speaks. Mom is deep in thought and I wonder if she can ever forgive the only man she has ever loved.

· *Twenty-Five* ·

"I THINK IT'S TIME TO CALL THE AIRLINE," Mom says without looking up from her sewing.

The comment hits me hard. It has been nearly a week since that day in court. I realize how, deep inside, I have given up hope that this trip will ever end. It's hard to believe how one phone call and a simple reservation could send us back to normal life. Something about this country makes one forget there's a wider world out there.

"We're not quite done here," I respond, finding it too demeaning to mention the final divorce papers she needs in order to leave the country without Moradi's consent. Lately it has been hard for us to communicate simple facts.

She continues to sew the loose button on her blouse and for a while I'm not sure she has heard me.

We are alone at Aunt Soraya's. My aunt and uncle are out. When Mom called and asked me to join her for lunch, I welcomed the chance and thought maybe I could persuade her to take me to the cemetery where Grandpa is laid to rest. The first time I asked, she said, "I refuse to visit any of their cemeteries and forbid you, too." And I knew that by 'their' she meant the new regime's. "My loved ones will forever live in my heart. As for a grave, I see this whole country as the burial of many beautiful people."

She has stood by her word and never showed interest in going to Shiraz to visit Marjan's grave. Having read her note from the plane, and especially after her reference at the courthouse, I picture her finding closure as she buries Emily—the doll—in some secluded garden in Tehran. Then again, such thoughts may be an indication that I, too, need a closure for Marjan's story.

I'm still angry about Mom's sudden decision to forgo the money that was coming to her, too angry to even bring it up. We haven't had much time to talk, but like it or not, there are a few issues to discuss. Most of all, I need to tell her about Colonel Moradi's recent letter.

It has been three days since Mr. Eskandary gave me the small envelope. "From your father," he said. The four-line letter is dry and formal. In it, Moradi has asked me to meet him in private before I leave for the States. "Please do me this favor and in return, I will do anything you ask me to, anything at all."

I have read his note enough times that by now it is memorized. Still, no one else knows about it. I haven't responded and am not sure what to do. So the crumpled piece of paper sits in my pocket and stays on my mind.

Knowing my Mom, soon it may be too late to bring up the matter without causing some hurt feelings. On the way here, I had no trouble rehearsing what I wanted to say. Now, sitting across from her, I'm once again tongue-tied.

"I haven't heard from Mr. Eskandary," Mom says. "Has he contacted you?"

"No, and I'm worried. We need the documents to get your exit permit."

She puts the blouse on her lap and crosses her hands over it. "I won't be needing any," she says before pinning me down with a firm stare. "I'm not going anywhere."

My laughter sounds as nervous as I feel. "That's not funny!"

"I'm not trying to be funny." She gives her attention back to her blouse.

"I don't get it."

"I intend to stay here," she says in her most serious tone. "I'm finally home, Yalda. This is where I'd like to live for my remaining years."

My gasp surprises even me. *Stay here and do what?*

Mom cuts a piece of thread with her teeth, wets one end in her mouth and holds the needle against the light coming through the window. I study her profile as the thread finds the needle's eye. I want to adjust to this new surprise, but am filled with too much disappointment. It's as though I have just received the result of a bad exam, one that all along I had expected to fail, yet had hoped for a miracle.

I should have seen this coming! She seems so changed that I can no longer guess what she's thinking. Sitting there with crossed legs on the couch, she even looks different. I've denied the obvious for some time, but now that it's out in the open, I wonder if I could have done something to stop it. Like a seed waiting for a good rain, Mom's old sentiments have flourished through this reunion. How could I even think of interfering when for the first time in a long time my mother seems so utterly happy? Then again, is she happy enough to forsake her American life? Me?

"Where did I go wrong, Mom?"

She stops her sewing and looks at me, wide-eyed. "My decision has nothing to do with you, honey. And don't you go thinking it was an easy one to make." She sighs. "I liked my life in the States. But it took me less than a day to realize this is where I really belong."

"Belong?" I don't mean to raise my voice. "What about your life back home?"

She stares at me. Hard. "This *is* home."

I laugh in anger. "And your daughter? Your friends? Don't any of us matter to you?" Her eyes are shaming me for thinking such thoughts, but I am on a roll now. "You're giving up twenty-four years of accomplishment—not to mention freedom—just so you can live *here*? I thought you had moved on."

Mom puts her sewing on the sofa and stands. "Almost twenty-five years," she corrects me, "but no, we Iranians don't move on. We may move, but we keep our country, our people, and a heavy baggage with us." She smiles sadly. "I was in the US, but all these years, I've secretly lived here. Isn't it amazing to find out that my sisters never stopped seeing my 'empty place' this entire time?"

This must be another one of her translated expressions, but I'm too outraged for trivial questions. I throw a hand in the air. "And *that* makes it okay to dump me?" I know I'm using guilt as my last weapon. "What am *I* supposed to do with your *empty place* back home, Mom?"

She sits next to me and gently holds my face in both hands. "I'm not dumping anybody, sweetheart. You're an adult and no longer need me to take care of you."

The warmth of her fingertips feels good on my wet cheeks. What has happened to the strong Yalda?

As Mom goes on to explain the reasons that led to this decision, her soothing tone brings back old memories. It was always the warmth of her body and the tenderness in her voice that soothed my pain more than any medicine could.

"America is a wonderful place to live, to pursue a dream, and to grow," she says. "It's like a greenhouse that nurtures its flourishing plants. But look at me." She motions to her body all the way down to her toes. "I'm a cactus, not a greenhouse plant. The cactus needs this harsh sun, the dry desert air. At this age, I can only find happiness in my natural habitat, among my own kind." And she recites a line of a Persian poem,

"*Pigeon with pigeon, dove with a dove,
birds of a kind, fly in harmony above*"

I look at Rana as if for the first time. Here she is, across the globe from Chicago and sounding more Persian than ever. The way she now pronounces *"Amreekah"* makes me want to smile. The change is evident even in the way she gathers her slim legs up on the sofa. Maybe I have denied my mother's Irnanian-ness long enough.

I press my eyelids shut, hoping to open them to a whole different scene. I envision life the way it used to be. Back home Mom's accent was diluted, negligible, but it was always there, wasn't it? I had admired her difference, her exotic looks, her otherness. When she showed up at my school wearing hand-knit sweaters, wool slacks and high-heeled shoes, she stood out among other mothers in their blue jeans, sweat shirts and sneakers. She even walked differently, was seldom in a rush, never running. Aware of her differences as I may have been, I never saw this coming.

Mom goes on down a list she must have prepared and concludes, "Besides, with a dual citizenship, I will keep my other passport and can visit you any time I want."

Visit? What would it be like to live far away from the only person I have known as family? Where would she live here? How will she survive without an income in this male-dominated society? And worse, I can't imagine the day when she may actually need Moradi's support. It's no comfort to realize that no matter how much I have learned about this country's divorce law, I know little about their social rules. In a place, where a single woman isn't allowed to stay at a hotel, could she find work?

Mom's calm expression couldn't be further from the storm within me. She seems so relaxed that, for a moment, I wonder if she even cares.

"My life is right here, among my family," she says and I want to think there's a hint of desolation in her voice. "It always has been."

"Not with me? Are you telling me that you've picked your sisters over your daughter?"

"No." She shakes her head. "I won't be living with my sisters. You're forgetting I also have another daughter to think of." She looks at me sideways. "Vida and Bijan will move to Tehran, but if necessary, I'd even move to Shiraz to be near them." She pats the back of my hand. "I couldn't be more proud of who you've turned out to be, Yalda–*jan*. But my job is done. You don't need Mom to see to your needs any more. I promise I'll come to you any time you should need me. As I get older, I'd rather be among family, and not be a burden to you."

"Did I ever give you the impression that you were a burden?"

She smiles. "Of course not. But someday I will be."

She speaks matter-of-factly and I can't believe how calm she is about everything. My anguish has done nothing to diminish the subtle joy in her smile or the ray of hope in her dreamy eyes. This can't be her only reason. All of a sudden a brand new discovery hits me. The image that pops into my head becomes clearer with each passing second. This is even harder to absorb, but I can think of no other explanation for the glow in Rana's face.

Is my mother still in love?

I study her more intently. Little wrinkles radiate from the corners of her sparkling eyes and her soft complexion shows a night cream shine. I notice she is wearing her favorite green eye shadow and I think there's even a touch of mascara. As far as I know she has no social plans today. It's a crazy notion, but I can't help wondering if Moradi stopped by earlier.

Is mom now "the other woman?" And why not? Maybe a role reversal is precisely what Parisa deserves. The vision is so perfect that I smile inwardly.

Mom gets up. "I sure could use some tea. How about you?"

I don't respond, but follow her into the kitchen.

"It's different for you," she goes on while turning up the dial on the electric samovar. A pot of tea sits on top of the samovar all day, ready to be served if someone drops in. And someone usually does.

Mom finds a towel and starts drying the tea glasses that are sitting on the dish rack. "The hardest part was to let you go. It isn't easy for me to accept America as your true home, or to admit that you need to go back to your normal life."

Normal life. America. The words take me back to Paul, to law school and to the job search ahead. I've enjoyed my vacation, but this chaotic lifestyle and the constant attention we receive overwhelms me. Somewhere deep inside I miss my carefree Sundays, when I wear a t-shirt and curl up on the couch with a good book. I long for a day when no one's watching me.

Poor Paul is so left behind that I have hardly had a chance to think about him. But I miss him. He would understand how confused I am. I can just see him making his special coffee and offering support as I try to untangle the complicated knot of my dual life. I still haven't talked to Mom about him and who knows if it will ever come to that. I've called Paul a couple of times, but somehow this place makes it harder to picture him.

Mom lines up her reasons for staying and leaves them there for me to see, like pieces of washed laundry on a clothesline. Of all people, I should be able to understand what it means to be "out of place." Whenever I've had enough of Islamic this and Islamic that, I draw comfort from knowing that soon I'll be back home and it will be over. I can hardly wait to return to my familiar habitat. Is that how Mom felt for all those years?

"I will be fine," she says. Maybe she will. But "fine" doesn't mean having freedom. I've seen the shrouded women who are not even allowed the simplest joys of life. Mom is letting go of her liberty just so she'll be near Vida. I can understand her need to do something for the child she has neglected, but isn't Vida all grown up, too? Does she even need her?

"Have you talked to Vida about this?"

Mom's eyes darken. "She never asked for any of this, if that's what you mean. I think Parisa has raised her to be too polite to express resentments, but I can feel it. I know that given a choice, she would have had Parisa at the *aghd*. It was Parisa's voice that should have given her permission to say 'I do.' Any fool can see who Vida's real mother is and I have come to terms with that. She can live without me. I'm only doing this so I can live with myself."

"What about me being alone, Mom?" I say and know how self-ish I sound.

"You won't be alone," she says and gives me a knowing look. My heart skips a beat. *She knows.* But then she changes the subject in her tactful way. "Has your father spoken to you since that day at the courthouse?"

I shake my head.

"Oh." She places the dried dishes in a cabinet, leaving out two large tea glasses in their gold-rimmed saucers. "So just what did he say to you at the wedding?"

There it is at last. Of course she knew. I recall how she looked at me when I returned to the room. How calm she seemed around Parisa. She acted so friendly that those who didn't know could never guess this was the same woman who had robbed her of a family. For all I know, Mom was behind my encounter with Moradi.

"You can't drop a bomb and change the subject, Mom. We're not done talking about your decision."

"Don't make this more difficult, Yalda. My mind's made up."

"Wow, Mom! How quickly this dictatorship has rubbed off on you."

She glares at me. "You think *I'm* the dictator? You're a fine one to talk. First you orchestrate my divorce and now you're telling me to go back to America and live in a place where I'll forever be nobody. You must have inherited the knack for ordering people around from your father!"

She mentions my father with no resentment and seems to expect me to be proud of the traits from his side of the family.

"It's got nothing to do with ordering you around and what is this 'nobody' business I hear? Things are different back home, Mom. Over there, everybody is somebody."

"That's not what I mean." She takes the glasses and starts pouring tea. "I receive plenty of support here, a true understanding. This is something that I rarely received outside of our little apartment in Wilmette. People here touch my heart, I have a role in their lives, that's what I mean by being somebody."

"That's beautiful, Mom, but affection is universal. Maybe you just didn't look hard enough for it." To say this, brings tears to my eyes.

"I did, but there was a difference I couldn't explain. I look back at my years in the US and wonder what happened to all the people I met along the way? Where are those college classmates, coworkers, or old neighbors? Then I come here decades later and everyone is there to greet me. Take Dayeh, for Heaven's sake! The woman can't even walk, but that didn't stop her from traveling a long distance just to see us." She looks into my eyes. "See what I mean?"

The problem is, I do see. But I say, "No, Mom. All I see is the impossibility of a life without you. What good is Chicago without Mom's place and our Friday nights?" This makes me cry even harder.

She throws her hands in the air. "I can't deal with you!"

Her tone reminds me of the universal mothers' threat of wait-till-your-father-gets-home and suddenly a question pops into my head.

"Did you put him up to that?"

"Up to what?"

"You know. The talk. How else would your Colonel know where to find me alone?" I am now so certain of it that I don't care how accusing I sound. Mom must have planned the whole thing. Did he even want to see me?

"Me?" Mom's laughter is pure anger. "Since when does Farhad Moradi do anything *I* ask of him?" She stops and lowers her voice. "I would never do such a thing, not without you knowing. We've had no discussions, whatsoever."

I don't know why this comes as a surprise. The fact that I'm staying across town from her, or that she has not shared much since our arrival, has allowed my imagination to create what it wants. Back home, such a talk would be no big deal.

I swallow hard and ask the question that has been brewing inside me. "Do you still love him?"

She gives me a fierce look. "Why are you doing this, Yalda?"

She is dodging my question and even though I worry that pushing it may fray the cord that connects us, I can't stop myself. "Isn't that the real reason you're staying?"

Her long silence tells me more than any words could. Finally she responds in her evasive way. "Spoken like a true American."

I'm not sure if that's an insult or a compliment. "Mom, I *am* an American!"

She sighs. "I know." We sit in silence for a minute. "He has his woman," she says this like a closing argument and there is enough hurt in her voice to convince me. I realize how her dignity would guard her against whatever it is that she feels for the man. "I owe it to Vida to give her what she's been denied."

I let the change of subject linger there for a while before going back to more of what I need to hear. "There are some facts I don't know. My questions are bound to revive some bad memories, but if you stay here, I may never have this chance again."

She just nods.

"What happened between the two of you?" I ask, and when she doesn't respond I add, "I mean, when did things start to go wrong?"

Mom exhales hard. "Some facts are buried so deeply that even I don't remember the details."

"Come on, Mom. He was the only man in your life. What went wrong?"

"Ah," she says nonchalantly and waves a hand in the air. "A forgotten love is as good as none."

So there *was* love. I am hoping this will be the time when she remembers the love and tells me all about it, but instead, she calmly sips her tea and is pulled into another silence.

It's time for direct approach. "What made him find himself another woman?" I ask.

She looks at me and puts her tea glass on the counter. "I don't know," she says and the honesty in her tone tells me that has remained a question for her, as well. Her voice is calm as she adds, "I can only guess how painful this entire experience has been for you. How it must hurt to know you have a father, to meet him, yet not know him."

I'm not going to allow Rana to change the subject again. Nobody could understand how I feel, especially not someone who had a father like Grandpa Ameli. If I weren't so outraged, this would be a perfect time to bring up Moradi's note. Then again, maybe Mom already knows about that, too. Let *her* bring it up. "That's not an answer," I say.

"Who said I had an answer?" She thinks for a while. "If I had known what went wrong—or when—I might have done something about it. The problem was that I only learned of his second marriage when his wife was already expecting."

I stare at her, wide eyed. "She had a child?"

"No. A miscarriage. But it made no difference. He was finished for me. My love for him went out the window the minute he walked out of the door to be with another woman."

I open my mouth, but she raises a hand and says, "And if you don't mind, I'd like to see the end of such talk."

The pain is back in her lovely eyes and I hate myself for having caused it.

In her brief explanation, Rana has painted a clear picture of her past. How would I react if Paul left my apartment one day and I knew he was on his way to see another woman? The fact that Mom has kept her silence for over twenty-five years is beyond my comprehension. Maybe it's cultural, or maybe motherhood dictated such strength. But I'm amazed at how broken she was and yet managed to keep the pieces of herself together for me.

Mom's voice is back to normal as she says, "See what you lawyers do to a simple question?" She chuckles. "All I asked was what happened between you and your father."

I want to tell her how it feels to have lost a father twice. It was easier to deal with the fact that he didn't want me. All I needed for that was deep hatred. But this time it hurts more because I'm faced with a father I can't entirely hate. "Nothing happened," I say and immediately regret my harsh tone. A few minutes go by in silence. "I'm sorry, Mom. There's really nothing to tell."

"What did you say to him?"

I don't want to make too much of that brief encounter. "We just said hello."

"That's all?"

"Yes. Figuratively speaking."

She nods with understanding. "Some people just can't change. The man is obviously as aloof as ever."

I study her in disbelief. We're speaking of Colonel Moradi's failure to express his emotions, his inability to apologize for his transgressions, and all she has to offer is a generous excuse? I take a good hard look at Rana and all I can see is her vulnerability. It will be hard enough to leave her here, but even harder to know she will be near Parisa or worse, that Moradi may hurt her again.

For days to come, I keep Moradi's note in my pocket. He wants to see me, and I don't know what to decide. Every time I'm in public, I wonder how many of the men I see have multiple wives? "It's now legal," the lawyer has said. Legal? Why don't they just make murder legal? I have seen how bigamy can kill a woman from the inside.

Chapter

· *Twenty-Six* ·

"HE CAN'T MAKE A SCENE IN PUBLIC." I don't remember where I've heard the phrase, but it's good advice. I have agreed to meet my father in a popular café, but now that the taxi has dropped me off, I feel ridiculous. Could it be that I feared *I* might be the one making the alleged scene?

Earlier today, my father called—God, no matter how hard I try, the word 'father' still sounds strange in reference to Colonel Moradi.

My aunt picked up the phone.

"*Allo?*" she said and soon passed the receiver to me without another word. The look she gave me was enough to know who the caller was.

"When can I see you?" the mesmerizing voice said, not bothering with a greeting. He sounded self-assured.

Aunt Mandy gave me an inquisitive look. She was about to go to somebody's memorial service and I'd have nothing to do until dinnertime.

"How about this afternoon?" I blurted before I could stop.

I turned my back to my aunt and waited for Moradi's response. There was a pause for a few seconds. "Good. Four-o-clock?"

Simple as that. We had put an end to my days of inner conflict. So here I am, this time forewarned, rehearsed even.

Despite the early afternoon hour, the café is crowded and dimly lit. The air is filled with cigarette smoke. As soon as my eyes adjust to semi darkness, I look around for him. Almost everyone here is young and from the books scattered on most tables I assume Iranian students have also moved their work from their desks and libraries to local coffee shops.

"Yalda," Moradi's voice makes me turn around. With a few long strides he reaches me, gently holds my elbow and points to a set of stairs. "This way, dear."

"Hello," I say, not knowing what else to add.

We go up the stairs and into what seems to be a more private extension of the café. Except for a young couple in the corner, the place is empty, and judging by the way they lean into each other, I gather they must have sneaked in on a secret date. No sooner do we arrive than they each say something to Moradi and leave.

My father points to a round table that has two bistro type chairs on either side and I take one before my shaking knees give up on me.

"Thank you for coming," he says formally as he picks up a folded sign from the table and puts it face down. "The owner of this café is an old friend. He reserved this room for us. Feel free to loosen your scarf and relax, we'll have ample privacy." When I don't move he adds, "Hope you like iced coffee. I took the liberty of ordering for both of us."

How terribly typical of him to assume, order, and take charge. "That's fine," I say and know I'm already being judgmental. I do like iced coffee. Had it been Mom ordering ahead, I'd appreciate her thoughtfulness, her knowing and providing what I needed.

Despite his warm voice and benevolent tone, resentment is rising within me. I picture him in this "ample privacy" meeting his Parisa. Where was Mom while they sipped iced coffee? How long did that go on before my poor mother found out? I look at the man sitting across from me and once again he is just Colonel Moradi, not my father, not the one I had prepared a speech for, not the one I dared to imagine being embraced by.

"How does the *kommiteh* know we are ..." I say and hesitate. "... related?" He must know about my birth certificate and last name.

He taps his breast pocket. "I brought enough cash to send them away."

I am disgusted at how easily their law can be broken, but remind myself that the only reason I've agreed to meet him is because I want something.

"So you're an attorney," he says with a broad smile, taking some credit for it.

"Why the sudden interest, Colonel?" I ask and know I'm being rude.

"The interest is not 'sudden', as you put it." He looks down. "You'll never know the number of times I have wanted to do this." He sounds affectionate and I hate him for being so damned like-able. It was much easier to dislike him before we met. What a great actor he'd make. I look to the door and am grateful to see a waiter, carrying a tray. He places two tall glasses of iced coffee before us and adds a platter of dainty pastries. He asks Colonel Moradi something to which he shakes his head and says, "*Nah, merci.*"

Moradi waits for the man to leave before he speaks again. "Regret will serve me no purpose. I need to get past all that. But as I age, I feel compelled to do something for you, something that may help me to forgive myself."

Amazing how everything is about him.

"I don't need anything. Your concerns should be for Mom."

He nods. "Unfortunately, she doesn't seem to need me." It's clear how much he resents that. Something in his tone also tells me he has come to such a conclusion after having talked to Mom, though she has denied such a talk.

"Neither do I." The words fly out of my mouth before I can stop them.

He smiles a sad smile. "I deserved that."

"It wasn't intended as an insult," I say almost apologetically. But then realize I have nothing to apologize for. "Years earlier I might have answered differently, but now I'm finally at a stage in life where I don't need your help."

He gives me a wan smile. "God only knows the depth of my regret." His words sound like inner thoughts. "True that I can only blame myself, but by the time I came to my senses and realized what I had done, Rana had vanished with no forwarding address."

"And when was that?" There's a sting of sarcasm in my tone.

"Sometime around your first operation."

"Ha! As early as nine years later!"

He is quiet for a while and I can't read his face, then he clears his throat and says, "You were three when Rana relocated from New York to Chicago. She stopped sending letters to Vida and told her father not to tell me where she lived."

I'm not about to let him blame Mom. "Would you have done any differently if for three years your mail was returned?" He doesn't respond, so I continue, "What puzzles me is why you wouldn't give my mother a divorce." I sound harsh.

He glares at me. "Why would I? So the mother of my children could go and marry someone in America?"

"So what if she did? At least she'd do it *after* resolving her previous marriage."

My indirect reference to his bigamy makes him blush, but I have just begun. "You can stick to your convenient laws, rules set by men and for their own benefit, but there's a free world out there." This is the lawyer talking, not the girl and certainly not the daughter. "Where were you when 'the mother of your children' worked double shifts? Where was your generous support when she took your daughter from doctor to doctor to doctor?" I get up and pace the short distance available to me. I bite my lip. *Don't you dare cry, Yalda!*

His silence tells me he's searching his mind for the right response. As if this is a game of chess, I give him time to make the next move. He buys time while taking a pack of cigarettes out of his pocket and politely holds it out to me.

I shake my head.

"Good," he says, and I think how ironic it is that almost everyone here smokes, yet they all admire non-smokers. I watch him light his cigarette and take a deep puff. The smoke lingers inside him and comes out in fragments with the next words. "I want to believe it's not too late."

I laugh. What's this man's standard for 'too late'? I search for words that could equally hurt him, but what comes out of my mouth sounds rational, calm even. "Let's be practical, Colonel. It's already too late for me, but maybe not for my mother."

He seems puzzled.

I continue as planned. "Let's see just how serious you are about helping. It's about time you did something substantial for Rana, don't you think?"

A wounded look creeps into his eyes, but he sounds composed. "I've already asked her. Unfortunately, her response was much the same. That she doesn't need my help."

"Or maybe she does, but is just too proud to admit it."

He looks at me with newfound hope. "Just tell me, please Yalda Jan. Anything!"

I weigh my words carefully. "Give her financial independence. She gave up her money just so she could be free. But she'll need it."

I hesitate and hit him with my request just when I think he's ready. "Buy her a place of her own."

He raises his eyebrows and I'm not sure if that means he's surprised or getting ready to make excuses. He squishes his cigarette in the ashtray. "And I thought you knew Rana!"

"I do. But I also know more about her financial status than anyone else does. She has worked hard and saved enough to get by, but not enough to pay a huge rent in Tehran."

He laughs bitterly and shakes his head. "That woman is too stubborn. She'd rather die than accept a penny from me."

"Who said it should come from you?" I respond. Prepared. Rehearsed. "Buy it in my name and let me persuade her to live in it."

He considers my proposition for a minute. "You sure have thought this over, councilor, haven't you?" I detect a hint of approval in his voice.

"I have."

He finishes his coffee and lights another cigarette. "I'll do it if that's what you want."

How clever. Checkmate, Yalda. I realize I may have just helped him to accomplish what he came here for. Let him clear his conscience. This is no time for settling scores. I feel relieved at the success of my plan, but deep inside a subtle sadness returns.

For an entire month, I imagined such a meeting and secretly hoped it might offer what I've never experienced, an emotional encounter with my father.

In the most secret compartment of my mind, little Yalda would see her father enveloping her in his strong arms and finally be held in his loving embrace. Who knows? Had he approached me with love, I might have let my guard down. But there is this huge distance between us and I am too angry for a tender moment with the father I never had. It hurts to watch my last chance slip by. We have nothing more to say to each other. I'll never call this man 'Dad' and he was never *Baba* to me, the way he is to Vida. Colonel Moradi and I are two parties making a deal. If for nothing else, for Mom's sake I need to close this deal. Let him humiliate me with a favor.

"Yes. That's what I want." Announcing the verdict, my voice sounds unfamiliar and bears no emotion.

He doesn't seem to notice because he puts his hand over mine and gives it an affectionate squeeze. "Consider it done, my dear."

I pull my hand away and reach for my coffee. The bitter taste goes with how I feel. The words I had rehearsed become futile. I need to leave now. I put my glass down and pick up my purse.

He grabs my sleeve. "Please. Don't go just yet."

I remain seated, still clutching my purse.

"It's important that you hear what I have to say." His voice is tired, resigned. "Life is nothing but a chain of mistakes. Some we learn from, but most others are only horrible misjudgments on their way to becoming regrets." He closes his eyes as if to recreate a picture behind his eyelids. "You were just a baby. My baby. And nothing, not even your forgiveness, is going to help me forgive myself for turning my back on you." Misty eyes look at me and he stops talking.

I know the story, but I'm going to let him tell it again. Let him feel the pain, even though I'm feeling it more.

"I was too young, and the young don't know any better. You'll never understand my situation. There's a lot to be said about family pressure. We were all hoping for a boy, someone to carry my father's name. But then came a third girl. Not only did I have to banish my dream of an heir, but there was also another problem." He pauses and seems to realize how ridiculous he sounds. He locks his hands together and brings them to his chest. "People make mistakes all the time, Yalda *jan*, especially when they're young. Just remember that as you judge your father." He waits a little and we both listen to the sound of talk and laughter coming from the café below. His voice is tired when he finally says, "I'm a God fearing man. Divine justice has brought me my share of losses. I've paid the price—if you will. So all I'm asking now is your absolution."

"Ha! Paid the price? Why don't you ask Rana what the price was? She paid for a crime she never committed. To lose Marjan may have been *your* punishment, but what was Rana paying for?" I don't want to mention Parisa, but this is the time to let it all out. "You had that woman, someone to hear you cry, to offer you comfort. But what about Rana, whose only companion was a crippled child? And what did Parisa pay for having wrecked a home?"

I know I have gone too far and expect him to react, but instead he covers his face with both hands. For a few minutes neither of us speaks, then he says in a voice that is muffled under his hands, "Parisa and I lost our baby boy. Stillbirth." And he looks up through blood-shot eyes without bothering to wipe his tears. "The right price."

The room has turned too cold. What he has told me is so shocking that all I want to do is leave. I am unable and unwilling to offer sympathy, but his pain is so palpable that I have lost my grip on what I came here to do. So it wasn't a miscarriage. *A boy?* I want to hold his hand, pat his gray hair and offer this broken man some solace. But instead try to remember that he still was not alone. He had Parisa. Not alone, not like Mom. I am filled with images of the lonely Rana, how she worked week after week, month after month. I see her dressed in black, mourning the loss of her father somewhere far away with no family around to ease her grief. I see her carrying bags of grocery up the stairs, looking forward to Fridays, the highlight of a life in exile. No. He and his Parisa will have none of my sympathy.

This time when I get up he lets go of my hand. Still sitting down, he seems so much smaller. The wrinkles on his pale face appear deeper, unsightly even. Mom must have heard about the baby being a boy. I can just imagine what that did to her. Dead or alive, it had been a boy. This self-absorbed man isn't capable of grasping the depth of Rana's pain. Or mine.

"I'm sorry about your son." I lean on the last word, aiming at his heart. For a few seconds, my courtroom performance is back and I pause to make sure he feels pain. "And I assure you, I have not suffered the lack of a father. I'll never know how my mother did it, but she made sure I had a happy childhood. As for misjudgments, my training leaves little room for that." I hesitate, pin him down with a stare and add, "My mother has taught me to always have a good reason behind my actions. That way, I never have to say that I'm sorry."

The look on his face says, *"Touché!"*

I start to leave, then stop. "There's just one thing I'd like to know."

He looks up.

"What have you learned from breaking a good woman's heart?"

He stands up to see me off and when a few seconds pass, it's clear he is not about to offer a response.

Adjusting my scarf, I tighten the knot under my chin, turn, and leave without a proper good-bye. Unheld. Unkissed. Unloved.

As I look for a taxi through the fog in my eyes, I can still see the man back in that isolated room. He must be smoking another one of his cigarettes, and I hope he's feeling as crushed as I do. Like a child who has just opened an empty package, my anticipation has vanished and I feel utterly cheated. He and I may never feel more for one another than we do at this moment, and yet I am certain that no two people on earth could be more torn apart.

Chapter

· *Twenty-Seven* ·

L
EAVING IRAN, I have double the amount of luggage I came
with. My aunts have bought me all the handcrafts I've admired and Mom not only gave me a small rug to take back,
she has stuffed my suitcase with bags of pistachios and tons of dried
herbs. When I objected to the smell, she said, "You're going to need
even more if you ever make your favorite *Osh*."

My flight is not leaving for another couple of hours. It's now
two in the morning and we are all gathered at the airport's VIP
lounge, which is a large room resembling a hotel lobby. You don't
really have to be anyone important to be here. I'm told it costs about
the same as a night at a hotel, but is well worth it as there's no hassle
involved at check in.

A server has just brought us tea and pastries. So hard to believe
I've been away for nearly two months. I came here thinking this
would be my only chance to see the country, but with Mom now
staying back, I wonder. I still can't believe she is not going back
with me. Vida is sitting next to me, chatting and giggling as always.
I'm going to miss her bubbly presence.

The whole family has given up sleep to be here. Mom has been
awfully quiet, shedding silent tears now and then. I promise myself

I won't cry. This trip has had its share of drama and I'm not about to add more. Iranians seem to have no gray zone. They are either crying or laughing their heads off at silly jokes. I'd rather remember the laughter.

My father isn't here, but I have a feeling he will show up. He has not tried to contact me since our talk at the café. My last communication with him was through Mr. Eskandary, who brought me some papers to sign, making him my official representative to sign the deed to a house.

Regardless of how little I have seen my father, thoughts of him have been a constant part of my last few days. I hate him for making it hard to hate him and I hope he can see that when he finally shows up.

I look for Mom and find her sitting in a wing chair, deep into a small book. I walk over and realize it is the prayer book Dayeh gave me. I put my arm around her. "Good book, Mom?" I say jokingly.

She elbows me gently as if asking not to disturb her and starts mouthing the words she is reading. A minute goes by before she closes the book and explains, "Just read the travel prayer for you."

"Since when have you become so religious?" I ask and am genuinely interested.

"I'm not. I read that for you on Dayeh's behalf."

The thought of old Dayeh clutches at my heart. She's back in her village and it's clear that I'll never see her again.

"Good," I say and give her a pat in the back. "I don't need a fanatic Mom." And I laugh.

She frowns. "There's nothing wrong with being a good Muslim."

She's so serious that it's hard to believe she is the same Mom who back in the States had no religion. She now wears her scarf willingly and often prays. I have a feeling she actually draws comfort from that. Has her faith always been there? Did her religion stay dormant all these years and all it needed to come out was the right climate? Like quicksand, my mother's old culture is pulling her in and there's nothing I can do to stop that. *Will it push a new wedge between us?*

Aunt Mandy walks over. "Want to go shopping?"

I know she means to look at the duty-free shops, but considering how we have lately shopped and shopped, the suggestion makes everyone laugh. Nothing is going on, so a walk would be nice. "Maybe just a look?"

As soon as we are out of the room, she holds my arm. "Try not to look so morbid," she whispers. "This is what your mom will remember for a long time. A little smile won't hurt."

"I thought I was doing a good job of it."

We walk a few steps and she motions to a long hallway with bright lights and fancy display windows. "Sometimes they keep the best things at the airport. Let's take a look."

Indeed these shops seem to carry merchandise of a higher caliber. I shake my head. "I'm not really in the mood."

Most overseas flights leave at late hours and yet there's quite a crowd around us. For a while we don't talk, then I ask her, "Do you think Mom is making the right decision?"

She thinks for a moment. "We will see."

"So you're not sure, either."

"I've never been sure about anything Rana does." She sighs. "I guess only time can tell. She wasn't so wrong about taking you away, was she?"

It's good of my aunt to give Mom all the credit and I'm not about to argue how that wasn't entirely her decision. What would Grandpa Ameli say about this? Would he want Mom to live on her own in this city? I'm conscious of the fact that this may well be my last chance to put an end to my unanswered questions. "Do you think she still has feelings for *him*?"

Aunt Mandy laughs out loud. "Think? Honey everyone can see that!"

I stop walking. "Everyone?"

She dismisses my concern with a wave of her hand. "Of course. Even you knew. Why else would you ask such a question?"

"Then why would she divorce him?"

She shrugs. "Maybe pride?"

"And his new wife?"

My aunt links arms with me and says, "It's different here. We Persians have all sorts of love. For most of us, true love is spiritual, a feeling beyond worldly needs and it certainly has little to do with sex. I'm sure it bothers her that he loves another, but in her world, Farhad is the source of light. She can't reach him, but his existence is needed. He is the sun, regardless of how far they are."

I don't know that kind of love and suddenly what I feel for Paul seems mundane.

My aunt continues, "People may be in love with someone from their past, or someone new, even an image." She notices I'm not convinced and adds, "Call it Platonic, if you like. But true love comes from here." She taps her chest with a fist. "Especially when you're older."

"Do you love Uncle Jamshid that way?"

She laughs. "Are you joking? I love my husband dearly, and am most loyal to him, but that kind of love happens once in a lifetime. I'm way past it."

I don't want to ask any more personal questions, but somehow begin to understand.

We walk and enjoy the beautiful displays for a while. People are rushing about, pulling their suitcases. Announcements are made periodically and we pass a man lying on a bench with his backpack under his head.

"What does she think she may gain by staying here? She could go back home and love him all she wants from far away."

My aunt considers that. "I'm not sure her staying here has anything to do with him. She really wants to be close to Vida." She shrugs. "Who knows? There may be more than one reason. I've talked to Rana multiple times. Life here isn't comfortable, but it has a lot to offer."

While she explains how Rana will never be alone here, I picture my mother back home. I see her sprinkling salt on her front steps in winter, storing a small shovel and another bag of salt in the trunk of her car. I see her tucked away in her apartment watching soap operas as she waits for the next load of laundry to be done. Every Sunday she setts and re-sets her booth in the antique mall. The phone in her apartment rarely rings and hardly any visitors stop by unannounced. It's clear that despite all the shortcomings, she'll have more here. She doesn't have all the machines, but can hire a maid to help. She will be minutes away from Vida and will forever have her clan around her. I smile at the image of my lovely cactus having plenty of sunshine to keep her happy.

The long road ahead of me doesn't look so bad. I will adjust. My home is across the ocean. I'm not Rana. None of her reasons could keep me here another day. I have a life back in the States and it has taken me a trip to Iran to appreciate it. All my life I wanted to be my mom, but now it's clear how different we are. This is her habitat and I'm going back to mine.

Aunt Mandy and I circle the transit area and by the time we return, it's close to departure time. I don't see my father and realize he's not coming. What prompted me to expect otherwise?

Mom walks over and offers a wan smile as if to console me. She must know I feel like crying, but says nothing. Before we go downstairs, she leans into me and whispers, "Use the bathrooms here, if you need to. They're the Western kind."

I smile at her practicality and wonder if she'll ever stop seeing me as her baby girl.

"I'm okay, Mom."

We walk down the stairs in a group and say our goodbyes. Mom's hug is too tight, but I know she won't cry in public. "You will call me as soon as you land, no?"

I nod and just let my tears flow. Vida is next. The way she holds me makes me want to stay. Aunt Mandy is suddenly a basket case amid uncontrollable sobs. There is an entire family around me and I smile at how they are all talking at once. I look beyond them to the entryway. There's no sign of Colonel Moradi.

I turn and hug uncle Ardeshir, who is all of a sudden saying a whole lot in Persian. The sad tone of his voice is translation enough. Next is Uncle Jamshid. As I hug my male relatives I am grateful for the VIP lounge for allowing me to do this. No sooner has he let go than a large hand grabs my shoulders and twirls me around and before I can react, I have disappeared into my father's arms.

His embrace is too strong to fight, too loving to want to. I allow myself to be held and can hear the sudden silence around us. He holds me so tight that I can feel his heartbeat. His tears pour on my face, my hair, my scarf. A sound comes out of his throat. Is he sobbing? Am I? I think of how easy it would be to stay in this moment. But I fiercely want to deny the warm feeling that has enveloped my entire being.

Someone cautions it's time to go and he loosens his grip a little. I'm clinging to the fronts of his jacket, hanging on for dear life. He bends and kisses the top of my head and as soon as I let go, he turns around without a word.

My first instinct is to go after him, but my feet are heavy as lead. The circle of family closes around me. I stand on my tiptoes and look for him beyond the group, but he has vanished. Another loud announcement comes and I'm back to my senses. Before disappearing behind the black curtain, I look back one last time. There is my lovely Rana, standing among her clan, yet lonely as ever. *When will I see you again?* I blow her a kiss, the way I used to on those foggy mornings in front of my nursery school.

Entering the passenger area, I want to savor this dizzy, intoxicating moment. I won't let anything change it, not right away, not for the next moment. This time I don't feel the body search and can hardly hear the woman's questions. Even as I climb the stairs in the cold morning air and find my seat on the flight, something is pulling me back, an allure I can't describe. I tighten my seatbelt, making sure I remain in place and turn to lean my forehead against the glass.

As we take off, the sun is rising from behind the Elburz Mountains. It illuminates Damavand, the highest peak in the range, the snow-capped magnificence I have admired daily each time we left the house. In my mind I can hear the awe in Mom's voice narrating as we landed, when Damavand was just a name, when this place meant nothing to me. "There it is," she had said. How had I missed all the love, all the anticipation in her voice as she said that simple phrase? A ray of sun hits my window at an angle and the sprinkle of its rainbow colors gives the view below an ethereal glow. That mountain is magical. And if I peer closely, I can just see a day, years from now, when I return to this place. Maybe then I, too, will feel the urge to whisper, "There it is."

―

About the Author

ZOHREH GHAHREMANI is an Iranian-American author. Previously a pediatric dentist also teaching at Northwestern University Dental School, in 2000 she moved to San Diego to devote herself to writing. Since then, over two hundred of her essays, short stories, and vignettes have appeared in magazines and online. She is a bilingual author, and her first full-length book, The Commiserator, was in her native Persian language.

Her debut novel Sky Of Red Poppies was selected by KPBS and the San Diego Public Library as the citywide reading selection for One Book, One San Diego, 2012.

Zoe lives in San Diego with her husband Gary and close to their three children. When not writing, she enjoys painting and gardening.

Please visit her on the web:

www.zoeghahremani.com

CPSIA information can be obtained at www.ICGtesting.com
Printed in the USA
LVOW12s1436030813

346135LV00002B/4/P